T0035843

"Barratt refuses to look away or ignore the heartbreak and depredations imposed upon the Jews of Poland during the Holocaust. With writing both sensitive and courageous, she brings to life the physical, spiritual, emotional, and mental hardships that those forced into the ghettos endured. In the midst of the sorrow, though, are glimmers of goodness, light, and hope that will encourage the reader that God is still sovereign and that He can be found even in the worst circumstances. Through the power of story, Barratt shows that even the smallest kindness can change a life."

—ERICA VETSCH, author of the Thorndike & Swann
Regency Mysteries

WITHIN THESE WALLS *of* SORROW

BY AMANDA BARRATT

My Dearest Dietrich

The White Rose Resists

Within These Walls of Sorrow

"Far as the Curse Is Found" in *Joy to the World*

WITHIN THESE WALLS *of* SORROW

A Novel of World War II Poland

AMANDA BARRATT

KREGEL
PUBLICATIONS

Within These Walls of Sorrow: A Novel of World War II Poland
© 2023 by Amanda Barratt

Published by Kregel Publications, a division of Kregel Inc., 2450 Oak Industrial Dr. NE, Grand Rapids, MI 49505. www.kregel.com.

Scripture quotations are from the King James Version.

Library of Congress Cataloging-in-Publication Data
Names: Barratt, Amanda, 1996- author.
Title: Within these walls of sorrow : a novel of World War II Poland / Amanda Barratt.
Description: Grand Rapids, MI : Kregel Publications, [2023] | Includes bibliographical references.
Identifiers: LCCN 2022026927 (print) | LCCN 2022026928 (ebook) | ISBN 9780825447013 (print) | ISBN 9780825477546 (epub) | ISBN 9780825469060 (Kindle)
Subjects: LCSH: World War, 1939-1945--Poland--Fiction. | National socialism--Poland--Fiction. | LCGFT: Historical fiction. | Novels.
Classification: LCC PS3602.A777463 W58 2023 (print) | LCC PS3602.A777463 (ebook) | DDC 813/.6--dc23/eng/20220613
LC record available at https://lccn.loc.gov/2022026927
LC ebook record available at https://lccn.loc.gov/2022026928

ISBN 978-0-8254-4701-3, print
ISBN 978-0-8254-7754-6, epub
ISBN 978-0-8254-6906-0, Kindle

Printed in the United States of America
23 24 25 26 27 28 29 30 31 32 / 5 4 3 2 1

In memory of the millions who suffered and died in the Holocaust.
May their stories never be forgotten.

And to the pharmacists of the Apteka Pod Orłem:
Tadeusz Pankiewicz, Irena Droździkowska,
Helena Krywaniuk, and Aurelia Danek-Czortowa.

Soli Deo gloria.

Come, take this giant leap with me
into the other world . . . the other place
and trace the eclipse of humanity . . .
where children burned while mankind stood by,
and the universe has yet to learn why
. . . has yet to learn why.

Sonia Schreiber Weitz,
survivor of the Kraków ghetto

We were not heroes. It was just our bounden duty.

Tadeusz Pankiewicz

PRELUDE

Zosia
Kraków, Poland

THE SUN SHONE THE day I married Ryszard Lewandowski. Kraków, the city spun from a fairy tale, with its castle on Wawel Hill and medieval market square, with its gothic churches and meandering cobbled streets held a special kind of beauty as we stepped arm in arm from the doors of the Mariacki Church, its magnificent redbrick towers rising against a perfect blue sky.

My heart was full, beating with the promise of our future as Ryszard and I pledged ourselves to one another, as our family and friends encircled us at the festivities afterward and sang "*Sto Lat*," lustily chorusing their good wishes for us to live for "a hundred years, a hundred years!"

It was 1938, after all. The world still held a golden tint, war only a rumor nipping at the back of our minds. Germany's recent annexation of Austria . . . yes, it was troubling, but in a remote sort of way, rather like reading a stranger's obituary. Since the early '30s, we'd watched from afar as the man with the fiery oration and inkblot of a mustache rose to power on a tide of "Sieg heil!"

But war? Some considered it, but who really believed it would happen? Who could comprehend how war would sweep across Europe, how swiftly our lives would be caught up in its vortex?

I'd recently graduated with a master's degree from Jagiellonian University's Faculty of Pharmacy and now I was *Pani* Zosia Lewandowska, wife of a distinguished professor of law. As Ryszard and I ascended the stairs to his flat, I thought only of the life we were beginning together and the night before us, the first we would share as husband and wife.

"Do you think anyone minded we left the party early?" I asked, Ryszard's fingers woven through mine, my suitcase in his other hand.

"I did notice your father looking at me rather severely as we made our departure."

I didn't need to glance at him to picture the faintest of grins tugging at his lips. My laugh spilled out. "That's *Tata* for you. But what else do you expect from a man who's just given away his only child?"

We reached the second-floor landing. Ryszard set down the suitcase and curled his hand around my waist, pulling me against him. "You've always been your own woman entirely." He gazed down at me in the half light. "No one but you, Zosia Lewandowska, could give yourself away."

"And now?" Our lips were but a breath apart.

"Now"—he tucked a strand of hair behind my ear, fingers lingering against my skin—"we belong to each other." He pressed his lips against mine and my arms wound around his neck, our kiss deepening. He tasted faintly of wine and my senses swam with the warmth of his mouth on mine.

We should go upstairs. The thought came rather dizzily to my mind.

At a creak, we both started. Turned. The door to the left stood ajar—I was sure it had not been before—and a girl, bare feet peeking out beneath the hem of her robe, stood in the opening.

Her eyes went wide, the reddening in her cheeks visible even in the dim light. For several seconds, she stared at us, looking very much as though she wanted to sink into the floor.

My cheeks warmed as I wished I could disappear right along with her. What had Ryszard and I been thinking, kissing each other senseless on the second-floor landing?

"Good evening, Hania." Ryszard was first to speak, smoothing a hand over his disheveled hair.

"G-good evening, *Pan* Professor." Her voice barely rose above a whisper. Her thick brown hair hung around her shoulders, a match to her still-wide eyes.

"I don't believe you've met my wife, have you? Zosia, you remember Dr. Silberman? We met him last week when we brought over some of your things."

"I do, yes." I recalled the quiet middle-aged gentleman who helped carry my heavy crates of books up to Ryszard's flat.

"This is his eldest daughter, Hania. Hania, this is my wife, Magistra Zofia Lewandowska. We were married just this afternoon."

I stepped forward, smiling, hoping to ease her awkwardness. "I'm very glad to meet you." I still wore my understated wedding gown of pearl-hued silk, and doubtless my lipstick was hopelessly smudged, my swept-back curls disordered.

"I'm glad to meet you too." Her smile shyly unfolded. She swung a glance into the flat behind her. "I have to go. I'm not supposed to be up." She hesitated. "I hope you'll both be very happy." She flushed again.

We thanked her and Ryszard picked up my suitcase and took my hand. I couldn't help but smile at her, this young girl watching Ryszard and me as if we were film stars, as if there was something magical about us simply because we were newlyweds.

I did not imagine then how the years would stitch the fabric of our lives together, how the inexorable pull of war would bind us. Then, she was just a shy fifteen-year-old schoolgirl living in the flat below ours, and I was twenty-two, a bride blissfully in love.

Ryszard and I reached the third floor, and he unlocked the door of his flat. The moment the door shut, we fell into each other, and the rest of the world fell away.

The day I married Ryszard Lewandowski remains in my mind like the photograph snapped of us outside the church, sepia-tinted, me smiling up at him, his hand over mine, my arms full of lilies and carnations. The beginning of a beautiful dream.

But how quickly dreams dissolve into nightmares.

How quickly.

CHAPTER ONE

Hania
March 3, 1941

THE *KRAKAUER ZEITUNG* RESTS on the table, the bold lettering of its masthead staring up at us above the fold. It's only a newspaper, black type and fresh newsprint, the sharp scent of ink clinging to its pages. But as my gaze fastens on it, lying atop the cream cloth, fear lodges in my stomach like a cold, hard stone. Darkness has long since fallen beyond the windows, the faces of my family cast in the dim glow of the light above the table.

"Read it out loud, Adam." Mama sits stiffly at one end of our dining table. Beside her, my younger sister Rena twists the ends of her plait around her finger, wide eyes fixed on Tata. My fifteen-year-old brother Szymon folds his arms, inky black strands of hair falling over his forehead.

The paper rustles as Tata picks it up and unfolds it. "Ordinance. Sanitary, economic, and security considerations make it imperative to house the Jewish population of Kraków in a special, enclosed section of the city, the Jewish residential district. The Jewish residential district will be located in the district of Podgórze, on the far side of the Wisła River. Without exception, it is forbidden for Jews to live outside the area of the Jewish residential district. The following streets constitute its boundaries . . ."

Beneath the table, I clench my hands together in my lap.

"All Jews in the city of Kraków residing outside the boundaries of the residential district are ordered to relocate by the twentieth of March 1941. The allocation of living quarters will be handled by the *Judenrat* housing office. Non-Jews residing in the area designated for the Jewish residential district are ordered to relocate to the district of Kazimierz no later than the twentieth of March 1941. The allocation of flats will be handled by the Municipal Housing Office. Failure to comply with this ordinance will result in severe punishment. Signed, Governor of the Kraków District, Dr. Wächter." Tata refolds the paper.

This morning, Mama and I stood in front of an advertising pillar, reading the freshly printed ordinance in silence. I've had a whole day to absorb this news.

But hearing the decree spoken aloud is like taking in the words for the first time. Tata has many voices. When he treats a nervous patient, his voice is calming; when teasing me and Rena, his voice rumbles with laughter; when reciting kiddush on Shabbat, it is resonant; when whispering in Mama's ear, making her smile, it is loving.

Now his voice is blank.

It is Tata's blank voice that seals the words and their reality inside of me.

"At least we know now where we'll be going." Purplish circles bruise the skin beneath Mama's eyes. Each passing month imprints a deeper weariness upon her features, her skin sallow, iron-gray tendrils straggling from her chignon. "The rumors have gone on long enough. Podgórze is only on the other side of the river. It could be worse."

"Will we be able to come and go freely, or will they trap us in this ghetto like rabbits in a cage?" Szymon's tone has a cynical edge.

Ghetto. The stone in my stomach grows heavier, colder. This will not be the first time Kraków's Jewish population has been driven into a separate district of the city. It's as if we've gone back to the 15th century and are once again being forced into isolation.

The Germans have already established ghettos in Warsaw and other smaller towns in occupied Poland.

Kraków, the city of my birth and the capital of the *Generalgouvernement*—the Polish territory under German rule but not annexed to the Reich—is next.

"Surely they won't keep us prisoner." Mama twists her clasped hands atop the tablecloth.

"I wouldn't be so sure." Szymon shoves hair off his forehead. "The Nazis would like nothing better than to lock us all up. Anyone who can't see it is either delusional or stupid."

"Don't speak to your mama like that."

I start at the harshness in Tata's tone. In all my growing up years, my mild-mannered tata rarely raised his voice to us, disciplining his children with firm but quiet words, the shame we felt at having displeased him worse than the pain of any punishment.

"I'm sorry, Mama," Szymon says quietly. "I meant no disrespect."

"It's all right, Son." Mama gives a weak smile.

"We're fortunate to have been issued *Kennkarten*," Tata says. "Those who weren't can hardly show their faces on the street on account of the roundups. The Germans are forcing all the Jews out of the city. The rest is simply a matter of location."

"Frank and his higher-ups are tired of having their delicate tastes offended, ruling from a city polluted by Jewish filth and disease. They want their capital cleaned out, and this time they're not doing it by half measures." My brother's words hang in the air.

Neither of our parents disputes them.

"Do we have to go?" Rena's voice is quiet and uncertain. She's only twelve. How can she be expected to take in yet another way in which the foundations of our lives are slowly disintegrating?

How can any of us take it in?

"I'm afraid so, Renusia." Tata's words are gentle, but strain hovers beneath their surface. "It won't be for long. Until the war is over, perhaps."

"Where will we live?" Rena asks, as if resigned to the inevitability of the ghetto.

The months since the autumn of 1939 have taught us the best way to adapt is to accept, and the sooner one accepts, the sooner one can begin to adapt. So much we've accepted that should be unacceptable, so many times we've adapted to what should not be borne . . .

"It says the Judenrat will arrange housing. They'll find a flat for us, I'm sure." I make my voice confident, comforting.

"Better for us to go now than to leave the city only to be forced into the ghetto later. This way, at least, we won't be among strangers. And surely once we're in the ghetto, we'll have some peace." Tata is back to the tone he uses in his consulting room, the calm, unquestionable logic that has settled many a patient's fears.

What he doesn't say is the people being rounded up as illegal residents because they failed to qualify as essential laborers and obtain Kennkarten authorizing them to remain in the city are no longer able to choose where they relocate but are sent to the transit camp on Mogilska Street, and from there deported wherever the Germans see fit to send them. Tata's reasoning is by moving into the ghetto voluntarily, at least we're the ones choosing when and where we go. It's as close to autonomy as ground acorns are to real coffee, but what other options do we really have?

Mama draws a long breath. "It will be difficult, but we are used to that now. And if this is the worst we must bear, we will be all right."

The strained resignation in Mama's voice gives rise to a sudden, unaccountable urge to scream. I bite my bottom lip to stop myself.

If this is the worst we must bear . . .

Six days after the announcement crackled over the radio—*Early this morning, German troops invaded Polish territories without a declaration of hostilities*—our occupiers arrived in Kraków, columns of helmeted soldiers, the unified stamp of their boots harsh on the cobbled street. At first, we reassured ourselves by telling each other it wouldn't last long. Somewhere along the way—when exactly did it happen?—as the net of occupation spread across Denmark, Norway, the Netherlands, Luxembourg, France, and Belgium, as loudspeakers and newspapers broadcast German victory after Germany victory, we stopped believing that delusion.

Now it's: *If this is the worst we must bear . . .*

Since the September dawn when Hitler's troops marched into Kraków, the Jewish population of the city has had to bear a great many worsts.

The first edict came only two days after the Germans arrived: Jewish businesses, market stalls, and shops had to be marked with the Star of David, making them targets for plunder. That December, the SS cordoned off Kazimierz—the center of Kraków's Jewish community—searching homes, confiscating valuables, and looting synagogues. They ripped rings from women's fingers and threw priceless Torah scrolls and prayer books into the streets, trampling them in the mud.

I'll never forget the night three uniformed Germans pounded on our door with their rifle butts, then burst into our flat, demanding to know where we'd hidden our valuables and cash, helping themselves to whatever they pleased. The fact that the place under the floorboards where we'd concealed Mama's diamond ring and what was left of our savings went undetected was a swallow of victory in a meal of humiliation.

One after the other, the decrees came in such rapid succession it soon became difficult to keep up with all the restrictions imposed upon our daily lives. The occupiers ordered the formation of a Jewish council—the main purpose of which was to communicate and enforce the edicts issued by the Generalgouvernement. The first order carried out by the Judenrat was to levy a tax on all Jewish Poles whose ancestry went back four generations. A census was conducted to ensure every last one paid.

In November 1939, the governor of the Kraków District published the order: all Jews over twelve years of age must wear an armband on their right upper sleeve—a blue Star of David on a white background, the exact dimensions for which were listed in the edict. Now whenever we set foot outside, we're easily identified; before it was not always so easy to tell who was Jewish and who wasn't.

Jewish physicians can no longer treat non-Jews, so Tata lost more than half his patients. We are forbidden to gather for prayers or hold services in the synagogues. We're issued special ration books with precanceled coupons, reducing our rations to barely above half those allotted to Gentile Poles. We can no longer use public transportation; walk in the Planty, the verdant park encircling Old Town, save for a small section where Jews are still allowed; or enter the Rynek Główny, Kraków's main square, renamed Adolf Hitler Platz. We're forbidden cinemas, theatres, cafés, and restaurants, except the few marked *Nur für Juden*—for Jews only. We can't sit on park benches, so when our feet are aching from walking everywhere, because we're also not permitted to own automobiles or motorbikes, we're not even allowed a moment's rest on a public bench. We can no longer access our savings, as bank accounts held by Jews have been frozen. Jews cannot own businesses; the most profitable enterprises have been taken over by Germans, the rest by Poles.

Jewish men and women between the ages of fourteen and sixty are subject to compulsory labor, which means at any time one might be rounded up on the way to work or to the market and made to sweep the streets, shovel snow, or do whatever the Germans assign. Since the beginning of this year, everyone has to spend eight days a month shoveling snow; those who don't get the stamps on their identity cards certifying they fulfilled the requirement are in danger of being deported.

Near the end of 1939, the decree barring Jewish students from state schools and closing Jewish private schools was issued. Oh, how my throat swelled and my chest burned to hear Rena sobbing quietly into her pillow when she could no longer attend school. It didn't affect Szymon or me because by then, all secondary schools had been closed by order of the occupiers. In this it didn't matter whether one was Jewish or not.

We've grown used to ordinances and edicts. *You are forbidden to do this. You are ordered to do that.* With each one, we tell ourselves this can be endured. We find ways to adjust and maintain an appearance of normalcy and comfort ourselves with the brittle hope that perhaps this decree will be the last. So much has already been prohibited, so many forced out of the city.

What more can they want from us? What else can they take?

When we ask each other these questions, no one is looking for an answer. But with characteristic German efficiency, they have one ready.

An answer.

A ghetto.

• • •

Zosia
March 4, 1941

The second winter of the war is as bitter as the first. Though it's the beginning of March, the damp chill in the air retains its ice-edged bite. Wind cuts through my coat as I hasten through Old Town. A tram clatters past, its blue-and-white body outlined by the dirty gray sky, the faces of its passengers blurred behind the windows. The rising prices of food and coal means I must count every grosz, so instead of taking the tram, I walk to and from Magister Borkowski's pharmacy to my flat on Starowiślna Street, now Alte Weichselstrasse. Renaming its streets is one of the many ways the occupiers have attempted to Germanize the capital of the Generalgouvernement since their arrival.

Golden warmth emanates from the windows of a restaurant, the light glistening on the slush-coated cobblestones. *FOR GERMANS ONLY* is displayed prominently on the door. I pause, the glow shadowing the figures inside, men in uniform and women in sleek evening gowns, dining in the restaurant's dim intimacy.

I walk on, shivering, glad it isn't snowing, at least. Loudspeakers spit the latest edict into the frosty air. The occupiers installed them on major streets to transmit their propaganda, and their drone has simply become part of the landscape, as commonplace as swastika flags. The words, first spoken in German, then repeated in Polish, form a dull blur in my ears. It's about the creation of the Jewish residential district in Podgórze, announced only yesterday. The ordinance is on every advertising pillar.

Governor-General Frank, ruling over his administration from Wawel Castle, and his officials have been issuing edicts to drive the Jews out of Kraków since last spring, first by voluntary relocation, then forced eviction. It seems they're determined to rid the city, now inhabited by thousands of Germans, of its entire Jewish population. "Sanitary considerations," read the announcement in the *Krakauer Zeitung*.

A chill seeps into me, deeper than the cold. I quicken my steps, blending into the crowd of pedestrians hurrying along the sidewalk, men and women wrapped in winter woolens, carrying market baskets or briefcases, bent against the wind. Beaten down by it.

By all of it.

I reach my flat several minutes later, the front door closing behind me. I mount the stairs, feet aching after the long day at the pharmacy and the walk home. Footsteps tap behind me and I turn, pausing on the second-floor landing.

Hania hurries up the stairs, head bent.

She glances up and I draw a sharp breath.

Mud streaks her cheek and the front of her coat, the kerchief knotted under her chin slipping loose.

"Hania, what happened? Are you hurt?"

She shakes her head. "I'm fine."

"But just look at you—you're covered in mud." I can't help but notice how worn down she is, shoulders slumped, cheeks wind chapped.

"Some boys came by while we were shoveling snow and decided to have a bit of fun. They threw snowballs at us, only the snow was muddy, so . . ." She gestures to the dirty splotches on her coat. "But I'm all right, really."

"No one tried to stop them?" The anger flaring in my chest escalates my voice. I know the type, adolescents who think it great sport to torment the Jews, showing off to their friends as if inflicting pain on those deemed defenseless somehow makes them tough.

Hania shrugs.

In the year and a half Kraków has been under occupation, the sum of suffering and humiliation endured by the Jewish people makes youths hurling snowballs seem small in comparison. Though the act itself may be of little significance, it's a sign, a symptom, of something far greater and far more frightening. Hatred against Jews has always existed in Poland, its seeds implanted so deeply few question their existence, much less seek to uproot them. In Kraków, there has been, to a certain degree, a peaceful accord, or at least a tacit kind of tolerance, Jews and non-Jews sharing business relationships and occasionally personal friendships. But in the centuries of Jews and Gentiles dwelling side by side, prejudice and persecution have run like poison through the artery of society.

Perhaps it shouldn't come as a surprise the degree to which the Poles have joined in the oppression of their Jewish neighbors. The Germans have only stoked the fires of time-honored tradition.

Hania's stocking has a rip at the knee. I look closer. Dried blood encrusts a nasty abrasion. "What happened to your knee?"

"I got hit with a snowball that must have had a rock in it. I slipped and fell. It's only a scrape."

Those pigs. Those vile, filthy *pigs*. If I'd been a passerby, I would not have stood by, even if Hania had been a stranger.

But I have, and the remembrance floods me with shame. Once, in the early days of the occupation, I watched as a rabble of youth made sport of an elderly man, an Orthodox Jew, mocking him and pelting him with garbage as he swept the street alongside others pressed into forced labor. The old man kept pushing his broom, head lowered, shoulders stooped, as if unable to bear the weight of his shame. I've watched German soldiers beating Jews in the street and rounding them up for work details, shearing the beards and sidelocks of Jewish men. Against the occupiers we have little recourse. But as Polish youths tormented that elderly man, I could have done something. Or at least tried.

Even as I tell myself I would not stand by, one does not know until the moment comes. Courage is strong until it is tested.

I stare at the mud on Hania's cheek and the dried blood on her knee and feel a little sick. "Come upstairs and let me have a look at your knee. I've a little tea left. You look as if you could use something warm to drink."

"That's kind but I can't, I'm afraid. Mama went to see if she could buy some bread. She sent me on ahead to help Rena with supper." She pauses, smiles sadly. "I'd say maybe some other time, but we won't be here much longer."

"Yes." I want to tell her how sorry I am, how terribly sorry it has come to this, but I'm suddenly at a loss for words. For the right ones, at least.

"You've heard then? About the Jewish district in Podgórze?"

"I think everyone has by now."

"We have to be out by the twentieth. Tata is making plans. He'll have to give up his practice, since there won't be any Jewish people left in the city for him to treat. But there will be plenty of need for doctors where we're going, so I'm sure he'll be very busy."

"Is there anything I can do?"

She hesitates. "We'll have to leave a lot of our belongings behind. This morning, Tata was talking about who we might be able to give some things to for safekeeping. If it's too much, we understand . . ." She looks embarrassed, her voice uncertain.

"Of course. Whatever I can do. And please, if there's anything else your family needs, tell your parents they have only to ask."

"I'll speak to Tata tonight." She glances toward the door. "I should go. Rena will be needing my help."

"Be sure to put a bandage on that first. You don't want an infection. Though as a doctor's daughter, I suppose I don't need to tell you that."

She gives a faint laugh, a remnant of the days before war stole the brightness from her smile. "I will." She pauses, looking into my eyes. "Thank you, Zosia."

I nod, gazing steadily back at her. Since the day I came to live in this building as the wife of Ryszard Lewandowski, an uncommon bond has grown between us, two women separated by a flight of stairs in a middle-class block of flats on Starowiślna Street. Now a swastika flies above Wawel Castle, and what separates us has nothing to do with distance.

The door closes behind her and I turn. On the third floor, I reach into my handbag for my key and unlock the door. Inside, I take off my coat and unwind my scarf and hang them on the rack. I should prepare supper, but the day has left me worn, too tired to care whether I eat.

I cross the sitting room and enter the adjoining bedroom. I tug the chain on the lamp and kick off my shoes, then stretch out on the bed. Light casts a glow through the shade, but it does little to dispel the dank chill. Coal is scarce, and what little there is comes dear, so I rarely light the stove. The gnaw of the wind never leaves my bones, even when indoors.

Silence gathers, collecting in the air like particles of dust. Most of the time, I manage to forget—or at least pretend I do—but each evening I dread returning to the flat, knowing the silence is waiting for me. War allots little space to dwell on personal griefs. One continues on, quietly endures as best one can. Loss has left its imprint on so many homes. At least I am alone, at least I have no children . . . though sometimes, I'm overwhelmed by an ache so fierce it takes my breath. For a child to care for and cherish. A small piece of Ryszard to hold onto.

I should be grateful not to have a child. Many women whose husbands are gone are left struggling to provide for their families.

Gone.

The word echoes, its syllables an empty shell. It explains nothing and it explains everything.

One morning, the most ordinary of mornings, Ryszard was sitting across from me at breakfast, gulping his coffee, wiping his mouth with a napkin, and rising from his chair. He kissed me goodbye, a hurried brush of his lips, the kind of kiss couples share out of habit when their minds are already with the day ahead.

Recollection has a strange way of centering on certain details while others remain in shadow. I don't remember the last words we spoke to one another. I've run through those moments so many times, trying to remember, but it's as if they're just beyond my reach, or my mind has simply lost them. But the click of the door as it shut behind him reverberates through me now as clearly as it did then.

It was the sixth of November 1939.

Because of the outbreak of war, Jagiellonian University had not commenced the academic year, but as time went on, plans had been made to reopen the university. Mere days before classes were scheduled to resume, SS-Sturmbannführer Müller, chief of the *Einsatzkommando* in Kraków, ordered the rector to convene a meeting of all professors for the purpose of giving an address on the Reich's views on higher education.

But it wasn't a meeting. Müller's speech lasted five minutes. The university had opened the academic year without permission from the German authorities, proof it was a breeding ground for anti-German attitudes. Everyone, Müller said, except for the two women professors, would be deported to a concentration camp. Those who resisted would be shot.

The next day, I joined the crowd of wives and relatives gathering outside the barracks where the professors were being held, clutching parcels of food and clothing. We waited in the cold for what seemed like hours until they permitted us a brief visit with our men.

Ten minutes. Sitting across from each other, unable to touch, a few whispered words when the guard wasn't looking. Ryszard's face was battered and swollen—a guard had hit him with a rifle butt when Ryszard protested the rough treatment of a colleague. He told me he had hopes they would soon be released, that someone would realize the senselessness of arresting nearly two hundred academics and intervene. I wonder now whether he truly believed it or if he said it only to comfort me.

Two days later, the men were loaded onto a train bound for Germany. After a brief imprisonment in Breslau, they were transported yet again.

This time to Sachsenhausen.

Each day, I told myself my husband would soon come home, rereading the few letters he managed to send, even after I'd memorized every word, kneeling in church until my knees could no longer bear the ache, begging God to keep him safe and restore him to me.

At the end of January, I opened the door to the postman holding a square box.

I signed for the package, carried it inside. Beneath the brown paper wrapping lay a letter.

This is to inform you that on 13 January 1940, the prisoner Ryszard Lewandowski died at Sachsenhausen. Cause of death: pneumonia.

The box contained Ryszard's ashes.

For long minutes, I stood in the sitting room, clutching the box, eyes dry.

Then I started to scream.

Over a hundred professors were released at the beginning of February and the release of others followed in the coming months. Those who survived returned to Kraków gaunt, almost unrecognizable. At least a dozen professors died at Sachsenhausen. Others never recovered from their ordeal, dying not long after they arrived home.

It wasn't until the professors returned to Kraków that I learned the truth. Before, I could not understand it. Ryszard had been one of the younger men, only forty years old, and had never been in ill health. One of those who'd been with Ryszard told me how after hours of standing at attention in subzero temperatures, an elderly colleague of theirs had fainted. Ryszard had lifted him up and supported him during the rest of roll call, but one of the SS noticed and beat Ryszard severely before ordering him to stand at attention on the *Appellplatz* for the rest of the day.

By nightfall, Ryszard had collapsed. He never regained consciousness.

I'd sat opposite this well-spoken gentleman, one of my husband's colleagues. The cup of tea in my hand grew cold as he spoke of the strength Ryszard had been to others, of how on Christmas Eve he'd led some of the men in singing "God Is Born" and spoken a few words of hope on a night spent far away from their dear ones.

The professor pressed a scrap of paper into my hand, its edges tattered, the page stained and worn, some words almost illegible. He'd found it among Ryszard's few belongings and kept it with him during his imprisonment. And now he gave it to me. These words, penned in a hand I knew so well.

There is evil and there is good and there is the space between. We are given free will to choose where we stand. Evil thrives when good men choose the space between. We cannot

The last sentence stood unfinished.

CHAPTER TWO

Zosia
March 18, 1941

DR. SILBERMAN ANSWERS THE door in his shirtsleeves. In the years I've known the Silberman family, I don't recall ever seeing him without a coat and tie.

"Pani Lewandowska. Please, come in."

"Thank you." I follow him into the flat. Suitcases and a trunk are scattered throughout the sitting room, an assortment of items cluttering the chairs and side tables, the wallpaper darker in places where frames once hung. In the dining room, Pani Silberman and Rena are busy packing dishes into a crate, their movements rushed, almost frantic.

"Faiga, Pani Lewandowska is here." Dr. Silberman turns to me. "If you'll permit me a few moments, I'll gather up what we have."

"Of course."

He leaves the room and I turn to the women. "Good evening, Pani Silberman. Hello, Rena." It's strange, somehow, to be in their dining room, greeting them as I would on any other ordinary day, when nothing about the present situation is in the least ordinary.

"It's kind of you to come." Hair straggles from Pani Silberman's chignon. "I hope you'll pardon the disarray."

Only a housewife as fastidious as Pani Silberman would think to apologize for the state of her home at a time like this. She's always taken such pride in it though. The times I've visited, I've often seen her lovingly straightening a piece of bric-a-brac, smoothing the lace doilies on the side tables. One would be hard put to find so much as a speck of dust anywhere.

"Please, don't apologize." I hold out the cloth-wrapped loaf of bread. "I brought you this. I thought you might not have had time to think about supper today."

"Thank you, that's very kind." Pani Silberman continues to empty the china cabinet. "Rena, will you take that to the kitchen, please?"

Rena brushes sawdust from her hands. I smile as I hand her the bread. She gives me a little smile in return, but her eyes remain somber as she leaves the room. Pani Silberman kneels and places dishes in the crate. Spilled sawdust scatters the floor around her.

"Here." I cross the room and bend down beside her. "Let me help you."

She glances up, face taut. Fatigue has drawn circles beneath her eyes. "Thank you," she says quietly.

I reach for the plates and help her pack them in the sawdust. The crate is full by the time Dr. Silberman returns, Rena with him, each carrying an armload. They set the items on the table.

I rise and wipe my hands on my skirt. On the table is a silver coffee set, a tablecloth of finely worked lace, a volume with the word *Photographs* embossed in gold, and four framed photographs. One of a young Dr. and Pani Silberman on their wedding day, the second of a seated middle-aged couple with children of various ages gathered around them, taken probably several years before the Great War. In the third, Pani Silberman holds a round-cheeked baby, her smile radiant. Baby Hania looks up curiously at her tata rather than at the camera. Pride and love shine from Dr. Silberman's eyes, a memory preserved in muted black and white. The last is of the Silberman family, taken only a few years ago. They look as if they're on holiday, the peak of a mountain rising in the background as they stand, smiling, windblown, the carefree moment captured by the camera.

I look up from the photographs to find the Silbermans watching me, faces drawn tight. They are holding themselves together by threads.

"I'll keep them safe for you."

Dr. Silberman nods. "We know you will."

Pani Silberman regards me with the same steady assurance. "It's good of you to do this for us."

The weight of their trust settles on my shoulders. I heard the crashes and thuds the night SS men searched the Silbermans' flat, robbing them of their valuables, of possessions woven into the fabric of their family for generations. The items on the table are all the more precious because they've already lost so much. It humbles me to be entrusted with them.

"There's no need for thanks." I swallow. "I only wish it did not have to come to this."

"It won't be so bad." Dr. Silberman gives a slight, sympathetic smile, as if seeking to reassure me. Shouldn't it be the other way around? Though what reassurance could I offer that wouldn't taste false? "Podgórze is only on the other side of the river. We'll manage. Until the war is over, at least."

Shame fills me and then anger flares quick at its heels. That these good people are on the eve of being forced from their home isn't the worst of it. Non-Jews have lost their homes as well, ordered to pack their belongings and vacate as the Germans requisitioned the best residences in the city. But though we are all at the mercy of the occupiers, the Silbermans are being uprooted because of the simple fact of their religion and birth. It's wrong. So terribly wrong.

And I can do nothing to stop it.

"Yes, of course you will." Do I say it to reassure them or convince myself? Maybe it's futile on both counts.

Dr. Silberman stacks the framed photographs and wraps them in the tablecloth. "I'll help you carry everything upstairs."

I should be going. Doubtless they still have much to do this evening. This is their last night in their home, and they must surely wish to be alone as a family. But I can't leave without saying goodbye to Hania.

I turn to Pani Silberman. "Is Hania here? I'd like to say goodbye to her if I could."

Pani Silberman nods, her faint smile tinged with sorrow. "She's in the kitchen."

"Thank you," I say quietly.

The Silbermans' kitchen is at the back of the flat, the door ajar. In the doorway, I pause. Hania stands at the kitchen dresser, an absent look in her eyes as she packs a hamper with cooking utensils.

"Hania?"

She turns, as if startled, perhaps pulled out of some memory. "Zosia, I didn't hear you come in."

"I just came to collect what you have for me. Your father is going to help me bring it upstairs. Is there anything you'd like me to keep for you?"

She hesitates. "No, but thank you. It eases my parents' minds to know our things will be safe with you."

The murmur of voices from the dining room filters into the kitchen. "I wanted to say goodbye."

She nods, presses her lips together.

"We may not be neighbors anymore, but we won't be far away. Perhaps you might visit. You're always welcome." Even as I say the words, I wonder how easy it will be for the inhabitants of the ghetto to move freely outside its boundaries.

"I'll come if I can." Hania's voice is hesitant, as if she wonders the same. She lifts her chin. "I'm sure we'll see each other soon." How young she looks, chin bravely lifted, even as she blinks as though forcing back tears, standing on the precipice of a future that promises no certain footing.

For an unguarded moment, her eyes hide nothing from me. In them is everything she does not say, a world of fear and uncertainty and loss.

The ache in my chest expands. I want to tell her everything will be all right, but I can't because I don't know if it will.

Instead I keep my smile strong. "Then there's no need to say goodbye."

"You're right." She smiles, a forced steadiness in it, only the slightest waver at its edges. "Why should we say goodbye?"

• • •

Hania

At last the long day draws to an end. Part of me is glad to put it behind me, yet another part wishes I could slow time, stretch out these final hours in the place I've called home as long as I can remember. Despite the hardships we've faced since the war began, despite everything that has been taken from us, we still had our flat. The familiarity we found within its walls gave us a measure of security, or at least the illusion of one as the storm raged outside.

Now its loss is added to the others.

We finish packing long after dark and sit down to supper, the last we will share around our table. Tata sold it to Pan Woźniak, our landlord, along with the furnishings in our sitting room. For them, Pan Woźniak paid a third of their value. We weren't in much of a position to haggle. In any case, we couldn't have moved them to the ghetto.

Though I'm hungry, I have to force myself to swallow the cold potato pancakes and chew the bread Zosia brought. We speak little, the scrape of our forks uncomfortably loud in the silence. No one feels like eating, except maybe Szymon, but we do anyway, forcing bite after bite until we finish the meal. Strain betrays itself in the faces of my family, as if we're but echoes of the selves that once filled this room with liveliness and laughter.

Mama offers to help with the dishes, but she looks so worn, I insist she leave it to Rena and me. In the silent kitchen, we repeat the routine begun long ago, continued evening after evening, year after year. I wash and Rena dries. I wipe the table and she sweeps the floor. There's no point in bothering with chores in a house that will no longer be ours after tomorrow, but we do not ask each other whether we should do them. We simply complete the tasks in silence, as if tonight is nothing more than the end of another day in an unbroken string of ordinary life.

Before leaving the kitchen, I pause to glance once more around the room, making sure everything is scrubbed and tidy.

I pass the sitting room on my way to bed. How strange and vacant it looks, suitcases, the trunk, and crates piled on the floor, the walls bare. Tata sits in his favorite armchair, muted lamplight casting his features in shadow. Through the days of preparation, he's remained strong for us, but now he slumps in the chair, eyes distant, almost dazed, the cracks in his control settling into his face. Though not an imposing man in height or build, my tata has always seemed so handsome and distinguished, a twinkle never far from his eyes. I ache to see how he has aged, how the light has left his gaze.

I pause beside his chair and bend to kiss his cheek. "Good night, Tata."

He reaches up and pulls me close for a moment, his cheek scratchy against mine. I breathe in the dusky scent of his pipe tobacco. He doesn't smoke as often as he once did, but he must have done so tonight, perhaps seeking some small comfort from the familiar habit. "Sweet sleep, my Hania."

I leave him there, sitting alone in the quiet room.

Rena is already in bed when I come into our room in my nightdress after brushing my teeth in the lavatory. I cross the room, the floorboards cold against my bare feet, and slip beneath the sheets, pulling the eiderdown to my chin.

"Good night, Rena," I call softly.

She doesn't echo my good night as she usually does. Maybe she's already asleep.

I close my eyes, listening to the murmur of my parents' voices down the hall and Szymon moving about in the room next to ours.

Sometime later, as I drift in the space between wakefulness and sleep, a voice whispers, "Can I come into bed with you?"

I open my eyes.

Rena stands beside my bed, a slight shadow in a pale nightgown.

I scoot over, making room for her. She crawls beneath the covers, resting her head next to mine on the pillow. It isn't until she's beside me that I realize she's shaking.

"Renusia, what is it?"

She doesn't answer, her body trembling.

I wrap my arms around her. "Shhh," I whisper. "It's going to be all right."

"I'm so afraid." Her voice is small. "I wish I wasn't afraid. I wish we didn't have to go."

It's the first time she's spoken about our move to the ghetto since the night we read the edict. Since then, she's been withdrawn, retreating into herself like a small animal into its burrow. It's worried me to see her so, but each time I've asked, she's always insisted she's fine.

My heart squeezes.

Why is this happening to us?

"I know. I'm afraid too." I haven't spoken the words aloud, and to voice them now feels like a confession. "But we'll be all right. You'll see."

"How long will we have to live there?"

"A few months, at least, maybe a year. Until the war is over." Will that day ever come? Germany and its allies have conquered and occupied most of Europe. Never would we have believed they could be capable of such victories until they achieved them. How are they ever to be overcome? The thought fills me with a panicked kind of despair, and I push it away before it tightens its grip.

"What will it be like?" Her breath warms my cheek. She's still shaking but less than before.

"Not as nice as this, probably. But we'll have our own things with us, and we'll make it as much like home as we can. It doesn't matter where we are so long as we're together. That's always the most important thing, no matter what happens. Now, try to sleep."

Rena's eyes drift closed as her warm body nestles against mine. Minutes pass as her breaths lengthen and she relaxes in sleep, and I wonder how much of what I told my sister will be true.

CHAPTER THREE

Hania
March 19, 1941

THIS HOUSE HAS HELD so many chapters of our family, each memory a page. There, I took my first steps, hoisting myself up by the arm of the sofa and tottering across the room into Tata's outstretched arms. Or so Mama always told the story. The dining room where our family has shared so many meals and memories, where we gathered around the table every Friday evening as Mama lit the candles and spoke the Shabbat blessing, the room aglow with light. With life.

My footsteps echo through the empty rooms. In the kitchen doorway, I still. Mama stands at the stove, running her hand along the edge of the oven, touching it lovingly as if it were a child. Her back is turned, her head bent.

"Mama?"

She turns, eyes glistening. "Hania." She swipes a hand across her cheek. "I didn't hear you come in. I was just having a moment, I suppose."

"Tata wanted me to tell you everything is ready," I say softly.

She touches the stove again, a wordless goodbye. I wait silently in the doorway. The kitchen is chilly and has a slight dusty smell from packing. I draw a breath, conjuring the scents of challah and cholent, potato kugel and spiced apple cake. Meals prepared with care and shared with warmth and love, so much a part of the simple cadence of our lives.

A prayer fills my heart for strength I do not have. ADONAI Eloheinu, the King of the Universe, has guided our people for thousands of years. Surely He will guide us, even now.

Mama turns. "We mustn't keep them waiting." Her voice is cracked but strong. She leaves the kitchen with dry eyes and straight shoulders and doesn't look back.

I follow her through the house and out the door. It closes behind us with a click. Its finality seeps into my heart and turns it cold. We pass no one on the stairs, and for this I am grateful. I do not want to encounter any of our neighbors, to see their pity or relief at our departure. Only Zosia bothered to say goodbye. I suppose it's easier for them to act as if we never lived side by side, as if we never existed at all.

We step into the damp March day where the rest of the family waits outside the building. The rented horse-drawn cart is piled so high with furniture and mattresses and crates that I have my doubts about whether the rickety conveyance will reach Podgórze intact. Tata, Szymon, and Rena stand around the cart, bundled in coats that bulge from the many layers they're wearing.

"I'm sorry to keep you waiting." Mama carries her handbag, hair smooth beneath her hat, armband with the blue star fastened neatly over her fur-collared coat.

Tata searches her face, a silent question passing between them.

She gives him a gentle smile, an assurance she's all right. "Did you give the key to the administrator?"

"I saw him earlier this morning."

"Good then." She's holding herself together, my mama. Perhaps she senses if her grip on her own frayed edges loosens, the rest of us will disintegrate into tatters.

Four suitcases rest on the pavement beside the cart. Szymon grabs the largest. I take another, leaving the smaller two for Mama and Rena.

As Tata climbs onto the cart, I look up at the row of third-story windows to the second one on the left. Zosia's window. The curtains are drawn and no figure stands silhouetted behind them, looking down at us. Somehow, I'm glad she isn't watching us go. It's better like this. I was afraid I would cry when we said goodbye, but I didn't want to acknowledge what both of us tried to deny, so I blinked the tears away as my throat ached.

Tata tugs on the reins and the cart rolls forward, the rest of us walking alongside it.

Only once do I glance over my shoulder at the building of buttery stucco with its delicate iron balconies where red geraniums bloom every spring, my girlhood home.

My eyes sting, but it's because of the wind, only the wind . . .

The cart rattles on and the shadow of our former home slips away.

As we make our way down the street, I sense the gazes of passersby upon us. Some stare with open disdain, others lower their eyes and quicken their pace.

"Hey, Jews! Don't come back," an adolescent youth in a ratty felt cap yells from the sidewalk.

I stare at him, wind tangling my hair around my cheeks. He elbows his companion and points at us as we pass. His companion winds up and hurls something at us, a rock or maybe a rotten apple. I tense but refuse to duck.

Thankfully he does not have very good aim.

"Good riddance, Jews!" Their jeers chase us down the street.

The relentless chill seeps through my clothes, but despite the cold, sweat soon collects beneath my armpits from the layers I'm wearing. With every step, the heavy suitcase bangs against my shins. Rena walks beside me, hair hanging in two plaits down the front of her woolen coat, armband drooping, eyes straight ahead. The pair of bony horses plod onward, hooves clopping on the pavement.

The closer we draw to the Third Bridge, the more clogged Alte Weichsel-strasse becomes. Soon we're caught up in a mass of others streaming down the muddy thoroughfare, making the same journey. Families pushing handcarts, wheelbarrows, prams, carrying suitcases, sitting crowded on carts heaped with furniture and odds and ends or following behind as we are. Women in elegant fur coats, their husbands in thick overcoats. Bearded men in black gaberdines and felt-brimmed hats. Families whose clothes are patched and worn.

Cart wheels creaking. Hooves clattering. Voices murmuring. Somewhere in the crowd, a baby cries. We cross the bridge over the Wisła, ornate iron spires dark against the unwashed sky. The lapping of the river merges with the steady tramp of footsteps. My shoulders ache from the weight of the suitcase. Icy wind rises off the river, scraping my cheeks and chilling me bone-deep.

Our journey to the ghetto passes in the space of a blink and the span of a lifetime. Somehow it is both. And neither.

Part of me is ready to arrive, to face what awaits us and set down the heavy suitcase. The other part wishes we could keep walking until we come to a place without occupation and edicts and the world walling us in. If such a place exists. If we could find a way to reach it.

But we're caught up in the crowd and it's too late to break away.

On we trudge, steadily forward, weighed down by the burden of our belongings.

Finally the gate stands before us. Men in the cap and armband of the *Jüdischer Ordnungsdienst*—the Jewish police force established by directive of the occupiers—keep order along with a few uniformed Germans. A queue of people and carts waiting to enter the ghetto snakes onto the street. At the gate, German police check everyone's papers.

Tata draws up on the reins and we wait beside the cart. Orders barked in German and Polish cut the air, sharp as the wind. My fingers ache from gripping the handle of the suitcase. The line drags forward. I stare at the half-built wall rising on either side of the entrance. How tall will it be when finished?

We reach the front of the line. Two German police approach our cart, their brimmed caps straight, holsters belted at the waist of their uniform greatcoats.

"Kennkarten." One holds out a gloved hand for our identification while the other strolls around our cart, hands behind his back, inspecting it.

The officer checks Tata and Mama's papers, then Szymon's. His gaze flicks over me as I hand him mine. I do not like to admit it, but to be in the presence of any German in uniform makes me shake inside. I know what they are capable of too well not to be afraid.

After a cursory scan, he returns my Kennkarte and waves us through. The cart trundles onward. Should we be sorry or relieved to be granted entrance?

As we pass through the gate, I suddenly find it difficult to breathe, as if a band has tightened around my chest. I suck in air, the cold sharp in my lungs. Rena walks beside me, wide eyes taking in Zgody Square, the cobblestoned expanse edged by buildings and teeming with luggage-laden men, women, and children. The guards at the gate, the frantic people hurrying in all directions, the collective tension thickening the atmosphere . . . all of it leaves me disoriented, adrift. Already, I ache for the comfort of familiar surroundings.

I glance at Mama. Wind tugs wisps of hair loose from her chignon, her cheeks reddened with cold, her lips pale. She scans the square, one hand clutching her traveling case, looking as lost as I am inside.

My parents need me to be strong. Rena and Szymon will be looking to me as an example. I grip the suitcase handle, swallowing my sorrow.

We're only across the river, after all.

After queuing for our housing assignment and wandering the ghetto asking strangers for directions, we finally arrive at Czarnieckiego Street. Somewhere on this street is the building to which we've been assigned. The cart clatters over the uneven cobblestones, wheels churning through puddles and splattering us with muddy water as we trudge past dingy buildings crammed alongside one another, their stuccoed facades crumbling and weatherworn. The buildings, the cobbles, the barren limbs of the trees planted at intervals along the sidewalk . . . everything is brown and gray. Even the sky is a faded pale gray.

Tata draws up on the reins in front of a four-story tenement building.

I swallow. Inside, it will be better. Surely.

Tata climbs down from the cart, pulls the housing assignment from his overcoat. He smooths the paper with his hand, squints a little as he checks it against the address.

"This is not the right place?" Mama asks, her voice pathetically hopeful and a little desperate as she stares up at the building's decaying exterior, the crumbling stucco revealing the bricks beneath.

"It matches the address on the housing assignment," is all Tata says, taking Mama's suitcase. He turns to Szymon. "Stay with the cart. We'll find out where we're supposed to be and start bringing everything inside."

Szymon swings onto the cart and holds the reins, cap tipped low over his eyes as he surveys the building with a grim expression.

The four of us approach the entrance. The door creaks when Tata opens it, and we follow him inside.

It takes a moment for my eyes to acclimate to the dusky light. We cross a small foyer with a cracked tile floor. One hand clutching the suitcase, the other trailing the peeling banister, I ascend the stairs behind my parents, Rena at my side.

One flight. Two.

Three.

The suitcase jostles against my legs with every step.

Four.

"Which flat did they say it was?" Mama asks, out of breath.

"This one, I think." Tata rummages in his pocket for the key the man from the housing office gave him. He sets down Mama's suitcase and tries the key.

The door swings open. We step inside.

In the doorway, we stop.

Four people—three men and an old woman—sit around a table. A middle-aged woman with a wrinkled apron around her broad waist stands at the stove stirring the contents of a bubbling pot. A folding bed is shoved up against one wall of the cramped kitchen and a clothesline sags across the room's length, shirts and undergarments almost brushing the heads of the people at the table. The odor of boiled cabbage hangs in the air.

Everyone stares at us. Rena sidles closer to me.

"Good day to you all," Tata says in the courteous tone he uses to greet patients. "I'm Dr. Adam Silberman. This is my wife, Faiga, and our daughters, Hania and Rena. We've been assigned housing in this flat."

Chair legs scrape as one of the men rises. "Mietek Birnbaum." He's about Tata's age, tall and wide-shouldered, his hair beginning to gray at the temples.

"But I think you must have the wrong place. This flat is already full. Let's see your housing assignment." He sticks out his hand for the paper. Tata gives it to him, and Pan Birnbaum scans the wrinkled page, rubbing the back of his neck.

"My apologies if we've disturbed you unnecessarily."

"No, no." Pan Birnbaum glances up, a crease between his brows. "This is the flat indicated on the housing assignment."

"But if there's no room available, I can speak to the housing office about reassigning us."

Yes. I take in the kitchen with its dirty window and peeling paint, the laundry drooping on the line, the strangers around the table eyeing us as if we're the last people they want to see. *Let's go somewhere else.*

"Wouldn't do any good." Pan Birnbaum sighs, hands back the paper.

My hope deflates slowly, painfully.

"The whole district is full, every building on every street. You'd better come with me. I'll show you to your room."

"Where are you going to put them?" The woman at the stove stops stirring, voice sharp.

"Current regulations are no fewer than three people for every window. Two windows, six people. There are two windows in your room and only three people. It could be worse, Pani Hirschfeld. There will be just seven with the Silbermans."

"But we're so crowded already." Pani Hirschfeld's voice turns shrill. "What does it matter how many windows there are? Surely seven people can't be expected to live in one small room."

"Actually." Tata's tone is quiet, apologetic. "There are five of us. My son is outside with our cart."

"That's quite all right, Pan *Doktor*," Pan Birnbaum says.

"Eight people," Pani Hirschfeld breathes.

"You heard what Birnbaum said." One of the men looks up from the nub of a cigarette, smoke curling between his stubby fingers. "Regulations. If you don't like it, take it up with the Judenrat. Or the Germans, if you prefer."

Pani Hirschfeld's mouth opens. Then she clamps her jaw shut and turns back to the stove.

Pan Birnbaum motions us to follow him. "This way, please."

We file past the people at the table and Pani Hirschfeld at the stove. She stirs vigorously as we pass, her lips sewn tight.

I want to tell her it's not our fault. We don't want to be here any more than she does. She should blame the Germans, not us.

Pan Birnbaum leads the way through a narrow passage into a room crowded with a bed, a sofa opposite, an armoire in the corner, and two mattresses on the floor. There's barely enough space to walk single file. "My family and I live here," he says as we pass. "My eldest son and his wife sleep in the kitchen."

He pushes open a door at the back of the room and steps aside to let us precede him.

The room is the size of Tata and Mama's bedroom at home—if anything it's a little smaller. An iron-frame bed is pushed against the far wall. Near one of the windows stands another bed. Suitcases and crates are stacked in jumbled piles, clothes spilling out of the open mouth of a trunk.

"They'll have to move some of their things to make room for yours, but that will not be a problem."

Maybe not for him, but what about Pani Hirschfeld?

"The, ah, facilities are in the courtyard. There's a water tap, outside too, I'm afraid, so we have to haul our water upstairs. Stove seems to draw all right though. My wife is out at the moment, but when she returns, you can speak to her about the kitchen arrangements, Pani Silberman."

"Thank you." Mama gives Pan Birnbaum a polite smile.

"The Hirschfelds arrived yesterday and we've been here only a week ourselves, so we're all still settling in. If I can be of any assistance, don't hesitate to ask."

"Thank you, Pan Birnbaum. That's most appreciated." How calm Tata sounds.

"Mietek, please." He gives a brief smile. "Well, then. I'll leave you to your unpacking." Pan Birnbaum shuts the door.

I lower the suitcase to the floor, taking in the faded yellow wallpaper that's ripped in places and discolored in others, the water stains on the ceiling, the two grimy windows, the tiny black bugs scattering the floorboards like spilled sand.

Eight people. In this room.

My throat tightens as if I'm being suffocated.

Tata sets down the suitcase. Mama simply stares, face chalky with disbelief. Rena's eyes search mine, seeking answers I do not have. Only this morning I woke in the room I've called mine since childhood, with its rose-colored wallpaper and shining floorboards. In my heart, it's still home. But that home is no longer ours.

How are we to keep ourselves clean in such a place as this? How are we to live at all?

"I'll start bringing everything in." I somehow expected Tata to say, "We'll make it better," or, "It's not really so bad," but he says neither of those things.

Perhaps because he knows there's no use, or perhaps because he feels as help-less in the face of this reality as we all do.

Mama nods, as if waking from a daze. "The cart has to be returned by five o'clock. We'd best get started."

"The children and I will manage. I don't want you tiring yourself out going up and down those stairs."

"Adam, I'm fine."

"There's plenty for you to do unpacking in here." Tata touches her arm. "Leave it with us, my dear."

"It won't take long at all." I move toward the door, eager to breathe fresh air instead of the dank staleness of the flat. Or maybe simply eager for a few moments of escape.

"We'll give everything a good scrubbing straightaway." She turns to Rena and me, makes an attempt at a smile. "How many times have I told you girls a little soap and water can do wonders?" Despite her brave words, she looks around our new living quarters as if she's asking herself how this can possibly be real.

For her to be reduced to this, my mama who has always taken such care with her housekeeping, such pride in making our home a comfortable and pleasant place . . .

"All the time. Isn't that right, Rena?" I force brightness into my voice. Better than to give into tears, though tonight, in the darkness, I am not sure I will be able to hold them back. Later, when no one can hear, then I will cry.

As I follow the others out, I glance over my shoulder. Mama stands in the middle of the dismal room in her fur-collared coat, our suitcases at her feet.

If this is the worst we must bear . . .

• • •

April 29, 1941

Walls surround us.

Rising three meters high, the newly built wall is an impenetrable barri-cade, sealing those within the ghetto off from the world outside. But it's the ridged half circles crowning the wall that make my stomach twist with a familiar sense of dread.

The top of the wall is shaped like a row of tombstones.

It's as if they have enclosed us in our own private cemetery. Perhaps that is what the Germans intend this place to become.

Where no wall has been built, there are fences of barbed wire. Even the windows and doors of buildings bordering the Aryan side have been bricked off or sealed with bars. The ghetto is a month old, and its demarcation lines are fixed in place. I've heard it said there are over twelve thousand people living in a space where around three thousand used to reside.

Some rumors are as flimsy as cigarette paper, but this is one I can well believe.

I hurry home, one among a dingy crowd. Dusk paints the sky in smoky tendrils, signaling another day in the ghetto is drawing to a close. Each morning, a large portion of the district's population passes through one of the four gates under guard to work in factories or perform other labor for the Germans, returning at the end of the day. In the evenings, the teeming cauldron of humanity bubbles over as the ghetto takes on a semblance of ordinary city life. People throng the streets, hastening about errands before the approach of curfew forces them indoors. In the past month, a handful of shops have been established, even a few restaurants and cafés frequented by those who can spare the złotys for a cup of ersatz coffee or a meal. Tata used what pull he has to get Mama a job at one such restaurant on Limanows-kiego Street.

Others cluster on sidewalks and street corners for a bit of conversation, to hear and tell the latest rumors and exchange news. The flats are so crowded that gathering on the streets, even in inclement weather, is preferable to remaining indoors. At least one can breathe a little air not tainted by the stew of odors that invariably collect when too many bodies are crammed into too small a space.

Of course, out of doors one runs the risk of bored SS passing through the ghetto and deciding to amuse themselves by beating passersby for some nonexistent infraction or shearing or yanking out the beards and sidelocks of Orthodox men, taunting them while the men stand, trickles of blood trailing down their faces where the shears clipped skin.

A trio of boys kick an old ball in the street, their high shouts carrying on the damp air, as if their confinement has been forgotten for a few moments and they are simply children, happy in their game.

I quicken my steps. They kept us later than usual today and Mama will be worried. Six days a week, I report to the *Arbeitsamt*—the labor office in the ghetto—where lorries wait to take a group of us outside the district to clean a military barracks or, on other days, to storehouses where we load heavy crates of foodstuffs onto trucks. At the end of the first day, we had to show our Kennkarten so our names could be put on a list. Whoever failed to report the next day, the German policeman said, would be severely punished.

After I came home and nearly collapsed from exhaustion, Tata wanted to try to obtain a better job for me, ready to exert influence with someone at the Arbeitsamt. But after the German policeman's speech, I didn't dare let my tata make such an attempt. I do my best to hide my weariness, to not taint our few hours together with dread of what the next day will bring.

I reach our building and let myself in. At the bottom of the stairs, I pause, staring wearily upward, then trudge up the four flights without stopping to rest on the landings. I step inside our flat.

Pani Hirschfeld stands at the stove, gripping a wooden spoon in midair, the other fist planted on one ample hip. "So now you're going to ignore me, is that it?" She slams down the spoon. The pot boils over.

"Will you shut your mouth?" Pan Hirschfeld mutters, slumped at the table, a half-smoked cigarette between his knobby fingers. "You're wearing on my nerves."

"*Your* nerves? What about my nerves? But why think about me? Why consider your wife at all?"

Hunched in the corner, Pani Hirschfeld's mama darns a sock, squinting at the stiches, deaf to the row in the kitchen.

I cross the room, giving Pani Hirschfeld a wide berth. During their last quarrel, we heard an awful crash from the kitchen. I never figured out who threw what. The Birnbaums' door is ajar, so I don't knock before stepping inside. Pani Birnbaum sits on the sofa, cleaning a shoe with a brush. Pan Birnbaum faces the peeling wallpaper, staring at it as if it's a window. Their room is emptier than usual. Pan Birnbaum's two sons, daughter, and daughter-in-law must not be in yet.

"Hello, Hania." Pan Birnbaum turns, giving me a tired smile.

"Good evening, Pan Birnbaum." I edge my way between the furniture and beds to the door of our room.

"Hania, you're so late," Mama says as I step into the right half of the room.

An old bedsheet strung across a clothesline divides the space in an attempt at providing a modicum of privacy, though we can still hear every sound made on the other side of the makeshift wall.

"They kept us until the work was finished." I shrug out of my coat, hang it on a nail.

"Where was it today?" Mama folds a towel, tidying our half of the room.

"The barracks at Montelupich Prison." I sit on the bed Rena and I share, kneading the sore muscles in my shoulder. Though we receive a bowl of soup in the afternoon—as if one bowl of soup is a fair exchange for a day's labor—my empty stomach aches for food, my body for rest.

"Why do they send you there? One would think they had enough prisoners for such work."

Some of the others in my labor detail voiced this question in the lorry on our way back to the ghetto. One of the men, cradling his injured arm, bitterly suggested it's because the guards find us entertaining. Though we women haven't been beaten yet, the men are often subjected to kicks and blows, beginning afresh each time the guards change, which they do often, as if everyone wants a piece of the fun.

To Mama I say only, "Maybe they like the way we do the work."

Pani Hirschfeld's shouts and Pan Hirschfeld's gruff rejoinders reverberate through the flimsy walls, the quarrel in the kitchen reaching a crescendo.

Rena picks up a book and holds it in front of her face.

Mama sighs, raising her gaze to the ceiling. "Really, how people can behave like this . . ."

Footsteps stump into the room, followed by a heavy creaking of bed-springs on the other side of the curtain. Pan Hirschfeld mumbles something under his breath.

"Where are Szymon and Tata?"

"Szymon isn't back yet . . ." Mama's voice fades. I look up as she presses a hand to her chest, face chalky.

I rush to her. "Mama, are you all right?"

She nods, eyes closed.

I turn to Rena. "Fetch Mama's medicine. And some water."

With a worried glance at Mama, Rena scurries from the room.

"Let's get you lying down." My arm around her shoulders, I guide her to the bed.

Rena runs in with a glass, fills it with water from the pitcher, and rummages for Mama's medicine in the drawer of the bedside table. She finds the packet and measures out some of the powder, adding it to the water.

I support Mama's shoulders while she drinks, then help her ease back against the pillow. "Do you want me to find Tata?"

She shakes her head. "He'll be home soon. I'm fine." Waning light from the window falls on her still-pale face. "The pain is already fading."

I lower myself to the edge of the bed, sitting beside her while Rena hovers nearby.

Finally, a trace of color returns to her cheeks.

"Are you feeling any better?" I squeeze her clammy hand.

"I'm all right now. I'm sorry if I frightened you. May I have another sip of water, Rena?"

I rise. "I'm going to make supper. Stay with her, Rena. Fetch me if the pains grow worse."

In the kitchen, Pani Hirschfeld sits at the table, eating a bowl of soup. She ignores me as I check the coal in the stove. The embers are dwindling, so I scoop a few chunks from the bin and feed them inside.

As I'm shredding potatoes into a bowl, the door opens and Szymon comes into the kitchen. He takes one look at sulking Pani Hirschfeld and shrugs. "I see we've had another evening of domestic bliss." A grin tips one side of his mouth.

Though I'm worn out and worried about Mama, I fight back a laugh.

"Glad I wasn't here to witness that touching scene. Where's Mama?"

"She isn't feeling well, so she's resting."

His brow tightens. "More pains in her chest?"

I nod, add a little flour to the shredded potatoes, and stir them together to form a dough of sorts. "Long day?"

"They took extra time counting us at the gate." His grimy hands carry a metallic scent from the nails he spends all day sorting.

I form the mixture into cakes and place them in the skillet. Tata comes through the door, finished with his shift at the community hospital, and goes straight in to Mama when I tell him she isn't well. The potato pancakes sizzle.

Life, in its own weary way, somehow goes on.

CHAPTER FOUR

Zosia
May 2, 1941

SPRING BRINGS RAIN AND drab skies, as if nature cannot find it in herself to flourish her splendors, the sun to unfurl its warmth upon the streets of Kraków while on the other side of the Wisła, the walls of the ghetto rise high.

Three days after the Silbermans left, I came down with a cough, which ripened into pneumonia and kept me in bed for nearly a month. I didn't realize until I started to regain strength how much time had elapsed during my illness. Easter had come and gone, my memories of the month of April as blurred as if I'd passed them in a haze of anesthetic.

Last week, I returned to Magister Borkowski's pharmacy and asked my colleagues if they'd heard anything about the Jewish residential district. The ghetto has been closed, they said. Its population can only leave under certain circumstances, mainly for work in industries deemed essential by the Germans.

Perhaps you might visit.

What sort of fairy tale had I been living in? As if the inhabitants of the ghetto would be allowed to pass through its gates whenever they chose. Perhaps I said it because it's what I wanted to believe. Of course they'd want to keep them behind the wall. Hadn't that been the point—to make Kraków free of Jews? My colleagues seemed surprised by my interest. They were glad the Germans had gotten rid of the Jews. And who really bothered about what happened to them anyway?

"Some people," I said simply. "Some people bother, and the Jews certainly do."

Magister Borkowski looked at me strangely while the young apprentice gave a laugh and said I could sometimes be quite absurd.

The next day, I attempted to obtain a pass to enter the ghetto, but according to the official I spoke to, a lady such as myself would not find the Jewish district at all to my liking. He seemed to think he was paying me a terrific compliment by calling me a lady, as I was, after all, still only a Pole. If I'd flirted or flattered, I might have had better success, but I did neither, and my polite insistence that someone now living in the ghetto owed me a debt I needed to collect (who could imagine a Pole would wish to enter the Jewish district for any other reason?) quickly put a damper on his charm and I left without the permit I sought.

I leave Magister Borkowski's and step out onto Grodzka Street, now christened Burgstrasse. A large number of our customers are German—the officials, police, and SS posted to the capital, some of whom have sent for their wives and children to join them in the city. I serve our occupiers with flawless German and a cool, professional manner while heat burns in my chest for all they have done to us—every oppressive edict, every ruthless punishment, every hour of fear for ourselves and the ones we love.

My steps clip on the sidewalk as I make my way along the stately thoroughfare lined with shops, cafés, and elegant residences. In the distance, the towers of the Church of St. Andrew rise against lowering clouds, its weathered stones a testament to the centuries it has stood watch over the present and the past.

"Zosia Lewandowska, is that you?"

I turn at the voice behind me as a woman approaches.

Her familiar features break into a smile. "I thought I recognized you."

"Irka, how good to see you." I smile warmly at Irena Droździkowska, my former classmate at university. By the time I arrived for my first semester, she'd already completed three years of studies, earning her master's degree the following year. We began one of those easy university friendships formed in snatches of conversation while dashing from one lecture hall to the next, Irka's almost-graduate confidence guiding me through those first uncertain days as a student.

How distant it all seems now.

"What are you doing in Old Town?"

"I work at Magister Borkowski's pharmacy, just down that way. And you?"

"My mama needed some thread. I've been to three shops and still haven't been able to match the shade."

Pedestrians pass as we stand in front of a shop window. I take her in, her compact figure in a simple jacket and skirt, blond hair drawn back in a chignon beneath her hat, keenly intelligent eyes.

"It's been so long."

Her expression is thoughtful. "It has, hasn't it?" Her eyes soften. "I was deeply sorry to hear about your husband. How long were you married?"

"Nearly two years."

One year and seven months. How fleeting and yet how indelible.

"What happened to those men is unspeakable. My tata was taken a few days after the arrests at the university. He's a teacher. Used to be one, anyway, at a secondary school. Taught German, actually. They released him, but not before he spent seven months in prison."

"How terrible." So many intellectuals seized, not only in Kraków but across Poland. Imprisoned, deported, or simply gone. Taken away and never heard from again. "How is he now?"

"He's not been the same since he returned." She presses her lips together. "The spirit breaks even when the body remains strong."

Silence falls between us for a moment. A flock of pigeons wheels away as a tram rolls past.

"Where do you work now?" I ask. "As I recall, you left Kraków for a time."

"I was working at a pharmacy in Rybnik, but I came back to Kraków as soon as I could after the war broke out. Are you on your way home?"

"I was, yes," I answer, the abrupt swerve in topics somewhat jolting.

"Mind if I walk with you?"

We fall into step, continuing along Burgstrasse. Thickening clouds darken the sky, the air close, nature's unspent breath poised to release as rain.

"To answer your other question, I've been at a pharmacy in Podgórze for over a year. The Apteka Pod Orłem, owned by the Pankiewicz family. Their son, Magister Tadeusz Pankiewicz, has been its manager for some years."

"The Pharmacy Under the Eagle," I murmur.

"It's in Zgody Square."

"Zgody Square. But isn't that . . . ?"

"The pharmacy is inside the Jewish residential district."

"I thought all Polish businesses had to relocate."

Irka leans close, as if we're girlfriends gossiping on an afternoon stroll. "They made an exception, if you can believe it. They offered Magister Pankiewicz a pharmacy in the city, formerly owned by Jews, in exchange. He turned it down. He said if he abandoned his pharmacy now, there'd be no chance of him getting it back after the war. It's been in his family for many years, and he didn't want to lose it. Not to mention he found the prospect of taking over property not rightfully his thoroughly distasteful."

"The authorities actually allowed this?"

"It took some persuasion, but they came to an understanding. As Magister Pankiewicz says, bribery is a most infallible method." Irka smiles dryly. "He told the officials it would be in their best interests to keep a pharmacy open in the ghetto to prevent an epidemic. You know how the Germans are about diseases. He managed to convince them in such a way it was as if they had the idea and he was simply following orders."

My mind reels as I absorb Irka's words. In an ordinary world, pharmacists serve whomever comes into their establishment. But in this new world where Jews live enclosed by walls for no other reason except they are Jews, the idea of the Germans permitting a Pole to run a pharmacy in the ghetto is almost unbelievable.

"And you're permitted to work with Magister Pankiewicz?"

"I've been issued a pass authorizing me to come and go, but Magister Pankiewicz lives in the duty room, so he's available at all hours. Between the two of us, we manage to meet the demands, though I admit at times we're nearly run off our feet. There are over twelve thousand people in the district and only one pharmacy."

Something stirs in my chest. Through Irka, could I find a way to reach the Silbermans?

"You don't happen to know how one might go about obtaining a pass? Not such as yours, of course, but to allow one temporary entrance. I've friends there. Former neighbors. I should very much like to look in on them, take them a few things. I tried to obtain one, but the official I spoke to didn't think a woman like myself had any business going into the ghetto."

"Someone ought to tell *him* the women forced to live there haven't any business there either." Irka cuts her voice low. "It could be arranged. Magister Pankiewicz has managed to get passes for a few of his acquaintances." For a moment, she regards me. "Would you ever think of taking such a position?"

Her hushed words still me inside.

Thunder rumbles overhead, a low shifting of the skies.

"What do you mean?"

"If a position at the Apteka Pod Orłem became available, would you con-sider it?" Still, that sharp assessment in her eyes.

"Is there such a position?"

"There may be."

"Then, yes." My words are fast, firm. "I would."

"You wouldn't like to think about it first?"

I can fold up my quick words and tuck them away like a handkerchief no longer needed. *I need time to think and consider.* But something awakens inside me, something that has been numb since the moment the letter arrived from Sachsenhausen with typed words that emptied my future and left me cold.

I refuse to surrender to the numbness again.

"There's no need. Please speak to Magister Pankiewicz."

She studies me a moment longer, then nods. "I'll ask him tomorrow."

For several minutes, we continue in silence. The first splatters of rain land fast and wet on my cheeks as we stop, facing each other at the corner of Alte Weichselstrasse. "How is it?" I ask in a quiet voice. "For the people behind the walls?"

She draws a long breath. "It's remarkable, really, what one can learn to endure. Poverty and degradation, the dailiness of their reality. It's not a life, but they find a way to live."

"And the pharmacy?"

Irka pauses before answering, simply, "We do what we can."

• • •

May 6, 1941

There's little a woman can't take on if fortified with the right hat.

The lady behind the counter told me that when I bought a hat for my interview with Magister Borkowski in the days when one still went shopping for such a frivolous purchase. I wanted something elegant and suitable for a professional woman, and she'd helped me choose a simple black felt hat with a slightly upturned brim.

Standing in front of the oval mirror hanging near the door, I set the hat upon my head, slanting it at just the right angle. I study my reflection an instant longer, my hair in a low roll at my nape, my best suit—a tailored burgundy jacket and skirt—neatly pressed. The woman in the mirror presents a picture of calm composure, gaze steady, cheeks only a little flushed, revealing no hint of the nerves beating wings in my stomach.

Then I pick up my handbag and leave the flat. I'm to meet Magister Pankiewicz at a café on Floriańska Street. Before Irka and I parted ways, I gave her my address, and yesterday morning a note arrived from Magister Pankiewicz requesting to meet for an interview.

I can't help but wonder what sort of man Magister Pankiewicz is and why he chose to remain in the ghetto. Are his motives merely to retain his family's pharmacy, or does he hope to make a profit off the Jewish people confined in the closed district? Or is he simply practicing his profession as one would at any pharmacy? I didn't put these questions to Irka, partly because I was still shocked a pharmacy operated in the ghetto at all.

Since I was a child sitting in Mass, I've trusted in God's providence, but since Ryszard's death, I've found it difficult to pray as before. How easy it is to seek God in the hope He'll bend His will to ours. How the silence mocks us when it seems our prayers have gone unheeded. I still pray, but my faith feels slight, cracked almost, in the face of the brutality and losses of war.

Yet if God has some purpose for me, I pray He will show me.

I alight from the tram and reach the café a few minutes later, pausing in front of the plate glass window to smooth a few flyaway strands before drawing a breath and pushing open the door.

I pause on the threshold. Customers sit at circular tables, drinking coffee, smoking cigarettes, reading newspapers, conversing with companions. The clink of cups against saucers mingles with the undercurrent of conversation.

I scan the room's occupants, attempting a modicum of poise. It's only now I realize I've no way of recognizing Magister Pankiewicz. I don't even know if he's a young man or an older one. I should have asked Irka.

"Pardon me, please," I ask a passing waitress. "Do you know if a Magister Tadeusz Pankiewicz is here? He's expecting me."

"Oh, yes. He's right over there." She gestures to a corner table where a man sits, reading a newspaper.

At that moment, he glances up and our eyes connect. He folds the newspaper and rises, making his way toward me. "Magistra Lewandowska?"

"You must be Magister Pankiewicz." Despite my nervousness, I find myself smiling. He's younger than I expected, surely no older than thirty-five, brown hair slicked back smooth, charcoal-gray double-breasted suit and pinstripe tie suggesting a man of sartorial taste.

"I am indeed. I'm very glad to meet you." He holds out his hand, a smile at the corners of his mouth. His clasp is firm yet warm. "Come." He motions for me to precede him. "I have a table for us over here." He leads me to the corner table and pulls out my chair.

I glance up at him. "Thank you."

He takes a seat across from me and signals to a waitress. After the waitress takes our orders and bustles away, Magister Pankiewicz folds his hands atop the table, studying me.

I regard him evenly in return, shoulders straight, my handbag in my lap.

He smiles again, slight, charming. "Thank you for meeting me."

"Yes, of course. I'm most interested to hear about your pharmacy."

He leans back in his chair, completely at ease. "Perhaps you might begin by telling me something of yourself. Your professional qualifications, as it were."

Despite his gallantry, the fixedness of his intelligent gaze tells me I've a test to pass. I clasp my hands atop my bag, palms moist. "In 1934, I passed my *matura* at the Queen Wanda State Secondary School of the Humanities. After that, I studied at Jagiellonian University's Faculty of Pharmacy and earned my master's degree in 1938. Following my graduation, I obtained a position at Magister Borkowski's pharmacy on Burgstrasse. I've been in his employ ever since."

The waitress returns bearing a tray with cups and saucers. After she leaves, Magister Pankiewicz picks up the bowl of sugar. He'd ordered sugar along with his coffee, but I didn't have the ration coupon, so had declined. "How do you take your coffee? One spoonful or two?"

"Thank you, but I'm fine."

"I insist. Come now, Pani Magistra. One spoonful or two?"

I laugh, letting myself be won over. "All right, one. And thank you."

He drops a spoonful of sugar into my cup, then one into his. He takes his time stirring his coffee, steam wafting from the cup, the spoon clinking against its edges. I stir my coffee and take a sip. Warm richness slides down my throat. The coffee is made of roasted acorns—only the Germans and those with the right black-market connections can get real coffee these days—but the sweetness of the sugar blends with the nutty taste, masking its bitter tang. I can't remember when I last had such a treat.

Magister Pankiewicz sits back, thoughtful as he regards me. "Magistra Droździkowska told me about your husband." His eyes are kind. "Professor Lewandowski must have been an exceptional man. I'm sorry not to have known him."

"He was, yes." I swallow. "A most exceptional man."

"Perhaps you'd care to hear about the Apteka Pod Orłem."

"Irka told me it's been in your family for many years."

"My father opened the pharmacy in 1910. Even before his retirement, I acted as its manager. I believe Magistra Droździkowska told you the pharmacy is in Podgórze."

I nod.

"We had a flat above the pharmacy, but my family had to move along with everyone else. The German authorities wanted to close my pharmacy and install me as the manager of one in the city center." He speaks in a low tone, our conversation one among a hum of voices. "So far, I've managed to avoid this."

"Considering the people you must've dealt with aren't known for their tractability, that's rather impressive."

He chuckles quietly. "Even the sturdiest branch has a point at which it will bend. It's simply a matter of ascertaining its location." He leans forward, gaze penetrating, and for the first time I shift beneath his scrutiny, afraid I'll somehow be found lacking. "You are aware, Pani Magistra, that if you accept a position at my pharmacy, you'll be working among Jews within the confines of their closed district."

"I'm aware."

"You've no objection?"

For so long, I've felt purposeless, powerless. If I might somehow do good, even if only in a small way, even if only as a pharmacist caring for people as my profession has taught me, then how can I not do what I can? It's not right, what is happening to the Jewish people, and I cannot stand by, an indifferent witness to the suffering of others.

My gaze is steady as it meets his. "Why should I object? I know there are a great many who are glad to see the Jews behind walls, but I've never been one of them. If they are forced to remain in this closed district, we must offer whatever aid we can. Certainly a pharmacy is a vital part of that." I hesitate. "At least, that is my view of things."

"Some believe the Jews have a tendency to spread disease, especially confined in such close quarters, and might see working in the Jewish district as putting their own health at risk."

"I'm not afraid of that. Besides, the risk of disease will be greater if they're unable to obtain medicine that could prevent its spread."

"That's just what I told the official who wanted to shut me down." He rubs a thumb across his chin. "There's another question I'm afraid I have to ask. You are of Aryan descent, are you not?"

"Yes," I say, though the question seems irrelevant. "None of my grandparents or parents were Jewish, if that's what you're asking."

"I only ask because, under the terms of my being permitted to operate the pharmacy, I must employ solely Aryan staff. I know several pharmacists in the ghetto, all extremely qualified, but I'm regrettably unable to offer any of them a position." He picks up his cup and takes another drink.

I'd forgotten about mine. I sip the now-tepid coffee, regretting not having drunk more while it was still hot.

"Very well, Pani Magistra."

My cup rattles against its saucer as I set it down.

"Magistra Droździkowska and I are in need of a qualified pharmacist to assist us. She may have mentioned how busy we are. I can pay you a salary of . . ." He pauses, then names a sum a little less than my salary at Magister Borkowski's. "It's not a very lucrative offer, I'm afraid. But the position is yours, if you're willing to take it."

I already live modestly and have only myself to support. I can manage a small decrease in pay. Apart from that, what else is there to hold me back?

I draw a breath, letting it out slowly. "Thank you, I accept."

A small frown creases Magister Pankiewicz's brow. "You're quite certain? Take a few days if you like, think it over. I'm in no hurry."

I'm not certain. But time will not increase my clarity, only allow room for hesitation. And really, what is there to be sure of anymore? War has shown us how friable our certainties are and perhaps have always been. There is only the moment before us. And what we choose to do in it.

"That won't be necessary." My heart beats fast, but my words are firm. "I've made up my mind."

CHAPTER FIVE

Zosia
May 12, 1941

TO THOSE WHO DWELL outside its walls, the ghetto is a place of mystery, a snapshot on the other side of a barbed-wire fence, a blur beyond the smudged window of a tram.

A world visited only through glimpses.

I approach the intersection of Podgórski Square and Limanowskiego Street. The pale arches of the main entrance to the ghetto stand ahead. My steps slow. Topped with scalloped crenellations and emblazoned with a Hebrew inscription, a Star of David crowning its center, there's a mocking elegance about the gate. A high wall capped with the same rounded half circles stretches on either side of the main entrance, a sentry box to one side, sealing off the street. Policemen stand guard, holsters at their belts.

JEWISH RESIDENTIAL DISTRICT

The words are inscribed across a nearby sign in German and Polish.

The street bustles with carts rattling past, women in trodden-down heels carrying market baskets, men with newspapers under their arms. As they pass the gate, no one stops, no one looks, no one pays attention. Perhaps the ghetto walls blend so seamlessly into the landscape they are no longer paid heed. Or perhaps it's simply easier to pretend the gate and what lies beyond it doesn't exist. That way there are no twinges of unease, no pangs of fear.

I check my watch. Five minutes past nine. Magister Pankiewicz said he or Irka would be at the main gate at nine o'clock on Monday morning. Minutes trail by as I wait, standing a few meters away.

A tram glides down the street and through one of the gate's high arches. Trams flow into the ghetto streets and out of them without stopping, like trains moving fast through the darkness of a tunnel and coming out the other side into bright light. Of course Jews are forbidden to board these trams and passengers prohibited from getting off until beyond the district's boundaries.

Irka hurries through one of the pedestrian entrances and rushes up to me. "Sorry I'm late." She presses a hand to her midsection, out of breath. "I had to finish up a couple of things in the laboratory. I hope I didn't keep you waiting long."

"Not at all."

She unclasps her bag. "I have your pass here." She rifles through her bag and hands me a folded slip of paper. "Permit to enter the district. Valid for two months, after which Magister Pankiewicz will arrange to have it renewed."

I study the pass authorizing the pharmacist Zofia Lewandowska to enter and exit the ghetto, an official stamp—an eagle above a swastika—near the left corner.

"They won't let you in or out without it, so keep it with you at all times."

"I understand." I open my handbag and place the pass inside my Kennkarte.

"Right then. This way."

I match her brisk pace as we approach the policeman at the gate—one of the Blue Police, as Polish policemen are commonly known, on account of their navy uniforms. Though Irka only left a couple of minutes ago, she presents her Kennkarte. He inspects her papers before returning them, and she moves on, waiting for me a few steps past the gate.

"Your papers?"

I hand him my Kennkarte, the identity card for non-Jewish Poles gray instead of dingy yellow.

He opens my Kennkarte and inspects the document inside. "You are employed at the Apteka Pod Orłem?"

"That's correct."

His gaze skims over me—my burgundy jacket and skirt, my small black hat at an angle, a basket over one arm, my envelope bag beneath the other.

"I've not seen you at the gate before."

"It's my first day." I keep my gaze level.

"What's in the basket?"

My stomach gives a little twist. I had not expected this. "My smock. And some food, as I'll be here all day."

"Open it."

I pull back the cloth. My smock is folded alongside a round loaf of bread, several potatoes, and a small head of cabbage. The policeman rummages through the basket. Beneath the loaf lies a cloth-wrapped sandwich of bread and beetroot marmalade—my actual dinner. The rest is for the Silbermans.

"A lot of food for one person."

"It's not only for me." I punctuate my words with a smile. "My colleagues will have some too. I brought it for us to share, as it's my first day."

"Not to sell to the Jews?"

I frown. "Of course not. Why would I want to do that?"

He assesses me a few seconds longer.

Sweat collects beneath my armpits.

"Very well." He returns my papers. "Proceed."

I pass through the small arch of the pedestrian entrance.

Irka waits for me on the sidewalk. "He searched you?"

"Only the basket." I draw a slow breath.

"You brought food for your friends, didn't you?"

I nod, stomach still tight, and return my papers to my handbag.

"What did you tell the policeman?"

"That we were going to eat it. I hope you like cabbage." A laugh escapes like a rush of breath.

"My favorite." She laughs. Then her grin fades. "It is possible to bring things in, if one knows how to go about it." She pauses. "You live on Alte Weichselstrasse, right? Then you won't often use this gate. The entrance at the intersection of Zgody Square and Kącik Street isn't far from the Third Bridge. It's the gate nearest the pharmacy. Come." With that, Irka strides onward and I hurry to keep up.

At first glance, we could be on any ordinary thoroughfare in Kraków. The pair of women crossing the street, the man carrying a ladder, the girl washing a shop window—all wear the familiar armband, but there is outwardly little to suggest we've entered a district accessed by guarded gates and hemmed in by a wall. It's strange, somehow, the indifference of externals.

We pass a street sign, the Hebrew letters indecipherable.

"All the signs are in Hebrew." Irka must have noticed my confusion. "It's one of the first orders the Germans gave, for all signs to be replaced with ones in Hebrew, which many here don't know how to read, especially younger people. The sign above the pharmacy is the only one in the district still in Polish. So far no one's said anything about changing it."

I don't need to ask why the authorities ordered this done. Inscribing everything in Hebrew is yet another way of deriding the Jews for their traditions, a further reminder of their isolation.

Irka leads the way at a breathless clip, far too quickly for me to absorb my surroundings, much less gain a sense of direction.

"The streets clear out during the day when many leave the district for work. There are several enterprises outside the ghetto that employ Jewish workers, factories and so forth, and people are always getting picked up off the streets and taken to do various labor. There are workshops inside the district too, along with shops, cafés, a community hospital, a hospital for infectious diseases, an infirmary for the elderly and disabled, and an orphanage. It's become quite its own community." Irka neither pauses for breath nor slows her stride.

A pair of uniformed men, a different sort of armband on their sleeves, stroll down the sidewalk. On the left side of their chests a bold yellow badge in the shape of the Star of David stands out.

"Who are they?"

Irka glances in their direction. "Members of the Ordnungsdienst. The OD handles the majority of day-to-day policing duties in the district. You'll see a lot more OD men and navy blues around here than you will Germans. They enter the district only on occasion, though there are some of them at the gates."

I hesitate before voicing the question. "What's it like? Working here?"

She doesn't answer right away. "The duties themselves are much the same as anywhere else. But it is . . . different. I can't explain exactly how. I suppose when one comes to understand the sort of life people lead here, one feels a duty to help however one can." She pauses. "We're on Targowa Street now. The pharmacy is just at the corner."

At the corner stands a building, the words *APTEKA J PANKIEWICZA* lettered on the glass above the door. Though some of the buildings in the square are old and dilapidated, there's a quiet elegance to this one with its sandstone facade, an iron balcony at its upper story.

Irka opens the door and I follow her inside, awash in the familiar intermingling of herbs universal to pharmacies. Magister Pankiewicz stands at a long front counter, a high cabinet filling the wall behind him. Porcelain canisters and labeled bottles line its shelves in orderly rows. Crowning the cabinet, above a clock, a carved eagle perches, wings spread, a patriotic homage to Poland's white eagle.

Magister Pankiewicz glances up from a prescription. He wears a pressed white coat, a bow tie at his throat, hair combed back. "Back already?" He sets the prescription on the counter. "Did you make out all right at the gate?"

"One of the navy blues searched Zosia's basket, but otherwise no difficulties."

"Good. The Blue Police don't give us much trouble. You'll get used to them soon enough."

"I'm sure," I say, as if being searched on one's way to work is simply an ordinary part of the day.

"Well then, Pani Magistra." A smile brackets the corners of Magister Pankiewicz's mouth as he rounds the counter, takes my hand, and grips it warmly in his. "Welcome to the Apteka Pod Orłem."

• • •

Hania

We assemble in the courtyard to be counted. The men in our group are already there, clothes stained with sweat and grime, faces weary in the waning light. My wrinkled dress clings to my sticky skin, rank with perspiration and—maybe I'm imagining it—the stench of the latrines we scrubbed today.

Hunger gnaws my stomach as the guards count us.

Soon this day will end. Soon I will be home.

Home. The word stills me. The ghetto, with its tombstone walls and eight people living in one room? That is a prison.

But my family is there, and so it is somehow also home.

The guards finish counting us, and I wait for the order to board the lorry. It doesn't come.

"You've done good work today," the tall guard addresses us. "You deserve a reward."

We stare at him warily. The men say he's always the first to beat them. What does this mean, praise from a German? Out of the corner of my eye, I glance at the taut faces of the men and women around me. We just want to return to the ghetto and our families.

"*Ja*," the other guard says cheerfully, the thickset one with the red face. "Good Jews deserve a reward. How about a song?"

Maybe they've gone crazy. The thought passes through my sluggish mind.

"'Rosamunde' is a good song. Do any of you know this song?"

We remain silent.

"Surely someone does. It's a popular tune." The red-faced guard hums a stanza under his breath. "Certainly, you remember. Don't you?" An undertone of warning enters his pleasant tone as he addresses a man in front.

"I remember now," the man says in a quiet voice.

"Good." The tall guard smiles. "Excellent. Then you will start everyone off. Come now, nice and loud."

We look at each other, uncertain what to do.

The guard pulls out his pistol.

My breath freezes.

The man's voice wavers as he begins the song. Others join in, voices blending in weak chorus. We're singing the Polish lyrics instead of the German ones, but the guards don't seem to care.

"Louder, louder." The red-faced guard claps his hands. "Everyone, together."

My lips move as I sing the next verse with the others. The guards clap along, laughing loudly at us. Spent from hauling heavy loads, from scrubbing their toilets, our voices are tuneless.

My chapped fingers form a fist at my side. Wind blows strands of hair into my face.

"Sing, sing!"

Our pathetic chorus blends with the laughter of the guards. The jaunty words, the faces around me tight with fear and strain and humiliation, the red-faced guard clapping along converges into a blur.

My nails dig into my palm, my voice wooden.

Soon I will be home. Soon this day will end.

But there is no end and so the words are comfortless.

• • •

Zosia

Irka is right about the work. My first day at the Apteka Pod Orłem differs little from my time at Magister Borkowski's. Irka quickly acquainted me with the pharmacy's layout. The dispensing room where customers come with prescriptions in hand or to seek out a remedy for a particular ailment, and the adjoining prescription room where medicines are prepared. The duty room where the pharmacist conducts professional meetings and stays if on night duty and where Magister Pankiewicz now lives, and the materials room where the stock of herbs, tinctures, syrups, and other pharmacopeia are kept. And finally the laboratory, where medicaments are distilled and equipment, such as the fume hood and Kipp's apparatus, are stored and used.

But the Apteka Pod Orłem is more than a source for medication. Here, people come to meet with one another, read newspapers, discuss the political situation, and seek news from Magister Pankiewicz about the state of life outside the ghetto. "In many ways," Magister Pankiewicz says, "we're rather like an embassy, representing a world quite different from the one around us, a world of singular freedom."

It's into this, a world of singular freedom behind ghetto walls, that I've arrived.

Dr. Silberman isn't among Magister Pankiewicz's acquaintances, and though Irka recalls filling a prescription for a Pani Silberman, she doesn't know where I might find the family. I determine to make my way to one of the hospitals in the hope someone might know where Dr. Silberman lives. In the late afternoon, Irka calls me into the dispensing room and introduces me to a physician from the community hospital. The man, who not only knows Dr. Silberman but works with him, writes down their address.

I leave the pharmacy at six to begin my search for the Silbermans. On the stoop, I pause, staring out across the wide cobblestoned expanse of Zgody Square. At its northern end stands the gate, finished in the same style as the main entrance, its rounded arches an unbroken string.

Unmarked gravestones.

Only now do I realize what the wall resembles, and a chill trails the ridges of my spine.

Columns of men and women file through the entrance, drifting across the square like shadows in the fading daylight.

I pass unnoticed through the throng, carrying my basket. On a street corner, a woman peddles Star of David armbands, though the people hastening by pay her little heed. Nearby a man purchases a pack of cigarettes from a boy hawking them from a tray around his neck.

Several minutes later, I reach Czarnieckiego Street. At least I hope it is. The sign in Hebrew isn't much help one way or the other.

My heels click on the sidewalk. Though the ghetto may be only across the river, far more than distance separates Czarnieckiego Street from the middle-class elegance of Starowiślna, the grand thoroughfares of Old Town. Dilapidated buildings line the street, the cobbles cracked, spindly trees spaced along the sidewalk. There's a tiredness about the narrow street and drab tenements, a dull poverty. In the hazy light of early evening, people stand talking in pairs or clusters, snatches of conversation ebbing and rising.

I scan the numbers on the buildings until I come to the address written on the wrinkled pharmacy letterhead. Outside the tenement, a man stands smoking a cigarette.

"Pardon me, do you know if Dr. Silberman and his family live in this building?"

He sucks down another drag before glancing at me. "Fourth floor. First door on the right."

"Thank you." I move past him and let myself inside.

The instant I draw a breath, I'm hit by the staleness of damp must and something rank and unwashed. I hurry up the narrow stairs. The higher I climb, the more oppressive the air becomes.

On the fourth floor, I rap on the first door on the right, then wait, basket over my arm.

A square-framed woman with tired eyes answers my knock. "Yes?"

"I'm looking for the Silbermans. I was told I'd find them here."

"If it's Dr. Silberman you want, he isn't in."

"Actually I came to see Pani Silberman and her daughters." I offer a smile, but her face doesn't soften.

"You'd better come in then."

I step inside a dingy kitchen. A middle-aged woman stands at the stove, the room stuffy with the scents of cabbage cooking, stale cigarette smoke, and musky bodies. A girl around Hania's age bustles about, laying the table with plates. On the sagging bed against the wall, a man bends to unlace his boots. In the corner an old woman sits, mending a shirt.

"Good evening," I say, as everyone's gazes turn toward me.

"I'll take you to Faiga." The woman who let me in eyes me with interest. Does she notice my lack of an armband?

"Thank you." I follow her out of the kitchen and through a narrow passageway.

She knocks on a closed door.

"Who is it?" a man calls.

"There's someone here to see the Silbermans."

"I'll be right there." A minute later, a man opens the door, shirt untucked, a few buttons yet undone. "Sorry. I was just changing."

The woman leads the way through a room so crowded with beds and furniture one nearly has to turn sideways to pass. A younger man snores on one of the mattresses.

How many people live in this flat?

The woman raps on the door of the adjoining room. "Faiga, there's someone here to see you."

Soft footsteps on the other side, then the door opens. Pani Silberman presses a hand to her throat. "Oh, Pani Lewandowska, what are you doing here?"

"It's good to see you, Pani Silberman."

"Please. Come, come. Thank you, Pani Hirschfeld."

I step inside and she closes the door. "How good it is to see you." Pani Silberman clasps my hand, her work-roughened fingers cold in mine. "But how did you get in? Did you get a pass?"

A bedsheet draped over a clothesline partitions the space into two rooms. Rena steps out from the right half.

I smile at her. "Rena, how are you?"

Her smile is a little shy. "Hello, Pani Lewandowska."

I turn to Pani Silberman. "I work at the Apteka Pod Orłem on Zgody Square now. I started today."

"However did you get such a job?"

"Magister Pankiewicz's colleague is a friend of mine from university. She told me about the position."

"Ah, I see." She leads me into their half of the room, the space cramped with two beds, an armoire against the wall, a bedside table, a folding bed, and a chair. Pani Silberman hastens to pick up the towel draped over the chair's back. "Please, sit. I'll bring some tea."

Absurdly, my eyes sting. It's always been her way. No sooner would I call at their home with a magazine or book I thought Hania or one of the other children might enjoy than Pani Silberman would invite me in with a "So kind of you to always think of the children, Pani Lewandowska. You'll stay and have a cup of tea? And a slice of poppy seed cake? I baked it yesterday." Really, there was no refusing her. Nor did I want to, for I'd never tasted such poppy seed cake as Pani Silberman baked, so moist and rich. We'd chat while I savored a slice and she sipped tea, and Hania and Rena would tell me about school.

I take in the striped bedsheet drooping on the line, the stained and yellowed wallpaper, the furniture crammed so close one can scarcely turn around without bumping into something, and an angry despair rises in my throat.

I find a smile for Pani Silberman. "Thank you, that's very kind, but I'm afraid I can't stay long. How are you?"

"We get on all right." Pani Silberman pulls her cardigan tighter around herself, chafing her arms. "Adam has work at the community hospital and Szymon is at a nail factory. I have a job in the kitchen at a restaurant. Hania cleans for the Germans."

"Is Hania here?"

Small lines form between Pani Silberman's brows. "Not yet. Sometimes they keep her late."

"How many people live with you?"

"We share the flat with two other families. There are fourteen of us altogether, but everyone is here only after curfew."

Fourteen people in a flat no larger than mine. This is not poverty, for in poverty one still has freedom. This is a degradation.

"How can anyone expect you to live like this?" Maybe I should not speak it aloud, but the words come before I can check them.

"It's not so bad, really." She presses her lips together for an instant, her eyes betraying what she keeps silent. "We manage. The Birnbaums are very nice people. Pan Birnbaum used to be an accountant, and Pani Birnbaum and I get on well together."

"Do you have enough food?"

"They issue rations. And it's possible to buy a little extra, if one has the money."

I set my basket on the bed. "I brought you a few things."

Rena comes to stand by my side while I unpack the bread, cabbage, and potatoes. She picks up the round loaf and turns to Pani Silberman, holding the bread. "Look, Mama."

Pani Silberman places her hand on her daughter's shoulder. "So kind of you, Pani Lewandowska."

The door opens and Hania comes in.

Pani Silberman turns. "Hania, look who's come to pay us a visit."

"Zosia." She stands in the entrance to their half of the room, staring at me. Her dress is wrinkled, armband slipping below her sleeve, the strands escaping her drawn back hair falling in limp tendrils around her cheeks. "What are you doing here?"

"I work in the ghetto now, at the pharmacy on Zgody Square. I'll be coming into the district six days a week. They issued me a pass."

"You'll be working here?" Her quiet words hold disbelief. "But why?"

"The man who owns the pharmacy, Magister Pankiewicz, needed a qualified pharmacist. And I thought if I worked in the ghetto, I could bring you food and whatever else you need."

She frowns. "This job, you took it for us?"

"Not only for you. The district is full of people and there's only one pharmacy. That's reason enough. Now." I turn to Pani Silberman. "Whatever it is you need, tell me and I'll try to bring it in. Prices will be lower on the outside."

"But would that not be dangerous?" Pani Silberman looks uncertain. "If you were discovered doing such a thing?"

"There's no law against me bringing a little food when I come to work. You can pick it up at the pharmacy in a couple of days or send one of the children."

"I'll give you some money."

"We'll worry about that later, all right?" I say gently. "For now, just make me out a list of what you need."

I chat with Rena while Pani Silberman writes me a list. Rena asks who lives in their flat now, if the geraniums are blooming yet, what's been happening in the city, as if the Silbermans have been away for years instead of a few weeks. Hania goes to sit on the bed, reaches into a basket of mending, and takes out a sock to darn.

"So many questions, Rena." Pani Silberman finishes the list and hands it to me. "Here you are, Pani Lewandowska. Whatever you can do."

I scan the list with its modest requests—*kasza*, a spool of black thread, acorn coffee. "Of course." I slip it into my handbag, then pick up the empty basket. "I should be going. Please give my regards to Dr. Silberman."

"Adam will be sorry to have missed you."

"If there's anything you need, please, come to the pharmacy. If I'm not there, you can leave a message with Magister Pankiewicz."

Pani Silberman nods, a gentle smile on her lips. "It's good of you to come."

Hania sets her darning aside and rises. "I'll show you out."

I say goodbye to the others, then follow Hania through the adjoining room. Before entering the kitchen, I pause, facing her in the semidarkness of the passage. From the kitchen comes raised voices—a woman's shrill tone, followed by a man's brusque reply.

"Is there anything I can do?" I ask quietly.

Hania glances down at her hands. I notice how red and cracked they are, doubtless from whatever work she's doing. They must be painful. She needs ointment. I'll see she gets some.

She puts them behind her back, as if to hide them from me. "There's nothing. Nothing you could do, at least. But I'm . . . glad to see you."

Our eyes meet and I read in hers what she does not speak. Life in this place has been a harsh awakening.

There's no time for the conversation my heart wishes we could share. To sit together and talk as friends should. For her to speak of the burdens she carries, the truth of their life in this place. For me to question and listen and offer what I can.

So I say only, "We'll meet soon, yes?"

"Yes." A faint smile touches her lips. "Soon."

I leave the flat and turn my steps in the direction of the gate, but the squalor of the ghetto remains with me.

Alone in the room I once shared with my husband, in my flat on the other side of the river, all I saw today runs through my mind. The people who came to the pharmacy seeking prescriptions and an oasis of momentary peace, the dreary streets thronged with all the bustle of an ordinary city, the walls topped so elaborately with scalloped ridges, the dismal flat smelling of cabbage and shared by fourteen.

Hania's eyes, a little lost, beginning to harden with a dull endurance of reality.

Tomorrow I'll return to the district and show my papers to the policeman. He'll search my basket and I'll pass through the gate. Spend the day compounding medications and filling prescriptions, the familiar duties anchoring me in a place that resembles a distorted mirror of a normal world.

Irka's words, spoken the day we met in Old Town, return now, an echo. *We do what we can.*

Even when there seems so little we can do.

CHAPTER SIX

Zosia
October 16, 1941

THE GHETTO GROANED BENEATH the weight of its inhabitants, but it was not enough for the rulers of the Generalgouvernement. No, more room must be found. More room to accommodate the Jews from the surrounding districts ordered to move to the ghetto.

Thousands made their way to Podgórze. The authorities denied the Judenrat's request for the boundaries of the Jewish residential district to be increased, so the new arrivals scrambled to secure lodgings in already overcrowded flats.

Yom Kippur, the holiest day of the Jewish year, was set as the deadline for the relocation. Instead of spending the day in fasting and prayer, people queued outside the gates in the spitting autumn rain, There are no coincidences with the Germans.

It's estimated over 17,000 people now reside within these walls. In many flats, three families share one room. People are living in cellars and attics, sleeping wherever they can find a place. We're busier than ever dispensing medications, the pharmacy crowded with acquaintances who gather to discuss the progress of the war. Germany invaded Russia in June, the two powerful countries no longer allied. Optimists say Hitler's defeat is inevitable, while others grimly predict that if the German army continues to advance, they'll soon be in Moscow.

Two weeks after the ghetto gates closed behind the last of its new inhabitants, I'm in the materials room preparing an ointment of zinc oxide when the door opens.

"I'm just finishing up." I keep at my task without pausing, pressing the pestle into the mortar to grind the ingredients into a paste.

No answer. I glance up.

Magister Pankiewicz stands in the doorway, Irka at his shoulder.

Their expressions need no translation.

I lower the pestle. "What is it?"

"There's been an announcement." Irka's voice is quiet, her features strained.

"Governor-General Frank has issued a decree, effective immediately. Any Jew caught without a valid pass outside their assigned district will be summarily executed." Magister Pankiewicz pauses. "Any Pole found giving refuge or aid to such a Jew will be dealt with in the same manner."

The words collect in my chest like unspent breath. It's no secret that people find ways of slipping out of the ghetto. Some of the policemen at the gate, even a few German guards, are willing to look the other way in exchange for a few złotys. Food is cheaper on the Aryan side, and some have become adept at sneaking out to purchase goods to smuggle into the ghetto, while others leave to sell their valuables. Before, being caught by the wrong person might earn one a beating or a fine. But now . . . ?

Execution.

"As far as the Germans are concerned, we're following their orders. In supplying medicines, we violate no decree. But if our aid extends beyond the boundaries of the district, if one of our acquaintances came to us requesting help in leaving the ghetto for any reason, well, there's no need to repeat myself."

"Is it still possible to stamp a prescription, so they can leave that way?" If a particular medicine isn't in stock at our pharmacy, it's often possible to obtain a pass to leave the ghetto for the purpose of going to another pharmacy if we stamp and write a note on a prescription stating a medication is unavailable at the Apteka Pod Orłem. Many times we've done this, even if we had the medicine, since the pretext enables someone to carry out errands on the Aryan side. I've done it several times for the Silbermans, allowing Hania or Szymon to purchase food outside the ghetto. In this way, they supplement the family's income by selling any extra provisions they bring in.

"For the moment, but I wouldn't be surprised if that comes to an end before long." Magister Pankiewicz crosses to sit on the edge of the table, takes his pipe from the pocket of his white coat.

"Already there's no chance of anyone getting a pass to go to another pharmacy on Sundays, since we're now ordered to remain open every day of the week," Irka says.

Magister Pankiewicz methodically packs and lights his pipe, a crease between his brows. "It will be far more dangerous now for our friends to handle their own affairs on the Aryan side." He takes a drag, whelming the room in the musky-sweet scent of tobacco. "Our passes enable us to enter and leave the district at any time. I know for you both to take on more than you already do would be a great deal to ask."

"I'll do it." Irka's words are quick, decisive. "Whatever is necessary."

I nod. "Both of us will."

"If it were to be found out the role of the Apteka Pod Orłem extends beyond the sphere of our profession, they'd shut us down, for one thing." He rises, looks at Irka and me in turn. "And that would likely be the least of it."

My stomach tightens.

"Every day we see the way life is here. How can we not help?" Irka says simply.

"We must do what we can." Though I may not fully understand the implications of my words, I mean them as fervently as I want Poland to be free, as I once wanted love.

Magister Pankiewicz nods. "Of course we must."

We look at each other and, in the small room hazy with tobacco smoke, it seems we all catch our breath a little.

God has granted us free will. The occupiers who strip the Jewish people of the most fundamental freedoms have exercised theirs.

Now the three of us, standing in the back of an unremarkable pharmacy, must exercise ours.

Is this resistance? Or is it simply our duty, as members of the human race, to alleviate suffering and oppose those who inflict it?

To answer the second we must commit to the cost of the first.

There is a sacredness to our vocation, one rooted in tradition passed down through the ages. Behind the preparation of medicines and dispensing of prescriptions, inbred in each of us dwells a desire to heal. Or at least to aid in healing in our own humble way.

War is not a disease for which a cure can be prescribed. Nor can we hope to mend the misery of life behind these walls.

But we are pharmacists. No matter how severe the sickness, if a remedy can provide a glimmer of relief, we will give it.

In serving, we find purpose.

• • •

Hania
December 27, 1941

"Achtung! Achtung!"

The words are an echo at first, distant, then drawing nearer. I stop on the sidewalk. A black car drives slowly down the street, the loudspeaker mounted on its roof spitting a string of words in German onto the frosty air.

"You are ordered by the *Stadthauptmann* to surrender your fur coats and all items made of fur, without any exceptions, to the authorities at the offices of the Judenrat by four o'clock today. All Jews found in possession of furs after four o'clock will be subject to severe penalties. Achtung! Achtung!"

The car passes by as the order repeats over the loudspeaker. People turn to one another on the sidewalk, low-spoken conversations flurrying on the early morning air.

I scramble to make sense of it, this strange, unexpected order. The German army is fighting the Russians on the eastern front. It's cold there, freezing. If their soldiers are suffering to such a degree the Germans are reduced to taking our furs, could it be things are starting to go badly for them? Now America has entered the war, maybe the Germans fear the coming year will bring an end to the victories of 1941.

Or perhaps it's simply a new kind of humiliation. Maybe that's how the Germans amuse themselves. Instead of playing cards, they sit around and devise new ways to increase the misery of the Jews.

I glance down at my coat. How elegant and grown-up I felt the first winter I wore the chocolate-brown wool garment with its stylish fur collar. In the ghetto, with little coal to heat the flat, I'd taken to wearing it inside.

I draw a breath of air as cold and sharp as the point of an icicle. Then I turn, carrying the empty market basket, and make my way down Limanowskiego Street.

Someone will need to take our furs to the collection point.

Tata and Mama must work today and Szymon's already at the nail factory. I'd best get going.

The first sound to reach my ears inside our flat is Pani Hirschfeld's sobbing. Ever since the night OD men took her mama, she cries all the time. The Germans issued an order for the population of the ghetto to be decreased on account of overcrowding, and the Judenrat and OD had to carry it out. Kennkarten were inspected and lists drawn up of those selected for resettlement. That is the word the Germans use: resettlement. Everyone speculates, but nobody knows what it really means. We'd heard rumors about the order, but there were so many rumors. How could we be prepared for the terrible night when OD men pounded on doors and rounded up the people whose names were on the list?

I can still hear Pani Hirschfeld's screams as the OD led her mama away. I could see it in their eyes; they did not want to do it, to take an old woman from her family. They are Jews too, but they must carry out the Germans' orders or the same fate may fall upon their own families.

At first, we didn't know where the people on the transport had been sent, but several days later word spread in whispers. Someone had returned to the ghetto and told how the train had stopped in the Lublin region. The guards forced everyone out and ordered them to disperse to the surrounding villages. In the following weeks, a trickle of others made their way back, having nowhere else to go and wanting only to be with their families, but Pani Hirschfeld's mama wasn't one of them. No one knows what happened to her.

Now, husband and wife face each other in the kitchen. Pani Hirschfeld clutches a fur coat against her chest.

"Give it to me, Lola."

"I don't—"

"I know you don't." Pan Hirschfeld sounds tired. "But you heard the order. We have no choice."

Pani Hirschfeld curses the Germans, loudly.

"Keep quiet. Do you want to be arrested?"

"Why are they taking our coats?" Rena whispers as she dries the breakfast dishes.

"I don't know." I sigh. "I suppose the Germans want them for their soldiers."

"Women's fur coats?" Rena scrunches her nose. "They'll look silly wearing those."

Despite how angry and miserable I am, I grin at my sister's expression. "I hope they look utterly stupid, and the Russians laugh when they see them. It would serve them right."

I pass through the kitchen and the Birnbaums' room. Pani Birnbaum sits on the bed, cutting a fur collar off a coat.

I step into our room. My parents stand next to their bed, Mama's fur-trimmed coat lying atop it. Tata's hand rests on Mama's shoulder. They both turn to look at me.

"Back already?" Mama asks. "Did you buy the bread?"

I set down the basket. "I hadn't reached the bakery when the order came over the loudspeaker. I'll go back for it."

"Shall I take the coats then?" Tata picks up his tie from the back of the chair.

"No, Tata. The line will be long, and it will make you late. I'll do it."

He nods and I retrieve Mama's sewing basket. I slip out of my coat and sit on the bed Rena and I share, the coat in my lap.

"It's just the fur they want, then? We can keep the rest of the coat?" I glance up. My parents don't seem to have heard me.

Mama runs her fingers gently over the soft fur trim, as she had when Tata gave her the coat for their fifteenth anniversary. I could still remember how her eyes had shone when she'd tried it on for the first time.

Then and there, she'd kissed Tata, rare in front of us children. Such joy, on both of their faces.

Now Tata presses his lips to Mama's forehead. "Someday, when this is all over, I'll buy you another one."

She leans into his embrace. "It doesn't matter," she murmurs. "That coat is worthless compared to you and the children."

I take up the cold metal sewing scissors, snipping the stiches, ripping out the threads. The fur collar comes away in my hands. I stare at it.

Never have words like Pani Hirschfeld used about the Germans been spoken in our home, and never before would I dream of saying them.

But as I cut away every last piece of fur from my once-beautiful coat, I choke them back while my hands shake and my heart twists from the swallowing pain of how completely powerless I feel.

Winter's bitter breath pierces through my now-collarless coat as I stand in the queue. Outside the Judenrat building near the main gate, women, men, and a few children form a line snaking down the sidewalk, arms loaded with bundles of furs. Snow falls from the blanched sky, thick flakes landing on my bare head and leaving cold blotches on my coat. The collars and linings from my coat and Mama's, the fur lining of my boots along with Rena's, Mama's muff, and Tata's fur-lined leather gloves fill my arms. We didn't risk keeping a single item. The Germans might conduct a search. Better the loss of our furs than our lives.

Minutes drag. Without the lining in my boots, my feet are soon freezing. I stamp in place to keep the blood flowing. People enter the building with their arms full and leave empty-handed.

The queue trudges forward.

My foot slips on a slick patch of sidewalk.

Breath whooshes from my lungs.

Lurching backward, I struggle to right myself, brace for the impact—

A steadying hand grasps my shoulder.

"Careful there."

Gasping, still clutching the furs, I turn.

Wind blows my hair away from my cheeks as my gaze tangles with that of the man who broke my fall.

"Thank you." My voice is a little breathless.

His brow furrows. "Are you all right?"

"I'm fine. The ground is icy, that's all."

The line plods forward and we move with it. I face forward, eyes on the back of the woman in front of me. Down the line, someone coughs. I glance over my shoulder.

I almost look away. Almost.

His nearly black hair curls at the ends, in need of a trim. He's perhaps a few years older than me, his cheekbones angular. They could be called chiseled, if he hadn't been existing on rations, but now his face is as lean as the rest of him. Over one arm, he carries a fur coat and several fur trimmings.

He notices me watching him.

His lips form the smallest of grins, a crevice deepening on the left side of his mouth.

If I wasn't so cold, a blush might heat my cheeks.

But I'm cold, shivering, so it doesn't.

We move forward again. I shift my grip on the bundle in my arms.

One of the collars falls onto the snow-coated sidewalk.

I bend to pick it up.

So does he.

We reach for the collar at the same time. My hair falls in a curtain around my wind-chapped cheeks. Our hands brush, the briefest of touches.

I snatch the collar, stand upright. "Th-thank you." My tongue stumbles over the simple words.

We're standing so close the smoke of our breath converges, mingles. I swallow, gaze falling on the furs over his arm. The coat is a soft reddish-brown. "That's a nice coat."

His lips angle upward, but the gesture holds no warmth, only bitterness. "It's my *babcia*'s. She loves this coat."

I nod, hoping my eyes show I understand.

"Better to cut it to pieces than hand it over to them," he mutters in a voice almost too quiet to hear.

I draw a sharp breath, the dangerous words dangling between us.

"My apologies." He truly does look sorry. "I shouldn't have said that."

"No," I say quietly. "I understand."

The queue drags forward as we near the entrance. I turn away as I follow the line.

A minute passes before I look back again.

He's gone.

My gaze swivels up and down the street.

A man strides away from the line, his coat-clad figure receding.

I sense instinctively why he has left the line. What he intends to do.

Severe penalties . . .

I glance away, fast, the furs a thick weight in my arms. Around me, people shuffle forward, waiting to enter the Judenrat building.

Where we'll surrender our furs, so German soldiers will be protected against the frozen winter on the eastern front, so they'll have the strength to keep fighting, so the war will be won for the Reich.

The people shivering in the queue are only handing over their belongings because they're afraid of the consequences of disobedience.

Something hot and hard rises inside of me. The occupiers take our businesses and homes, trap us behind walls, force us to labor in their industries for a few pitiful złotys or a ladleful of soup, steal winter coats from old women and fur linings from young girls' boots, and we do nothing to stop them, because really, what can we do? How confident they are in their ability to terrify us into submission.

With that, I make my decision.

I look around. Everyone is either watching the door or staring at the ground.

Three steps is all it takes to slip out of line.

My heart thuds. I force myself to walk slowly away from the queue.

Someone will notice . . . any second I'll hear boots pounding behind me, a harsh shout ordering me to halt . . .

I glimpse the back of the man's coat as he rounds the corner.

I quicken my pace, clutching the bulky furs. The street blurs in the flurrying snow. The sidewalks are mostly empty, and the few people out walk with hurried steps.

I stop, scanning the street. The frost of my breath clouds in front of my face. A woman trudges down the sidewalk, carrying a bucket of coal.

What if I can't find him? What if I left the line for nothing?

I keep walking.

A flash of a dark coat as the man disappears down an alley.

I break into a run, stumbling over the slick cobbles.

If I don't catch up to him, I'm on my own.

I hurl myself into the alley, my breaths ice in my lungs.

He pauses at its end, stance rigid, as if he senses he's being followed.

"Wait." I gasp the word.

He turns, framed by derelict buildings rising on both sides, his cap pulled low.

I rush toward him.

He frowns. "Did you follow me?"

"Please." My voice sounds small, like a frightened child's. Not like a bold woman who left the line and dared the consequences. "Let me come with you."

"Where?"

"Wherever you're going to destroy your babcia's coat."

"How did you . . . ?" He shakes his head. I can't tell whether the gesture means no or is simply an expression of disbelief. "Are you sure you want to come?"

"I don't want the Germans to have my mama's furs. I'd rather burn them."

The force of my words seems to surprise him. "All right." He nods. "Come with me." He leads the way through familiar streets and less-familiar alleys and courtyards, through a gateway and into a courtyard, freshly fallen snow coating the dirty slush beneath.

A wooden privy stands in one corner of the yard, the icy air sharp with the familiar stench of waste.

He scans our surroundings, eyes alert, cautious. He glances at me. Cold reddens the tip of his nose. "I'll be back in a few minutes. I need to get a couple of things. Hold these." He dumps his furs on top of the pile in my arms, the load now so high I can barely see over it. "If anyone asks, you're on your way to the Judenrat building."

I nod, shifting my grip on the bulky furs. I'm not certain what he plans to do, but I sense this isn't the moment for questions.

"I won't be long." He brushes past me, his steps crunching quickly across the snow-covered courtyard.

Time stretches as I listen for footsteps. Twice someone comes into the courtyard to use the privy and both times I trudge toward the gateway, loaded down with furs, as though I'm on my way to the Judenrat building. Thankfully, it's too cold to dawdle, and each time they pay me little heed as they hasten into the privy.

At another set of footfalls, I pretend yet again to be walking away from the privy, but this time it's my comrade, returning with a shovel. He begins to move the crates and assortment of odds and ends mounded against the building, working quickly, throwing glances over his shoulder.

I watch, stunned, as he shifts the junk to one side, revealing a trapdoor inset in the side of the building. Hinges groan as he pulls it open.

He scoops the furs from my arms and tosses them through the opening, then turns to me.

"You go first. I'll follow and close the door."

I stare into the yawning mouth of the cellar, hesitating only an instant before I crouch and grasp the top of the ladder. Rung by rung, I descend into the darkness until my feet touch packed earth. Seconds later, he scrambles down after me, the slam of the trapdoor behind him immersing us in a blackness so complete it's suddenly difficult to breathe.

A flicker of light. The beam of an electric torch illuminates the outline of a low-ceilinged cellar.

I face him. Light casts shadows over the silver tapestry of cobwebs, over the planes and angles of his face. "What are we going to do?"

He sets the torch on the ground and shucks off his coat. "Dig a hole. Bury them. If we burned them, remnants in the stove could give us away." He picks up an armload from the junk piled in one corner—crates, a pram with only one wheel, and a battered coal scuttle. "This way, no one will be able to tell what we did or didn't do."

I hasten to help, and my coat soon becomes streaked with dust. Once we've moved everything, he picks up the shovel, stabs it into the hard-packed dirt, pushing down with his foot.

"Can I help?"

He tosses a shovelful of dirt to the side. "There isn't another shovel, I'm afraid."

I search for something to use, almost giddy when I glimpse a rusty coal scoop in a dark corner.

He raises a brow but doesn't say anything when I start to dig, pushing the coal shovel into the hardened dirt and flinging scoopfuls to the side. We work in silence, save for his panting breaths as he churns up the dirt and the thump of shovelfuls landing on the pile.

Finally, we finish the shallow pit. He leans on the shovel while I gather the furs and carry them to the hole. He takes his furs and drops them inside. I add ours to the pile, the trimmings of Mama's coat last.

I run a dirt-streaked palm over the sleek fur.

I didn't give it to the Germans, Mama.

We fill the hole, tamping down the dirt with our shovels.

When we've packed the dirt as best as we can, he takes the jar he brought, unscrews the lid, and sprinkles water over the area. "It's a trick my tata taught me," he says at my questioning glance. "Evenly distributes the absorption. Sometimes when they search a cellar, they pour water over the ground. When it soaks into one area more than the rest, it tells them something's recently been buried there. Then they dig and find it and . . . well, you can imagine what sort of things happen to the people who hid whatever it was."

I shiver. "Then you've done this before?"

"This isn't my first time digging in a cellar."

We replace the pile of junk and step back to survey our work.

"Even if you moved the junk, you wouldn't be able to tell." He reaches into his trousers pocket and hands me a folded handkerchief. "You'd better wipe off your hands."

I take the handkerchief and clean my palms as best I can. "Do you think they'll search?"

"Possibly. We'll find out, I suppose."

I return the handkerchief. "Did you plan this?"

He scrubs the dirt-stained handkerchief across his own hands. "I'd thought about it. I found the cellar not long after we moved in. But something came over me, standing in that line." He shoves the handkerchief into his pocket. "Maybe it was talking to you."

"I'm not usually this daring," I confess.

"Really?" A grin tugs at his lips. "I never would have guessed."

I'm grateful the scant light hides the sudden heat in my cheeks.

He shrugs into his coat. "I'll go first." He puts the jar in his pocket and hands me the shovel and electric torch. "Take these."

He scales the ladder. I stand at the foot, shining the torch toward the opening as he shoves against the trapdoor. It creaks and falls open with a thud. He scrabbles up and disappears. I flick off the torch and clamp it under one arm, clamber up the ladder carrying the shovel. He takes the shovel from me, then grabs my hand and I scramble out.

In the next instant, he shuts the trapdoor and we move the crates, so they once again conceal its location, working fast and in silence, attuned for the sound of footfalls. We finish and I brush myself off as best I can.

My comrade has a streak of grime across his cheekbone. If someone sees . . .

"You have a spot." I point to my face, indicating where it is.

He swipes the back of his hand along his cheek. "Thanks."

The mark remains. "You didn't quite . . ." I reach up and smudge the pad of my thumb across his cheek, grazing the warmth of his skin as I wipe away the dirt. The contact lasts a second. Scarcely more.

"Thanks," he says again.

I've danced with boys before, and once Poldek Ferber held my hand when he walked me home from school, but I've never touched a man so boldly. I'd be embarrassed, maybe a bit guilty, but wiping dirt off a man's face is really not all that significant after one has just defied a German order outright.

I should be getting back. Rena will worry. By the time I reach the flat, I'll need a suitable explanation for the length of my absence. I don't want to lie to my family, but they'd only worry if they knew what I'd done. "Well." I hesitate. "I'll say goodbye then."

"Goodbye." Our gazes hold. Beneath his fraying cap, his eyes are a deep, rich brown. The bridge of his nose has a small bump in it, as if he broke it once. I wonder when it happened and why.

I chide myself for studying him, for noticing how nice-looking he is. Doubtless there are no shortage of girls eager to walk with him on Krzemionki Hill, a grassy slope near the wall where courting couples often stroll on Sunday afternoons. He's probably already seeing someone. Either way, it doesn't matter to me.

I move past him, though not without a tug of reluctance.

"Wait."

I turn.

"My name's Romek." That half grin again, a little shy. "Romek Weinberg."

"Oh." A laugh escapes. Though we spent the past hour mutually risking our lives, neither of us thought to ask the other's name. "Hania Silberman."

"It's a pleasure to meet you, Hania." His voice is warm, the words strangely formal for a courtyard that reeks of a privy.

"And you, Romek." I test the name, savoring it like the first taste of a sugar-dusted Napoleonka.

"I'll see you again, I hope?"

I nod, my smile shy. "Goodbye." I hurry across the courtyard, ducking my head to hide my flushed cheeks.

I'll see you again.

Through the rest of that gray December day, I carry his words in my heart like the memory of a song.

CHAPTER SEVEN

Zosia
December 31, 1941

THOUGH THE ADVENT OF 1942 is little cause for celebration, that doesn't stop us from putting on bright faces for the occasion. Any excuse for a few hours' reprieve from reality, a harkening back to happier times. After the last prescription of the day has been filled, the ladies of the Apteka Pod Orłem hang up our smocks, holiday spirits high as we prepare to celebrate Sylwester and the end of 1941.

I arrange pastries on a platter alongside a tray of sandwiches. Irka and I procured the sandwiches and Tadeusz, who possesses an indefatigable ability to produce something out of nothing, supplied the confections. Our prewar selves would have scoffed at this fare compared with the sumptuous array once laid out at festive gatherings, but now our mouths water at the platters of thinly sliced bread layered with pickled herring and dubiously comprised pastries.

Irka carries in a tray of glasses and places it on Tadeusz's desk. "I hope this is enough. I'm not exactly sure how many are coming tonight. Though if we run out, there are always plenty of empty medicine bottles." She grins and I laugh.

Tadeusz strides into the duty room, his white coat exchanged for an elegant charcoal-gray suit, a pocket square peeking out of his coat.

"Have you got the wine?" Irka calls.

"A bottle of plum vodka and"—he flourishes the second bottle—"white wine."

"Well done."

A comma of a dimple deepens at one corner of his mouth. "For you, only the best."

Irka laughs, straightening his tie. "Give them to me. Our guests will be here any minute."

Helena Krywaniuk bustles in, pretty in a cardigan the color of ripe cherries, brown curls framing her round face. She joined our staff as a trainee at the beginning of December and at twenty-three is the youngest of our group, yet to complete her degree, her studies interrupted when the occupiers closed Jagiellonian University.

The demand for our services—those sanctioned by the occupiers and otherwise—has never been higher. The pharmacy now also functions as an unofficial and illegal post office, ever since the Germans closed the post office in the ghetto earlier this month. Nearly every day we pass through the gate with letters or small parcels tucked in our dresses or the lining of our handbags, food smuggled in shopping bags or baskets, jewelry or valuables someone asked us to sell for them on the outside concealed beneath the false bottoms of our bags or in our brassieres.

We pharmacy ladies stroll past the guards, diamond bracelets in our brassieres and black-market meat in our baskets, and smile at the police so they don't search too closely.

"The Rosners are here." Helena stands aside as Herman Rosner steps into the duty room, snowflakes dusting his coat, violin case in hand.

"Good evening." Tadeusz greets the celebrated musician with a hearty handshake. "Honored you could join us tonight."

Herman Rosner's younger brother Poldek follows with his accordion case. "Evening, everyone."

"Welcome." Tadeusz grips his hand. "Delighted to have you with us. Come. I'll pour you both a drink."

I hasten forward. "Let me take your coats."

Herman sets down his violin case and shrugs out of his overcoat.

"We're so eager to hear you play." I take their hats and coats. "My husband and I had the pleasure of attending one of your performances in Kraków some years ago. Rosner's Players deserves only the highest praises."

"Thank you." Herman smooths a hand across his dark hair. "But I'm afraid there are no Rosner's Players anymore, just Poldek and me. Most evenings, we play at the Variete Café." He gives a faint, ironic smile.

Once Rosner's Players was a highly sought-after orchestra, performing in nightclubs and restaurants in the grand cities of Europe. Now the brothers play at one of the finest establishments in the ghetto to an audience of its elite. It's said even Germans frequent the café to listen to the famous musicians.

I carry their coats to the laboratory as footsteps and voices announce the entrance of more guests. As I return to the duty room, the Silbermans arrive, coats snow-sprinkled, cheeks red from the cold.

"I'm so glad you could come." I greet Pani Silberman and the children in the doorway. "Here. Let me take your coats. But where is Dr. Silberman?"

"He had to do an emergency operation at the community hospital." Hania unbuttons her coat, now bare and shabby without its collar. The edict ordering everyone to give up their furs has only compounded the misery of winter in the ghetto with its drafty rooms, coal hard to come by.

Pani Silberman unwinds her scarf. "It's quite the party."

"The Rosners are here, so we're sure to have good music." As I drape their winter garments over my arm, I notice someone has sewn linings made of blankets into them to add a layer of warmth. "You'll have some refreshments, I hope. There are sandwiches and some lovely pastries with jam in them."

Rena looks up at Pani Silberman. "Can we, Mama?"

"Why not? Let's go and say hello to Magister Pankiewicz and then we'll have something to eat. You'll excuse us, Pani Lewandowska?"

"Of course."

Pani Silberman and her two youngest wend their way through the guests milling in the duty room.

"It's a nice party," Hania says. "I've always wanted to hear the Rosners. Tata promised to take me sometime, but we never had the chance." Wistfulness tinges her smile, a trace of regret. She's lost weight the past months and her eyes no longer hold the soft innocence they once did, a wary sharpness to them that comes from seeing things as they are.

Though I'm in the ghetto nearly every day, we only meet when she comes to the pharmacy with a prescription for her mama's medicine or to collect the food I smuggle in a little at a time. Rarely is there an opportunity to exchange more than a few rushed words.

"How are you all? And please don't say fine because I know it isn't true." We stand near the doorway, their coats still over my arm.

"We're no worse." Her lips tip upward, but there's no humor in her smile. "Szymon is slipping out sometimes now, going over to the other side to buy food."

"How long has this been going on?" As Tadeusz predicted, it's no longer possible to leave the district on the pretext of obtaining medicine at another pharmacy. Since the October edict, the ghetto has become even more impenetrable.

"A couple of months. There's a farmer outside the city who sells eggs, cheese, even chickens." Hania lowers her voice. "Szymon has even smuggled in live chickens to sell to some of the Orthodox families."

There are those in the ghetto who, in spite of everything, still observe the laws of their faith, preferring to go without than eat meat that hasn't been killed by a ritual slaughterer. But for Szymon to take such a risk for a chicken . . .

"And if he were caught?" My voice is urgent. "What then? He can't keep doing this, Hania."

She nods, eyes troubled. "I've tried to tell him, but he won't listen. Not even to Tata. He says he knows how to handle the navy blues." She hesitates. "Please don't mention this to anyone. Mama already worries so."

"I won't. But it must stop. If it's a question of more food, come to me." In the months since I began bringing food into the ghetto, I've become very good at buying—and indeed selling—in the places of the city where illegal trade thrives and it's possible to purchase goods beyond the quantities officially issued on one's ration card.

"I'll talk to him." Her eyes meet mine. "Everything you bring us . . . it helps a great deal. Especially Mama. It's not easy for her to have to work as she does. She's so tired all the time." She looks across the room where Pani Silberman stands talking with Tadeusz, a soft smile on her lips. "The extra food . . . it is a gift to us."

"I only wish there was more I could do."

Helena ushers in more guests, and we step aside to let them pass.

"I should put these coats away, see if Irka needs help. The music will start soon. Why don't you go and have a pastry?"

Across the room, Rena takes tiny bites of her pastry, as if to savor it as long as she can. Szymon chews a sandwich, the other hand in his pocket, looking awkward and out of place.

"I will. It looks as if Szymon could use some company. He's never been much for parties." Hania shakes her head with half a grin.

When I return from stowing the coats in the laboratory, I pause on the threshold.

Irka and Helena hand around glasses of plum vodka and wine while Tadeusz pours at the improvised refreshment table. Everyone has made an effort to dress for the occasion, the ladies in carefully pressed prewar fashions, the men in suits. A trace of perfume lingers in the air like a forgotten melody.

Only someone observing closely would notice their elegant clothes show fading and wear, the etchings of weariness marking features prematurely aged by the strain of life in this walled-in city.

Less than three years ago, they were professors, doctors, businessmen, musicians. Respected. Well-to-do.

Now they live separate from the city, labor in factories, queue for rations, their future decided by the occupiers' decrees.

Their presence here tonight forbidden.

Tadeusz's rich laugh rings out, a glass of vodka in one hand as he chats with Poldek Rosner. Never is the manager of Apteka Pod Orłem more in his element than when entertaining. I cross to help Irka at the refreshment table. For once in the ghetto, the crowd only adds to the atmosphere of conviviality.

The Rosners tune their instruments and the hum of conversation dwindles in anticipation. I find a place along the wall next to Helena, Irka standing nearby with Tadeusz, the Silbermans across the room.

Instruments poised. A breathless pause. The opening bars of a waltz flit onto the air, Herman's bow a blur as it flies over the strings, Poldek's accordion a lively accompaniment.

Though no one dances, the notes dance for us. The blinds are drawn, the room aglow with lamplight, and though the night is black and cold beyond the windows of the pharmacy, a special warmth emanates from the music and reaches into us all.

The Rosners play waltzes, tangos, classical pieces, popular tunes, these musicians who have taken the stage across Europe offering the occupants of a pharmacist's duty room the gift of music tonight. Perhaps nowhere else in Kraków would such a gathering be possible—Jews and Christians meeting freely, sharing the joy of a moment like this.

A world of singular freedom . . .

Herman strikes up a new melody, one unknown to me, but from the expressions on the faces of those around me, familiar to many. He draws the bow slowly over the strings, eyes closed. With tears as true as any shed by man, the violin weeps. Transporting us beyond the ghetto walls, beyond even this night, to the place where music and the soul meet.

When the last notes fall away, there is no applause. Only silence.

Its own refrain.

CHAPTER EIGHT

Hania
May 31, 1942

SUNDAY AFTERNOONS ARE MY scrap of sunlight. When I lie awake listening to the Hirschfelds quarrelling on the other side of the makeshift curtain, when I'm queuing for rations or standing in line to use the stinking privy, when the familiar ache of hunger hollows my stomach and fatigue drains my body as I drag myself up the stairs at the end of another long shift at the brush factory where I now work, I tell myself it will soon be Sunday. It does not diminish the reality of life in the ghetto; even when I am dreaming of Sunday, I am still hungry and tired, burdened by the cares of the present and fears for the future that are a constant of our lives. But the fleeting hours with Romek Weinberg on Krzemionki Hill are a bit of sunlight to tuck into my palm for when the days are gray and cold.

On this warm spring afternoon, breathing fresh air, couples strolling, women chatting, I can almost imagine we're in one of Kraków's parks.

Yet the round-topped wall marking the boundary of the ghetto is an ever-present reminder that the freedom we find on Krzemionki Hill is only an illusion.

Today the atmosphere is subdued, unsettled, people clustering in small groups. From their tense features and low voices, the same topic forms the sum of their conversations.

Resettlement.

For weeks there has been talk that something is coming, that because of overpopulation, the number of inhabitants in the ghetto is to be reduced. Two days ago the order came: everyone residing in the district must report for registration. To remain in the ghetto one must receive an *SS und Polizeiführer* stamp on their Kennkarte. Nothing definite was said about the fate of those denied the stamp, but it's rumored they'll be resettled in newly built labor camps somewhere in the east.

Those employed in enterprises deemed "essential" have a greater chance of obtaining the coveted *SS und Polizeiführer*, but some say bribes can smooth the way with the right official. Because Tata is a doctor at the community hospital, the official stamped his Kennkarte without question and Tata's authorization also covered Mama and Rena. Szymon and I also got the stamp on account of our jobs.

Which is better? To be chosen to stay or to go?

Always the familiar is preferred above the unknown.

"What are you going to do about your babcia?" I ask as Romek and I climb the steep incline, the scrubby grass under our feet well trampled. He came to our flat last night but stayed just long enough to tell us he, his mama, and younger sister Adela had received authorization to remain in the ghetto. Only his babcia had failed to get the stamp.

Stubble shadows Romek's jaw, the strands of dark hair falling over his forehead slightly stringy. He looks wrung out, as if he hasn't had a decent night's sleep since the announcement about the registration. "I won't let her be sent on a transport. Not when we don't know where it will end up, not after what happened last autumn. What would have become of her? When the train stopped and the guards threw everyone out, what would she have done?"

He pauses, as if he expects me to answer, but then continues before I can.

"She would have suffered from hunger and cold, and unless someone took her in, she would have died, just like a lot of them did." He glances at me, his jaw clamped tight. "My babcia is sixty-nine years old. I'm not sending her into the unknown alone."

"No, of course not." The memory of Pani Hirschfeld's mama standing in the doorway in a coat and kerchief, a suitcase in her hand, framed by the white light of the OD man's electric torch, has branded itself upon my mind.

For such a thing to happen to Romek's gentle babcia . . .

It must not.

"I don't trust what we hear about these camps in the east. They say there's enough food, that people who work will be paid wages. I've even heard talk of a reading room and a cinema. A cinema? Can you believe it?" He gives a humorless chuckle, shakes his head. "How do we know conditions there won't be worse than they are here? After what we've been hearing about the things happening in other places—" He cuts himself off. "It's best to stay together."

I chafe my arms, though a warm breeze wafts across my skin. Not long ago, a terrible rumor went around the ghetto of a village in eastern Poland where some one thousand Jews lived as they always had, for no ghetto had been established there. During Pesach, on the night of the Seder, SS and German police entered the village and ordered all the Jews to gather in the square. That night, they forced some of the men to dig ditches in the forest, and in the morning they marched everyone to the forest, lined them up at the edge of the ditches, and shot them all, even the children.

Recalling it makes me shake inside. Perhaps it's only a rumor. For how could something so unthinkable be true?

I swallow, trying to shake the horror of it. "What about her papers?"

"I've been running around talking to everyone I can think of, trying to find a way to get her the authorization." He draws a heavy breath. "We don't have much in the way of valuables, even if someone would take a bribe. So many people are trying to arrange something, and I don't have enough pull."

We reach the top of the hill and stand together, the sky a pure blue ribbon above the rust-brick arches of the wall.

"Maybe Tata knows someone who could help."

"I wouldn't want to cause your family any difficulties—"

"No, Romek. Tata would want to help if he can. We'll go and ask him right now." Usually we linger at the top of the hill. He spreads his coat on the ground for me to sit on and leans back on his elbows in the grass, the sun warming our faces as we savor the fleeting moments of our time together. But it will be evening soon, and a sense of urgency fills me to do whatever we can for Romek's babcia.

"You're certain?"

I nod. "There may be nothing he can do, but we can at least try."

We make our way down the slope, our hands brushing as they often do when we walk side by side. Each time, I wait for him to slip his fingers around mine, but his hand always remains at his side. Sometimes I wonder what it would be like to hold his hand, how it would feel if his fingers enveloped mine.

Is it wrong to indulge in such girlish daydreams when we live on the brink of so many unknowns?

"Look! Over there!"

I turn at a man's shout. A crowd gathers; a commotion of raised voices and people gesturing at something in the distance.

I glance at Romek. "What is it?"

"I don't know." Romek starts back up the hill and I hurry to keep pace with his long strides.

A man flounders past on his way down the hill.

Romek stops him. "What's going on?"

"They're almost at the gates." The man flings his arm in the direction of the wall, his eyes dilated with panic. "SS. A detachment, at least." Then he stumbles down the grassy slope without looking back.

We push through the throng. Down in the distance, beyond the wall, stretches the Aryan side of the city, a forest of spires and rooftops, the afternoon sun glinting on the far-off ribbon of the Wisła.

Far below, ranks of men in gray-green helmets march down the street. From where we stand, they could be toy soldiers, a child's plaything. It's strange not to hear the strike of their boots on the pavement, as if we're watching a newsreel without sound, but my ears reverberate with the rhythm still.

Rifles at their shoulders, they pass down the street in unified columns, marching toward the ghetto.

I stand beside Romek, wind stirring my hair, heart turning to ice.

"What are they doing?" a woman asks, voice pitched high with fear.

Fingers close around mine and I glance at Romek, his features set in hard lines as he takes in the scene below us. I grip his hand.

"Surrounding the ghetto," a man says. "That's what they are doing."

I lay on my side, Rena's slight frame nestled into my warmth, her breathing quiet, steady. In the blacked-out darkness, the flimsy bedsheet separating us from the Hirschfelds is its own kind of moonlight.

A fist strikes a door. Once. Twice. Hard.

The knock on the door and the beating of my heart join as one.

In the blue-black darkness, I glimpse Tata, half-raised in bed.

Boots. Muffled voices somewhere below us.

"Open up. Ordnungsdienst."

Szymon sits up in bed, blanket tangled around his knees.

Rena stirs. "What's happening?" she mumbles.

"Shhh," I whisper. "Keep still."

Springs creak. Tata's shadowy form rises. I slip from bed and cross to the window where he stands, a hand at the curtain, pulling it back enough to peer out.

Light flickers from a second-floor window in the building across from ours, its glow spilling waxen onto the cobblestones below.

It's happening again. First the OD knocking on doors, rounding people up, then the silent march through the ghetto, out the gates . . .

"What is it, Adam?" Mama whispers.

"The OD are going door-to-door."

Szymon joins us at the window. "There's going to be an *akcja*. It can't mean anything else."

"At least we have the stamp," Mama says in a weary voice.

I'm ashamed by my raw sense of relief that our family received the authorization. It could easily have been otherwise.

Tata has arranged a bed for Romek's babcia at the infirmary for the elderly and disabled. She'll be safe there until the akcja is over. Then she can return to her family.

Raised voices and banging on doors bleed through the walls. The heat of Tata's body radiates through mine as I stand at his side. I ache to lean my head against his chest, draw comfort from my tata's strength as I did when I was little and frightened of the dark.

Pan Hirschfeld's spluttering snores and Pani Hirschfeld's whimpering moans indicate they still sleep. They both got the stamp, as did the Birnbaums.

"Let's try to sleep if we can." Tata's voice is drained. "There's nothing we can do tonight."

I ease between the sheets beside Rena and pull the eiderdown to my chin.

In the broken silence of the night, the ghetto waits and I wait with it. The minutes fall one upon another like raindrops plinking from a rooftop's eaves. One after the other after the other. Each draws us nearer to dawn. Each pulls us closer to darkness.

CHAPTER NINE

Zosia
June 1, 1942

FROM EVEN THE WORST of nightmares one eventually awakens. The images fade, the dreams recede. Even the most vivid are, in the end, unreal.

But the scene unfolding beyond the dispensing room window is not a nightmare.

They fill Zgody Square by the hundreds. Men, women, mostly the old, but the young are there too—children with their parents, infants in the arms of their mamas. Carrying bundles and suitcases, those awaiting deportation collect in the square as sunlight glitters from a brilliant blue sky. Families in traveling clothes, old women in coats and kerchiefs, men in black gaberdines and felt-brimmed hats.

OD men with truncheons and German police with rifles patrol the crowd.

This is how they are to go, then.

Herded into the unknown while we watch from the pharmacy window.

Two automobiles drive through the gate at the northern edge of the square, the sun glinting off their windshields. One of the automobiles stops and two officers emerge, sweeping their gazes across the crowd.

A hefty German policeman drags a girl in her teens away from an older woman.

"Mama!" Her strangled cries reverberate through the window. "No! I want to go with you. Please, let me go with her."

Beside me, Helena makes a sound, a soft involuntary cry. Irka presses her lips together. Tadeusz's jaw tightens.

The four of us stand at the window, staring out across the sea of humanity gathered in the square, only a pane of glass to separate us.

"They're coming here." Panic rises in Helena's voice.

I nearly drop the bottle of digitalis but manage to set it on the counter of the prescription room before rushing after Irka. Helena stands at the dispensing room window, Tadeusz behind her.

Two SS officers stride toward the pharmacy, revolvers in their hands, a black-and-gray Alsatian on its lead. The clatter of their boots rings out on the cobblestones.

Helena's face blanches. "What do they want?"

Tadeusz turns away from the window and calmly takes his place at the front counter. Irka and I follow him.

The door opens. The SS come in.

We stand behind the high counter—three women in white smocks, Tadeusz in his pressed pharmacist's coat.

I swallow, throat parched.

"May I help you?" Tadeusz's tone is steady as he addresses them in German.

The two officers approach the counter, the measured tread of their boots resounding on the floorboards, the Alsatian trotting alongside them, pointed ears pricked.

My breath emerges shallow from my dry lips.

Their gazes slide over us beneath their black-brimmed caps with the silver death's-head emblem, traveling with slow deliberation over the room and each item in it—the counter with its cash register and brass scales, the cabinet behind us lined with labeled canisters and bottles, the framed image of the Blessed Virgin and the infant Jesus on the wall, the carved eagle keeping vigil above the clock. Then their eyes settle again on us.

Steel clanks against marble as they set their revolvers on the counter.

Without removing his gaze from us, the older of the two officers withdraws a cartridge clip and takes cartridges from a pouch, placing them onto the counter one by one.

Four. Four cartridges.

I can't breathe.

Methodically, he loads the revolver. Each cartridge slides into the magazine with a hollow click.

One. Two.

Out of the corner of my eye, I glimpse Helena gripping the edge of the counter.

Three. Four.

Our Father which art in heaven . . . I mentally chant the prayer, the words all that penetrates the fog in my mind. *Hallowed be thy name* . . .

Will they start shooting at us from the right? Or from the left?

A ghost of a smile edges the officer's lips. He regards us a moment more, rotating the revolver with a motion of his wrist. Then, without a word, both officers swivel toward the door, the Alsatian with them. Boots recede.

The pharmacy door shuts.

The four of us stare at one another. No one speaks. Helena's face is ashen.

My gaze lands on the window as the officers stride onto Zgody Square. The older SS raises his revolver. Someone shouts.

Sweat trickles down my shoulder blades.

Gunfire explodes.

A doctor in a wrinkled white coat bursts into the pharmacy. Irka presses a vial of valerian drops into the hand of one of his colleagues as the doctor stumbles toward the counter.

"We need," he gasps out, "more sodium bromide."

"For how many?"

He struggles to catch his breath, forehead glistening with perspiration. "At least ten doses. No, better make it twelve."

I run into the prescription room, open the cabinet, scan the shelves for the bottle of sodium bromide, grab it off the shelf, and withdraw a paper packet from a drawer. I count out the tablets, working as fast as I can, close the top of the packet and hurry out to the dispensing room, passing Tadeusz. I thrust the packet at the doctor across the counter and he rushes out again.

All afternoon, we've worked without stopping as doctors, nurses, and OD men rush into the pharmacy for sedatives to calm the agitated. Digitalis for those suffering cardiac distress. Spirit of ammonia to revive the many who've fainted from the heat.

We give them everything they ask for.

But, God forgive us, it is nothing. A drop of water in the face of an inferno.

I pause at the window. The crowd surges toward newly arrived lorries, pushing and trampling to claim a place. The SS stand to the side, talking among themselves as they observe the mad scramble to board the conveyances.

The door opens. My heart jolts as two officers enter the pharmacy.

What now? Have they come to finish what their comrade started?

"Good day." One of them gives a curt nod. "Who is the owner of this pharmacy?"

Tadeusz comes into the dispensing room to stand behind me. "I am," he replies in the same level tone as before.

"Good. Then you will be able to tell us how to get to the balcony."

As Tadeusz directs them, I notice the square leather cases slung over their shoulders.

"Thank you most kindly." The officers turn to leave.

"Wait." I draw myself up, my voice flint.

They turn slowly, their features registering surprise.

"Where are they being taken—the people in the square?" I'm not sure why I ask, why I let myself believe I'll get the truth.

"They are being resettled in labor camps in the east where they will be put to useful work." The officer's words are clipped. "They are fortunate." He nods again, and they exit the dispensing room.

Minutes later, their reasons for asking about the balcony—and the purpose of their cases—become apparent with the clicking of cameras, sharp and staccato, above us, the sliding crank of winding film.

"Propaganda photographs," Tadeusz mutters. "I suppose even the devil wishes he could keep a record of hell."

I swipe the back of my hand across my forehead, drained of any response as the sounds of history being recorded merge with the misery of the crowd. I lean one hand against the edge of the counter, shoulders slumped, eyes sliding shut.

"Schnell! Out, out!"

My gaze snaps up.

"Out, out!" The Germans pull people off the lorries as if unloading sacks of meal, throwing their luggage out after them with crashes and thuds.

A woman bends to pick up her fallen suitcase. A policeman beats her with the butt of his rifle, shouting a stream of indecipherable words. Blood drips from the side of her head. The lorries empty, the Germans dragging and shoving their occupants who trip over their luggage and each other as they clamber down. Some don't bother to reclaim their baggage but stand aimlessly, hands empty, eyes distant. Those who hadn't found a seat look on, their silent terror visible even to us.

Why order everyone to board the lorries if they weren't to be used as transport to the station?

Of course. The propaganda photographs. To preserve for the historical record how well the Germans treated those being resettled.

"Schnell, schnell." The shouts mingle with screams and cries, forming a score of panic as the Germans drive the surging crowd toward Lwówska Street.

The sun beats down. An old woman drops her bundle and trudges on as if forgetting she ever carried it or cherished the items it held. A woman carries a toddler in her arms. A gray-haired woman leans on the arm of an elderly man. Onward goes this human tide, onward toward the gates.

Then the square is empty, filled with littered belongings and a silence so complete in another time and place one might call it hallowed, but now it is only cold.

Half-open suitcases, contents spilling onto the cobblestones. A bundle the size of a prayer book encased in blue velvet. Splatters of blood browning in the sun.

Remains.

CHAPTER TEN

Hania
June 4, 1942

ROWS OF WOMEN AND girls, a few men among them, hunch over tables threading bristles into wooden laths while shots fragment the air. It's been three days since the first transport left the ghetto, and the akcja pauses but does not stop. No one ventures outside except to go to their jobs or for food. Many are afraid to even stand near a window, as the cordon of *Sonderdienst* and SS around the perimeter don't hesitate to shoot at shadows. Trams no longer travel through the streets, as if the Germans want no witnesses to the acts committed here, as if someone might glimpse the suffering these walls contain and let it be known what is happening. Cut off from the outside world, we can do nothing but wait.

Sharp bursts of gunfire erupt. Then silence, the room echoing with unanswered questions and unspoken fears. A few minutes, a half hour later, more firing from the direction of Zgody Square. The square has a new name now—the *Umschlagplatz*, the assembly point for the deportations.

It's a bitter kind of irony that a square, the name of which means *concord*, would be chosen for such a terrible purpose.

The authorities were not satisfied with the number of people who reported for resettlement, so last night and into the morning, the Germans conducted a search. Through the long, sleepless hours, we sat in darkness, listening to the heavy tread of boots in the street, the rifle blows against doors, the staccato report of shots, the weeping. They came for the Hirschfelds, even though both had the stamp. Pani Hirschfeld begged, sobbed, screamed. They took them anyway.

My fingers move by rote inserting the tufts of bristle into the holes in the wooden lath, my sweat-dampened hair clinging to my neck in the stifling heat. My mind travels to Zgody Square, pulled by a force I cannot stop. What is happening there? How empty will the ghetto be tonight, and which of our friends will be among the absent?

I lift my head at a commotion at the door of the workroom.

A woman rushes down the aisle between the tables.

Mama? I start to my feet, dropping the bristles, the half-finished lath clattering to the table.

She reaches me, her chignon windblown, breaths rapid.

"What's happened?" My tone is sharp, my heart thudding fast.

Mama presses a hand to her midsection. "They took your tata to the Umschlagplatz."

"What?" The word is a gasp. People at the tables near us look up from their work, watching us with furtive interest, but I barely pay them heed.

"He was on his way to the community hospital this morning and they took him. I don't know anything more."

"But that's . . . that's not possible. Doctors are exempt from resettlement. How do you know they took him?" Surely this is a mistake. It has to be.

"I went out to buy bread—"

"It's not safe to be out on the streets with the patrols."

She doesn't seem to have heard me. "On my way, I met Henryk Szydłowski. He's an OD man now, but he remembered your tata from when he was his patient. When he passed me on the street, Pan Szydłowski recognized me and told me he saw your tata on the Umschlagplatz."

"Maybe he was there to help. Some of the doctors are seeing to the people there."

The numbing buzz of the drilling machine fills my brain.

Tata.

"I came to tell you I'm going to Zgody Square, so you know"—she swallows—"if something happens."

"Mama, no. You can't." I grip her arm.

She jerks from my grasp. "I have to find my husband." She grits the words, a fierceness in her eyes I've never seen before. "I have to see him, Hania," she says, voice quiet now.

"Then I'm going with you."

"No, you must stay here—"

"I'm going. He's my tata." Without giving her a chance to argue, I pick up my handbag, slide its strap over my shoulder, and thread my way through the aisles between the tables to where our foreman stands, speaking to another worker.

"Pan Ehrlich, I'm sorry to interrupt."

He glances at me. "What is it?"

"I'd like permission to leave early today. They took my tata to the Umschlagplatz." I pause. "Please. I have to find him."

Pan Ehrlich nods. He's strict, but a fair boss, and one of us. "Fine. But if I were you, I'd keep away from there. Doesn't matter if you've got the stamp, they're taking people off the street now, anybody. You're crazy if you think they'll let you leave the Umschlagplatz."

I swallow. "Thank you." I turn to Mama and we move toward the door. "Where's Rena?"

"She's at home. She doesn't know I've come."

We exit the brush factory. It's like stepping into a furnace, the air is so hot, the sun blazing. We pause outside and I glance up and down the deserted street. My skin prickles in the stillness, the strange absence of any sign of life.

Shots reverberate in the distance. My body tenses.

I look at Mama, her face hard-set.

Then I walk on, gaze constantly roaming, keeping as close to the shelter of buildings as I can. My heart pounds, but somehow I'm not afraid, not for myself.

The streets are empty, as if the ghetto is a slate that's been wiped clean. The few people we pass startle at the sight of us, then hasten onward. Mama's cheeks are flushed, her features tight. Neither of us speaks, the tap of our shoes echoing in the silence.

And once we reach the Umschlagplatz? What then?

We should have a plan, but then we turn down Targowa Street and a shot rings out. Louder and closer than before.

My throat dries. *Please,* ADONAI, *protect us. Please guide us to Tata.*

Zgody Square stretches before us, backdropped by a startling-blue sky. Men, women, and children carpet the broad expanse, some huddled in groups, others sitting on the ground or on suitcases, packed together in a swell of humanity surely numbering into the thousands.

Near the edge of the crowd, an SS man beats an old man with the butt of a rifle. "Get up," he shouts, striking him again and again as the man tries to shield himself from the blows. "You miserable crippled *hund*, get up."

A pair of crutches lies discarded on the cobblestones.

He only has one leg.

The SS man is beating him, and he only has one leg.

Only a few meters from where we stand, a dark puddle stains the cobbles, glassy in the sun.

If I allow my mind to absorb what's happening around me, I won't be able to keep walking. I suck a breath tinged with a coppery odor that needs no definition. Then we move forward into the thick of the crowd, its mass closing around us like water over our heads.

How are we ever to find one man among hundreds, thousands?

"Pardon me." I tap a woman on the shoulder, and she turns. She wears a floral dressing gown, bedroom slippers, her hair loose around her shoulders. "Have you seen Adam Silberman? He's a doctor at the community hospital. He has brown hair like mine, not very tall, wearing a—"

"He's wearing a gray suit, a nice suit." Mama breaks in. "Have you seen him?"

The woman only stares. Not at us. Just . . . stares.

We move away. I crane my neck, searching every face for Tata or at least someone familiar.

"Adam Silberman? Have you seen Adam Silberman?"

People stare at us, expressions listless, vacant, shake their heads or murmur a few words, and we continue on, pushing deeper into the crowd, stumbling over discarded luggage.

Through a gap in the throng, I glimpse a bespectacled man, his wiry height standing out in the tightly packed multitude. Rena's friend Dola's tata. "Mama, look, there's Pan Goldner." I shoulder through the crowd, Mama following. "Pan Goldner! Pan Goldner!"

He turns. "Hania, Pani Silberman, what are you doing here?"

Mama rushes up to him. "Have you seen Adam?"

His high forehead is shiny with sweat. Behind his gold-rimmed spectacles, his eyes are grave. "You should not be here."

A few steps behind Pan Goldner stand Dola and her mama. Pani Goldner carries her coat over her arm, her hat tilting at a jostled angle, two suitcases at her feet. Dola clutches a small traveling case, cheeks pink from the heat, taking everything in with frightened eyes.

"Please, Pan Goldner." My voice is urgent. "Have you seen him?"

Pan Goldner nods. "I'll take you to him."

As we pass, Dola's eyes find mine. "Tell Rena I'm sorry I couldn't say goodbye."

I swallow the dryness in my throat. "I'll tell her."

There's no time for more words as Pan Goldner leads us through the press of the crowd. The scents—sweat, refuse baking in the heat, and sharpest of all, fear—choke every breath of the sticky air.

Pan Goldner steps aside, gestures. "There."

Tata stands with his back to us, as if staring at something in the distance.

"Tata," I cry at the same time Mama calls, "Adam."

He turns and I catch my breath. The right side of his face is swollen, a purplish-red bruise beginning to show around his eye, the shirt beneath his suit speckled with dried blood, his tie loosened. Shock comes over his face at the sight of us.

Mama throws her arms around him. "Oh, Adam. Thank HaShem we found you."

He holds her tight, face stricken with the slow draining of horror. "What are you doing here?" His voice is rough, almost angry.

She draws away. "We came to find you. I met Henryk Szydłowski, he said you were here. What happened?"

"You weren't caught in the akcja?"

"No." I raise my voice to be heard above the melee. "We came because of you."

Relief passes briefly over his haggard features. He takes me by the shoulders, looks me in the eyes. "You need to leave. Take your mama home and stay there." He pushes out the words, his swollen jaw making it difficult for him to speak, but the urgency in his voice is unmistakable.

"What about you?" Mama's voice cracks, desperate.

"I'll be all right. They'll need doctors wherever they're sending us. Someone has to take care of all these people. Now go." He pulls Mama into his arms, crushes her against his chest, kisses her hair, her lips, pulls her close again. "Please, Faiga. Please go now."

Mama is crying, tears running down her cheeks. I fling my arms around him, and he wraps his around me, holding me fiercely. The drone of the crowd, the shouts of the Germans, and the reedy cry of an infant surround us, but they barely penetrate. I cling to my tata, my face pressed against his shoulder.

I don't want to let go. How can I let go?

"Tata." My eyes burn with tears, but they don't fall. "I love you, Tata."

He whispers something into my hair, a blessing in Hebrew, the words too low for me to catch. Then he pushes me away. Because he must. Because he knows I can't let go on my own.

There are two kinds of pain. The first is physical, measurable. The second is so deep, so great, one feels no pain at all. The body cannot register it, nor the mind comprehend it.

Tata's face remains strong, as if for us he keeps himself from breaking. "I'll send word as soon as I can. Don't worry. I'll be all right. The Germans need me."

Mama nods, face wet with tears.

"Tell Szymon and Rena—"

Shots crack the air. The crowd surges. Women scream.

I need to get us away from here.

I take hold of Mama's hand, my body so numb I'm surprised I'm still upright. Mama's damp fingers clutch mine as we fight our way through the current of bodies. I push forward, as if clawing my way above water, unable to breathe until I break through the surface.

Sunlight glitters, the heat suffocating. The crowd fades into a blur of colors, a woman's red dress, a doctor's white coat, the gray-green uniforms of the German police.

"Halt! You there."

I keep walking toward Targowa Street, pulling Mama with me. They're not shouting at me. Why would they be shouting at me?

"For the last time, halt! Or I'll shoot."

I spin.

An SS man stands a few meters away, a revolver in his hand.

The barrel aimed at me.

• • •

Zosia

Blood glistens in the unrelenting sun, a spreading blot of crimson pooling on the cobblestones. Sprawled in the blood is an old woman, shot by an SS man.

Dear God, are You watching? Are You weeping? Or have You stopped Your ears and closed Your eyes and abandoned Your chosen ones to their fate?

The square is a sea of uniforms—helmeted German police positioned along the tenement buildings, armed with rifles and machine guns, SS officers with revolvers, OD men carrying truncheons, Polish police with pistols. This is the first time during the deportations that the Blue Police join the Germans, brought in as reinforcements. Though the navy blues are doubtless here on direct orders from the occupiers, their complicity turns my stomach. Once they were ordinary policemen. Today they stand alongside the enemy, not only as witnesses but as participants in their crimes.

Throughout the morning, as before, doctors and nurses rush into the pharmacy for bromides and pain medications, bandages to dress the wounds of the injured, emetics to treat several who managed to get hold of cyanide. Tadeusz gives out everything free of charge, refusing payment from anyone who offers, though in the frantic haze of activity, few do more than grab the items and rush back out to the square. Every now and then, someone awaiting deportation succeeds in slipping into the pharmacy for medicine or to give us messages to pass on to their families. I take the bits of paper they press into my hands and promise to deliver them as soon as I can.

I return to the dispensing room with a packet of iron pills for a woman, one of our frequent customers. I draw up short. An SS officer stands at the counter, talking with Irka. A shiver skitters down my spine. It's the officer who came into the pharmacy and loaded his revolver at our counter. Now he converses with Irka in German. The woman awaiting the iron pills and three others who must have just come in dart anxious glances in his direction.

I step behind the counter and am about to hand the woman her pills when the officer asks, "And who is this?"

Irka turns to me. "This is Frau Lewandowska, another of the ladies employed by Herr Pankiewicz. Zosia, this is Sturmscharführer Kunde."

An amiable smile touches Sturmscharführer Kunde's lips. "Herr Pankiewicz certainty knows how to surround himself with attractive company."

I'm not certain what to make of his presence, nor do I like accepting a compliment from someone who very nearly shot me and my colleagues only a few days ago, but I manage a brief nod, setting the packet on the counter. "What is your business in the district, Herr Sturmscharführer?"

"I'm one of the officers in charge of Jewish affairs coordinating the resettlement. Making sure it all goes off smoothly." How unremarkably he states it, as one might say, "I'm a bank clerk," or "I manage a dry goods shop."

"Do you expect it to take much longer?" I match his conversational tone, though my voice is a bit strained.

"These things are always more trouble than one expects. We're running a bit behind schedule today. Worst of it is the heat. It's like a furnace out there." He takes off his cap and sets it on the counter, pulls out a handkerchief and wipes his perspiring face.

"Sturmscharführer Kunde is meeting some people here at Commander Spira's request," Irka says.

The name gives me pause. Symche Spira, the chief of the Ordnungsdienst, is known throughout the ghetto as a collaborator who executes the orders of the occupiers with fanatical obedience.

"There are some Jews he wishes to perform a service for, so I've come to stamp their Kennkarten."

Stamp their Kennkarten?

"Would you care for a glass of something while you wait? Vodka, perhaps?" Irka's smile is so poised one might believe she enjoys nothing better than playing hostess to the SS.

Kunde tugs at his collar. "I'd give a king's ransom for a glass of good vodka." He leans his forearm on the counter. "You've tempted me, Fräulein Droździkowska. You shouldn't do that, you know. I'm on duty."

"We won't tell." Irka dimples conspiratorially up at him. "Will we, Zosia?" She glances at me. *Play along,* her gaze demands.

I give a nervous smile. "No, of course not."

"Excuse us for a moment, Herr Sturmscharführer." Irka touches my arm and I follow her into the prescription room. "Keep everyone here," she whispers. "Don't let any of them leave."

"Have you any idea who that man is?"

"I know what I'm doing." She throws the low words over her shoulder as she heads toward the duty room.

Kunde stands at the dispensing room counter, hands behind his back, staring at the eagle atop the cabinet.

I breeze around the counter. "I see you've noticed our eagle."

Kunde glances at me. "Fine piece of craftsmanship."

"It is, isn't it?" I open a drawer and feign straightening its contents. The woman waiting for her iron pills gives me a look of confusion, almost distrust. As though she thinks I'm purposefully ignoring her. If not for Kunde, maybe she'd speak up or simply take the pills, but now she stands nervously waiting with the others. There are only two now, a man and a woman. The other man must have left.

You'd better know what you're about, Irka Droździkowska.

A young OD man enters the pharmacy, followed by a woman and three men.

"Sturmscharführer Kunde?"

Kunde turns. "Yes?"

"Commander Spira ordered me to bring these people to you."

Tadeusz and Irka come into the dispensing room, Tadeusz carrying a tray bearing a bottle of vodka and a glass.

"Ah, Sturmscharführer Kunde, isn't it?" The tray clinks as Tadeusz sets it on the counter. "How are you doing?"

Kunde nods. "Herr Pankiewicz. Your ladies have been very good company." He gives a little smile.

"Glad to hear it. Quite the heat wave we're having this week, wouldn't you agree?" Tadeusz opens the bottle. He pours a shot of vodka into a glass and slides it across the counter to Kunde. "Here. See what you think."

The customers cast furtive glances toward Kunde and the group near the door. They might have given up and left by now, but the new arrivals and the OD man now block the exit.

Kunde picks up the glass and swallows half.

"Good, isn't it?"

"Excellent." Kunde sets the glass on the counter. He glances at the group clustered near the door, motions them forward. "If you'll just bring your Kennkarten here." He withdraws an *SS und Polizeiführer* stamp and a small inkpad.

They come forward, each holding several identity cards, belonging to family members, no doubt. Leaning on the counter, Kunde stamps them, stopping periodically to drink from his glass, which Tadeusz keeps refilled with the ease of a skilled bartender.

Irka chews the corner of her bottom lip.

Kunde stamps the last one and hands the woman her Kennkarten.

"Thank you, Herr Sturmscharführer," she says in a quiet voice. Likely these people paid the OD chief enormous bribes for him to persuade Kunde to dole out the coveted stamps. Obviously they had the money or valuables to do so, giving them the advantage over many who could never afford to buy their way off the transport. But as the woman takes her family's Kennkarten, relief washes over her strained features.

The group and their OD escort file out of the pharmacy. Kunde closes his inkpad and drains his glass for the second time.

"Herr Sturmscharführer, might these people not also be given a stamp?" Irka gives Kunde her most charming smile.

He frowns, as if confused. "Which people?"

"There." Irka gestures to the three customers near the back of the room. "Seeing as you're already here."

The pieces fall into place. Had I not been so tired, I might have realized what Irka intended earlier.

"It would be so little trouble." Somehow I remember how to tip my chin, to deepen my smile, to be pretty, persuasive. Like these stamps are for fun, a game, instead of what decides whether one must board a train bound for the indefinite.

Tadeusz doesn't interject. He's smart enough to know what a woman's influence can accomplish.

Kunde regards us. Then he chuckles, his laughter a little loud. "Why not? Give me their Kennkarten and I'll stamp the lot."

I leave Irka's side and cross to where they stand. "Give me your papers," I urge quietly as Tadeusz refills Kunde's glass. "Come. Quickly."

They hesitate less than a moment before the man reaches into his wallet, the women into their handbags. As they hand me their Kennkarten, their eyes meet mine, silently asking if this is a trick, begging it not to be.

I spread the identity cards in front of Kunde with a smile. "Here we are."

Irka folds her arms on the counter, leaning forward, chatting with Kunde as he stamps the Kennkarten.

Finished, Kunde returns the stamp and inkpad to his pocket, swallows the remainder in his glass, picks up his cap from the counter, and settles it atop his head. "Now I must be going."

"Come and have a drink with us whenever you like." Tadeusz is as good an actor as Irka. If I didn't know better, I'd think him and Kunde to be on friendly terms.

"If there's more where that came from, I certainly will." Kunde nods to Irka and me. "Ladies." He pivots on his heel and leaves the pharmacy.

Tadeusz turns to the group hovering near the back of the room. "Apologies for keeping you waiting. Here are your Kennkarten. Everything should be in order."

"I came to give you a message for my brother and now there is no need," the man says as he returns his Kennkarte to his wallet. "No one will believe it when I tell them what has happened. I'm very grateful to you all."

"There's no need," Tadeusz says quietly. "It was simply a matter of chance."

"It was more than chance, Pan Magister. More than chance."

"You'd better wait here until things calm down. Irka will show you to the materials room. Later, you can leave by the back door."

I pass the woman her packet of pills.

"Thank you, Pani Magistra." She puts it in her handbag. "How much for these?"

I name the price. As she counts out the złotys, I turn and glance out the window at the throng gathered in the square.

What kind of world is this where the future of people like these hangs on the caprices of men like Kunde?

Near the fringes of the crowd, an SS man raises his revolver, shouting something indistinct as he aims it at two women who seem to be walking away.

The women stop, as if in response to his command.

One turns, a slight girl with brown hair.

My heart stands still.

Hania and Pani Silberman.

Why are they here? The Silbermans all got the stamp.

Hania reaches into her handbag, holds something out to the SS man. Her Kennkarte?

He doesn't lower his revolver.

There's no time to think. I round the counter, shove open the door.

Someone calls my name—Tadeusz, maybe—but I don't stop.

The sun beats down, its heat overpowering. I rush out into the square. What if I'm too late?

One of the Blue Police approaches the SS man, stopping slightly in front of Hania and her mama. I draw up short.

The Polish policeman says something to the SS man, gestures in the direction of Lwówska Street. After a moment, the SS man holsters his pistol and both men head toward Lwówska, leaving Hania and Pani Silberman standing in the square.

Hania turns. Our eyes lock. She gives a small, warning shake of her head. *Don't come closer.*

Before he fades into the crowd, the Polish policeman glances back at Hania and Pani Silberman as they walk quickly, eyes straight ahead, in the direction of the pharmacy.

I return to the pharmacy, passing the automobile parked near its entrance, its seats loaded with briefcases stuffed with valuables stolen from the deportees by the SS.

Hania and Pani Silberman come through the door.

I pull them inside.

Sweat glistens on Pani Silberman's face, her skin unnaturally pale.

I put an arm around her shoulders, ushering her through the dispensing room. "This way. Quickly." I hurry them down the corridor and into the laboratory. If the SS search the pharmacy, the Silbermans can slip out the back entrance.

"Here. Sit down." I lead Pani Silberman to the stool in the corner and turn to Tadeusz, who had followed us in. "Some water."

As he leaves to fetch a glass, I crouch in front of Pani Silberman sitting limply on the stool, head bent. "Do you feel faint?"

"A little." Her voice is breathless.

"Let me help you off with your jacket." I ease her jacket from her shoulders and loosen the collar of her blouse in an attempt to cool her.

Tadeusz returns with a glass, fills it at the laboratory sink, and gives it to Pani Silberman.

She finishes the water in a few swallows and hands it to Tadeusz. "Thank you, Pan Magister."

"How's the faintness now?" I ask.

"Better. It must have been the heat." She falls silent. Tadeusz hands Hania the refilled glass. "Here. Drink this."

Hania takes the glass. Her hands shake as she raises the water to her lips and gulps it down.

I go to her, gently take the empty glass from her hands.

She looks at me, eyes glazed. The distant crackle of gunfire reverberates through the pharmacy.

"They took him," she whispers. "They took Tata."

A stranger who happened upon the square might ask when it had rained. For the weather has been sunny and warm for days.

They would ask because who could believe the reason the cobbles glisten wet? Who could imagine the day's events except those who witnessed them?

Who could comprehend the darkness that can be conceived beneath a summer sun, a clear blue sky?

I stand outside the pharmacy, gripping my handbag, the vacant square stretching before me in the hazy summer twilight, strewn with bundles and suitcases abandoned on the march to the station. After it was over, carts came around to collect the dead, but the sluice of their blood still pools on the pavement and in the gutters.

Every night the ghetto has been surrounded, Tadeusz's friends have filled the pharmacy, fearing they'd be rounded up if they remained at home. They sit up in the duty room listening for sounds in the street and slip out the back door in the early hours. Irka, Helena, and I have spent nearly every night at the pharmacy, snatching a few hours' sleep in a chair, afraid if we left, the guards wouldn't allow us to return. I've gone home only once the past four days. I need to return to my flat, if only for the night, to sleep and wash and eat a hot meal.

I walk on without looking down, the cobbles slick under my shoes. Silence hangs like smoke in the square, the stillness stark against the day's events.

An officer in navy uniform approaches, his solid frame shadowy in the fading light. The man whose intervention saved Hania.

His long strides span the distance between us. We're almost at the point of passing each other, and I'm about to do exactly that, when his voice stops me.

"You should not be out here." It's a commanding tone but a low one, as if he doesn't need to shout to be obeyed. "It's still not safe on the streets."

On another day, I might heed him, but I'm tired, so terribly tired, and I only want to leave this place for a few hours of precious sleep, enough to gather the strength to return. I keep walking.

He stops in front of me, his strong-shouldered figure blocking my path. "Perhaps I wasn't plain enough. They will shoot you. They don't care whether you're a Pole or if you have a pass. Here they can do whatever they like and there's no one who can question them."

"I work at the pharmacy. I need to go home." My voice, which I'd meant to be strong, betrays me.

"I know who you are." He regards me. I doubt much gets past that blue-gray stare. "I'll escort you as far as the gate. See you come to no harm."

"Fine." I fall into step beside him, too tired to argue. I've seen enough the past four days to know he speaks the truth. They could shoot me as easily as any of the people who fell in the square.

We continue in silence. We've seen each other at the gate for months, but as far as I can recall, never spoken beyond the necessary words exchanged as I hand him my pass and he returns it, as he searches my bags, maybe a brief *good morning* or *good evening* from time to time. His jaw is set, his stride firm, his gaze straight ahead as we cross the littered expanse of the square. Again I wonder if he meant to intervene or if it was only by chance Hania and her mama managed to reach the pharmacy.

"In the square today, there was a young woman. An SS man had his revolver pointed at her when you stepped in. Because of what you did, she was able to get away. Why did you do it?"

"What I do and why is my business." He glances at me, pace slowing. "Why do you ask?"

I hesitate, not certain what to make of his answer, whether I should give a reply as oblique as his or speak frankly. No matter his motives in regard to Hania, he took part in what happened. Though I never saw him fire a single shot, beat, or even shout at anyone, he still participated. Not only today, but every day he stands guard at the gate, enforcing the orders of the occupiers, complicit in the suffering of the people imprisoned here.

My chest burns, the horror of what I saw today calcifying into searing heat. Perhaps because it's easier to feel anger than grief, to rage rather than to break, though what I witnessed has left me shattered in ways beyond repair.

If I'm not careful, all control will slip from my grasp, and I'll scream at this man the way I've wanted to scream all day.

I draw an uneven breath. "The young woman is someone I know. She and her mama came to the square because her tata was there. He had the stamp. They took him anyway."

"Stamps mean nothing to them. They're just a formality." He doesn't look at me, his strides lengthening as we approach the gate.

"What do you mean?"

He turns, his gaze penetrating. "When we cease to believe another living soul shares the same humanity as ourselves, anything is possible." Without another word, he leads me to the gate where German police stand guard. He leans forward, his voice low, his breath stirring the wisps of hair near my ear. "If you'll take my advice, you'll wait until this is over before coming back here. But if you must return, ask one of the guards to escort you to the pharmacy. Bribe them if you have to."

"I will. Thank you." I'll be back within a day, but he doesn't need to know that.

He nods, once and firmly, strong features impenetrable. Then he walks away, leaving me at the gate.

I show my pass to the guard. After searching my bag, he motions me through. I don't pause until I'm well past the entrance, then my steps slow, every part of me bone weary. I cross the Third Bridge, blending into the throng of pedestrians. Two young women hurry past, laughing. A little boy in short trousers stops by the railing to peer into the water below while a woman calls for him to come along.

People going about the bustle of life, the end of an ordinary day.

How is it possible? How can a child's laughter carry on the evening breeze while less than a kilometer away the cobblestones are stained with blood?

CHAPTER ELEVEN

Hania
June 20, 1942

EIGHT DAYS. THEN THE akcja ceased.

In the week the ghetto was surrounded, seven thousand people were deported. At least a hundred were shot in the square and in the streets. Others, when faced with separation from their families, chose to swallow cyanide rather than be sent into the unknown.

The corpses were buried in a mass grave at the Jewish cemetery in Płaszów, the streets cleared of baggage and debris. Almost everyone had at least one member of their family taken. Entire families are missing. Those who are left recollect their experiences and number their losses. Others are silent, their shock and sorrow a burden too great to form into words.

Only a few days after life returned to a semblance of normalcy, a new edict was posted. The district is to be reduced. Several streets, including Czarnieckiego, are to be returned to the Aryan part of the city. Krzemionki Hill has been cut off from the ghetto, so there will be no more Sunday walks in our little patch of green, forgetting for a few moments the walls that surround us.

Everyone residing on the now-forbidden streets has only a few days to move. It's as if we're watching the spring of last year repeat itself, only this time there's a heightened sense of panic. Everyone is desperate to get a good place for their families and be settled by the deadline.

We trudge down the street in the early twilight, one of many trundling their belongings through the ghetto in these last hours before curfew. Most of our furniture had to be left behind as we'd no way of transporting it, but we packed what belongings we could in suitcases and a trunk.

It isn't like before, when we left home. There are few pleasant memories attached to the squalid room we shared with the Hirschfelds. But as I look back once more before we turn the corner, pain sticks its knife into my heart, past the calluses and into soft flesh.

The last place we were together as a family.

"So, Rena." Romek walks alongside us, he and Szymon hefting the bulky mattress. "Did Hania tell you about the man in the flat below ours who plays the violin?"

Rena glances at him but doesn't answer. Since Tata left, she's barely spoken, her eyes distant, hazy almost, as if her mind is somewhere else, beyond our reality.

"He's no Herman Rosner, but we like to listen to him."

A pause, then in a soft voice, Rena asks, "What does he play?"

A small smile forms on my lips as Romek replies, "Wieniawski, Mozart, Statkowski. All sorts of things."

That Romek would make an effort to cheer my sister at such a time speaks more than words of the kind of man he is, giving of himself to others even as he carries his own burdens.

The same day Tata was taken to the Umschlagplatz, half the residents of the infirmary for the elderly and disabled were loaded into lorries and driven to the station, where they boarded the trains for resettlement. Romek's babcia was among them. Romek assured me he doesn't blame Tata—who could imagine they would touch elderly people in such an institution?—but I've seen it in his eyes, the guilt mingled with grief. He blames himself for not protecting his babcia.

How well I understand. For do I not ask myself if I could have done something? Do I not blame myself for walking away, leaving my tata in that desperate crowd?

I fall into step beside Romek. "Thank you."

"I have a little sister too, you know."

I glance down, our trunk bumping over the cobblestones as I pull it behind me. "She hasn't been the same since . . . Tata always took care of us. When he was with us, we felt . . . protected, I suppose. That sounds foolish, I know."

"There's nothing foolish about that." He pauses. "It's hard to go on without them. But we must. For them, we must go on."

How many times has he repeated that to himself?

"And you're not without those who care for you and your family." His eyes are gentle as they look into mine. "Not so long as I'm here."

His words surround me with warmth. "I haven't thanked you yet for letting us come to stay with your family. It will be good not to be with strangers. To be with you." My cheeks heat. I had not meant to say it that way.

The corners of his mouth soften. "I'm—we're very glad to have you join us."

We reach the building where the Weinbergs live. Gripping the trunk with one hand, I open the door and hold it for the others. We make our way up the steep stairs, Romek and Szymon heaving the mattress. On the third floor, Romek shifts his grip on the mattress and knocks.

Pani Weinberg opens the door. "Good. Just in time to eat with us." There's no mistaking the resemblance between mother and son—the same sculpted cheekbones and deep-brown eyes. Even her cheek creases in the same place as Romek when she smiles. "Let me take those for you, Pani Silberman." She reaches for the suitcases Mama carries. "Adela, help the girls with their luggage. Come in, come in."

• • •

October 26, 1942

Summer becomes autumn, but in the ghetto, the chill that crackles in our bones and leeches the warmth from the sky, and the fading of the daylight hours into deeper nights are our only signs of the passing of the seasons. For those who don't leave the district for work, the world has been whittled down to a few drab streets, the Aryan side of Limanowskiego a glimpse beyond a thick fence of barbed wire. With the reduction of the ghetto, barbed-wire fences have been erected in places where the boundaries of the district were constricted. Sometimes I pause at the fence and stare out at trams clattering past—since the reduction, they no longer run through our streets—horse-drawn carts clopping along, people hurrying by. I wonder where they're going and if any of them remember we are here. They can see us as easily as we can them. Perhaps they prefer not to look. Perhaps it's easier not to remember or at least to pretend to forget.

In the first weeks after the deportations, we waited for word from Tata, from anyone on the transports, but no letters or messages of any kind have reached us. People scrounge for any scrap of news about their families, and rumors from sources said to be reliable run rampant.

It's as if the thousands marched out of the ghetto in June evaporated into empty silence. I do not understand it, and yet my lack of understanding is somehow more frightening than any of the rumors.

Mama and Rena work with me at the brush factory now. In return for long days of labor, we receive a ladleful of soup in the afternoon, but we all must work, for in the event of another akcja, the unemployed are at far greater risk of deportation. Tension simmers in the ghetto as rumors of an impending akcja spread, but no one knows when it will be, who will be taken.

I string bristles onto a wooden lath. The rough bristles and wire used to leave my hands a mass of cuts and scrapes, but my fingers are accustomed to the work and are tough with calluses now. Beside me, Mama hunches over the table, working slower than usual, a sheen of sweat on her forehead and upper lip, though it's drafty at the long tables far from the small stove at the other end of the workroom.

I nudge her and she glances at me, face pale, almost gray. "Mama, are you all right?" I whisper.

"Just having some of my pains." Her voice is a little breathless. "I'm fine. Go back to your work."

As the hours drag, I keep a close watch on Mama. She continues working, pain tightening her face. Worry sends little jolts through me as I thread the bristles, fingers moving mindlessly.

A clatter. Mama doubles over, clutching her chest.

I barely have time to catch her as she slumps against me. "Pan Ehrlich, Pan Ehrlich." I cradle her in my arms, shouting for our foreman.

The women around us stop their work, staring at us.

Rena bends over Mama, fear frozen on her face. "Mama, Mama, what is it?"

Pan Ehrlich rushes over.

"My mama. She's been having pains all morning. I must get her to the hospital."

Pan Ehrlich takes in Mama's colorless face and labored breathing. "You'd best take her there straight away."

"Can my sister come too?"

"Yes, all right."

"Is there anything I can do?"

I glance at Adela who's run over from across the room. "If we're late getting back, tell Szymon where we are. Tell him what's happened."

Adela nods, eyes full of concern. "I'll tell him."

I'm already rising, pulling Mama up with me. She droops against my chest, scarcely able to stand.

"Help me, Rena. Support her other side. We're taking you to the hospital, Mama. Don't worry. Everything will be all right."

Rena gets on Mama's right side and together we half carry, half drag her from the workroom and out of the building, not even stopping in the cloakroom for our coats.

Mama is thin, but so are we. We struggle down the street, buffeted by a scouring wind.

Breath rasps in and out of my lips. Faster.

She has to be all right. She has to be all right.

I push myself harder, bent under Mama's weight, Rena stumbling along on her other side. The streets are all but empty with most people at work, so we pass no one who can help us. Finally, we reach the entrance of the community hospital. Rena lets go of Mama to open the door and we lurch inside.

"Please." My voice is hoarse. "We need help."

A man in a white coat comes out of a room down the corridor, takes one look at us, and rushes over. "Give her to me."

Carefully, I transfer Mama into his arms. He lifts her and carries her down the corridor, calling out to a passing woman in a white uniform. She hurries after us into a room. He settles Mama on the bed, pulls his stethoscope from around his neck.

I rush to her other side, drop to my knees beside the cot, grasp her hand. "She was at work and she just collapsed. She's been having pains all morning. She has them sometimes from her angina but never like this."

Bending over her, the doctor presses his stethoscope against her chest, brow furrowed.

Someone touches my shoulder. The nurse. "Wait outside, please."

I glance at the woman, Mama's clammy hand limp in mine. "But my mama—"

"We'll take care of her, but you must leave us to do it," she says, voice quiet but firm. "Go on now."

I release Mama's hand and rise on shaky legs. Rena, still standing in the doorway, follows me out.

The nurse shuts the door behind us.

Silent tears slide down Rena's cheeks.

Please, ADONAI, *preserve our mama, as we trust in You.*

Standing in the empty corridor, I swallow back the swelling in my throat and pull my sister close.

· · ·

October 27, 1942

I sit beside Mama's hospital bed, holding her hand. Shadows drape the ward, the room lined with close-set beds, most filled with patients. Mama lies on her back, eyes closed. I trace her with my gaze, her sallow skin stretched over hollow cheeks, the strands of the loose plait falling over her shoulder the color of ash, the white sheet outlining the sparseness of her flesh. The hands that once cradled her babies, kneaded challah, and polished the Shabbat candlesticks are worn to bone, her fingers papery in mine. The sharp knife of war has whittled away her softness and strength bit by bit, sorrow by sorrow.

Mama stirs, eyes flickering open. "Hania. How long have you been here?"

"For a little while." I smile, glad to see her awake. "How are you feeling?"

She shifts and I rise to adjust her pillow. "Better today."

The doctor told us Mama suffered a mild heart attack. Strain and over-work have left her health in a fragile state. I told him we would do anything to help her, and he shook his head and said, almost sadly, that here, with the way life is, there's so little that can be done. But he says she may well recover, and the medicine will help.

She settles against the pillow. "How are Szymon and Rena?"

I smooth the sheet before sitting down. "Both well. Szymon will be here later. Rena sends her love." Children are only permitted to visit under special circumstances. I reach for my handbag and withdraw a folded sheet of paper. "She asked me to give you this."

The page rustles as she unfolds it. "Bellflowers."

"Remember when we used to gather them on holiday in the mountains? Rena said since she couldn't go and pick them for you, she would sketch them instead."

Her smile softens the lines in her face. "Tell Rena they're beautiful. I'll smile every time I look at them." She rests the paper atop the sheet. "And Romek? How is he?"

"He's well."

"He's a nice boy, don't you think?"

My cheeks heat under my mama's knowing eyes. "Yes, he is. Very nice."

"Your face tells far more than your words. You care for him, don't you?" She smiles, a gentle question in her voice.

I flush even more. "How do you know?"

"A mama knows these things. And it is not hard to see the feelings between the two of you." A tender sadness tinges her gaze. "Someday, when you are a mama, you will know what it is to have dreams for your children. So many dreams I have lost. But Romek, he is the kind of man I have always dreamed of for you."

"Me too." My voice snags in my throat. In our lives before, how often were moments like this lost in the clamor of the everyday?

How closely we would have held them if we'd known how easily they break.

She brushes the back of her hand across my cheek. "You must be tired after your long day. Go home and have your supper." I open my mouth to say I'm not really hungry and can stay longer, but she continues. "Do as I say. You may be old enough to fall in love, but you're still my daughter."

I smile. "All right." I rise and pick up my handbag, then bend to press my lips against her forehead as she did when we were small, tucking us in and kissing us good night. I linger there a moment, breathing in the remnants of her scent. "I'll come again tomorrow."

I leave the hospital, the sky dusky with the approach of evening, the air mild for October. Józefińska Street teems with people. Two OD men shoulder through the crowd, features tense. The air seems to crackle.

Something is happening. Or about to happen.

Mama. She's my first thought. My next is Szymon and Rena. I need to find them.

I quicken my pace. In the throng clogging the sidewalk, I catch sight of Romek's familiar brown cap and lean frame.

"Hania!"

We rush toward each other. Rena and Szymon run up behind him.

"There's going to be an akcja tomorrow." Romek's words are fast, urgent. "It's all over the ghetto."

"Are you certain?"

"The chairman of the Judenrat had a meeting today at SS headquarters. They warned him to keep it quiet, but he talked, and now everybody knows." Szymon's face is taut. "Some people coming back from work saw a detachment of Sonderdienst marching toward Podgórze. By tonight, the ghetto will be surrounded."

Fear pounds in time with my pulse. We cluster together, the ghetto boiling over around us. "Has there been any word about who will go on the transport? Are they making lists?"

"No one knows," Romek says. "There's been nothing said about another registration. Maybe the lists are already drawn up."

During the June akcja, patients in the hospitals were dragged from their beds—those recovering from operations, the elderly, the disabled—and put on the transports along with the rest.

"We need to get Mama out of the hospital."

Romek's brow furrows. "Can she return to work?"

I draw a shaky breath as the realization of what we must do comes flooding over me. "She can barely stand. And she can't stay in the flat during the akcja. We'll have to hide her until it's over."

"But where?" In the hazy twilight, Rena's eyes are strangely bright.

The pharmacy. But it's in Zgody Square, right on the Umschlagplatz, and could be searched. I can't put Zosia and Magister Pankiewicz at risk by asking such a thing of them.

Romek looks at me. "What about the cellar?"

"Is it well concealed?" Szymon asks.

"Some people hid there in June, and they didn't find them."

There isn't time to ask ourselves if we're doing the right thing. By the time we find an answer, it could be too late.

"It's the best place." My heart thuds dully. "We should go now."

"She'll have to sleep down there," Szymon says. "In case they take people during the night."

I nod. "I'll stay with her. At least through the night."

The four of us start toward the hospital, Romek at my side. "I'll stay too."

"You don't need to do that. We'll be fine."

"I won't sleep anyway. I can at least keep you company." He slides his fingers through mine. There's a steadiness to the roughness of his palm, the strength of his fingers, the joining of our hands while the world spirals around us.

We reach the hospital, hurry through the corridors and into the ward where Mama has a bed, our footsteps clattering in the silence. A nurse glances up from bending over a patient's bed but makes no move to stop us.

We reach Mama's bed. Her eyes are closed, one hand resting over her chest, her fingers partially covering something. Rena's picture.

"Mama." I lean over the bed. "Wake up. We have to talk to you."

She opens her eyes. "Hania." Her voice is groggy. "Why are you all here?"

"There's going to be an akcja tomorrow, Pani Silberman," Romek says gently. "We're taking you home until it's safe for you to return."

"Now? Tonight?" She struggles to sit up.

"It must be tonight. Romek will carry you. Szymon"—I turn to my brother—"ask the nurse to fetch Mama's clothes."

Szymon nods and heads across the ward.

"It's all right, Mama." I help her sit up. "We'll take care of you."

Szymon returns several minutes later with Mama's clothes. The nurse rolls a screen around the bed for privacy, and Rena and I help Mama dress. She's stronger than I expected, but by the time we finish, she needs to lean back against the pillow to catch her breath. Rena sits with her, an arm around her shoulders, while I step from behind the screen to where Romek and Szymon wait.

"She's ready."

Romek comes behind the screen. "All ready, Pani Silberman?"

"I suppose so." Her eyes search mine. "Hania, are you certain about this?"

My chest squeezes. Because, no, I'm not certain at all. "If there's to be an akcja, we don't know what will happen to the people in the hospitals. There's a place for you to hide. You'll be safe there."

"Don't worry, Pani Silberman. We'll look after you." Romek steps toward the bed. There's something tender about how gentle and respectful he is toward her. "Can you put your arms around my neck?" He lifts her carefully. I walk beside him, keeping a close watch on Mama, the four of us leaving the ward and the patients in its beds behind. A few raise their heads, gazes following us as we pass. I do not meet their eyes.

The crowd on Józefińska has dwindled. It's as if everyone has heard the news and no longer needs to seek it, as if there's nothing left for them to do but return to their homes, gather their families, and wait.

Perhaps some are acting instead of waiting. Perhaps others are seeking places to hide, taking measures to protect the vulnerable from whatever tomorrow may bring.

We walk home as the last traces of the sun fade, darkness slipping over the streets.

• • •

Zosia
October 28, 1942

Fear's hot press in my throat, I hurry toward the ghetto. The morning air is soft, springlike, the sky cloudless above the spires of the Third Bridge. It's nearing eight, earlier than when I usually arrive at the pharmacy, but I couldn't sleep. Finally I dressed and left my flat, needing to reach Podgórze.

What awaits the ghetto today? What will this akcja mean? Who will be taken? Who will remain?

Yesterday people crowded the pharmacy as word of the akcja spread. Everyone sought to find out what was being said, asking us if we knew anything. They came to us for tranquilizers, nerves teetering on the point of shattering. Few had prescriptions, but we dispensed them anyway. How could we refuse when even we didn't know what the next day would bring? Others came to buy hair dye to darken their gray strands in an attempt to restore an appearance of youthful vitality and thus be deemed fit for labor. Some asked us for Luminal to sedate small children and infants. Many had prepared hiding places, and a baby's cries could betray them all.

I quicken my pace, nearly running across the bridge. There will be something we can do, someone we can help. If nothing else, we are witnesses.

Father in heaven . . .

The words crumble, dissolving into dust.

Prayer, once sacred, holds only cheapness now.

The Zgody Square gate stands ahead, a wall of gray slabs against a pale-blue sky.

Two policemen flank the gate.

Germans. Not Blue Police.

I approach the entrance and reach into my handbag for my Kennkarte and pass.

"Good morning." I make myself smile as I present my papers.

Impassive eyes beneath a steel helmet scan over me. The policeman doesn't look at my papers. Nor does his expression soften under my smile. "What is your business in the Jewish residential district?"

"I work at the Apteka Pod Orłem on Zgody Square."

"Only those with special authorization from the Gestapo are permitted to enter the district today."

"If you'll look at my papers, I'm sure you'll find everything in order."

He opens my Kennkarte, sparing the creased pass with its official stamps and signature a few seconds of his attention before returning my papers. "Your pass is not valid today."

Not valid? No. I must get into the ghetto. "I was told nothing of this when I left yesterday." I make my voice as inflexible as his. "I've been at the Apteka Pod Orłem nearly two years and not once have I or my colleagues been turned away."

"No one enters the district today without the express authorization of the Gestapo. There are no exceptions."

Gunfire rings out. I start, tensing.

What's happening?

I reach into my handbag and withdraw from my pocketbook every złoty I have with me—which doesn't amount to much—and show him the bills. "Perhaps you might accept this."

He hesitates, the tension of some inward debate passing across his still-boyish features. "No one enters the district today without the express authorization of the Gestapo." His voice is clenched. "I will not repeat myself again. If you do not desist, you will be shot."

I stare at the guard, his rigid stance, his rifle. Then I turn and walk away, because what else can I do?

"Zosia."

I glance up.

Irka rushes toward me, her coat unbuttoned. "Where are you going?"

"They won't let us in." My voice shakes. "Only those with authorization from the Gestapo are permitted to enter the district today."

She pulls in a sharp breath. "Tadeusz?"

"I don't know." It's the first I've thought of him. He urged us to return home, told us he could manage until morning. He couldn't have left the ghetto last night.

One of us is still there.

Irka draws herself up. "I'm going to try—"

Shots spatter in the distance.

The sound trembles through my body.

We look at each other. Reflected in her eyes is the same desperate fear my own surely hold. So many people trapped behind the walls, at the mercy of whatever unknown is about to unfold.

Hania. Hania and her mama and brother and sister. I haven't seen any of them in several days. I should have tried to get them away from there. They could have slipped out of the ghetto, stayed with me for the duration of the akcja.

Why didn't I try?

Minutes pass as we stand in the street, two women staring at the guarded gate.

. . .

Hania

All day, they keep us in the windowless workroom. No one knows what's happening outside. But we hear the shots. Round after round.

It goes on for hours.

I become a machine, attaching bristles to laths at a feverish pace. When I look up, I'm met with strained features and red-rimmed eyes, fear drawing shadows on the faces of the men and women sitting in rows.

When we took Mama to the cellar, we found others already there. An old couple, a middle-aged woman, and two children. They didn't want another person in their hiding place and the middle-aged woman nearly came to blows with Romek. Finally he convinced them to let Mama hide with them. They'd done a poor job concealing the trapdoor and he'd help them if she could stay. But nothing could persuade them to let us remain with her overnight, so we left her there, in the dark hole of the cellar, with strangers.

This lath hasn't been drilled correctly, so I have to jab a pin through the holes to thread the wire through.

The pin slips, penetrating the pad of my thumb.

I quickly stick my thumb in my mouth, the taste of metal on my tongue. Then I wipe my finger on my skirt and bend to my work again.

My hands are shaking.

Mama, Mama, Mama.

Finally, Pan Ehrlich dismisses us. The akcja is over. We can return home.

Chairs scrape and footsteps shuffle. Whispers rustle through the people around us. No one speaks any louder.

I exit the building into autumn sunlight, Rena beside me. The silence seeps damp and heavy into my skin.

Then it is before us. The aftermath. Men and women swarm the street, running into buildings, rushing in a dozen directions. Women weep in each other's arms. A man stands alone on the sidewalk, head bent, shoulders shaking. A horse-drawn wagon draped with a blood-splattered sheet trundles down the street. The sheet flutters loose, exposing a tangle of naked bodies, a woman's head dangling back, empty eyes staring up at the sunny sky.

I walk faster, Rena following. The cobbles are strewn with suitcases and bundles, stray shoes, patches of blood dark in the sun. An old woman lies face down on the curb, the back of her head shattered by a bullet.

Urgency pulses through my body, a second heartbeat as we push through the crowd of the searching, the grieving, the numb.

I pound down the street and through the gateway, into the courtyard.

There I skid to a stop.

The cellar door yawns wide, a gaping mouth. Someone moved the crates and broken furniture Romek and I placed to conceal the trapdoor.

Then I'm rushing forward, stumbling down the ladder, missing the bottom two rungs entirely. There's a vague sensation of pain shooting through my twisted ankle, but it doesn't penetrate.

"Mama?" I blink in the darkness. "Is anyone there? The Germans are gone. It's safe to come out now."

I grope my way forward, shadows and outlines coming into focus. The junk piled in the corner.

The blankets on the floor.

I drop to my knees on the hard-packed dirt, running my hand over the blanket, the one we brought for Mama. My fingers brush against lumpy canvas and I pull it toward myself.

I gave Mama this rucksack with a jar of water, a loaf of bread, and cold potato pancakes wrapped in a cloth. I open the bag. A hunk of the bread is missing, the rest is untouched.

I scramble to my feet and up the ladder. She's in the flat. Someone must have helped her there. She didn't think to take the food and blanket with her.

Rena stands at the mouth of the cellar, staring into its black void.

"She's upstairs." I pull myself out, scraping my knees, not caring. "They must have realized it was safe to come out."

I burst into the building, my panting breaths heavy in my ears as I run up the stairs.

The door to our flat stands wide open.

Deep gashes gouge the wood, smashed by an axe or rifle butt.

Fragments of glass crunch beneath my feet as I step into the kitchen. As if from a distance, I notice the overturned table, the flung-open kitchen dresser, the shattered dishes on the floor.

I walk through the open doorway into our room. The bed Pani Weinberg and Adela share lies on its side, our bed frame an iron skeleton in the corner, mattresses a heap on the floor, slashed down the middle. Feathers scatter the floor like bits of snow. A few drift in the air as if stirred by my entrance.

Deep inside my chest, a crack spreads.

Footsteps. I turn. Rena appears in the doorway, staring at the room, its ruins and its emptiness. Her dress hangs on her scrawny shoulders, her face framed by the plaits wound around her head small and young . . . and knowing.

"Mama," she breathes the word. "Mama." Louder this time. It's a child's wail, broken and lost, but laden with a grief that has no boundary in years.

I can't move. My ears ring. My breath won't come.

Mama.

This time the cry is mine. Soundless in my throat.

Tears slide down her cheeks, her sobs fill the room.

Somehow I force my legs to move. Somehow I cross the room and put my arms around my sister. But my body, my heart, everything is numb.

Rena sobs into my chest. "No!" The garbled word emerges as a scream. "Why did they take her? Why?"

I can't speak, my throat hot and swollen. I hold her while her body shudders with the force of her gasping cries.

I hold her because I can do nothing else.

How long do we stand in the center of the room, my head bent, my arms around her? It doesn't matter. What is time but a continuation of pain?

Pani Weinberg and Adela enter, faces ashen. Their mourning wordless. Romek follows. His anguished eyes meet mine. Rena hasn't moved, her tears muffled against me.

He walks toward us. And then his arms come around me.

Around us.

I lean into his chest without letting go of Rena. Rest my cheek against the strength and warmth and steadiness of him.

"I . . . can't . . . breathe." My voice is a rasp.

"I know." His hand circles my back, slow and even. Tracing the same pattern again and again. "I've got you. I'm right here."

Tata, scooping my toddler self up from a fall, gathering me in his arms, his scratchy cheek against mine. *I've got you, my Hania.*

Mama, bending over my bed when I was sick, her cool palm smoothing my burning forehead, face gentle in the lamplight. *I'm here. Mama's here.*

A sound wrenches from my throat, ripped from deep within. I don't have the strength to hold it back any longer. Guttural sobs wrack my body and I surrender to them.

Romek pulls me tighter and I weep until I go still in his arms. Until every crack within me has turned to shards.

CHAPTER TWELVE

Zosia
October 29, 1942

WE RETURN TO A ghetto that is barren and stripped. Even the air carries the silent burden of sorrow. It is difficult to comprehend and impossible to bear the full enormity of such a loss—six thousand deported in a single day—so each mourns for their own, and in that way, their grief becomes collective.

Hundreds were killed in the ghetto. The Germans barged into the hospitals and infirmary for the elderly. Anyone who couldn't walk was simply shot where they lay. At the orphanage, SS men ordered the older children and their teachers to march to the Umschlagplatz. The younger ones were loaded onto trucks. No, loaded is too human a word to describe how they threw the littlest children inside, one on top of the other, like sacks of meal. No one knows where they were taken.

Tadeusz himself barely escaped deportation, forced to join the deportees in the square when the Germans searched the ghetto. Only after the officer in charge of the akcja checked his papers was Tadeusz able to return to the pharmacy. Had they taken him with the others, there would be nothing we could do.

Less than ten thousand remain in the ghetto.

And us. We are still here too.

I walk quickly through the ghetto in the waning twilight, a kerchief knotted beneath my chin, a basket over my arm. Even as we listened to recounting after recounting of individual tragedies, even as Tadeusz gave us the news of who had been taken—so many names, so many friends—I told myself the Silbermans were still here. Hania, Rena, and Szymon, healthy young people employed in useful enterprises were among those most likely to be kept off the transports. Though there had been young, working people selected for deportation when loudspeakers ordered all workers to assemble in front of the Arbeitsamt yesterday morning. With a motion of an officer's hand, no criteria applied save his whims, some had been kept behind instead of leaving with their work groups.

I tell myself the Silbermans were not among them because I can't consider the alternative.

I reach the run-down tenement on Józefińska. It's safer for our friends to come to the pharmacy, to meet inside the relative freedom of our walls, so I haven't visited the Silbermans since they moved, but Hania gave me the address.

Hinges whine as I open the door and step into the dusky interior. Narrow stairs wind upward and I mount the treads until I reach the third floor.

My stomach roils, the raw gash defacing the door silent evidence of recent destruction. I raise my fist and knock, dread breaking over me.

The door cracks open. On the other side stands a dark-haired young man in a worn shirt and trousers.

"Are the Silbermans here?"

He has pronounced cheekbones and a guarded expression, and he takes my measure as though he's trying to decide if he has reason to be wary of the strange woman at his door. "That depends on who you've come to see."

"I'm a friend of Hania's. I work at the pharmacy on Zgody Square." Most are aware of the pharmacy and the reputation of its owner as a decent man. "Is Hania here?"

"She's inside." He steps aside to let me pass.

Strangers crowd the kitchen, sitting around the table and on an iron-frame bed pushed against the wall. The room has a smell of musty dampness, overlaid by the rotten odor of cooking cabbage. A carbide lamp casts a grimy light. Electricity in the ghetto is now cut off every evening for a few hours. "They're through here."

The wary-eyed people at the table watch us as we pass. The man opens a door, lets me precede him.

Hania sits on one of the beds, stuffing a shoe with newspaper. On the other end, Rena sits cross-legged, bent over a book.

Hania rises. "Zosia?"

"I was so worried." I rush across the room, drop the basket on the bed, and wrap her in my arms. She smells of stale sweat and boiled cabbage, her frame fragile as cracked china, and I hold her close before drawing away.

Then I see her eyes.

Eyes numb with a pain so deep it stills my breath.

"The others?" Somehow I form the words.

"Szymon's all right. But . . ." Hania shakes her head, her breath shuddering in. "Mama collapsed at the brush factory a few days ago. The doctor told us she'd had a heart attack." Her voice is as hollow as her eyes. "When we heard about the akcja, we knew she wouldn't be safe in the hospital, so we took her to the cellar in our building. We thought she could hide until the Germans left. When the akcja was over . . . she wasn't there. We don't know what happened."

Pani Silberman. Gentle, kind Pani Silberman. "Hania, I'm . . ." My voice fades. "I'm so sorry."

One would think, after everything, we would have found the words to speak in the face of another's loss. Instead language fails us. Grief defies vocabulary. Time and experience don't give us new insight into the incomprehensible. Each loss only grows heavier, harder upon those that came before.

Rena watches us silently, her book in her lap. The young man stands in the doorway, his hand shoved in his trousers pocket, something hard and broken in his face. The woman and the girl on the other bed are also silent.

"Why didn't you come to me?" I ask, my chest scraped by an almost physical pain.

"Why?" Hania's voice cracks, a trace of anger in it. "What would you have done?"

"I could have . . ." I shake my head. *Could have* is meaningless now. "I don't know."

I don't know what I should have done, but I know what I did not do.

• • •

Hania
November 10, 1942

Stillness settles over the flat as it does each night, though there is rarely ever silence. With ten people crowded into one room and a kitchen, there's always the groan of a mattress, always someone sighing or moaning or snoring, the sounds telling of how each person passes the night.

The hours between when the flat quiets and sleep overtakes my body are those I dread most. The day places a barrier between me and my thoughts— one riddled with cracks and chinks but a barrier nonetheless. In the void of the night my barricade crumbles, leaving me nowhere to hide from my questions and fears, the despair kept at bay by the day.

I roll onto my side, Rena asleep beside me. When the three of us shared the bed, we had to lie like spoons in a drawer, and if one wanted to turn, we all had to shift positions.

I no longer need to cling to the edge of the mattress. The empty space in a bed once warm with the heat of three bodies is now a silent presence, an accusation of its own.

I should never have left her. Why did I leave her?

Mama.

A floorboard squeaks. The shuffle of a footfall. I raise my head, make out the shadow of someone crossing the room. Romek?

The door creaks as the figure steals out.

I ease out of bed and pull the covers up over my place, pick my way around the beds and mattresses occupied by the lumpy outlines of sleeping people. Romek's mattress is empty, the covers turned back.

I edge the door open and step into the kitchen. Romek sits at the table, staring at a small collection of items in front of him by the sputtering light of a carbide lamp. I rest a hand on his shoulder, his warmth radiating through the threadbare cotton of his shirt.

At my touch, he turns.

"Hania, what are you doing up? It's after midnight."

"I heard you leave. I wondered why." I'm careful to whisper, mindful of the man and his adolescent son asleep on the bed against the wall and the pallet on the floor.

"Couldn't sleep. I thought I'd sit here for a while."

"Do you mind company?"

He glances at me with an almost-smile. "Please. Stay if you like."

I pull a chair close and sit beside him. "What are you doing with these?"

On the table is a wad of złoty notes, a pair of diamond earrings, and a gold pocket watch.

"It's all we have left." His voice is weary. "It's not enough."

"For what?"

He scrubs both hands across his face, draws a long breath. "We can't go on like this, Hania."

I meet his eyes. "What do you mean?"

"They won't stop. The transports to this place of which we know nothing, from which no word returns. We've told ourselves they need us to work, but they don't care about our work. These stamps, these . . . these blue cards, they're nothing but a means to make us believe some of us have a chance. But they take the workers along with everybody else, take whoever they want. They'll keep reducing the district—only last week another reduction—keep taking more and more people. Until one day, no one is left. It's . . ."

"What?" I say, voice firm, though my throat is dry.

"For a long time, there have been rumors about what's happening to the people on the transports. I told myself it was only talk, but after the last akcja, how can anyone believe they're sending those people to work? If it were the young, the strong chosen for resettlement, I could believe this, but the old, the sick from the hospitals, the children thrown into the trucks . . ."

"But if not to work, why send them? If they are taking them somewhere"—I swallow—"else, why go to the trouble of putting them on trains? We've seen how easily they kill. If they mean to simply do away with them, why not do it here?"

"I don't know." He sighs. "How have we let ourselves be deceived for so long? Perhaps because we want it to be true, to think these mythical camps where thousands of people live do exist. To believe anything else . . . we would have no hope left." The defeat in his voice turns me cold, a slow numbing to ice.

"Surely." My voice isn't quite steady. "It could still be possible."

"Perhaps." His gaze holds mine. "But to trust in what may be possible is to close our eyes to reality."

If Romek's words were new, they could be denied, dismissed. But everything he speaks is but a voicing of thoughts I've kept silent. Telling myself it cannot be true . . . it cannot be true.

I can't let these words reach my heart. I can believe them, or at least not deny them, but I can't let them touch me.

"What do we do?" I ask softly. "What can we do?"

"We need to find a way to get you and Rena, my mama and sister out of here. Szymon and I too, but what's most important is to get the four of you out."

"Leave the ghetto?" It's more statement than question.

"Yes." He leans toward me, so close our foreheads nearly touch. "We need to get false identification papers so you can live on the Aryan side."

I've heard talk of such documents, rumors like everything else. If one can get hold of a Kennkarte belonging to a real person or obtain a good forgery, it's possible to pass as an Aryan Pole. Provided one has the skills of an actor and the nerves of a very good liar.

"How does one get such papers?"

"They can be bought, for the right price. The better the documents, the more costly they are, from what I hear." He picks up the pocket watch, rubs his thumb over its case. "When we found out my tata had fallen during the invasion, I knew it was up to me to do as he would have. His place became mine." Raw desperation tightens his face. "I must find a way to get my mama and sister out. If they stay here . . ." He shakes his head. "And you. I must find a way for you and Rena too." He lapses into silence, both of us lost in our own thoughts.

An idea slowly unfolds.

"I might know someone who could help us."

"What do you mean? Who?"

"Zosia. The woman from the pharmacy. Remember I told you we used to live in the same building? Before we came to the ghetto, we left some of our valuables with her for safekeeping. If she sold them for us, we could use the money for the documents."

"What does she have?"

I return to the past, to our flat, long enough to remember but no more. Lingering will only bring pain. "There's a lace tablecloth and a silver coffee set." There are the photographs too, but those are worth nothing except to us. "And Mama's diamond ring is here with us. Zosia might be able to get it appraised. Would it be enough, do you think?"

Romek considers this. "It would be a start. Do you think it's still there, what you gave her? I ask only because we also placed some of our valuables with friends. Last winter, before the post office was shut down, I wrote asking if it could be arranged for one or two of the items to be returned to us, but I never received a reply. They either have the stuff and aren't keen on the prospect of parting with it or our things have long since been sold."

"No, Romek. Zosia isn't like that. She's here in the ghetto almost every day, doing whatever she can to help, taking no care for the risk to herself. She would never steal from us." I reach for his hand, closing my fingers around his broad palm. "We will find a way," I say softly. "And if there's no way to be found, then at least we will know we tried."

CHAPTER THIRTEEN

Zosia
November 13, 1942

"I'LL JUST SAY GOODNIGHT." I stop in the doorway of the duty room, my coat on, carrying my handbag.

Tadeusz sits at his desk, staring at a sheet of paper in front of him. He doesn't look up.

"Is everything all right?" Maybe I didn't speak loudly enough. "Tadeusz?"

He raises his gaze.

The look on his face. As if all life has been drained out of him, body and soul.

"The others, are they still here?"

"Helena's gone already, but Irka's in the materials room."

"You'd better have her come in. There's something you both need to hear."

"What's happened?" I ask quietly, even as my chest tightens.

He hesitates. "Just tell Irka to come in, please, Zosia."

"Yes, of course."

In the materials room, Irka stands in front of the cabinet, putting a bottle away. She closes the cabinet and turns. "I thought you'd gone."

"Tadeusz asked me to fetch you. He has something to speak to us about."

Perhaps noticing the restrained urgency in my voice, Irka follows without question.

Tadeusz sits in the same posture as I left him, except now he stares at the curtained window instead of the page upon his desk.

"What is it?"

His eyes focus on Irka. "Dr. Heim was just here."

"Dr. Heim from the community hospital?" Irka asks.

"I picked up a letter for him in town yesterday. He came back later and left the letter with me. He wished me to read it."

"Who is it from?" Irka lowers herself into the chair near the window.

"Dr. Heim's sister. She managed to leave the ghetto shortly before the last akcja. She . . . Let me read what it says." He picks up the two sheets of creased paper from his desk, studies them a moment. "She begins by writing that she arrived safely in Lwów. Then she goes on, 'On my journey to Lwów, I passed through the village of Bełżec.'"

Bełżec. I've never heard of it before.

"When I arrived at the station, I noticed another train on the tracks nearby. This train did not have passenger carriages but the sort of wagons used for the transportation of freight or livestock. German police stood outside the cars armed with rifles.

"I wondered what sort of freight the Germans guarded so carefully, so I waited outside the station, hoping I might be able to detect something of what was going on. The wagons were closed, so I could not see inside, but then I began to hear sounds coming from within. For a moment, I did not understand what they were, but then I realized there were people in the cars, groaning, crying out for help. People begging for water, for bread. What conditions were inside the cars, I cannot say, but I can only imagine from the sounds I heard how horrible it must have been. I noticed something else too, a peculiar odor in the air when the wind blew a certain direction. A scent of burning, as if there were a fire somewhere nearby. There was another smell too, a strange, foul stench. I do not know how to describe it nor if it can be described, but there was a sweetness about it, a nauseating sweetness. I did not know then what caused it, but somehow, I sensed something terrible was at its origin.'" Tadeusz reads without infliction, without pauses, his mouth simply the vehicle by which another's words are formed.

"I met a woman in the village, and we started to talk. I told her I was a stranger in the area and remarked upon the unusual smell, asking if she knew what it was from. She did not want to tell me at first, but once she began to speak, the words poured out of her. There is a camp in the forest, about half a kilometer from the station. Since March, trains have arrived almost daily, destined for this camp. Sometimes, she said, the cars wait for days on the siding until their turn comes. When those living in the village pass by, they hear the pleas and cries of the people trapped inside, but they can do nothing to help them.

"The woman said at first she did not know what was happening in the forest, but in time, she heard talk. What she heard she could scarcely believe, but as the same account was repeated, she realized it must be true. Once the cars arrive in the forest, the doors are opened and those still alive are ordered out by the guards. They are told by an SS man they are at a transit camp and are to be taken for disinfecting. The men are separated from the women and children, they are made to undress and leave their luggage, then they are herded into chambers with signs indicating they are entering a bathhouse. Once everyone is inside, the doors are sealed and poisonous fumes pumped into the chambers."

I can't shut out Tadeusz's voice. I can't even move. I can only stand frozen as the words come and come and come.

"Within twenty minutes, everyone inside is dead. The chambers are then opened, and the bodies taken away. Day after day, this procedure is repeated. For many months, they buried the bodies in pits, but now they are burned. Clouds of smoke hang over the forest from the incineration of the corpses."

I am supposed to absorb these words. I cannot. How can the mind comprehend what is incomprehensible? The enormity.

The finality.

"I write this to you and to all who yet remain in the ghetto to beg you to dispel any illusions about the fate of the people on the transports. This is where they are being taken. This is what is happening to them. Do not think you will be spared this fate, but by any means you can, escape. Escape before it is too late." Tadeusz lowers the letter.

No one speaks. This is a silence not meant to be filled.

Irka sits motionless, face ashen.

My heart is a pulsing pressure in my chest. I stand in the duty room, still wearing my coat, holding my handbag, but I am scarcely aware of my surroundings, of anything at all.

We do not know the woman who wrote this letter nor the one from the village. Perhaps it is the concoction of an unstable mind, scenes not of reality.

But it is not.

Images conjured by the letter's words run through my mind like a film. Such a place as the woman described requires organization. How could members of the human race so forget their own mortality that they would invent the means by which to murder thousands? How can human beings turn against their fellow man so completely? It is surreal, inhuman. And yet who but humans are its orchestrators?

Thousands have been deported from the ghetto.

But it is not the thousands that overwhelm me. It is the faces of those who passed through the door of the pharmacy. Each with their own set of fears and joys, ways of hoping or despairing. Men. Women. Children. Families.

Lives.

Long ago, my tata told me of a friend who'd worked as an engineer for a railway. Once, as the train raced onward, the engineer spotted a child playing alone on the tracks. The train drew closer, but the boy didn't move. In a panic, all the while shouting to the child to get out of the way, the engineer tried to stop the train. But it was traveling too fast to be stopped or even slowed. He could do nothing but watch as the train struck the child and killed him.

The story returns to me now as clearly as the day Tata told it to me.

For we are living it.

Only thousands are stranded on the tracks instead of one.

And the train travels faster, faster, faster.

• • •

November 15, 1942

For two nights, I do not sleep. Images break through my mind in flashes, waking nightmares. Scenes from the akcja, visions of the camp at Bełżec, the smoke rising over the forest without end.

Like the one driven by the engineer, the train of the Nazi plan to extermi-nate the Jewish people of Poland bears down upon the ghetto, speeding too fast to be stopped or even slowed. For what could be the reason for such a place as the camp at Bełżec if their purpose is not total annihilation?

I must pull them away from the tracks. I must pull them away from the tracks while there is yet a chance.

Since the letter arrived, I've thought of nothing else.

Every week brings fresh upheaval. A labor camp is being built at Płaszów, on the outskirts of Kraków. It's now certain the camp is intended for the inhabitants of the ghetto, but how many will be sent there and when, and what will happen to the rest? People grab at rumors, try to predict what will come next, as if by their conjectures they can manage to stay one step ahead of the Germans.

On Sunday, I return to the flat where the Silbermans live. This time it's Pani Weinberg, the mother of the young man whose name I've learned is Romek, who answers the door and ushers me into the kitchen.

Hania stands at the table, shredding potatoes into a bowl. At its other end, Rena slices a loaf of dark claylike bread while Pani Weinberg's daugh-ter, Adela, darns a sock. They turn as I step inside, the basket over my arm lighter than usual. The rise of prices in the street markets, where goods are sold illegally, means my resources don't stretch as far as they once did. I've been selling Ryszard's clothes and books to purchase food for the Silbermans and some of our other customers at the pharmacy. These days, leather-bound volumes of classic literature are sold for a pittance, while butter and meat are all but unattainable luxuries.

"Hello, girls."

Hania doesn't smile, but her features ease a little. "Zosia, we weren't expecting you."

"I've brought a few things. I thought I'd save you the trouble of coming to the pharmacy."

"That's kind." Hania sets the potato in the bowl. "I was going to come to the pharmacy tomorrow. There's something I need to ask. Can you spare a few minutes?" She lowers her voice, glancing at the man in a tattered sweater who sits on the bed, smoking the nub of a cigarette.

"Of course, yes. I wanted to speak to you as well. Would you empty the basket for me, please, Rena?" I hand the basket to Rena, and she sets it on the table, lifting the cloth to peer inside, Adela close beside her.

The door opens and Romek and Szymon troop in, arms loaded with what looks like broken furniture, cheeks blotchy from the raw November day.

"Mama, we got the wood."

"Good." Pani Weinberg chafes her arms. "On a day so cold, we certainly need it."

"Good day, Pani Magistra." Romek nods to me then steps past to feed the wood into the stove.

Szymon follows, his nose and the tips of his ears red from cold. "Hello."

"Hello, Szymon."

"If there's one good thing about the district being reduced, it's all the furniture nobody takes the trouble to move anymore." Szymon drops his armload into the woodbox near the stove and heads into the adjoining room.

Hania steps to Romek's side as he finishes lighting the stove, says something to him in a voice too low to catch. A look of accord passes between them, but there is more than accord in the way their eyes meet. It's not a look between lovers but of two people with something strong and deep and true between them.

It stills me, Hania and this young man regarding each other in this way.

Romek brushes his hands on the knees of his trousers, faces me. "Would you care to join us in the next room, Pani Magistra?"

Within minutes, we're sitting in the adjoining room with its water-stained walls and crammed-together beds, me in a chair, Hania and Romek on one of the beds, Pani Weinberg on another. Szymon stands near the window. Rena and Adela are still in the kitchen. I clasp my hands in my lap, the dank chill making me glad I'm still wearing my coat.

Everyone looks at me, waiting.

How to form the words? How to find them? To voice what the letter held is to speak of a thing so terrible it is beyond language.

But to keep silent is a crime.

"Two days ago, a letter came into Magister Pankiewicz's hands . . ." I speak the truth contained in the letter, faltering slightly but forcing myself to go on, keeping my description as brief as possible.

When I finish, they sit silent. Stricken.

"The letter ended with a plea for everyone who can to escape while it's still possible. I will do whatever I can to get you out." I look at each of them in turn. "All of you."

As soon as I voice the words, I wonder if I've spoken too hastily. When I came here today, it was for the purpose of speaking with Hania and Szymon. I did not even think of the Weinbergs.

But how can I not help whomever I can? I'm not foolish enough to believe my capabilities are boundless, but surely it's possible to help a few. For Dr. and Pani Silberman, it's too late, and grief swallows my heart at this reality.

The children are still here. The Weinbergs also.

For them, there's yet a chance.

"Romek and I have already spoken." Hania's eyes are intent on mine. "We hoped you might be able to sell some of the things we left with you. We thought to use the money to purchase Aryan papers."

"Do you have a contact who can provide you with the documents?"

Romek hunches forward, fingers linked between his knees. "I've been making inquiries."

"And discovered a good set of false papers costs a small fortune." Szymon's eyes flare, a thatch of hair falling stubbornly over his forehead. "I say forget the false papers and join up with one of the partisan units fighting in the forests. At least if we die, it will be as human beings instead of letting them lead us like cattle to the slaughter."

"These partisan units you speak of," Romek says, "they do not always welcome people like us. One would think anyone willing to fight the Germans would be accepted as a comrade, but there are a lot of Poles who think they're better off letting the Nazis deal with us." He glances at me. "I mean no offense to you, Pani Magistra."

I nod. "I understand."

"Perhaps there is good to be found in fighting in this way." Pani Weinberg's voice is quiet but firm. "But we know nothing of how to join such a group. Even if we did, do you want your sisters to become partisans too, Szymon?"

Szymon shoves a hand in his pocket, lowers his head.

"Obtaining Aryan papers and finding a way to live outside the ghetto, this is what I think we should do." Romek's tone carries a decisive calm far older than his years. "The victory of the British in North Africa surely means the war is beginning to turn and Germany's defeat is no longer a hope but an eventuality." He pauses. "Is not to live to strike back?"

Romek's words settle into the silent room. From the kitchen comes the clatter of dishes, the undertone of voices.

The choice about their future—what few choices there are—is not for me to make. We outside the ghetto endure the pangs of occupation, the fears too, but no one who has experienced both worlds could rightfully compare our circumstances. Though I enter the district almost daily, I remain isolated from its realities insofar as I am not directly affected by them.

Still, I can offer what I have.

"For a time, there were certain men, Poles, who delivered to the pharmacy envelopes containing false papers. Since the district fell under the jurisdiction of the Gestapo, it's become almost impossible to get a pass to enter the ghetto, so they can no longer make these deliveries. But perhaps Magister Pankiewicz knows someone who can supply the necessary documents. I don't need to tell you such an undertaking is not without risk." I meet their gazes. "There's no assurance of safety outside the ghetto. But there is a chance."

Romek nods. "That's all any of us can hope for."

"And what about you?" Though her features are pale and spent, a steady resolve emanates from Hania's eyes. "Whether we stay or go, we will always be in danger, but you . . . you are already safe."

The weight of their gazes rests on me. If I were to be caught helping even one Jewish person escape the ghetto or aiding them on the Aryan side, well, the edict states it clearly enough. No one is exempt from the consequences.

But who would I be if I watched the train surge toward the boy on the tracks and did not stretch out my hand to him, even if I risked being thrown under the wheels myself?

For it could easily be me stranded on the tracks and I would not want another to stand by.

"Do you know," I say softly, "I don't believe any of us are safe anymore."

CHAPTER FOURTEEN

Zosia
November 26, 1942

DO YOU HAVE A *light?*

To anyone else, the words are nothing more than a simple remark, a commonplace question easily exchanged with a stranger or acquaintance. Now the sentence is a link, the connection between my contact and me.

How strange to think I have a contact.

At 6 o'clock, a man will be sitting on a bench reading the paper in the square near the statue of Grażyna and Litawor. You'll ask if he has a light, he'll offer you one, and invite you to join him.

My steps tap along the pavement as I mentally repeat Tadeusz's instructions.

With winter's approach, the chestnut trees along the Planty's paths reach empty branches toward a washed-out sky. In my gray coat, my black hat slanted over my eyes, I blend into the sparse crowd of Poles and Germans, an ordinary woman out for a stroll before curfew. Exactly as it should be.

I near the small square across from the statue. There are several benches.

All are empty. I angle my wrist, glancing at my watch. Eight minutes before the hour.

I cross to the edge of the square. Facing the statue set in a grove of trees, I make a show of studying the marble rendering of the knight Litawor and his wife Grażyna from Adam Mickiewicz's narrative poem.

To meet at a statue depicting a scene, albeit mythical, from a battle between Lithuanians and their Teutonic enemies seems grimly appropriate.

Wind scuttles a few leaves across the path. Over the dry rustle of the leaves comes the steady tread of footsteps.

Without moving my head, I turn my gaze the barest amount as a man in an overcoat and fedora comes down the path.

In the next moment, he'll sit on a bench and open his newspaper and I'll approach him.

Do you have a light?

I hold my breath, feigning absorption in the statue.

His footsteps don't slow. He's walking away.

Minutes trail by. More pedestrians pass but don't stop. An old man in a coat and muffler sits heavily on one of the benches and lights his pipe. He has no newspaper.

What if the person Tadeusz arranged the meeting with—the contact who's to provide the false papers—isn't coming after all?

I stare at Grażyna, resolute in armor. I won't leave until I'm certain there's no one meeting me.

A man approaches, stride firm, the brim of his cap hiding his features.

I keep my eyes fixed on the statue, my profile turned just enough to follow his movements.

He looks up.

Even without his navy uniform, there's no mistaking the solid frame, the strong features.

The policeman from the ghetto.

If he notices me, he's sure to recognize me. It's too late to turn and walk in the opposite direction.

I sense the instant he catches sight of me. But his eyes don't connect with mine nor does his expression in any way acknowledge recognition.

He'll pass through the square and continue on his way. Then I'll be able to breathe again.

His steps slow. He sits on one of the benches opposite the statue with the unstudied ease of any passerby taking a few minutes to rest and enjoy the view.

He reaches into his coat and takes out a rolled newspaper.

Surely there's some mistake.

He unfolds it and begins to read, his face all but hidden by the front page of the *Krakauer Zeitung*. I stay where I am, watching him.

If he knew the real reason I'm here, he could have me arrested. Or maybe he'd do it himself.

Enough. Either he is my contact or he isn't. I won't find out which by standing here.

I reach into my handbag, withdrawing the slim cylinder of a cigarette. A cigarette I borrowed from a pack in Tadeusz's desk, because I don't smoke.

As I approach the bench, he doesn't look up from his paper.

"I'm sorry to disturb you." I roll the cigarette between my fingers. "But do you have a light?"

He glances up. Maybe it's my imagination, but it seems a glimmer of surprise penetrates his gaze. "Certainly." He folds the newspaper. "Would you care to join me?" he asks, my question and his reply fitting as neatly as two pieces of a puzzle.

The old man with the pipe has since left, the paths around us deserted as the evening chill sets in.

"Thank you." I sit on the other end of the bench.

He reaches into the pocket of his coat, pulling out a battered lighter. I put the cigarette to my lips as he flicks his thumb across the wheel of the lighter. He leans toward me. A bluish flame flares in the fading light.

"There are certain documents you wish to obtain?" he asks, low voiced.

I hesitate. There are no more innocuous predetermined phrases between me and unchartered waters.

"Is such a thing possible?" I hold the cigarette between my fingers.

"That depends on what you need."

I'd been prepared to trust the person Tadeusz arranged for me to meet. After all, I need these papers. Though the man across from me on the bench could pass for a factory worker in his well-worn coat and cap, all I can see is the uniformed officer standing at the gate, a holster at his belt, enforcing the dictates of the occupiers.

I fight the urge to rise and run. But if he's working for the Germans, I've as good as incriminated myself already.

I meet his eyes, my stare direct. "Why are you here?"

"It would appear I'm meeting you."

"You know that's not what I mean. I didn't expect . . . You're not the sort of person I expected."

One corner of his mouth edges up a fraction. "Considering the circumstances, that ought to be a point in my favor."

"But you're a . . ." A policeman? A collaborator? "You work for them."

Hands resting on his knees, he regards me evenly. "Not by choice."

The way he states the words, the guardedness in his eyes briefly falling away, exposing something hard, almost angry, shakes me unexpectedly. Anger may not be an emotion that should encourage trust, but somehow the bluntness of it gives rise to the sense that, in regard to the occupiers, we share a common feeling.

And what he said could be true. Shortly after the Germans arrived, the existing Polish police force was pressed into service by order of the General-gouvernement. Not reporting for duty was considered desertion and severely punished. Perhaps few know better than he the lack of choices afforded one in a country under occupation.

Can one trust what one reads in another's gaze? Or do eyes lie as easily as lips? War has taught neighbors to betray neighbors and decent people to tell falsehoods. We ration trust because there are few dangers greater than giving it away.

"How do I know you're telling the truth?"

"How do I know you won't denounce me? You know who I am, after all."

Something shifts between us as his eyes hold mine. Part trust, part tacit agreement, our gazes joining like a handclasp to seal a bargain. I've all but demanded him to prove himself, but he's asked no similar questions of me. This man is not naïve. How then does he trust me?

"Now, what is it you need?"

"Six Kennkarten and baptismal certificates. Can they be obtained?"

"With some effort, yes."

"Are they good documents?"

"They aren't the sort of shoddy job any *Schupo* or navy blue can pick out with a glance. I speak from experience. The Kennkarten themselves are genuine, not copies."

The only way to obtain a genuine Kennkarte is from a person who has one. Or, I suppose, from the office that issues the documents.

It's probably best not to ask too many questions.

"The better the documents, the higher the price from what I hear."

"I'll make sure you're dealt with fairly."

I frown. "You're not the one who supplies the documents?"

"I'll see to it you get what you need."

A pair of young SS lurch down the path, their laughter boisterous. One straightens his cap and the death's-head insignia on its brim winks silver in the toneless light.

I stare at the cigarette between my fingers, smoke trailing from its smoldering end.

We sit in silence until they pass.

"When will they be ready?"

"A couple of weeks, at least. You'll need to give me their photographs, so they can be properly affixed to the Kennkarten."

"I'll get them as soon as possible."

I give him each person's details for the Kennkarten, and he repeats them back to me. Then he stands. I drop the cigarette on the ground and rise, facing him.

"We'll meet in a week's time, at the same place and hour. Bring the photographs."

"They'll be ready."

"Fine. I'll see you then."

I nod, wondering if he's thinking as I am—we'll be seeing each other much sooner than next week, at the gate tomorrow or the day after.

He turns and walks away, his figure fading into the shadows.

• • •

Hania
December 14, 1942

The boundaries of our world have been severed in two. Zone A and Zone B—the two districts divided by a barbed-wire fence. Zone A is designated for working people, Zone B for the unemployed. Once again, the weary scene of people trundling through the streets, burdened by belongings. Few bothered moving furniture. Why continue to cling to one's possessions when nothing about this new division feels permanent? Many destroyed their furnishings by hurling them out upper-floor windows rather than leave them behind for the Germans to plunder. Teetering mounds of tables, armoires, and sideboards fill the courtyards, the battered wreckage of former lives.

Families kept together thus far are now separated by the demarcation line. Wives from husbands, siblings from each other, the aged from their children—only the working in Zone A, only the nonworking in Zone B. The only exception is young children who are allowed to remain with their working parents in Zone A. Because our flat is already located there and all of us are employed, we did not need to move.

The pharmacy—the small oasis of freedom behind ghetto walls—is in Zone B. To make sure no one crosses the boundary, OD men are posted at the fence and a pass is required to travel from one zone to the other. So far, it's been possible to obtain this pass from the OD for certain reasons, such as to pick up medicine at the pharmacy. Those unable to get a pass gather at the fence to meet family and friends. Standing on opposite sides of the barbed wire, shivering in the wind and snow, they snatch a few moments of conversation.

Construction of a camp at Płaszów progresses by the day. Each morning, groups of workers from the ghetto march the two kilometers to the camp, where they labor to level the ground and put up barracks, returning in the evening exhausted and half-frozen. The camp is being built on the site of two Jewish cemeteries and they are paving its roads with the uprooted tombstones.

I should be immune to the desecration of all we hold sacred by now, but my chest burns when I hear how, by order of the Germans, they ripped the tombstones from the ground and leveled the earth, scattering the bones of the dead. My grandparents are buried there.

Zosia has found a contact to supply us with the necessary papers. We gave her photographs for our forged Kennkarten, and she passed them on. She smuggled out Pani Weinberg's diamond earrings and Mama's ring and sold them, along with the valuables we left with her before coming to the ghetto.

Our papers will be ready soon, Zosia says.

Let it be soon.

Hope, as I once understood the word, as I once felt its life-giving pulse, no longer exists. For how can one hope for oneself when all who share these boundaries begin and end each day under a question mark?

We do not hope, but we wait. And in one there is something of the other.

CHAPTER FIFTEEN

Zosia
January 18, 1943

THE TRUDGING DAYS OF winter pass, the city gripped by endless, driving cold. Shortages are rife, stomachs empty, coal difficult to obtain.

It's hard outside the ghetto but far worse within it. Since the November decree announcing that Jews are only allowed to live in one of five enclosed ghettos—of which the ghetto in Kraków is one—while the rest of the Generalgouvernement has been declared *judenrein*, clean of Jews, the ghetto has seen an influx of new arrivals. Some rounded up and brought by force, others making their way there for lack of anywhere else to go. Trapped in the nonworking zone, slowly starving on the rations allotted them, many pace the barbed-wire fence, begging for food from the inhabitants of Zone A. But people can't feed their families, let alone give to strangers, so beggars are lucky if someone tosses them a crust of bread.

We help as best we can, giving them food and tea laced with alcohol to warm them, dressing their frostbitten fingers and toes, and providing ointment for their sores. It's growing more difficult to obtain even common medicaments, and though we turn no one away, there are many we can do nothing for.

It's no secret the ghetto's days are numbered. As the camp at Płaszów fills, the ghetto's inhabitants dwindle. Soon men and women we know and countless more we do not will be marched to the barracks being erected on the site of the desecrated cemeteries or vanish into the abyss of the transports.

But not the Silbermans and the Weinbergs. So help me, not them.

My worn boots slip on the icy pavement, wind slicing through my coat, my breath forming crystals of ice against the damp wool of the muffler wound around my head like an old woman's shawl. At the gate this morning, as he returned my pass, Sergeant Kamiński—for that is his name—slipped a tiny square of paper into my hand.

Third Bridge. 7 o'clock.

For weeks I've waited for word the documents are ready. I didn't expect it to take so long, but there could have been difficulties. I had, after all, asked for six sets of identification papers. After leaving the pharmacy, I rushed home to retrieve the money—the profits from everything I managed to sell. Now I cross the bridge, the river a frosted slate of ice, tinged gray as the sky deepens from navy to black.

Sergeant Kamiński stands on the pedestrian walkway, facing the Wisła, his collar turned up, cap pulled low. He turns as I approach.

"I hope I haven't kept you waiting long."

"Not at all. Let's walk, shall we?" He offers his arm.

It's only after I've fallen in step beside him that I realize how easily, thoughtlessly even, I took his arm. No different than when Ryszard and I used to stroll together. Have I really become so quick at adapting to whatever role the situation requires me to play? Anyone who sees us will assume Sergeant Kamiński and I are a couple. Likely married, since neither of us look young enough to be youthful sweethearts.

Should the thought make me want to pull my hand away?

We continue over the bridge. On the other side of the frozen river rises the silhouette of the blacked-out city.

"Did you bring the papers?" I cut my voice low, though there are few pedestrians on the bridge at this hour.

"It's not good news, I'm afraid." Tension maps his profile in the meager light. "There was a raid on the flat where the work was being done. The Gestapo arrested the man in charge of the operation."

Shock comes in a swift and nauseating rush. "How did they find out?"

"Someone must have denounced him, or someone he provided with documents was caught and told the Gestapo where they got them from, though how they knew his name, I don't know."

I draw a breath, the dry air scraping my lungs even through my muffler. "Did they find the papers?"

"The whole place was ransacked. I don't know what's left, but anything they found, they certainly took with them. I haven't been back there."

"And the others?" Were there others? I've only had contact with Sergeant Kamiński.

"They're keeping their heads down. Going into hiding if they can." We reach the end of the bridge and continue along the street.

"But you're still here."

"My involvement was limited. Not that it would matter if the Gestapo found out. I'm better off staying where I am." He glances at me. "It was my cousin who did the forgery. He sold the documents because he thought he could make something for his trouble, but he did want to help."

"I'm sorry." Perhaps I should say something else, something about his cousin being all right, after all, in the end, but we both know it wouldn't be true.

He nods and we continue on in silence. Bits of snow swirl in the air, landing on my wind-stung cheeks.

For weeks we've waited for the papers to be ready. Counted on them. Hoped for them.

It's all been for nothing. We've waited for nothing.

"The people these papers are for, they're in the ghetto, yes?"

"Yes." My voice is quiet.

"There are others who do such work, you know. I'll make inquiries if you like."

"You would do that?" I stop on the sidewalk, my hand falling from his arm, snow eddying around us. "Why?"

Darkness outlines his hardened features, breath exhaled from his lips like smoke. "Perhaps the better question is why are you doing it? You and the others at the pharmacy, why do you stay? You know what you risk, yet you would risk more."

I face him, shivering in the wind. "Surely someone who has spent even a day in that place should not need an explanation."

He nods, eyes grim. As if he understands there comes a point when one is willing to risk everything simply to act. To defy the bitter paradox of a world where to take a life is not a crime but to preserve one is. "I can't promise anything, but I can see what could be arranged."

I hesitate, looking into his face.

There's a line between trusting someone for a moment and giving them your trust. If only it were easier to mark where one ended and the other began.

I draw a breath. Then I nod. "Whatever you can do, I'd be grateful."

• • •

Hania
January 21, 1943

"They're sending me to Płaszów." Romek drops into a chair without taking off his coat and cap.

The words slice through the air and into me. "What?" I stand at the stove, broth dripping from the wooden spoon in my hand onto the floor. I barely notice it.

"No, Romek," Pani Weinberg breathes.

"They need more workers for construction. Half the men in my work detail were selected. We're to report in the morning."

"Will you be returning in the evenings?" Pani Weinberg's voice holds a particle of hope.

Romek leans his forearms on the table, scrubs a hand across his face. "We'll stay in barracks at the camp. We're permitted to take whatever we can carry."

Each week, fresh transports leave for Płaszów. It's all everyone talks about, going "up the hill." Will everyone be sent to Płaszów eventually or only a portion of the ghetto's inhabitants? If only a portion, what will happen to the rest? It's rumored the ghetto will be liquidated; do they intend Płaszów to take its place? Everyone is asking these questions, but as usual, nobody has the answers.

"What about our plan?"

Zosia asked me to meet her at the fence, sending a message via the pharmacy's new delivery boy who carries medicine to people waiting on the other side of the barbed wire in Zone A. I went, eagerly expecting the news that the papers were ready. Instead she told me the man who was to supply the documents had been arrested.

We would try again, she said. She wouldn't rest until we were away from this place.

But as we stood whispering on opposite sides of the barbed wire, though Zosia tried, she couldn't hide the defeat in her voice.

"The rest of you will continue with the preparations. Once the papers are ready, Magistra Lewandowska will help you make arrangements on the Aryan side."

Pani Weinberg twists her clasped hands atop the table. "What about you?"

"In Płaszów, it will be much harder to escape, if not impossible." In spite of myself, my voice rises. "You must not report."

"If I'm not there tomorrow morning—" He glances up at me. "They'll come looking for me."

"But if you're away from here, they will not look for you outside the ghetto. You could hide with Zosia." Yes. He can stay in Zosia's flat for a couple of weeks. Just until we have the documents.

Could I ask such a thing of my friend? If she were found sheltering one of us . . .

I want to press my eyes shut against the thought.

But if she knew Romek was being sent to Płaszów, where the difficulties and dangers of escape will be far greater, surely she'd agree to hide him.

Romek shakes his head. "Even if I could arrange to leave tonight, I would be a danger not only to her but also to our plan. If she were caught sheltering me, how would you all get out without help from someone on the other side? I won't risk the chance for the rest of you."

"But you'll go to Płaszów?" Still gripping the wooden spoon, my voice hard-bitten, I must be a mirror image of Pani Hirschfeld. What am I coming to?

What are we coming to?

"It's a labor camp, Hania. Not a transport to the east. It's barely two kilometers away."

And the ghetto was supposed to be only across the river.

Somehow the thought makes me want to break down and cry until there are no more tears left.

"They're going to a lot of trouble building this camp, so they must intend it to remain in operation for some time." He turns to his mama. "In any event, we wouldn't have been able to stay together on the Aryan side."

Vaguely I'm aware of a bubbling on the stove and I turn to stir the soup. The steam rising from the pot fans my face with welcome warmth, but it doesn't reach inside me. Every part of me is tired, so tired I could lie down and sleep, just sleep and nothing else. Sometimes I wonder if the will to endure is slowly seeping out of me, like air from Szymon's old bicycle tire. The hole was small, so the air didn't leak out all at once, yet the day still came when the tire buckled.

Chair legs scrape as Pani Weinberg rises. "I'd best start packing your things." Her voice is heavy with resignation. "You'll need plenty of warm clothes and some of them may need mending."

"No, Mama. I'll do it." Romek rises and comes toward his mama. He places his hands on her thin shoulders as if to guide her back into the chair.

The remnants of a beautiful woman are still present in Pani Weinberg's face, her elegant cheekbones and deep-brown eyes, but standing before her son, she's aged and frail. "Please, Romek." Her eyes are steady on his, her voice firm. "Let me do this for you."

His throat bobs as he swallows. "Thank you, Mama." His hands fall away.

Pani Weinberg walks into the bedroom and shuts the door.

Romek stares at the closed door and I press my lips together. I won't look up from peeling potatoes to see him coming through the door of the flat each evening. When I wake in the night, shaking, I'll no longer be able to listen for the even cadence of his breathing and let it steady my own ragged exhales.

During the long hours at the brush factory, I live for the moments when we're all together, the only time I know everyone is safe.

I stir the soup hard. The whitish broth speckled with bits of potato and cabbage slops against the side of the pot.

After tomorrow, I won't know if Romek is safe.

Romek turns to me. "Sit with me, Hania." It isn't a question, but his voice holds one.

Wordlessly, I move to the table and take the chair nearest his.

He resumes his seat, still wearing his cap and coat, as if he's forgotten he has them on.

I fold my hands atop the scarred tabletop, staring at my reddened knuckles and ragged nails.

"Once you're on the Aryan side, you must never let down your guard, not for a moment, not with anyone. There are plenty who'd gladly turn you in to the Germans for a few kilos of sugar or a carton of cigarettes." He takes off his cap, runs a hand through his hair. "It won't be easy, this kind of life."

"I know. But we'll have Zosia to help arrange things. We won't be alone." Though anger at him still twinges, it's only because I care for him so much. I don't want him to worry about us.

"Look after them for me, Hania." His voice is quiet. "Mama and Adela. I know you may not be able to stay together once you're out of the ghetto, but you will do what you can?"

"Of course. You don't have to ask. You must look after yourself."

"The work will be hard. But I'm strong and not afraid of hard work. You're not to worry about me."

"You know I will." I smile sadly.

"Things are going pretty badly for the Germans on the eastern front, if reports are to be believed. Even their papers are talking about 'withdrawing according to plan.' It's just a matter of waiting until the war comes to an end."

I nod, words of assurance drying up on my tongue. I know nothing of the future, only that I fear it.

Silence falls. I trace him with my gaze, imprinting his face upon my mind, as if memory could capture a photograph one could carry and keep close. His nearly black hair slightly stringy and in need of a trim, his ears a bit too large for his angular features, stubble shadowing his jaw, the slight ridge on his nose where it was broken, the depths of his brown eyes. Every nuance, every imperfection, these I embed, these I remember.

And as I do, I find the worn edges beneath his strength, the fear he keeps hidden to show courage to others. Again, I wish to comfort him, not with false hopes but with something beyond words that are so often lacking. I reach across the space between us and wrap my fingers around his hand. His palm is calloused and hard, his fingers warm. His gaze rests on our hands, my fingers covering his, then his eyes soften as they find mine. "How beautiful you are."

The gentle awe in his voice catches something inside of me. I rarely look in a mirror, but if I did, I'd see a thin girl in her mama's worn cardigan, once-glossy hair limp around her face. Once, I might have believed him, but the beauty of the girl I used to be is gone. Like old straw, she has crumbled and become dry.

He turns his palm over, lacing our fingers together. "I wish I had a picture of you."

"If I had one, I would give it to you." Pasted into the pages of our old family album are snapshots of who I used to be—standing outside Wawel Castle with my brother and sister, surrounded by school friends in party frocks on my sixteenth birthday, laughing into the camera as I posed at the seaside.

More than a picture, I wish Romek could have known that girl.

"Someday you can have one taken for me." He lifts my hand and his lips whisper over my roughened knuckles with a tenderness that makes me ache. Past the calluses and numbness, past the emptiness that has swallowed up my heart, something stirs inside of me, fragile, unfolding. He raises his eyes, my fingers still twined in his, and draws our clasped hands to his chest. The steady rhythm of his heart radiates through my fingertips. "But I don't need a picture. For your face is always here."

I gather his words as gently as if they are porcelain and tuck them inside my heart with the memory of him.

• • •

Zosia
March 9, 1943

Rain pours as I walk toward the gate, pelting my coat and seeping through the kerchief covering my hair.

Sergeant Kamiński's navy-uniformed figure stands to the right of the entrance. Strange as it may seem, I've begun to look forward to our brief encounters each day. Though we exchange no more than greetings, as our eyes meet there passes between us a silent understanding.

He's done what he said he would, found someone who can supply forged documents. Though I did not ask, I suspect Sergeant Kamiński is no stranger to the underground for him to have such a connection. The

Silbermans and Weinbergs bribed an OD man to let them into Zone B, and I took their photographs for their new identity cards in the duty room.

Now again, we wait.

"Good morning." I'm careful to keep my expression void of any special recognition, my voice neither too low nor too loud as I hand him my papers.

He nods, rain dripping off the brim of his cap. "Good morning, Pani Magistra." Droplets fleck the gray cover of my Kennkarte as he scans my papers. Our hands touch as he returns them, but he doesn't pull away. His fingers briefly clasp mine and a jolt goes through me as I close my fingers around the twist of folded paper in my palm and slip it into my handbag along with my Kennkarte.

Our gazes lock.

He does not speak a word, but his eyes communicate enough.

My stomach coils in a way all too familiar.

I hurry through the ghetto. At the gate separating the two zones, I show my papers to the OD man, and he allows me through. I enter Zone B, passing a man with sunken cheeks and nothing but rags wrapped around his feet, passing an old woman carrying a bucket. I reach the pharmacy and push inside.

"Good morning, Zosia." Behind the front counter, Tadeusz hands a packet of pills to the messenger boy.

I greet them absently, continuing through the prescription room without pausing.

Once in the duty room, I don't stop to remove my damp kerchief and rain-splattered coat before opening my handbag and rifling through its contents until my fingers curl around the twist of paper.

I unfold it, smooth my palm across the small square.

Liquidation imminent. If they are to get out, it must be now. Do not attempt alone.

Narrow handwriting fills the scrap of paper. My fingers close around the note, balling it in my palm.

For weeks, the ghetto has lived under the shadow of its numbered days.

But this is a finality that seeps into my bones.

I do not know what will happen to the pharmacy and us during the liquidation. It doesn't matter. There's no time even to think of it. Tadeusz and Irka are already arranging places for several friends on the Aryan side. But we're not an organization with widespread contacts and resources. We're four pharmacists. And against this there is no remedy.

Standing in the duty room, the note crumpled in my fist, it's as if I stand on the crest of a hill, viewing the ghetto from a great height. The pitched rooftops, the crevices of familiar streets and alleys, the outline of the barbed-wire fences, the people wending its thoroughfares. So many people.

Then I see the train.

It hurtles down the tracks on a rise of steam, bearing down upon the figures thronging its streets, young and old, the able and the beggars.

Its course is set, driven by a force beyond our hands.

In the distance, yet drawing ever closer.

But I will reach out and pull away those I can.

God help me, that I might pull away a few from its path before it becomes too late.

CHAPTER SIXTEEN

Zosia
March 10, 1943

AS SERGEANT KAMIŃSKI RETURNED my papers this morning, our hands clasped long enough to transfer the note from my palm to his.

If you can help me, we must speak.

It's childish, really, passing notes as though we're in the schoolroom, but we can't talk openly at the gate. When composing the note, I deliberated about where we should meet. Not the pharmacy where Sturmscharführer Kunde drops by unannounced at least once a day, commandeering the duty room for private meetings with people who are probably informers.

In a café, anyone could be listening, and with the weather beginning to turn springlike, the parks are crowded with both Germans and Poles eager to be out-of-doors after the long winter.

I hesitated only a moment before scribbling my address at the bottom of the scrap of paper, along with the word *tonight*.

I'm in the kitchen washing dishes when the bell rings.

I rush through the flat and open the door.

Sergeant Kamiński stands in the shadows.

To find him standing outside my flat takes me momentarily aback. Somehow I hadn't fully expected him to come. "Please. Come in."

He steps inside.

I shut and bolt the door behind us and turn to face him. "Thank you for coming, Sergeant Kamiński. I hope it wasn't too out of your way."

"You asked me to come, so I did. And it's Janek."

"I'm Zosia." There's an unexpected intimacy to it, this offering of our names. We regard each other in the dimness, only steps apart. "May I take your coat?" I ask, the moment broken as fleetingly as it was formed.

He shrugs out of his overcoat and removes his cap, then hands both to me. "Thank you."

The well-worn coat carries his warmth, the scent of him—soap and an undertone of musk. I hang them up and lead him into the sitting room.

"Sit wherever you like." I tug the damp tea towel off my shoulder. "I'll just put this away."

When I return, I find Sergeant Kamiński—Janek—on the sofa, hands braced on his knees, taking in the room with its sofa and armchairs, the lamps on the side tables, the mahogany bookcase against the wall, only a sparse remainder of volumes lining its shelves.

It's strange to find a man in my sitting room, on my sofa, in the same corner Ryszard used to favor. Stranger still that I would think of it at such a time.

I move to the armchair. "I asked you to come because I thought here we could speak freely." I sit, clasping my hands in my lap. "Is there a date set for the liquidation?"

"I haven't been informed, but I expect in the next week or two. The new *kommandant* of the camp at Płaszów has been driving the workers to finish construction. When it isn't progressing at a pace to his liking, he takes measures to see that it does."

The way Janek says "measures" makes me feel faintly sick. "And the papers?"

"I should have them any day, but you must get these people out without delay. Papers will be no good to them in Płaszów. Or anywhere else they may be sent. How many are there? Six, was it?"

"Five. One was sent to Płaszów already."

"They're in Zone A?" At my nod, he continues. "I can see to it they get through at the gate." Since the division of the ghetto into two zones, the Zgody Square gate has been closed, the entrance at the corner of Limanowskiego and Węgierska now the only one in use.

"You've done this before?"

"There are few that haven't turned a blind eye from time to time. One can make a tidy sum out of people crossing to the Aryan side, not to mention when goods are smuggled in. There were those who managed to get out before an akcja, but the majority came back after it was over. Without papers or a good hiding place, it's too dangerous to remain on the other side."

"You must do very well for yourself." The moment I speak the words, I wish I had not.

He regards me evenly. "I don't take bribes."

I flush. "I'm sorry, I didn't mean . . ."

One side of his mouth tilts. "Don't apologize. There are plenty of us who do, as you say, very well for ourselves."

"When should this be attempted?"

"Early evening, around quarter to six. There won't likely be many Germans on duty. Don't send more than two at once. A larger group has a greater chance of attracting notice. If there are any OD men about, they may need to be bribed. Have the first group ready day after tomorrow." He pauses. "Once they're out, what then?"

"They'll come here until the papers are ready." I speak the words with far more confidence than I feel.

"There must be nothing to suggest their presence, no noise, no running water or moving about while you're away. Is there anywhere for them to hide in the event of a search or unexpected visitor?"

"Only the bedroom. But we'll manage. It's only until we have the papers." I hesitate. "Can we get them out, do you think?"

Why do I seek assurance from him when I know all too well there is none to be had? There are no certainties of safety or success, not when failure is as close as a single misstep, as simple as an encounter with the wrong person.

"It's impossible to predict the risks, no matter how thoroughly one plans. But"—he pauses, gaze meeting mine—"I believe we have a good chance."

That's all any of us can hope for.

Romek Weinberg's words return to me. Now Romek is in Płaszów.

Silence slips between us, seeping into the crevices and shadows. So often silence is cold, heavy with absence, but there's a warmth in this silence, in the glow of the lamp. Perhaps that is why I do not break it, allowing myself this one moment of stillness.

Lamplight softens his features, the set of his strong jaw, the deep lines webbing the corners of his eyes, his always vigilant gaze. His sandy-brown hair is touched with silver at the temples. Is he older than I thought or has loss weathered him beyond his years? Though we've known each other for over a year and given each other a measure of trust, what do I truly know of this man who wears the uniform of the occupation police and yet risks himself willingly to help others?

To glimpse beyond the surface of another soul requires one to give oneself in kind. Though a part of me wonders what it would be like to know him, I'm not sure I have anything to offer in return.

"Thank you for what you are doing." My voice is quiet, hesitant almost, the words poor compensation for what he undertakes and all he has undertaken.

In the shadowy lamplight, his features harden. "There's nothing for which to thank me."

"But there is. You've done—"

"If you knew what I've done, you wouldn't be thanking me." The words come rough.

In the eyes of the man skilled at concealing so much, there's no mistaking this. Shame. What did he think of as he spoke the words? What moment flashed through his mind, what face rose to his memory? What scenes does he relive again and again?

I do not voice these questions. Perhaps because it does not seem my place. Perhaps because another part of me is afraid of the answers. What has circumstance compelled from him? He's risked his life to help some, but has he been complicit in the suffering of others?

Are we not, every one of us, complicit in our own way? War lays bare the illusions that once led us to believe in our own decency. Our circumstances offer us no absolution. Only in our choices is there hope.

Janek Kamiński has made his.

"War gives us much to regret."

He releases a long exhale. "When I joined the police, I made a pledge to myself to use whatever authority I had for the good of others." He stares at the blacked-out window. "I haven't kept it. So many times I've done nothing but watch."

"That's not all you've done," I say quietly. "There's something my husband once wrote, something I remember often. 'There is evil and there is good and there is the space between. We are given free will to choose where we stand. Evil thrives when good men choose the space between.'" I swallow. "No matter what we lose in this war, our will remains. You've exercised yours in the past and will do so again. And perhaps it will not be in vain."

"Your husband must be a remarkable man." His gaze rests on the photograph in its oval frame on the side table. Ryszard and me outside the church. My arms full of flowers. His eyes full of love. The one photograph I couldn't box away.

"Yes, well." I glance away, down at my hands. "He was. He . . . died in Sachsenhausen." Perhaps I should pause there, but instead I rush on, say the rest before I can stop myself. "He was a professor at the university. They arrested him with the others, only he died before he could be released." I keep my gaze on my hands. It's safer than looking at Janek.

"I'm sorry."

How easily we repeat those words. We mean them to be full, but so often they are empty. To feel sorrow for another does not erase their pain. Yet Janek's voice holds no attempt at forcing sympathy. It's a statement, simply spoken, but with a depth of understanding that holds more than the flimsiness of words.

I raise my gaze. "Thank you." I twist my hands in my lap, eyes pricking with an unexpected burn. "Compared with the many whose losses are far greater than mine, I am fortunate."

His eyes hold mine. "Grief is not a thing to be measured. Only lived."

That depth of understanding again, the kind only experience can teach. "You sound as if you know of what you speak."

A shadow passes over his gaze, the barest glimpse of an unbound wound. Silence settles, lingering so long I begin to think we've spent all the words there are between us.

"My wife and daughter were staying with my brother when the war broke out. I thought they'd be safer in the country." He swallows, presses his lips together. "The Germans strafed the marketplace of the village. They were there."

"Both of them?" I can barely find my voice.

He nods.

The darkness beyond the curtains seeps into the room. No words come but those he said to me, and their very cheapness makes me swallow them. No right words . . . until these. "What were their names?"

"My wife was Celina. My daughter, Teresa." There's a gentleness to his voice, not familiar to me, but to him it seems tenderly so.

"They must have been beautiful."

"Yes." The memory of a smile whispers across his lips. "In every way. Teresa was five, so full of joy, light. So like her mama." He draws a long breath. "Why is it always the best of us?" He pauses. "I tell myself it's a kindness they're not here. They don't have to see what the world has become. Who I have become. But it isn't, and there's no use trying to find the sense in it because there is none."

"No," I say softly. "There is none."

. . .

Hania
March 12, 1943

For two years, the ghetto has been our existence. Now its self-made rulers have decided it must no longer exist.

Why this decision has been made, we do not know. There are never explanations. If they give us one, it is probably a lie. Perhaps there are some among us who still believe what the Germans say, or tell themselves they do. Like a man dangling from the edge of a cliff, they grasp at the only rope in front of them, even though it's frayed and already breaking.

I know better. In the ghetto, I have learned the cruelty of hope.

Still, I fight. Gather strength, not for myself but for Rena and Szymon, Pani Weinberg and Adela. For Romek. For Tata and Mama. Though they're not with me, I hear their voices in my mind, whispering words of courage, reminding me of their love.

For them—for all of them—I prepare for our escape.

Yesterday evening, Zosia came to our flat and gave us the news—within days, everyone will be sent to Płaszów or put on a transport. If we are to leave, it must be now.

For us, she's willing to undertake risk that would be incalculable if I didn't know exactly how our occupiers calculated it.

Once our papers are ready, we'll continue as planned. To pass on the Aryan side is to trade one set of dangers for another. Dangers we've spent hours discussing, albeit with limited knowledge. For the five of us to keep together would put everyone at risk. If one person comes under suspicion or—thinking about it twists my stomach—is caught, they could drag the others into the undertow with them. It will be safer for everyone if we separate. Rena and I together, Pani Weinberg and Adela together, and Szymon on his own.

We'll leave the ghetto in pairs—two today, two tomorrow, the last person following shortly after the others on the second day. Zosia will be waiting outside the gate to lead us to her flat.

We all agree Rena, the youngest of us, should be in the first group. There's risk in being the first, but now we've made our decision, there's more risk in remaining behind. At any time, we could be put on a transport or ordered to march to Płaszów.

Pani Weinberg will accompany Rena. I told Romek I would take care of his family and will do everything I can to honor my word. Tomorrow Adela will leave with me. Szymon will follow alone. Szymon reported for work, but Rena, Adela and I risked not going to the brush factory. If all goes as planned, we won't be returning.

Rena stands beside our bed, hands at her sides as I button her coat, letting me dress her as if she's a child.

"We'll only be apart for a day." I smooth the collar of her coat. "By tomorrow night, we'll be together again, safe, away from here."

"You can't say that. You don't know what will happen to us." Her words are matter-of-fact, but her voice wavers at the end, a punctuation mark of fear.

The same fear pounding a rhythm inside my chest reveals the uselessness of my words.

"You're right." I crouch on the floorboards, kneeling in front of her, looking up into her face. "I suppose I said it because it's what I want so much to be true. Mama and Tata would want us to do this, Rena." I reach out and take her hands, clasp them tight in mine. "They would tell us to take this chance. We will make them proud, you and Szymon and me. And someday, we will make them proud every day of our lives."

"Yes." Rena's plaits frame features that have lost much of their girlish roundness, her eyes bright in her pale face. "Mama and Tata would want us to try."

I rise and wrap my arms around my sister. Our parents would be proud of us, their children. They aren't here to hug her, so I do, tight and strong, like Tata's hugs, and warm and loving, like Mama's. Then I wind a scarf around my neck and put on my coat and we make our way into the kitchen, where Pani Weinberg and Adela wait.

"Are you certain you don't want to go with your sister?" If Pani Weinberg carries fear inside her chest, it doesn't show on her face.

I nod. The decision has been made. I won't change it now. "If there are any OD around, wait for a distraction before approaching the gate. You have a little money?"

"About thirty złotys, I think." Pani Weinberg's voice is raspy. What started as a cold has lingered for nearly two weeks, settling in her lungs. Zosia will need to dose her with plenty of codeine, so she doesn't cough. Pani Weinberg's illness is all the more reason for her to leave now, as anyone who appears sick is at risk of being put on a transport. I said as much last night when we decided who should be the first to go.

"Give it to them if you have to." It's a poor bribe but all we have. "There may be more than one navy blue on duty. The one you're looking for is tall, light-brown hair, about thirty-five. You're to ask if he's seen a woman in a gray coat. That will be his signal to let you through. Zosia will be waiting nearby."

"I know," Pani Weinberg says. We went through all this last night.

"We'd best go." I button my coat.

Pani Weinberg whispers something to Adela, pulls her close, then picks up her handbag and follows Rena and me out the door.

Tattered clouds hang in the sky as we make our way through the ghetto, our footsteps echoing in the quiet, the streets all but deserted, most people still at work.

Pani Weinberg's shoulders are straight, her chignon neat under her hat. Rena walks beside her, eyes fixed ahead, features empty of any emotion.

I go with them as far as I can, the gate within sight. We slip into a doorway, and they take off their armbands. I shove the crumpled pieces of fabric marked with the blue star into the pocket of my coat.

Pani Weinberg glances at me.

I nod.

Now.

I look at Rena. For barely an instant, I hold my baby sister's gaze. Then she and Pani Weinberg walk away, steps quick, toward the gate.

I stand in the doorway, a shadow, gaze following them as they approach the gate, a woman and a girl in dark coats. A fist encloses my throat.

Protect them. Please, protect them.

CHAPTER SEVENTEEN

Zosia
March 13, 1943

THE CITY WAKENS TO a gray March morning. A thin drizzle falls, the sun's rays hidden in the colorless sky.

Across the river, in Podgórze, helmeted SS flank the ghetto gate. Others, black-uniformed auxiliaries are posted around the perimeter. Reinforcements, proficient in the special methodology of an akcja, trained to carry out their duties with efficiency.

There can be only one reason for their presence today.

Somehow the official stamps and signature on my permit got me past the SS at the entrance, then past the guards at the barbed-wire fence separating the useful from those the Germans deem of no use.

In the dispensing room, Tadeusz, Irka, and Helena speak in whispers.

"The SS are everywhere." My words come fast. "They've cordoned off the perimeter of Zgody Square completely. The whole ghetto is surrounded."

"We know," Irka says quietly, her face drained. "We saw them when we came in."

"There's been no official announcement yet, but it seems it's what we expected." Tadeusz's voice is strangely calm, as if he's exerting great control over himself. "They're closing the ghetto."

I don't need to hear the words. I knew their truth the moment I drew near the gate. Weeks of waiting have led to this inevitable day.

I press my lips together. Hard.

"Did your friends manage to get out yesterday?" Helena asks.

"They got through at the gate. I took them to my flat. They're there now. Waiting for me to bring the others."

The others. Hania.

Get them out. Get them out. Get them out.

"Have you seen any of the navy blues?"

"Only Germans and their auxiliaries," Irka says.

Janek knew what we were planning today.

If there were a way, would he still try to help us?

Either the SS relieved him of his duty or he's unable to reach me. Whatever the case, I can't rely on him.

For weeks, time has fallen through my fingers like grains of wheat, golden kernels slipping from my hands, even as I fought to gather them, the precious grains scattering the dust.

Until my hands are empty.

There's no way out of the ghetto. Not with a cordon of SS around the perimeter, rifles at the ready, a human wall blocking anyone from escape.

"If we could hide them until it's over, I could still get them out." I turn to Tadeusz. "The place in the cabinet. It could fit one person. The attic. We could put the others in the attic."

Tadeusz draws a long breath. "If there was something that could be done, you know I would not hesitate. If these walls could keep them from whatever is to come, I'd bring them here. I'd bring them all here." He stares out the window overlooking the square, rain speckling the pane like teardrops. "But these walls are not an embassy anymore. There's no more freedom here than anywhere else in this godforsaken place." He turns to me. "They searched the building last time, the attic, everything. They should have gotten out before." The words are low, spoken almost to himself. "We should have gotten them out before."

I understand the logic of his words, but how can I accept it?

"We can't count on the protection of our passes, not anymore. Nor Kunde's favor. This will end. But what will be left when it's does?" He sighs, shakes his head. "I don't know." He looks at the three of us. "It's time for you to go. Return to your homes, wait until it's over."

I stare at him. "You're asking us to leave?"

"There's nothing more that can be done." He stands, backdropped by the cabinet in his white coat and burgundy bow tie, a weary resignation in his eyes. "Collect your things and go home. Now, while there's still the chance."

In October, it didn't matter that Tadeusz had a pass. They forced him into the square anyway. Somehow, by chance or providence, he was spared the transports—then.

"Is that what you'll do?" Irka asks. "You'll leave?"

"It doesn't matter what I do," Tadeusz says quietly.

I look at Irka and Helena. The three of us regard each other in silence. Of what are they thinking? Their parents, their families?

In this place, there is only one law, and it is no law at all. In these, the ghetto's final hours, we cannot assume we will be spared. They may decide they don't want any witnesses. We've seen too much already.

Irka draws herself up. "I'm not going. After it's over, you can dismiss me if you want to, but I'm not leaving."

"I'm not either." Helena's face is pale, but her eyes are iron.

"If we go now," I say. "We'll never know what we could have done."

"No, Zosia." Tadeusz's tone is firm. "Think for a moment, what would become of your friends if something happened to you?"

"Yes, you must go," Irka says. "Helena and I will stay."

I hesitate. Always I've had only myself to consider. What risk I took, I bore alone. Now others' lives depend on mine.

I nod. "All right. But I have to find Hania first. She needs to know her sister is safe."

"If anyone questions you, show them your papers." Urgency permeates Tadeusz's level voice. "Tell them you have authorization."

"I will." I start to move toward the door, then pause. The unknown dwells in the gazes of the three behind the counter. We've shared so much during these years together. Whatever comes, I count it an honor to have worked alongside them.

"As soon as I can." I swallow hard. "I'll come back."

Tadeusz nods. Irka eyes are resolute, a silent strength passing between us.

Leaving feels like desertion. But what else can I do? Sometimes there are no good choices. Still, we must choose.

I turn and leave the pharmacy.

Chaos surges in the streets. Men and women, families, hurry in the direction of the gate, carrying rucksacks and suitcases. Everyone in Zone A must line up to leave for Płaszów. OD men circulate the order.

I pass unnoticed through the swelling crowd, heading for Hania's building. SS patrol the streets. Gunshots reverberate, distant, terrifying. I keep walking.

Through a gap in the mass of people, I glimpse a slight girl in a brown coat, a rucksack on her back, caught up in the crowd flowing toward the gate.

"Hania!" I rush toward her. "Hania!"

She turns. The moment she catches sight of me, she pushes through the crowd, against its surging current. We run toward each other, meeting in the middle of the street.

I take her in—her coat bulky as if she's dressed in layers of clothing, the rucksack on her back, the dullness in her eyes.

"Zosia, what are you doing here?"

"I came to find you."

"We've been ordered to line up to march to Płaszów," she says as though telling me news I don't already know. Szymon and Adela rush toward us. They too wear layers and carry rucksacks.

"No." I shake my head. "We can hide you. There must be a way." Even as the words spill out, I search for a means to fulfill them.

"In a ghetto full of Germans? Where could we hide that they would not search?"

How can I accept there's nothing more I can do?

"Zosia, is my sister safe?" Hania's voice is a demand, a plea.

"They're both safe. I took them to my flat."

She exhales a breath, eyes falling briefly shut.

"Please." Tears shine in Adela's eyes. She blinks them back. "Tell my mama I'll be all right. Tell her I love her."

"I'll tell her," I say quietly.

People bump into us, moving past as if in a fog.

"We have to go." Szymon's voice is urgent.

"You will take care of her?" Hania's eyes meet mine, as fierce as her voice.

"I will protect her with my life, I promise you. Both of them."

The jostling crowd surrounds us. Shots shred the air. People scream.

"You are a good friend, Zosia Lewandowska," she says softly.

I shake my head. "If I was, I'd find a way to help you." I open my handbag and withdraw the folded złotys—not much but all I have with me—and press them into her hand.

"You don't need—"

"Take it." I close her fingers around them.

A look passes between us; in it lies all the words there are no time for. For an instant, the crowd fades, and it's just the two of us. Joined by the friendship we have known and shared. Women united by a bond more abiding than war.

"Thank you," she whispers. She smiles; it is cracked and full of sorrow.

I will protect them with my life, Hania. I swear to you.

Then she turns away and follows Szymon and Adela. The crowd merges around them, a pulsing, desperate tide.

Seconds is all it takes for Hania to disappear.

CHAPTER EIGHTEEN

Hania
March 13, 1943

WE STAND IN ROWS of five, waiting to march to Płaszów.

The street is an endless column, men on one side, women on the other, lined up according to their places of work, carrying suitcases and bundles, rucksacks on their backs. Like us, many wear extra clothing, the bulk of the layers in contrast to their thin faces giving them strangely unbalanced appearances.

I stand beside Adela in the group of workers from the brush factory. I'm not sure what time it is, but surely we've stood here over an hour. The straps of the rucksack dig into my shoulders. My stomach gurgles, but only my physical body acknowledges hunger. The unknown consumes my mind.

Rena is safe.

The words become the cord that keeps my body upright. Rena is safe. She is with Zosia. I looked into the eyes of my friend as she promised to protect my baby sister. Promises are fragile, I know this. But this one I clutch close. If Rena is safe, I can be strong.

In the row ahead of us stands a little girl of about six, tiny fingers tucked in the hand of the woman beside her, dark hair a cloud around her face. Quietly, she waits in line with the other women. Will the march to Płaszów be too far for her small legs?

Everywhere there are SS standing in groups, striding along the columns, shouting orders. OD men walk among the ranks, voices echoing on the damp air. "Anyone found in Zone A after all the groups have moved out will be executed immediately. If you know of anyone in hiding, step forward and tell us now and we'll bring them out to the lines."

No one steps forward. Shots resound. Somewhere nearby, they are shooting people. Again and again the distant charges come. My stomach cramps.

"Children under fourteen are to remain here. They will be taken to the children's home in Zone B and tomorrow they will be brought to Płaszów in lorries." Up and down the lines, the OD men issue the order, the words slicing through the ranks of women. Ahead of us, the woman holding the little girl's hand turns to the woman next to her. They speak in whispers.

There are other young girls in the line of women, and across from us, I glimpse boys in the line of men. Why can't the children leave with their parents today? Unease travels down my spine.

SS advance along the columns, carrying whips, hobnailed boots ringing out on the cobblestones.

"The child is too young. Take her out of line." Barked orders.

A woman's scream, feral, tearing. A child cries.

The two women ahead of our row exchange frantic whispers. The little girl stands patiently, waiting.

The SS comb the lines, pulling terrified children from the ranks. They draw closer, nearing our row. With them strides an officer in a black leather greatcoat. He is huge, a tower. In one hand he carries a submachine gun, in the other a whip. Near him, held by another SS, two dogs strain at their leashes.

"That's the new kommandant of Płaszów," one of the women in our row whispers.

My throat tightens, squeezed by a noose. If this man is the kommandant, what awaits us at the camp?

The SS reach the row ahead of ours. The woman stands perfectly still. The little girl shrinks closer to her.

"The girl must go to the children's home." One of the SS pushes into the row, grabs the little girl by the arm.

The little girl latches onto the woman's leg. "Don't let him take me, *Mamusia*."

The SS officer yanks harder, but the girl's arms are a vise around her mama's leg as she screams and cries.

"It's all right, Dina," the woman soothes. She turns to the SS officer. "If my child must go, then so will I." Her voice is cool, her German perfect.

The SS officer turns to the kommandant. "Fine," he says. "Send them both to Zone B."

The woman bends and pries her daughter's arms from her leg. Holding hands, mother and child step out of line.

As she walks away, the woman turns, looking back at the others. "Tell Samek Dina and I will join him tomorrow."

"I'll tell him," her friend calls back. "Don't worry."

The SS pull more children from the rows of men and women, their movements systematic, brutal. Shots fragment the air, the report of pistols and the *rat-ta-ta-tat* of machine guns. I clench my jaw to keep it from trembling. My shoulders throb from the weight of the rucksack. The wails and screams of women and children mingle with the shouts of the SS, anguish and cruelty joining in chorus.

Today is Saturday. Shabbat. Though our existence in the ghetto allows few to keep Shabbat as we once did, we did our best to observe the day however we could. The significance of today as the end of the ghetto does not escape me.

Finally we're ordered to move out. Other groups ahead of ours leave a trail of luggage on the muddy cobblestones. The OD men circulated the order that we're to leave behind whatever we can't carry on our backs, and it will be brought to the camp tomorrow. I don't believe them and am glad we decided to pack rucksacks. The Germans will pilfer what's left and search for valuables, and the owners will never see their things again.

The shuffling columns move toward the exit. We step over abandoned luggage.

SS officers—including the kommandant—stand at the gate, overseeing the groups as they pass. One of the SS orders a row to halt. I crane my neck, trying to see what's happening. A red-faced officer pulls a young woman from the middle of the row. She has something under her coat, supporting the bulge with her arms. He orders her to open her coat. She does, slowly.

"Hania," Adela breathes. "Look what's she's carrying."

The woman's open coat reveals a little girl, concealed in a shawl knotted as a sling against her chest.

The officer tears the child from the sling, the toddler's hysterical screams joining the distant rattle of machine gun fire.

"Please. Please let me have my child."

"Enough!" Another SS raises his whip.

"Please, I beg you—"

"Don't watch," I whisper to Adela.

I stare at my scuffed shoes as his whip cracks against her flesh. Once. Twice.

Again, we move forward, nearing the entrance. Beneath the watchful gazes of the SS, we pass through the gate. At the barbed-wire fence stand dozens of children pulled from the lines. Their little faces peer through the gaps as they watch the departing adults. Some are crying, others look on silently, as if searching for the parents forced to abandon them.

"Tata, Tata, take me with you," a boy shouts, waving his arm above his head. "I want to go with you."

No one answers him. We move on.

I cast a glance over my shoulder at the gate, rows of men and women flowing from its mouth. For two years, the ghetto has imprisoned our bodies. Now we are being released, not to freedom but to another prison. It's strange to wish to remain where we have known such suffering, yet even familiar miseries hold a kind of comfort when compared to the unknown.

Płaszów is a place of numberless unknowns.

At least we'll be reunited with Romek. I will the thought to comfort me, but it does not drown the sound of gunfire that reaches us even past the gate. My feet move by rote, my eyes stare straight ahead.

One shot, one life.

There are so many shots.

I can't think about it. If I do, I'll start screaming and won't be able to stop. If I think, I'll go mad.

OD men and a few SS flank our columns. Hundreds of people march ahead of us, hundreds more behind us. Our footsteps meld into a single sound.

For so long, my only glimpse of the outside world has been through barbed-wire fences. How startlingly ordinary everything remains. Workers throng the sidewalks, leaving their shifts at factories. Women hurry past with woven shopping bags over their arms.

A woman in a blue coat pauses on the sidewalk as we pass down the middle of the street. Her lipstick is the color of poppies. She stands watching us, rank after rank of men and women with armbands on their sleeves marching past.

What thoughts cross her mind? Is she glad to see us leaving the city?

A few others watch as we go by, whispering to each other. After the ghetto is liquidated, the city will be *judenfrei*. Have they heard the shots? Do they know how Kraków is being freed of its Jews? Many do not stop at all.

The woman in the blue coat moves on. I imagine her returning home, preparing supper for her family. Perhaps she has children and they will gather around the table, then she will tuck them into bed, kiss them good night.

She does not know what happened today. She does not know how children were ripped from the arms of their parents.

She does not know.

The rucksack on my back grows heavier with every step. We step over packs discarded by others ahead of us who could no longer carry them. People on the sidewalk fix their gazes on the cast-off items as if waiting for us to move on so they can seize whatever we left behind. No matter how much my burden punishes my shoulders, I refuse to leave my belongings for the greedy to retrieve.

I glance at Adela. Her pack is lighter than mine, yet she struggles beneath its weight. Breath pants from her dry lips, hair straggling around her pale cheeks.

"Not too much farther now," I whisper.

She nods, gaze dull and tired.

As if she were Rena, I reach for her hand. Her cold fingers clasp mine, her eyes meeting mine gratefully. Holding hands, we march.

The site of the former cemetery is on Jerozolimska Street, scarcely on the outskirts of the city. We're almost there.

We lived behind walls shaped like tombstones. Now we're moving to a cemetery.

Hundreds of feet tramp onward, the procession snaking down Jerozolimska. I shiver in the air's chill.

Our ranks slow. Adela and I are somewhere in the middle of the massive column stretching ahead and behind us.

Somewhere ahead of us, men shout, "Schnell! Schnell!"

Fear tastes bitter in my dry throat. My heart thuds as we move forward. Adela grips my hand.

Before us stands the entrance of the camp. Utilitarian iron gates. No elaborate scallops like the ghetto walls, no Star of David like the one that crowned the main gate of the ghetto before it was reduced.

SS men oversee our arrival. "Schnell! Schnell!"

Beneath a sky the color of frost, we pass through the gate. Row after row. We are in Płaszów.

I must be strong. It is not a choice but a necessity. There is no room in Płaszów for despair or grief or fear. If I do not find a way to cope with this new reality, I will disappear. And I will never see my sister again.

When we first entered the barracks, I thought: *This has to be a mistake. They can't expect us to live here*, even as I knew there was no mistake and we would, indeed, be living here.

Rows of tiered shelves three high fill the long rectangular room. There are no mattresses for the rough wooden bunks, each shared by two or three women. Next to the door stands a bucket of water in case of a fire and in the center, a small stove. A few windows spaced at intervals let in lengthening evening shadows.

That's all. That and several hundred women crowding the room—all of whom are also assigned to this block. Each barrack is called a block, and each has a woman in charge, known as the block elder. I absorb these strange words as I absorb everything around me. They are part of my vocabulary now. I must learn and remember them.

I chose a bunk on a bottom tier for Adela and me. That way we won't have to climb up and down to reach our bed. After I claimed our bunk, Adela sat down and hasn't spoken since, unfocused eyes staring blankly out of her pale face.

In the ghetto, though we dwelt several families to a flat, our rooms still possessed some of the trappings of our lives from before—women had stoves with which to cook, families gathered around the table for meals, we had real mattresses to sleep on, and some of our own belongings around us. Because of these externals, though we did not consider ourselves free, neither did we fully view ourselves as prisoners.

Now we've been sent here.

Some of the women claimed a place on a bunk, put down their belongings, and left the barracks to search for their husbands or sons. I'd do the same, except I don't want to leave Adela. I haven't seen Szymon since he left us to line up with the other men from the nail factory. Thousands of people were marched to Płaszów today and there were many groups still in the ghetto when we left. Szymon may not even be here yet.

And Romek? Does he know we've arrived, or does he think we escaped before the akcja? To see his familiar face in the strangeness surrounding me would be a relief. If I could rest in the warmth of his arms, even for a moment, perhaps a bit of my strength would return. Since he's been in the camp for weeks, he can tell us what to expect. Such information will be valuable in the days ahead.

I turn to Adela. "Are you all right?" I ask quietly. The clamor of the other women in the barracks, their voices at a variety of volumes, blend in the background.

She nods, but her eyes are glazed, her shoulders hunched.

"Let's eat something, all right?" Maybe after she's had some food, she might feel strong enough to come with me to search for her brother and mine.

I open my rucksack and rummage inside. The food we packed—two loaves of bread and a few potatoes won't last long. When will rations be distributed and how much food will we be allotted? I carefully portion out two slices from one of the loaves, handing a piece to Adela before returning the remainder to my bag. Taking my own piece in hand, I chew the stale bread slowly. Women around us also eat what they brought while others watch with hungry eyes.

It shames me how quickly I consider and discard the thought of sharing our food. Few of us were spared hunger in the ghetto, but never did I eat surrounded by others who have nothing.

The last bite of bread lodges in my dry throat. I swallow, wishing for water or tea to wash it down.

"Romek!"

At Adela's voice, I glance up. Romek and Szymon make their way down the aisle between the bunks, coming toward us. Adela jumps to her feet and Romek's arms swallow his petite sister in an embrace.

They are alive. They are here. I hug my brother and he clutches me as tightly as I do him.

After a moment, I step back. Adela keeps close to her brother's side, as if she's afraid he'll disappear. I look at Romek—really look at him—and my momentary relief shrivels.

In the few weeks he's been in the camp, he's lost weight, his ears protruding from his sharp-boned face. Dirt stains his coat and trousers, and stubble darkens his jaw. His eyes are different too. Harder. Darker.

"Is it safe for you to be here?"

"It should be all right for a few minutes," Romek says. "Everyone's trying to find their families."

So much has happened while we've been apart. So much needs to be said and we have only moments.

"Sit." I slide our rucksacks to the back of the bunk. Only three of us can squeeze onto its narrow edge, so Romek crouches beside us. In the meager light of the barracks, we huddle together, shoulders touching.

"Is Mama all right?" Romek asks, voice low.

"She and Rena got out yesterday." I hunch forward. "Zosia is hiding them."

A stifled sound of relief releases from his lips. "May HaShem preserve them and protect Pani Lewandowska."

"We'd planned to leave today, but the SS surrounded the ghetto."

"I'm glad you're with us, Romek," Adela says softly.

Though Romek gives his sister a tender smile, it doesn't warm his eyes.

"What is the situation here?" I lean toward Romek, keeping my voice down.

He swallows, glances at Adela. "We'd better be going before they close the gate to the women's compound." He rises along with Szymon.

"Wait. I have something for you." I dig through my rucksack, pulling out the remainder of the loaf. I stand and hand it to Romek. "Share this between the two of you."

His throat bobs as he swallows, holding the round loaf before shoving it under his coat. It's painful to see the hunger on his bony face. "Thank you."

"What aren't you telling me?" I glance back at Adela. "It's bad here, isn't it?"

The darkness hardens in his eyes. "Untersturmführer Göth, the kommandant . . . he is more dangerous than any German I've ever encountered. To
kill is sport to him."

My blood chills as I recall the giant of a man in the leather greatcoat.

"The other SS and guards are little better." He shakes his head, grimacing.
"Please don't tell Adela. She'll find out soon enough. I've learned, and both
of you must too, that to become invisible is the only way to live in this place.
Do nothing to draw attention to yourselves." He speaks quickly, as if trying
to cram everything he needs to say into as little time as possible. "In the
morning, the bugle sounds at five. You need to get up right away and make
up your bed. Make certain your blanket is straight, because sometimes there
are inspections. Then join the line in your barracks for coffee. Bring a cup
or bowl. At noon, you'll get soup, and in the evening, the block elder will
distribute bread. After you get your coffee, you must drink it quickly, use
the latrine if you need to, and then go to the Appellplatz for the morning
count. Under no circumstances must you arrive late to the Appellplatz. Do
you understand?"

I nod, mind racing to remember everything he tells me.

Romek glances at Szymon talking quietly with Adela. "I spoke with the
block elder and arranged for Szymon to stay in my barracks. I'll look out for
him as much as I can."

"Thank you." It's small comfort to know Szymon won't face the ordeal
ahead of us alone. The segregation of men and women has further severed
families already broken apart. Perhaps that's why the Nazis chose to separate
us—to rob us of the stability we give each other, and thus further render us
defenseless.

"We'll come and see you both as often as we can." He reaches out and
wraps his fingers around mine, cradling my hand in both of his, as if he's
missed the touch of my skin. Calluses harden his roughened palms. "Good
night, Hania."

For an instant, I savor the warmth of his touch, the gentle way he frames
my name on his lips. "Good night." I give him a small smile.

He lets go of my hand. "Come, Szymon." His voice is terse.

"I'll see you later." I squeeze my brother's shoulder as he passes.

Szymon glances at me, nods but doesn't smile. There's so little I can do to
protect him.

So little I can do to protect all of us.

Adela and I stand beside our bunk as the two men stride toward the door.
Emptiness yawns in my chest as they disappear out of sight. Though we are
in a barracks crowded with women, I've never felt more alone.

CHAPTER NINETEEN

Zosia
March 14, 1943

THE HEAVY HAND OF darkness settles over the lifeless streets as the four of us sit in the duty room, listening to shots coming from the direction of Zone A.

By the time I drew near the gate, it was too late to leave. Ranks of people stood waiting to march to the camp, the gate guarded by SS, chaos barely reined in, shots resounding somewhere nearby. If I'd attempted to approach the exit, I might have been forced to join the line and both my pass and my arguments would have proven weightless. There was nothing to do but return to the pharmacy, trapped for the duration as the final act unfolded.

Another burst of gunfire fractures the night. The SS must be searching the abandoned flats and empty buildings for people in hiding. We've no way of confirming this, but what else could be happening? Hours later, the shooting stops. I slump against the chair, body spent, heart numb.

Dim lamplight outlines Irka and Helena sitting on Tadeusz's divan, Helena's head resting on Irka's shoulder, while Tadeusz sits smoking his pipe, the surface of his desk scattered with ashes. His white coat is rumpled, his bow tie cast aside.

In the silence of the pharmacy, we wait for dawn.

Pani Weinberg and Rena will think something has happened to me. I left them with food and water but can do nothing about the unbearable strain they must even now be suffering.

Let them stay hidden.

The guards at the fence allowed residents of Zone A to cross into Zone B, though not the other way around. Friends came to the pharmacy to entrust valuables to our care and say a few words to us before leaving for the camp. Despite the risk of a search, we took whatever they gave us and concealed the items in empty drawers. People came running in, asking for sedatives for small children, so they might smuggle them to Płaszów in rucksacks or hide them in the ghetto. Luminal and codeine. It was what we had, and we dispensed it, yet we could do nothing to protect their little ones.

Tendrils of light steal into the duty room. I rise and cross to the window. The first rays of morning sun slant softly over the cobblestoned square. Tadeusz comes up behind me, whelming me in the aroma of pipe smoke that clings to his clothes. We stand a few paces from the window, the net curtain concealing our presence as people leave their homes and make their way to the square, according to the order issued yesterday. Everyone in Zone B is to report to Zgody Square for resettlement; anyone who fails to appear will be shot.

Families carry suitcases and bundles, rucksacks on their backs. Elderly men and women drift into the square, dressed in hats and coats, as if anticipating a long journey. A few of the old men have volumes bound in velvet beneath their arms—prayer books. A young woman cradles a swaddled bundle. She gazes down at the baby, her mouth moving as if she whispers words to soothe the infant. Mothers lead children by the hand. People stand in close-knit groups. Some sit down on their luggage.

Irka and Helena join us at the window.

The square fills.

The crowd waits.

How long do we stand at the window? I no longer count the hours. I'm scarcely aware they pass. What is time? Time measures life. Time is human.

There is no time. There is only death.

The SS herd group after group into the square. People without luggage or coats, goaded by shouts and blows, move in a catatonic state. They must be scouring Zone B for those in hiding, rooting them out from cellars and attics, whatever places they'd found to shelter themselves. Once in the square, the SS divide them into groups, an arbitrary choosing with indefinite criteria. Some remain in the square. Others, so many others, are marched away, out of view.

Bursts of gunfire, like empty voices, answer our unspoken question.

Sometimes they don't take them away. The wall of the building opposite the pharmacy is stained with browning red splatters, the cobbles below strewn with what, from this vantage point, appear to be bundles of fabric.

Only they are not bundles.

We stand at the window as if turned to stone.

In the distance, a large group flanked by several SS enters the square. I blink as what I have caught sight of comes into focus.

Children. Dozens of them. The SS walk alongside them, armed with rifles and revolvers. Older boys and girls hold the hands of the littlest ones. Their wide eyes take in the scene around them—the discarded luggage, the dark patches of blood on the cobblestones, the bodies strewn in the square. Tiny fingers cling to stuffed toys, another child's hand. So many enter the square alone. But these little ones are not only alone. They are lost

A girl with brown hair bobbed around her thin face walks near the front of the group, carrying a small boy on her hip, her gaze darting back and forth. A boy of about twelve, one of the older ones, stares straight ahead, eyes glazed with understanding. A little girl with a blue bow in her hair clutches a doll against her chest. Her hair shines golden in the sunlight.

"Dear God," Irka breathes. "Dear God . . ."

The SS march them through the square, pair after pair of small feet filing past. As she passes by, the little girl looks up at the window where we stand.

Her innocent eyes sear my soul.

She walks on, following the crowd, cuddling her doll against her heart.

The children disappear out of view. Silence . . . suffocating, empty . . .

Then the shots.

"One," Irka whispers. "Two."

Somewhere, in the inferno of my brain, I hear Irka counting softly. I clench my hands into fists at my sides.

God, where are You?

Is it really a prayer if He is not listening? For if He is listening, how, how, could He stay silent?

"Seven. Eight."

In my mind, I see her sweet, round face, hair shining in the sun, little arms gently clasped around her doll.

I see all their faces.

They will be afraid. So afraid. The thought rises above the roaring in my mind. I don't want them to be afraid. They are so small. Babies.

"Fourteen. Fifteen," Irka murmurs.

My nails gouge my skin. Wetness slicks my palms. Shots shatter in my ears. I stare unseeing out the window.

"Forty-one. Forty-two."

Are we all dead? Is this hell?

"One hundred seventy-five. One hundred seventy-six."

Screaming.

I turn.

Over and over, Irka screams, tearing at her hair.

Helena stands frozen, her hand clamped to her mouth. Tadeusz grasps Irka's shoulders, restraining her. Her screams turn to wrenching sobs.

"Zosia. Fetch the sodium bromide." Tadeusz throws the words over his shoulder as he grips Irka in his arms. "Quickly."

Somehow, I move. In the dispensing room, I fumble through the canisters and bottles, pushing them aside, searching for the one I need. I knock a bottle off the shelf. It crashes, shattering.

I locate the bottle of sodium bromide and return to the duty room. Irka sits on the divan, Tadeusz beside her. Helena still stands at the window.

A pitcher of water rests on a stand, a glass beside it. I fill the glass with water. My hands tremble uncontrollably as I open the bottle and shake out a tablet. I carry it to Irka, and Tadeusz holds the glass to her lips, helping her drink. He looks at me, mute anguish in his gaze.

I cross the room on leaden feet, drawn toward the window as if by some force outside of my control. I take my place next to Helena. She doesn't glance at me.

Beyond the window, out of sight, the shots continue. No one counts them. They come one after the other, one after the other.

Numberless.

CHAPTER TWENTY

Zosia
March 16, 1943

THE GHETTO HAS BECOME a city where the living are only memories. The stillness of its desolate streets amplifies the tap of my footsteps. Moonlight illuminates the empty buildings in a silvery glow, their shadows elongated in the darkness.

I quicken my steps. Though visible reminders of the liquidation have been erased—the debris cleared, the corpses taken away, and the blood scrubbed from the cobbles—I've no desire to linger in a place still fresh with the scenes of annihilation that left these streets devoid of life.

None of us came to the pharmacy yesterday. Tadeusz told us there wasn't a need. I stayed in the flat with Pani Weinberg and Rena because I couldn't face returning. I came back today because I could not stay away.

A creak, like a window opening.

My breath hitches. I stop on the sidewalk. Stillness has a way of magnifying the smallest sounds, but only the wind meets my ears. My frayed nerves must be conjuring what isn't there.

Someone whistles, a single note.

I spin around, craning my neck. Darkened windows stare back at me. One stands ajar.

Something flutters to the ground, landing at my feet. I flash a glance into the darkness around me before bending to pick it up. A scrap of newspaper, crinkled and damp, as if clutched in a sweaty palm. The moon throws light on the torn newsprint, the three words scrawled in pencil.

Please help us.

I stare up at the window where the note was thrown. It's closed now, the building shadowy in the night. No sign of whoever is or was there.

I crumple the note in my fist, sensing instinctively the need to hide it.

Someone is there, somewhere in that building.

How is it possible the SS didn't find them? How can it be that in the midst of so much death, someone is still alive?

I taste recklessness, raw like my heartbeat, but also need. Someone is calling for help and I must answer. There's no question of *if*, only of *how*.

The authorities permitted several OD men to remain in the ghetto. They, along with German police, patrol the streets. No doubt searching for sounds and signs of life, seeking to expose the hidden.

I fling a glance over my shoulder and down both sides of the street. Empty.

I dart toward the entrance and try the knob. The hinges whine as the door eases open. I slip inside, the door clicking shut behind me.

Darkness swallows me.

"Hello?" I call softly. "If there's anyone there, please come out."

Step by step, I grope my way down the corridor. I don't bother searching for an electric switch. Even if I found one, I wouldn't dare risk a light.

I stumble over something. My heart rams against my breastbone. As my eyes adjust to the blackness of the corridor, I make out a body sprawled on the ground.

Sucking in a breath, I keep walking. To the right, a door stands open. I step inside. The moon casts waxen light over the remains of the room. Chairs knocked over, a bed frame tipped on its side, a mattress ripped down the middle. My shoes crunch over broken glass.

A floorboard creaks. I still. Someone steps out of the shadows.

A young boy. Dirt streaks his pinched face. For breathless seconds, we stare at each other.

"Did you throw the note?" I pitch my voice low.

He nods, trembling. "Please, pani," he whispers. "Don't tell the Germans."

"I won't." I take a step closer. "What are you doing here?"

"We've been in the cellar." His eyes are white against his grimy face. His stained clothes reek of filth and urine.

"You hid in a cellar during the akcja?"

He nods.

"Are you alone?"

He hesitates. "My little sister is with me. She needs help. Please don't tell the Germans about us."

"It's all right. Don't be afraid. Where's your sister?"

"The cellar. The Germans searched, but they didn't find us. We hid under the coal. Mama made us a place."

"Is your mama with you?"

He shakes his head. "She told me she'd come back after the Germans were gone, but she didn't come. I think they took her away."

At the least, they've been hiding for four days. Four days beneath a pile of coal . . .

"Can you take me to your sister?"

He nods, stepping around the room's detritus, moving past me into the corridor. I follow as he navigates the darkness with ease. Near the end of the passage, he stops in front of a door and turns to me.

"Stay here. I'll get her." He opens the door and steals inside. I stand outside the door, listening to the patter of footsteps as he descends the stairs, straining for footfalls or sounds from the street. My nerves thrum as I wait.

The door opens. The boy emerges, carrying a baby.

Though I heard him perfectly well when he said his sister was with him, shock sluices over me at the sight of the child in his arms.

She isn't an infant, but how old she is, I can't tell. Her matted hair clings to her head and the odor emanating from her diaper stings my nose. She looks at me, eyes round, face dirty.

"Here, let me take her."

His grip tightens on the child. "Better not. She doesn't know you. She might start to cry."

"Did she cry when you were in the cellar?"

"Mama gave her medicine to make her sleep. Later, when she wouldn't stop crying, I gave her more. Mama showed me how."

"Where did she get the medicine?"

"At the pharmacy on Zgody Square."

Luminal then. In the darkness, it's difficult to examine the child for signs of an overdose.

They can't stay here. But I can't get past the police at the gate with a baby and a young boy. They'd know in an instant where the children came from.

"What's your name?"

"Leon Guterman."

"Listen, Leon. You know the pharmacy where your Mama got the medicine?"

He nods.

"The owner is a good man. I work for him. You can stay there tonight. Do you think you can make it there without being spotted by a patrol?"

He nods again.

"I'll take Sara."

"I can—"

"It'll be safer for both of you if you go alone. Hurry now, give her to me."

Leon's small jaw clamps as he stares at me, likely debating whether I can be trusted. He rubs his sister's back. "It's all right, Sara-bird. You're going to be all right." Then he passes the baby into my arms.

She whimpers, stretching out her arms to her brother, but doesn't cry.

Traces of Luminal are still in her system. And she's likely dehydrated.

Even in the darkness, anyone who saw her would know immediately she'd been in hiding. But there's no time to clean her and nothing to clean her with.

Shifting her in my arms, I unbutton my coat and close it around her. "Wait a few minutes, make sure the street is clear, then go to the pharmacy."

Fear darts through his gaze, but he nods.

I retrace my steps to the entrance, my eyes adjusted to the lack of light. I crack open the door and peer into the night. All is silent, the street empty.

Carrying Sara wrapped inside my coat, I hurry toward the pharmacy. Night air fans my cheeks. Sara whimpers in my arms.

"Shh, little one," I whisper. "We'll be safe soon."

Strangely, I'm not afraid. Purpose—only purpose—drives my steps. On either side of the street, the silhouettes of abandoned buildings rise into the night. I keep close to their shelter. The moon glimmers in the cloudless sky, lighting my path.

Footsteps.

My heart jolts. The figure of an OD man emerges. No time to duck into a gateway. I keep walking, slowing my steps, as though I've nothing to hide, as though I'm not concealing a Jewish child inside my coat.

I recognize him by sight as I do most of the OD. Tadeusz knows them better than I. Who will betray another to gain favors for himself, who can be trusted.

We approach one another. Beneath his cap with the OD insignia, his clean-shaven face registers surprise. As if he's as startled as I to encounter another human being in the desolation of the former ghetto.

Keep walking.

He stops. Blocking my path.

"Good evening," I say in a pleasant tone. It's impossible not to notice the bulge in my coat or the way I'm cradling it.

"You're one of the women who works for Magister Pankiewicz, aren't you?"

"Yes. I'm on my way there now. I forgot something."

Sara lets out a mewling cry. I tense as her whimpers increase in volume.

Not now, little one.

He takes a step closer. "What's that in your coat?"

"A child. Can't you hear her?" My voice is indignant.

He levels me with a probing stare. I gaze back at him, unflinching.

Do you have children of your own? Do you hope by following the orders of the Germans and enforcing their edicts, you might be able to protect those you love? She could be yours, this child in my arms.

"You'd best be on your way."

"Thank you," I say quietly.

He nods, his only response.

I walk past him. Sara's cries continue unstifled.

All the way to the pharmacy, my breath comes shallow, every sense heightened by a prickling alertness.

The abandoned expanse of Zgody Square stretches before me in the moonlight, the barbed-wire fences throwing shadows onto the cobbles. I approach the pharmacy and knock, my other arm supporting Sara.

Seconds expand.

I rap again, harder this time, my knuckles against the wood startlingly loud in the silence.

A rattle, then the door opens. Tadeusz stands inside, wearing a smoking jacket. "Zosia—"

I push past him, carrying Sara. "Don't say anything. Just let me in."

Leon arrived at the pharmacy out of breath and shaking from fear, having narrowly managed to evade detection by a German policeman. Now he sits at Tadeusz's desk, eating his second piece of bread. After I bathed Sara and fed her some bread softened in warm water, she promptly fell asleep on the divan. Besides a rash from her soiled diaper, she appears to have suffered no ill effects from her time in the cellar. I suspect Leon gave his sister most of the food and water their mama left them.

Leon told us Sara is ten months old, though from her size, I'd guess her to be younger. He's nine, but like so many children in the ghetto, there's a hardened weariness about his features, the aging of experience. Their tata, Leon said between mouthfuls, had been deported in October, but their mama continued to labor in a workshop mending military uniforms. As they prepared to leave for Płaszów, she heard the SS were pulling children out of the lines and decided to remain with her children in the ghetto. Instead of taking them to Zone B—Leon said she feared the Germans had something bad planned for the people there—she decided to make use of the hiding place she'd prepared in the cellar of the building where they lived. But there hadn't been room for them all, so after making sure the children were hidden, she left, telling them she'd hide nearby and return as soon as it was safe. She hadn't come back.

"Can they sleep here tonight? I'll find a way to get them out as soon as I can." Sitting on the divan beside Sara, I keep my voice low.

Tadeusz stands near the armoire, one hand in the pocket of his smoking jacket. "They can stay in the attic. I'll take up some blankets and make them a bed."

I brush a lock of still-damp hair off Sara's forehead, the soft exhalations falling from her parted lips telling of her peaceful sleep. "She'll have to be given something. We never know when Kunde or one of the other SS will turn up. Or anyone, really."

"There are others out there, you know, in hiding. Somehow they remained undetected during the searches. Some have come to me for food, medicine, asking me to get a message to someone."

I glance at him. "You didn't tell us this before."

"Irka knows. I've spoken to a couple of the OD, trustworthy men. We're making arrangements to get the people into Płaszów. The adults will slip into one of the work details coming to clear out the flats. In the evening, they'll return to Płaszów with the rest of the group. The children will be smuggled to the camp in furniture wagons."

"You think that's what we should do? Send them to Płaszów?"

"If we could arrange a place for Sara on the Aryan side, we could get Leon into the camp. He could pass as older. It's something to consider, if there's no other alternative."

My gaze falls on the young boy tucking the remainder of his bread into his coat. How can Tadeusz consider letting Leon go to Płaszów? If the children weren't here, I may have given vent to the swell of sudden, irrational anger. But I'm not angry at Tadeusz. Understanding a reality makes it no less painful, but I do understand. If someone is found hiding in the ghetto, they'll be shot. On the Aryan side, without false papers . . . the same end. Płaszów offers some chance of survival.

"If he went to the camp, he would be alone. I can't watch a child be sent to that place, not after . . ." I squeeze my eyes shut, unable to finish the sentence.

"We'll find a way. Until then, we'll look after them here." How simply Tadeusz speaks the words. As if we will not all face the consequences if the children are discovered.

Perhaps we, all of us, are beyond the consequences. They exist but they no longer matter.

"It's past curfew," he says. "You should stay here tonight."

I rise. "Pani Weinberg and Rena are waiting. If I'm not back, they'll only worry. I'll keep to the bystreets, avoid the patrols."

The glow of lamplight in the blacked-out duty room outlines Tadeusz's haggard features. He's aged since we first met. We both have. Then he was a debonair gentleman doing what he could to hold onto his family's business, and I was a young woman, sharpened by loss but still naïve, who thought accepting his offer would give my life a sense of purpose. Has it?

It really doesn't matter anymore.

"Then you'd best go. And Zosia." He pauses. "Take care."

I manage a faint smile. "You know I always do."

. . .

March 17, 1943

The tread of footfalls across the floorboards unsettles the stillness of the pharmacy. I start. Not only because the door has scarcely opened for three days, but because the steps are too heavy to belong to an ordinary pair of shoes.

Boots.

The sound of boots rarely heralds good news.

It's after five. Irka and Helena are already gone. Tadeusz and I—and Leon and Sara—are here alone.

Tadeusz greets whoever has come in.

I step out into the dispensing room, expecting to find Sturmscharführer Kunde, who seems to think the pharmacy—and Tadeusz's vodka—exists solely for his personal convenience.

On the other side of the counter stands a man in a navy uniform. He turns.

I haven't spoken to Janek since before it happened. *It.* Even my mind can scarcely form the word.

Liquidation.

The word evokes everything and, somehow, nothing.

At the sight of him in uniform, anger rises. Unfounded, but then is it? I don't know what he did during the liquidation. The trust that had begun to form between us has cracked under the weight of failure. My own as much as his.

"Pani Magistra, I was wondering if I might have a word."

I pause before nodding. "Certainly." I lead the way through the prescription room and into the duty room, Janek's even footfalls behind me. He follows me in and I close the door. Then I turn to face him, waiting for him to be the first to speak.

"Pardon me." Without preamble he unfastens the belt at his waist. It clanks as he sets the belt with its holster on Tadeusz's desk.

I watch, stunned, as he starts to unbutton his uniform.

He withdraws a small parcel and hands it to me. "I got them yesterday."

I take the thin package, warm from the heat of his body. I unfold the brown paper, revealing several gray Kennkarten alongside other folded documents. I open the one on top. Hania stares back at me from the small photograph, her hair carefully curled, eyes serious.

I once expected the moment I held the documents in my hands to taste of victory, but all I can think is *It's too late.*

I close the Kennkarte and refold the wrapping. "How much did it cost?"

"This was a favor to me." Janek does up his uniform and fastens his belt. "You'll need to add their fingerprints, and they must sign the Kennkarten with their new names. Crease them, smudge dirt on them, whatever you have to do so they don't look newly printed." He pauses, eyes holding a pain deeper than regret. "I'm only sorry . . ."

I press my lips together, saying nothing.

"Are they safe?" The question comes low, the roughening of his voice revealing unspoken strain.

"The woman and the girl? Yes. They are."

"The others?"

"They went to Płaszów."

The silence that follows speaks more than words.

"Did you know that day what would happen?"

"When I arrived on duty, they posted me and the other navy blues on the other side of the fence. The SS didn't want us in the ghetto. They must have figured we wouldn't have the stomach for it." His mouth thins, his voice grim. "I tried to reach you."

It changes nothing, our trying. Somehow, though, there's no anger left in me toward him.

"Do you think anyone got out at the last?"

"I heard some went down into the sewers, found passage that way, until the Germans got word and posted guards at the outlet. After that, anyone who tried was shot by the police as they came out."

I should feel shock or sorrow, but all that pervades is a sinking heaviness. They ventured everything on escape only to fall into the hands of the Germans just as they succeeded in reaching the other side. The futility of it, of all of it, empties me.

I must not allow myself to dwell on it. I can do nothing for the ones who are gone.

But they are not all gone.

I hesitate only a moment before giving voice to my secret. "Last night, on my way to the gate, I heard a noise at one of the windows." Janek listens as I tell how I came upon Leon and Sara, showing no sign of surprise at my admission that there are people alive in the ghetto, in hiding, asking for help. "They're in the attic. I've given the baby a sedative to keep her quiet, but I must get them away from here as soon as possible."

For a moment, he does not speak. "This thing you've done, it's not only a danger to you, but to the others who already depend on you." His features harden. "What would happen to them if you were caught sheltering these children? Have you thought of that?"

The reproof finds purchase. When I came upon Leon and Sara and made the decision to hide them at the pharmacy, I didn't think of the two already relying on me. I only saw children desperately in need. And I saw others. In the faces of the boy and his baby sister lived the faces of every child who made the journey across Zgody Square.

How does one measure one life against another? But I have. Over and over again. In offering help the Silbermans, I turned my back on others. Not by choice, but still I chose.

"And if I'd left them there, what would happen to them?" My voice is a demand, even as it chokes, not from fear or tears, but from the raging in my chest. "You're a policeman, you should have no difficulty answering that question."

He stiffens like a man physically struck but says nothing to deflect or deny my words.

"I need to get them out," I say, voice quiet now. "Tomorrow I'm going to give Sara a sedative and carry her out in a basket. Irka will go with me, distract the guards."

"You're going to smuggle out a Jewish baby right under the noses of the police?"

"If I told you the half of what we've taken out and brought in, you wouldn't believe it."

Letters, parcels, medicine, food, diamonds. Never a life.

"But if you were at the gate, it would help. The basket, it can't be searched."

The crevice between his brows deepens. "There's another reason why I'm here. My commander informed me I've been reassigned. As of five o'clock today, I'm no longer on duty in the district."

The words jolt through me. "Why?"

"Fewer police are needed now that the ghetto has been officially closed."

In time, it's said the walls and barbed wire will be removed and the streets reintegrated into the city. For now, the former ghetto remains closely guarded.

But my acquaintance with Janek Kamiński seems to be drawing to an end.

"I'm sorry I won't be able to help you," he says quietly.

I shake my head, even as my stomach twists. "We'll be fine."

"What about the boy?"

"There's a spot at the fence on Józefińska where the wire has been cut. Magister Pankiewicz says every child smuggler in the district knew it. If he could just get across . . ."

"He'll need to do it near the end of the day, before the workers leave, so there's some activity in the district, but not too early. If he encounters anyone, he should say he's part of the group from Płaszów. But"—he pauses—"he must not encounter anyone."

"I understand."

"After you get them out, what then?" He looks at me hard. "You're not thinking of having them in your flat?"

I glance away. I haven't spoken with Pani Weinberg and Rena and will do nothing without their agreement. But the children have nowhere else to go. Irka and Helena live with their families. I can't ask this of them. And there's no time for another place to be found.

"Sara will stay with me. I'll tell everyone I've taken in a friend's child. I'll need to arrange for a forged baptismal certificate as soon as possible, but I can't wait to take her out."

"And the boy?"

"For him to pass the same way would be . . . more difficult. I'll keep him hidden in my flat until I can make other arrangements."

It's a hard reality. One's physical appearance can be its own betrayal. Those best able to hide in plain sight are those whose features conform to assumptions about typically Polish looks. The same applies in the reverse. Leon also has a noticeable Yiddish accent. A simple check, the so-called "trousers test," is all it would take to confirm the truth.

There are plenty of *szmalcowniki*—blackmailers and extortioners—who, at the suspicion someone is Jewish, will demand payment for not turning them in. Others hand them over to the Germans for a reward of five hundred złotys or a few kilos of sugar. Shopkeepers, neighbors, passersby on the street—no one can be trusted, and the most innocuous person can turn into a dangerous enemy. Some are even Jews themselves who bought their liberty for the price of betraying other Jews to the authorities. To turn against one's own people is a terrible thing, but who among us knows what we are capable of doing to survive until the choice is before us?

"I know of a place."

I start at the low-spoken words. "Where? Is it in the city?"

"It's not far."

"But how do you know this place? These people, who are they?"

He pauses. "It's better you don't know."

It is better. I could be arrested and interrogated, and what I don't know, I can't repeat. But I must gain some idea, at least. "Have—have they sheltered others?"

"People have come to them for varying lengths of time."

"They would take him?"

"I believe they would."

That a place could be so easily found . . . how is it possible? "How much do they ask to be paid?"

"They don't. Ask for payment, that is."

"But why would they do this?"

Silence lengthens. "Because there comes a point when it becomes impossible to do nothing and justify one's existence as a human being." He swallows, presses his lips together. "I can make the arrangements, if you're willing."

Is this what's best? To give a young boy into the care of strangers? To separate him from his sister, when the bond between them remains the last thing they haven't lost?

But if it means a chance for them both . . .

Their mama did all she could to protect them. She chose not to go to Płaszów. As long as she could, she stayed with her children.

Did something sever inside her as she hid them in the cellar, or did she feel only the urgency of the moment? When she told them she'd return, did her voice catch or had her words remained steady and strong?

When she walked away, had she known she was leaving them for the last time?

The decision she'd made saved their lives.

And in making it, she'd almost certainly sacrificed her own.

I meet Janek's eyes and voice the question their mama isn't here to ask. "Will he be safe with them?"

For a moment, his exhale is the only answer. "They will care for him as well as they can. Beyond that, only God knows."

"There are no miracles in that." Weariness fades my voice. I want to be the woman as brave as her flung-forth plans, but deep down I am afraid. Not for myself, but for the burden of other lives and whether my shoulders are strong enough to bear their weight.

"No." He shakes his head, chest lifting with a heavy breath. "There are no miracles. But perhaps in doing what we can there is the hope of one. Even when there seems to be none."

CHAPTER TWENTY-ONE

Zosia
March 17, 1943

THE HARSH SCENT OF ammonia rises from the bowl as I stand in the kitchen, mixing the solution of diluted peroxide. At the other end of the table, Pani Weinberg alters one of my skirts to fit Rena, her needle flashing in the dim light, small lines of strain marking her brow, a distant expression on her features.

It's all too easy to guess where her thoughts take her. I kept my descriptions of the liquidation brief and withheld the worst of what I'd seen. I could not hide the whole of it and shock had drained their faces as they questioned me about whether I knew what happened to this person or that person, pressing for details I could scarcely bring myself to give.

When I told them Hania, Szymon, and Adela had been taken to Płaszów, they bore the news with a subdued resignation that spoke louder than grief. They didn't blame me. In fact, Pani Weinberg reassured me I'd done everything I could. But though they attempt to conceal their feelings, each time I glimpse their faces in an unguarded moment, I'm reminded of how I failed.

I set the bowl aside. "That's finished, then."

Rena glances up from brushing her worn shoes. Reaching up, she unpins the plaits wound around her head and wordlessly begins to unravel them.

I come to stand behind her. "Here. Let me help you." I loosen her plaits until her hair hangs around her shoulders, reaching nearly to her midback. A folded towel rests on the table, my pair of sewing scissors on top. I gather both and return to where she sits, lift up her hair, and drape the towel around her shoulders.

She has beautiful hair, rich brown, almost black, thick and wavy from the plaits.

It's a shame to do what must be done.

In the days since they left the ghetto, the three of us have discussed at length how they will live on the Aryan side. After some consideration we decided, rather than renting a room from strangers whose curiosity could easily lead to suspicion, they should stay with me, posing as friends of mine come to stay as boarders. No one will think anything of a widow taking in boarders to help meet expenses, especially when they are as innocuous as a middle-aged woman and a girl.

It's all straightforward, except for Rena. Two years ago, she lived in this building. During the time she's been in the ghetto, she's grown taller, the childish roundness of her face replaced by slight features and serious eyes. With dyed hair and cosmetics applied, she'll bear little resemblance to Dr. Silberman's youngest daughter.

Rena will use Adela's Kennkarte, the fictitious name matching Pani Weinberg's as mother and daughter. With her hair lightened, Rena will resemble Adela's photograph enough that the Kennkarte will suffice for a few days until we can replace the photograph with one of Rena with an altered hairstyle and appearance.

Now to carry it out.

"Are you ready?" I ask gently.

Rena nods.

I take up the scissors and gather a small section of her hair in my fingers. The scissors snip, bits of hair falling to the floor. Minutes pass as I work, the slice of the scissors filling the silence.

Pani Weinberg looks up from her hemming. "How are the children?"

After returning home last night, I told them how I came to discover Leon and Sara but haven't yet spoken of my intention to take in a baby. No matter my own feelings, I'll do nothing without their consent. If they show any hesitation, I'll make other arrangements for Sara.

"They stayed in the attic all day." I measure the ends of Rena's hair with my fingers, making sure the strands are even.

"What's to be done for them?" Pani Weinberg speaks softly, our conversation carried out in tones barely above a whisper.

"I've found a place for Leon. The man who obtained your papers knows someone who may be willing to take in a young boy. I can arrange for a baptismal certificate for Sara, take her in as if she were the child of a friend. I believe I can care for her, but to do such a thing . . . the risk will be greater for us all." I look at them. "I will do nothing without your agreement."

Pani Weinberg's hands still from their work, her features thoughtful. "For this child to survive what happened in that place, there is a purpose in it. Whatever we can do, we must. There is no question in this." She pauses. "But there's a better plan, I think. The other tenants know you work in the Jewish district. If you returned one day with a baby, people would question this, no matter what story you told. But if your boarders arrived with a child, the neighbors would not think so much of it."

"But whose child?" I frown. "You could not . . . What I mean is you are not . . ."

Pani Weinberg gives a quiet laugh. "No, you are right. I fear I would not make a very convincing mother of an infant. But if I were to, shall we say, have had another daughter, one older than Rena, who was no longer living and whose husband had been deported to forced labor in the Reich, what could be more natural than that I should care for my granddaughter?"

There's sense in this. Many of my neighbors are aware I work in the ghetto—such gossip has a way of getting around—and could easily draw dangerous conclusions.

"When will we do it?" Rena asks.

I draw a breath. "Tomorrow." At the alarm on their faces, I continue. "I can't risk keeping Sara at the pharmacy any longer. We have to move her."

Rena rises. Her hair frames her face, falling just past her shoulders. "Then we will be ready tomorrow. It is not so hard."

"So we're agreed." We look at each other. It takes effort to push back the trepidation hovering at the periphery of my consciousness. Like rising fog, it threatens to close in around me, obscuring sight when I most need clarity.

"Let's wash your hair. It's best to apply the peroxide damp."

Rena follows me to the sink. She leans over it as I wet her hair and lather it with a little soap. I rinse out the soap and squeeze the excess water from her strands. I glance over my shoulder. "Would you hand me that towel please, Pani Weinberg?" I pause, catching myself. "I'm afraid I must stop calling you that. We cannot separate ourselves from the parts we must play. They must become all there is, or we'll never be able to do this. From now on, you must use only your new names, even when we're alone. We must memorize the details of your pasts and you must be able to repeat them as if there has never been any other truth." I wipe my hands on my apron, meeting their eyes. "We will not make mistakes."

Rena, standing by the sink as she dries her hair with the towel, watches me, gaze solemn.

Pani Weinberg leaves the kitchen, returning a few minutes later with their Kennkarten and baptismal certificates to which we still need to add their signatures and fingerprints. She hands Rena the Kennkarte that was to be Adela's and returns to her chair with her own. "Why don't we begin by studying these? Then you can test us, and we'll see how well we know them."

I layer cotton wool pads around Rena's hairline, hoping to keep the mixture from touching her skin, then pick up the bowl of diluted peroxide and a small brush. My aim is for the result to look natural; for Rena to end up as a platinum blond wouldn't look right on a girl her age and would be more likely to attract suspicion than if we left her hair alone.

I dip the brush in the bowl and daub the diluted peroxide onto Rena's damp strands as she studies her Kennkarte, her lips moving silently. Despite my best efforts, it isn't long before scalded red splotches begin to appear on her scalp from the caustic solution. She'll need to wear a hat out of doors until the burns are gone. Rena bites her lip.

"I'm sorry. I know this isn't pleasant."

"It doesn't matter," Rena says quietly.

Soon blisters begin to form on my fingers, but neither Rena nor I complain. "Can you tell me your name?"

"Jadwiga Górska," Rena answers immediately.

"And when were you born?"

"On the twenty-ninth of May 1926."

"Your place of birth?"

"Tarnow."

"And who are your parents?"

Rena hesitates, looking to Pani Weinberg.

"Henryk and Agata Górski," Pani Weinberg supplies. "Your tata Henryk was born on the twelfth of October 1893. He died two years ago from pneumonia. Your older sister's name was Sylwia . . ."

As darkness falls and Pani Weinberg sews, we labor over a fabric of a different kind, stitching together the pieces of our new reality.

Later, in the hours when one cannot see to either side of the black tunnel of night, I lie in bed beside Rena and Pani Weinberg. I do not know if they are awake or if they find rest as the night deepens. My mind refuses to quiet, already with the day upon us even now. The plans set in place and what we must do to carry them out. The ways, so many ways, in which we could fail.

Sleep offers an escape from burdens I can never unshoulder by day, but I've slept little since the two days that ended the ghetto. Only when fatigue overtakes my mind will my body surrender. Still, it doesn't erase the memories, only stifles them. They hover on the fringes, shadows near enough to reach.

Beginning with what I saw . . . and ending with the people I could not protect.

As I drift toward sleep, one face rises above the rest.

Hania.

• • •

Hania
March 18, 1943

In the predawn darkness of the Appellplatz, thousands of men and women stand in perfect rows of five. Though the wind pierces through our clothes and into our bones, we do not wrap our arms across our chests for warmth or stamp our feet to keep the blood flowing. Every morning from half past five until all the prisoners have been counted, we stand in silent, shivering formation. Shoulders rigid, hands at our sides, eyes ahead. The SS are looking for people who do not stand straight enough, who shift their feet, who glance to the left or right. The smallest infraction—and often nothing at all—warrants the sharp lick of a whip.

At the front of each group, the block elders report to the SS on the number of prisoners in their block going to work, the number of sick prisoners who will remain in the barracks, and the number of prisoners who died during the night. The number of ill prisoners reported in each barracks is usually small. There's no use for people who can't work in Płaszów. What the rulers of the camp have no use for, they get rid of. Plain and simple . . . and to them, it's very simple.

We've been in Płaszów less than a week, yet already we understand this. We have learned many things in our time in the camp and we have learned them well. In Płaszów, there's no use for people who are slow to learn either.

Standing beside Adela, I clench my jaw to keep my teeth from chattering. Searchlights cut swaths through the frosty darkness, passing across our faces. SS men stride along the ranks, counting the prisoners to make sure the numbers match the reports. A slim officer advances down the lines of women, flicking his crop against his boot.

Shoulders taut, I fix my eyes on the back of the woman ahead of me. The soft clattering of Adela's teeth mingles with the voices of the SS echoing across the Appellplatz and the rhythmic slap of the officer's crop against his boot.

I struggle to stay alert, my mind sluggish, my stomach a hollow void. It's difficult not to drift away from the hunger, the cold, the shouts, away from the rows of prisoners carpeting the Appellplatz like a blanket of misery. To raise my eyes the barest fraction upward toward the expanse of sky as spilled-ink darkness fades to navy and imagine I am floating there. Far away from the bonds of earth, wrapped in the safety of the stars . . .

The whistle of a whip jerks me into the present. The SS officer hits a woman several rows ahead of us. The first morning we stood on the Appellplatz, when someone was struck, I wondered what they had done. I don't wonder anymore.

The officer continues down the rows. Time stretches. The sky lightens to a dingy gray. My legs ache, my feet turn numb from the cold.

"Achtung!" The order travels like a volley across the vast mustering ground. As the SS give the command, thousands of men and women stand at attention. I draw myself up, spine stiff, eyes facing forward as Untersturmführer Göth arrives on the Appellplatz. Accompanied by his two vicious dogs, he towers over everyone, even the other SS. My throat dries. My spine prickles.

"Mützen ab," comes the next command. In one motion, the male prisoners remove their caps, the sound of thousands of hands slapping their caps against their thighs reverberating across the Appellplatz.

The kommandant strolls between the ranks, his dogs ambling alongside him. I lose sight of him as he inspects the lines of men, but my pulse doesn't slow. Awareness of his presence overpowers the Appellplatz. We stand motionless as if willing ourselves to disappear. Even Adela's teeth have stopped chattering. The cold still penetrates my skin, but I scarcely notice or feel it. It's as if my body realizes it isn't entitled to succumb to or even acknowledge its needs.

The voices of the SS and OD men are the only sounds permeating the silence. Sparse rays of sunlight filter through the pale dawn.

A shot shatters the air.

I flinch. At my sides, my fingers curl into fists. I don't glance right or left or crane my neck to glimpse what has happened. In five days, Untersturmführer Göth has shot seven people during the morning count.

Somewhere in the endless rows of male prisoners are Szymon and Romek.

I refuse to let myself begin the thought, much less finish it. There are thousands of men standing on the Appellplatz, but fear stays, a hard stone in my throat.

By now, Untersturmführer Göth walks slowly along the ranks of women. Out of the corner of my eye, I glimpse him drawing nearer, accompanied by two SS. His dogs trot at his heels.

The women around me stand completely motionless. I hold my breath, my body rigid. Gravel crunches beneath his obsidian boots. I don't dare look at him. No one does. But I sense when he reaches our row, the weight of his gaze falling upon us.

He passes us by. I breathe again.

The remaining minutes of the morning count pass in a haze. At the order to form into *kommandos*, the ranks disperse, some to march under guard to factories outside the camp, others to join groups heading to workshops or labor details inside Płaszów. Szymon is among the fortunate ones who leave each day, as the nail factory has not been relocated inside the camp. The brush factory has been moved to a building in the industrial section, so Adela and I remain in Płaszów.

As everyone scatters, OD men keeping order, I scan the wide expanse of the Appellplatz. Amid the rushing crowd, a figure lies unmoving on the ground. From this distance, I can make out little apart from a brown coat, but it's enough. Relief, blessed but bitter, fills me with a pang. Neither Szymon nor Romek wears a brown coat.

Adela and I join the workers forming up to march to the brush factory. I step quickly into the back of the line, Adela beside me, two of a row of five. Within minutes, everyone has assembled, the OD man escorting us taking his place at the head of the line after counting us.

"March."

We link arms. I stand, second to the end of our row, Adela on my right.

"Right, left, right, left." The OD man sets our pace, and we march in time to his commands. Arms linked, we leave the Appellplatz. "Right, left, right, left."

"Did you see the Herr Kommandant this morning?" whispers the girl next to me. As long as we keep in step and don't look at each other, marching to and from the brush factory affords an opportunity for snatches of conversation.

I nod.

"Do you know why that man got shot?" She doesn't wait for an answer. "The Herr Kommandant said the man was too tall, told him to step forward, and he shot him. Can you believe it? Just because he was too tall . . ."

I don't answer. Can I believe it? How can I?

How can I believe a reality so horribly unreal?

"One to nothing," the girl mutters under her breath as we step in time down the muddy road. I understand what she means without having to ask.

Each morning, the count begins again, a daily tally, a deadly score. At first, I wondered what it meant when one evening a girl murmured to the woman squatting over the hole next to hers in the latrine, "Thirteen to nothing." The next time someone passed along the day's total, I understood. Thirteen was the number of Jews killed in the camp that day. The score on our side fluctuates, but it's always zero on the Nazis' side.

In this way, we number the dead of Płaszów.

CHAPTER TWENTY-TWO

Zosia
March 18, 1943

SITTING ON A PALLET in the low-ceilinged attic, I cradle Sara's warm weight against my chest. Once another woman's arms had sheltered her as mine do now. A mother holding her little one while she slept, breathing in the innocent sweetness of her scent, savoring her softness. Memorizing her features as if she knew every moment was as fragile as the child in her arms.

How small and vulnerable she is. How I ache to keep her safe.

Leon's wary gaze didn't leave me as I gave Sara the sedative, then held her as the Luminal began to take effect, her breaths lengthening, her body going slack.

At a quarter past five, he's to go to the fence. Janek will be waiting nearby. Tadeusz and I described to Leon the exact location of the cut wire. I trimmed his hair and washed his clothes, and Tadeusz gave him a cap to pull low over his eyes. Once Leon reaches Janek, he'll lead Leon to the people who agreed to take him in.

"Do you want to say goodbye?"

Leon nods and I pass his sleeping sister into his arms.

"I'm here, Sara-bird. Leon's here." He holds her against his chest, his touch both clumsily boyish and fiercely protective.

It's one of the hardest things I've ever done—telling Leon I'd found places for him and his sister to hide, but it would not be possible for them to stay together. He absorbed my words with the sober understanding of a child whose mind has been shaped by survival, not life, for whom a feeling of safety is something rare and little known.

Leon rests his palm on his sister's head as he whispers something in her ear. Words almost too quiet to catch, not in Polish but Hebrew. I glance away, not wanting to intrude upon a moment meant for the two of them alone, but not before he notices me watching.

He finishes and looks right at me, an almost defensive glint in his eyes. "I said a blessing over her. My tata used to say it over us, but he isn't here, so I did."

"He would be proud to know you did that," I say softly.

He stares at me, unblinking, jaw firmly clamped. Then he lowers his head to his sister's. The muffled undertone of voices filters from below. Kunde has been here well over an hour, arriving after I came up to the attic. Urgency thrums in my chest as the minutes tick away.

The creak of footsteps on the steps, then Irka emerges. "He's gone."

"Finally. I thought he'd never leave."

Ducking so as not to bump her head, Irka crosses the attic and kneels on the floor beside us. She looks at Leon, sitting on the pallet, Sara cradled in his skinny arms.

"I need to take her now, Leon." I keep my voice as gentle as I can.

Leon raises his head. His hold on his sister loosens as he releases her into my arms. Carefully, I lower Sara into the basket, lined with a cloth. My chest squeezes as I gaze at her, nestled inside the willow basket, her lashes a whisper against her cheeks, her lips softly parted.

Taking up my folded smock, I cover Sara with it, making sure it rests lightly, and there are crevices along the edges for air to seep in. Irka hands me a few potatoes and I place them atop the smock, away from Sara's face. Over the potatoes I drape a cloth, the same one I use to cover food purchased at the market.

It's a poor subterfuge. To smuggle her out in a suitcase or rucksack offers a better chance of concealment. But I've carried this basket in and out of the ghetto, past the police at the gate, more times than I can count. People rarely give a second glance at what they expect to see. And what they will see is a woman in a gray coat carrying a market basket. The woman who passes daily through the gate, a feminine face to enliven the routine of guard duty, smiling when needed, flirting if necessary, always innocuous.

Only what they expect to see.

Irka rests her hand briefly on the handle of the basket as if in benediction. Our eyes meet in the attic's half light.

I inhale deeply. "Let's go then."

The basket sways as I walk, its cloth covering securely in place. I carry it over my arm, as if it contains no more than a few groceries. The willow handle digs into my forearm, creaking beneath Sara's weight.

Weak sunlight filters from the pale sky as I stride down the street, Irka at my side, her hat at a slant, her handbag over her arm. Magister Pankiewicz's pharmacy ladies, inconspicuous in our familiarity.

As we approach the gate, I take the measure of the two Germans on duty. We aren't as familiar with the German police as we are the navy blues, but I recognize one of the men at the gate. Blockish features, older than most. The type who's just doing his job, probably glad to be on guard duty in Kraków instead of dodging bullets on the eastern front.

I glance at Irka. We might be out for an afternoon stroll, so serene are her features. My heart drums, the basket heavy on my arm. Sara sleeps on, soundless and still.

At the gate, we stop.

As she unclasps her handbag to take out her papers, Irka turns her smile on the older policeman. "Good day."

"Your papers?"

Irka shows her Kennkarte to the policeman.

He opens her identity card and scans the pass inside.

Shifting the basket, I open my bag to withdraw my own papers.

"It's a fine day, is it not?" Irka says.

The policeman grunts, then returns her papers.

Before he can even think to check her bag, I hand him my Kennkarte. He gives it a cursory glance. I wait for him to return my papers, Irka beside me.

"What's in the basket?"

My heart stops.

I lift a corner of the cloth, revealing the potatoes and my folded smock. No hesitation. No reluctance.

"A few potatoes. And my smock. I'm taking it home to wash." I drop the cloth. Smile.

His eyes flicker over me.

I look directly at him.

Seconds elongate, each slow agony.

He hands me back my papers.

Without missing a beat, I tuck my Kennkarte in my handbag. "Good day to you."

Irka and I pass through the gate. Keep walking, not a falter in our stride, without even a glance at each other. Every second I'm sharply aware of the basket's weight, of its contents, but I keep my eyes straight ahead.

Neither of us speak as we cross the Piłsudski Bridge, two women, side-by-side, backdropped by its looming iron archway. Not until it's time for us to part ways do we pause, standing in front of a shop window.

Only then do I realize my legs are shaking.

Now isn't the moment to speak of what we've just done or to absorb how close we came to discovery.

"I'll see you tomorrow." Irka's expression remains collected and I only hope mine is the same.

"Tomorrow then." I step past her, continuing down the sidewalk, basket over my arm. There's no deep exhalation, no rush of relief, no easing of the tightness in my midsection. Only alertness, an ever-present humming in my brain.

I may be out of the ghetto, but I've far from reached the end of this day.

They stand near the bedroom door, suitcases in hand, Pani Weinberg in the black hat and coat she left the ghetto in, her handbag holding her new Kennkarte.

I look at the young woman standing beside her. Gone is young Rena Silberman. In her place is sixteen-year-old Jadwiga Górska, dark-blond hair swept off her forehead and pinned at the sides, wearing an old coat of Helena's, a hat I bought secondhand—if she wore one of mine, someone might recognize it—concealing the burn marks on her scalp, lipstick tinting her mouth.

I hold Sara, her head resting on my shoulder. She's still under the effect of the Luminal. A relief, as someone in the building might hear if she cried.

Rena unraveled one of my sweaters and used the yarn to knit one for Sara, along with a matching hood, and Pani Weinberg stitched a dress out of a pillow slip. With the hood of soft blue yarn tied under her chin, the neat dress beneath her sweater, her face clean, Sara bears little resemblance to the baby in the cellar. Not Sara, I remind myself. Karolina Nowak, Agata Górska's granddaughter.

For hours last night, we labored over their new identities, embellishing them with the commonplace details found in the history of anyone's life. Whenever possible we chose fact over fabrication. The truth is far easier to remember—and far less likely to confuse—than invented fiction, and we've planned it down to the particulars of Ryszard's acquaintance with the Górski family.

What would my husband say if he knew what I undertook? With a sudden sharpness, I wish I could turn and Ryszard would be lying on our bed, arms behind his head, watching me with that look that said he knew exactly what I was thinking. Somehow I know he would stand by me in this, do all he could to preserve these lives no matter the risk.

But I'm alone and it doesn't matter, because I will do whatever I must for the ones with me now.

I swallow, throat dry. "Ready?"

Pani Weinberg nods. Any emotions they may be feeling are concealed behind calm expressions. In silence, we make our way through the flat.

The plan is to slip out without being seen, walk in the direction of Kraków's Main Station, and return to the flat as if we're coming home after I met their train.

It sounded straightforward, simple even, when we discussed it. But it all depends on our leaving the building undetected.

At the door, I stop.

"I'll go first, make sure no one's about. Take her for me."

Pani Weinberg sets down her suitcase and I pass Sara into her arms. Then I crack the door and peer into the landing, alert to the smallest sounds. The tread of footfalls on the stairs. The squeak of a door opening. The voices of my neighbors.

I wait, breath coming shallow as I measure the seconds. Then I turn, motioning them to follow.

They wait as I lock the door, drop the key into my handbag. I reach for Sara, leaving Pani Weinberg with the suitcase.

Time sharpens and blurs, magnifying every detail. The soft clatter of our footsteps on the stairs. Sara's weight in my arms. My own jumping heartbeat.

Down all three flights.

Into the foyer, our steps clicking across the floor.

The entrance stands straight ahead.

A creak.

We turn.

The door to the left of the stairs opens. Pan Burzyński steps out, a toolbox in hand.

I force a smile. "Good day, Pan Burzyński."

"Pani Lewandowska, how are you today?" As he speaks, he looks between me and the others, a small frown creasing his broad forehead.

"Very well, thank you." I turn to Pani Weinberg and Rena. Save for the slight stiffening of Rena's posture, they both appear perfectly composed. "I'd like you to meet my friends. This is Pani Górska and her daughter Jadwiga. And this little one"—I shift Sara in my arms—"is her granddaughter, Karolina." To Pani Weinberg and Rena, I say, "Pan Burzyński is the caretaker of this building."

Pan Burzyński steps forward. He wears a knitted vest over his shirt, his collar open, sleeves rolled to his forearms. Though he can't be much past his early thirties, his hairline is beginning to recede, aging his blunt features. "It's a pleasure to make your acquaintance, ladies."

"Very nice to meet you." Pani Weinberg smiles politely, her words echoed by Rena.

"They just arrived from Tarnow." I keep my smile in place. "They'll be staying with me from now on."

"Ah, I see." Pan Burzyński studies us intently. Or maybe it only seems he does. "You came in on the train then?"

Pani Weinberg doesn't falter. "Zosia met us at the station."

This morning, I'd telephoned the Kraków Main from the pharmacy to check the timetable. A train from Tarnow was scheduled to arrive at 11:40 a.m.

"She took us to a café before we came here." Somehow Rena makes her voice bright.

"How nice," Pan Burzyński says. Panic breaks over me in waves as his gaze settles on Rena. Does he see through Jadwiga Górska's bleached hair, cosmetics, and grown-up clothes? Does he remember Rena Silberman?

In my arms, Sara stirs, starts to fuss.

"Shall we go upstairs?" I turn to Rena and Pani Weinberg. "You must be tired after your journey."

"So pleased to have made your acquaintance, Pan Burzyński."

"Likewise, Pani Górska. If you and your daughter have need of anything at all, my flat is on the fourth floor."

Rena gives him a small smile. "Thank you."

Pan Burzyński nods, returns her smile briefly. "I look forward to seeing you both often."

I give a crisp nod. "Good afternoon, Pan Burzyński." I sense his eyes on us as we pass by him on our way upstairs.

In silence, the three of us mount the steps.

Inside my flat, Pani Weinberg and Rena set down their suitcases and take off their coats and hats. Sara's cries increase.

Pani Weinberg reaches out and unbuttons Sara's hood. "You must be hungry, aren't you, my little one?" she soothes. "I'll fetch her something to eat."

I step into the sitting room, still wearing my coat, and stand near the curtained window, rocking Sara in my arms, making soft shushing sounds. A headache beats in my temples like a pulse. I glance up as Rena comes in, carrying the suitcases. "You did well."

"I should put these away," Rena says, voice dulled by a weariness that runs deeper than the physical.

"What is it?" I ask gently.

She meets my gaze, still Rena Silberman beneath the blond curls and cosmetics, eyes wide, a little lost. For a moment, she doesn't answer. "I wish I wasn't afraid," she says softly. "It's so hard always being afraid."

"I know."

"If it were only for myself, I could bear it. But Szymon and—and Hania. I don't know what it's like where they are. I don't know if they're safe." She draws a shaky breath. "I don't know anything."

This bright girl's life should be full of hopes and plans, brimming with promise as she grows into womanhood. Instead, to survive she must live as a fugitive, fearing whether the people who were once her neighbors might recognize and betray her, never free from an impossible burden of strain, isolated from those closest to her.

What can I say? How can I help her find the strength she needs to face not only this moment but every day that lies between us and the end of all of this?

I go to her, Sara in my arms. "When I was a girl, not much younger than you, my mama became ill. They said she had cancer." I swallow. "She died only a few months later." I rarely think of that time, of the mother who had filled my life with hers for twelve years . . . and then left it so suddenly, as if death were a door slammed in my face.

Rena listens, a quiet understanding in her gaze.

"I tried to be strong, but I was so afraid to lose her. One does not understand that kind of fear until one lives it. Even then perhaps we do not understand." I pause, remembering. "But before she died, she told me something. She said to me, 'Strength is not to live without fear but to live in spite of it.'"

Little did my mama know when she spoke those words so long ago when they would again find me. Needing them now as much as I did then. Perhaps she did know—not what my future would hold but that her words would return to me someday, to give to another as she had given them to me.

"She told me God would show me how to find that strength when I could not find it alone." I look into Rena's eyes. "And I believe it will be so for you too."

CHAPTER TWENTY-THREE

Hania
April 19, 1943

SIX WOMEN DIVIDE ONE kilo of bread.

Bread in the camp does not mean bread as we once knew the word. Płaszów is its own reality, one where we are human, but our reality is not. We use the same words: *bread, work, time, cold,* but their meanings have changed. The old words, the old ways, are from a life we have begun to only half believe.

Now when I think of bread, I do not think of the loaves Mama once bought at the bakery, dense and fragrant, or the challah she baked for Shabbat, each loaf beautifully shaped into a plait, burnished tops golden brown, every sweet bite seeming to melt a little on one's tongue.

Bread in Płaszów is one-sixth of an oval loaf, black and claylike, half flour and half something else—one woman says it's sawdust—that sticks in your throat going down.

Sometimes I remember the other bread, recall the bakery shelves filled with fresh loaves, imagine having a whole loaf, two loaves, all to myself, savoring the richness of every warm bite, filling the void in my stomach until I am satisfied. My body craves those loaves of my memory, aches for any food beyond thin soup and sawdust bread.

In the ghetto, we had enough to eat to sometimes forget our hunger. The gurgling of our stomachs kept us awake at times and we always sought ways of obtaining more food, but for us, at least, it was still hunger as humans imagine it.

In Płaszów, hunger invades not only our stomachs but also our minds. Gnawing at our intestines and fogging our consciousness. When I rise from the bunk in the morning or bend to pick something up, my vision blackens at the edges and dizziness swamps me. No one must notice my weakness and I allow myself only a few seconds for my body to steady. I am terrified of fainting during roll call or at the brush factory. One of the guards will see and he will beat me. If he's feeling generous, that is.

However poor its quality, a ration of bread is like gold to us. Every crumb must be accounted for and distributed evenly, and each group of six has their own system for dividing the precious loaf. Often arguments erupt throughout the barracks over the slicing of the bread, sometimes so heated the block elder intervenes.

It's Fela's turn to portion the bread, which means the process will be completed with little disagreement. Before the war, she'd been studying to become a lawyer, and is the only one of us to whom even Balbina, always the first to start a quarrel, will listen. Fela sleeps on the bunk above Adela and me with her friend Genia. Young Pola and Balbina, who sleep on the top tier, make up our six.

The five of us cluster around the bunk as Fela measures each slice with a scrap of string before carefully cutting the lump of bread using a piece of sharpened tin. Once every crumb has been divided evenly, each person takes a slice. Sometimes there's a sliver of margarine or a blot of sour jam made from by-products from a raspberry juice factory, also divided six ways, but tonight there's only the bread.

"A few of us are going to recite the prayers for Pesach tonight," Fela says quietly as I pick up my piece. "Would you and Adela like to join us?"

Of course Fela would remember it's the night of Pesach. I knew it was soon from my rough counting of the weeks, but it's difficult to keep track of time without calendars to mark our days, no clocks, nothing but the blast of the bugle jerking us from sleep at five every morning. Somehow Fela, more than the rest of us, is able to keep a part of herself in the world outside Płaszów. Books and paper are forbidden, but sometimes at night she recites poems she's memorized by heart, the rise and fall of her voice unspooling the words like a Chopin nocturne.

Fela reminds me what it is to be more than a machine for the Nazis.

"Yes, we'll come." Though we have no candles to light, no wine to speak a blessing over, we can repeat the familiar, sacred prayers. We can still honor our faith and remember its traditions.

"Good." Fela gives me a quick smile.

Adela and I sit on the edge of our bunk. I stare at the small piece of bread in my hands. Even in the ghetto, we abstained from leavening during Pesach.

But we have nothing else. If we give up our bread, we will starve.

We did not choose this, I tell myself as I take a tiny bite from the corner of my slice, chewing slowly. "Fela invited us to join her and some of the others to say the festival prayers tonight."

"It's the night of Pesach, isn't it?" Adela eats her bread, leaning against the side of the bunk. "I forgot," she says softly.

"I had too." I reach under my kerchief, scratch at the bites on my skin. The misery of lice crawling over my flesh, breeding in my hair and in the crevices of my clothes, feeding on my blood, is one of the constants of life in Płaszów. The bites can become infected when scratched, but the prickling sensation against my skin is almost unbearable when I'm sitting still. Before I go to sleep, I'll take off my kerchief, sift my fingers through my hair, and squash as many as I can. It's one of the ways we spend our little free time—combing our clothes and bodies for the parasites, killing as many as we find. It doesn't seem to do much good.

"Yesterday, Fela told me—"

The door bangs open. Two guards barge into the barracks. "Out, out!"

Fear slams into my body. I instantly respond. Shoving the remainder of my bread into my pocket, I turn to Adela, making sure she's beside me before we follow the others.

The guards herd us out of the barracks, whips at the ready to strike anyone who moves too slowly.

We assemble outside our block. In the dusty twilight, long rectangular barracks built of boards squat on the road, high barbed-wire fences an outline in the distance.

As the barracks empties and the guards shout, I wait alongside Adela and the other women.

Wait. Another word to which the camp has assigned a new definition.

In Płaszów, to wait means to be powerless.

Splinters of wood dig into my raw palms. Mud sucks at my shoes with every step. Beneath the crushing weight of the beam, my muscles burn.

The guards marched us through the camp to railcars on the tracks a short distance outside the gate. Beams needed to be unloaded and hauled to building sites in the main part of the camp. We would take the night shift.

No questions followed this announcement. No one protested we'd just ended a twelve-hour shift at our various labor assignments. We simply began unloading the beams.

To ask a question, to act as if we have rights, to remind our captors of our humanity in any way is not only impermissible in Płaszów but punishable.

Three women carry one beam. They are enormous, these beams. I don't know what they weigh, but as my shoulders cry out in pain I imagine they are over seventy kilos. We trudge down the muddy road, bent like old women under our burden. I'm too tired to care what the guards shout at us, the vile names they call us as they goad us to work faster.

If a woman stumbles or moves too slowly, whips lash above our heads, landing on our shoulders like fiery tongues.

Adela walks ahead of me, supporting the end of the beam with her shoulder and hands, slight frame hunched beneath the load. She's too frail for this heavy labor. A month in Płaszów has whittled our bodies of strength, of weight. Everyone is thinner now, and Adela was small even before we arrived.

We were to keep Pesach tonight, honoring Adonai by reciting the text of the Haggadah and repeating the familiar prayers, though we had no unleavened bread or bitter herbs or any of the elements of a proper Seder. Perhaps I would have added a silent prayer of my own, though as I toil through the mud, I do not know what I would have said.

Do the Germans know the significance of tonight? Preventing us from observing this holy night is yet another means of degrading us, another way of reducing us to the machines they believe us to be.

Why is this night different from all other nights? The question asked by the youngest child during the Seder fills my mind.

We were slaves to Pharaoh in Egypt, and the Lord, our God, took us out from there with a strong hand and with an outstretched arm.

I hear the response in Tata's resonant voice, as we sat around the table laid with a fine white cloth, the faces of my family aglow in the flickering candlelight.

The memory stabs like a knife. Retreating into the past is an escape, but its price is bitter and full of pain.

We reach the building site and set down our beam. It thuds as it lands on the pile. Scrapes sting my hands, blisters form. I spit on my palms and rub in the moisture. My joints ache.

Breath comes in pants from Adela's chapped lips. "Why are they doing this to us?" she gasps.

"I don't know."

Because we are Jews.

"Here." I pull my handkerchief from my pocket and pass it to her. "Quickly. Bind this around your hand. It will help."

She nods and takes it from me, wincing as she wraps the fabric around the angry red skin of her right palm.

This is our third trip. How many will we make before the night is over?

We form into rows of five without being told. I glimpse Fela beside Genia a few ranks ahead of us as we move onto the road.

She turns, catching my gaze. *We are strong*, her eyes seem to say. *We can do this.*

Fela reminds me of Zosia, the same combination of gentleness and determination, the kind of person I've always wanted to be. Wisps of hair escape her kerchief to curl around her cheeks. Exhaustion doesn't diminish her loveliness, nor do the garish red stripes daubing her dress. Everyone's clothes received this treatment a couple of weeks ago. If someone attempts escape, the stripes and prisoner number painted on their garments will instantly identify them as an inmate.

Back and forth, from the railcars to the building site, we trudge.

Four trips. Five.

On the fifth trip, two women collapse. The guards beat them until they get up.

The camp surrounds us as we walk, dark slashes of electrified barbed wire against smoke-gray twilight, watchtowers manned by guards with machine guns, rows of rectangular buildings stretching over the sprawling complex.

We pass the building where the kommandant has his office. I don't dare turn my head to glance at the curtained windows. He likes to stand at the window and shoot at prisoners working nearby, pick them off one by one, as if they are targets put there so he might practice his aim. It's unlikely he would be in his office at this hour, but still I tense.

The guards report at the gate and we march out to the waiting railcars, their exteriors murky in the fading light. The doors of two of the cars stand open, revealing the stacked lumber inside. Adela and I clamber up the step and drag one of the beams to the door. The third woman waits below to help us. Gasping for breath, we heave the long, thick piece of lumber out of the railcar, then scramble down to pick it up again.

For the sixth time, we trek to the building site. Blisters break open on my palms. My muscles scream. I ache for the bread tucked in the pocket of my coat, the brief easing it offers from the pangs that consume my stomach.

I am strong. I can do this.

Fela's message bolsters me. I draw on my remaining scraps of strength as I heft the bruising weight, put one foot in front of the other. The tramp of our footsteps, the labored breathing of the women around me, my own heartbeat . . .

"Achtung!"

We come to an ungainly stop, still holding the beam.

Untersturmführer Göth stands at the edge of the street, putting a cigarette to his lips, his huge dogs, a Great Dane and a mixed-breed Alsatian, at his side. He wears a white button-down shirt, a Tyrolean hat with a feather in its brim, a holster at his wide belt. His gaze slides over us, a ragged line of women bent beneath the weight of the beams.

I stiffen.

Why is he here? Why isn't he sitting down to his evening meal or hosting one of his lavish, drunken parties?

Our guards approach him and salute, the men exchanging a few words. We wait for the order to march, but the directive doesn't come. Instead the kommandant approaches us. The tread of his boots reverberates in my ears.

The heavy beam turns my arms to gelatin. I fight to keep my grip on the rough lumber, my palms slick from sweat and broken blisters. Numbing fear spreads through my limbs. The kommandant strolls down the line of women, the end of his cigarette a smoldering coal, his dogs trotting at his heels.

The boots stop.

"That looks heavy. Is it too much for you?" His voice is cultured, almost pleasant. One could even be fooled into thinking he addresses the woman as a fellow human being whose welfare inspires his genuine concern.

"No, Herr Kommandant," the woman answers, her words barely audible.

"Are you sure? It really does look heavy. If it's too much for you, you're welcome to return to your barracks."

"Thank you, Herr Kommandant, but I'm fine. I can work."

The beams and the backs of the women in front of me hide her from view. But my ears cannot hide from the strike of the kommandant's fist or the woman's stifled cries. The sounds repeat one after the other, until there's a thud, like a beam hitting the pile, only this time it's her body hitting the ground. I can't tell what happened to her, whether she's dead or only injured.

The boots continue. Even at a distance, the kommandant is a huge man. Usually that's how we view him. From a distance. Now he's only a few meters away and his massive height and broad girth is overpowering.

He stops again. At Fela's row.

"What are you staring at so stupidly?" The words are addressed to Fela, his voice full of disgust.

Fela doesn't respond.

My end of the beam grows heavier as the other women struggle to bear the weight.

"I expect to be answered when I ask a question."

I flinch, anticipating the blows that will follow. But the kommandant doesn't hit her.

"Now, what were you staring at?"

"Nothing, Herr Kommandant." Fela's steady voice shows no fear.

"Nothing?" His faint chuckle ripples through the air. "If you have time to stare at nothing, perhaps you are not thoroughly occupied. We don't want anyone to be bored here, now, do we?" He turns to the women in Fela's group. "Put down the beam."

Immediately they set it down. It lands hard on the ground.

"Now, you pick it up."

A chill shivers my skin.

She won't be able to carry it. Three of us barely can.

But failure to carry out an order means she will be beaten . . . if she's fortunate.

Fela bends down and grasps one end the beam, straining to lift it. Grim determination emanates from the set of her slim jaw.

She stands, gripping the beam in both hands, and drags it behind her.

"Higher. Higher."

Fela pulls the beam down the long road, the slab of lumber bumping behind her.

The kommandant watches, his back to us, smoking his cigarette, his dogs at his heels.

If she can make it to the building site, perhaps she won't even be beaten. Perhaps the kommandant will lose interest in his human draft horses and return to his house. Perhaps—

The kommandant points at Fela. "Attack." The single word stabs the air.

The dogs bolt down the road, muscular bodies a blur.

At the last second, Fela turns, catches sight of them. My breath stops.

They leap on her, knocking her to the ground.

Fela's screams sicken the air. There is no word for this sound . . . this horror . . .

Somehow, we support the beam. Somehow, we stand motionless.

Fela.

Her name is a mute and endless cry.

The dogs snarl as their jaws tear her apart.

I stare at the ground, eyes glazing over the desecrated tombstones.

Screaming. Screaming.

Nothing.

"Ralf, Rolf."

The dogs bound back to their master, panting.

"Good boy. Good Ralf." The kommandant praises them, petting their heads. Untersturmführer Göth strides toward Fela's body, the dogs following him. He unholsters his pistol, aims.

A single shot.

The kommandant holsters his pistol and heads up the road toward his house, whistling.

I recognize the tune. Strauss. A waltz.

No one moves, even the guards, until he's gone.

"March."

The command snaps me out of my daze.

We move down the road, beams hoisted at the level of our shoulders. We pass the woman the kommandant beat. I barely glance at her. We walk fast, as if we've ceased to acknowledge the weight of our load, as if we truly have become machines.

We walk because we cannot run. But every fiber of our bodies seeks nothing but to get away.

A limp body lies near the edge of the street, next to the beam.

Don't look.

But I do. Only for an instant, but it's enough. The image burns my mind. Indelible.

Fela, quieting a quarrel with a calm word. Fela, smiling at me as I take my bread. Fela, whispering the words of a poem, lulling us to sleep with her voice.

Fela, beautiful and brave . . .

My throat aches. Group after group of women files past the remains of Fela's body.

We are silent.

The world is silent.

CHAPTER TWENTY-FOUR

Zosia
April 21, 1943

"COME IN, ZOSIA."

At Tadeusz's voice, I step inside the duty room.

A balding gentleman occupies the club chair, a cigarette in hand. Tadeusz sits at his desk, Irka on the divan.

"Why, Dr. Weichert. How nice to see you."

Dr. Weichert serves as chairman of the Jewish Mutual Aid—known as the JUS—which distributes food, clothes, and medical supplies donated by Jewish organizations abroad to various ghettos and labor camps. Due to his position, Dr. Weichert is permitted by the Germans to remain in the ghetto instead of moving to Płaszów. Of course, all activities of the JUS are closely supervised by the German authorities.

"Good day, Pani Magistra." Dr. Weichert greets me as I cross to sit on the divan next to Irka.

Irka turns to me. "We were just discussing the efforts of the JUS to provide aid to the people in Płaszów."

My interest sparks. "What sort of efforts?"

"Mainly delivering food and medical supplies to the camp, as well as distributing special items to specific inmates, such as letters, money, and parcels from friends on the outside. Because of my position, the authorities permit me to enter Płaszów to make these deliveries. They don't like it but, for the moment, they permit it."

"We'll be supplying Dr. Weichert with medicine to deliver to the camp. It will also be possible to send letters and parcels," Tadeusz says.

I absorb these words with growing eagerness. "Dr. Weichert, would it be possible for me to send a parcel to some friends?"

"Why, certainly."

"There's one person in particular I'm anxious to get a message to. I'd be grateful for the chance to send her something." Perhaps I can send parcels not only to Hania but others as well. "Are they allowed to keep what's sent to them?"

"The Germans consider confiscation their special prerogative. But we do our best. My associates in the camp aid in the distribution of such parcels." He takes a drag of his cigarette. "Have it ready in a few days and I'll pick it up before my next delivery, along with whatever supplies you can arrange, Pan Magister."

Tadeusz nods. "We'll do what we can."

Dr. Weichert takes his leave. Tadeusz shows him out, leaving Irka and me in the duty room.

She turns to me. "Your friend in Płaszów, she's the one you tried to help leave the ghetto, isn't she?"

I nod. Tried. I could do no more.

"What of the others? Has Pani Górska found work?"

"She took a position cleaning at a hospital for the Wehrmacht. She decided if she were employed where she'd have to spend a great deal of time among other Poles, the chances of someone suspecting her identity would be greater than if she worked for the Germans. No one notices the woman mopping the floor." My lips tilt.

"Has there been any word of Leon?"

"He's well. Sergeant Kamiński says they're looking after him."

On my way to the pharmacy the day after Leon left the ghetto, I met Janek. Knowing which way I walked, he'd waited for me. Leon managed to reach the fence and slip out of the ghetto and Janek led him to the people who took him in. Janek and I agreed to meet from time to time, so he can keep me informed about Leon's welfare and take a parcel from me to the people sheltering him.

"That's good news." Irka pauses. "It's been a strange existence these past weeks, hasn't it? I suppose it was a delusion to believe in the permanency of the ghetto until the end of the war." She gazes out the window overlooking Zgody Square. "Now what do we do?"

Her voice holds an emptiness I well understand. The ghetto has become a town of desolate streets and abandoned buildings, a place all but forsaken by life. The pharmacy remains open because Kunde continues to arrange for the renewal of our passes. But our only visitors—apart from OD men, German police, and SS—are the workers marched under guard from Płaszów each day, assigned to the task of clearing out the uninhabited buildings and sorting the furniture and belongings for storage in warehouses. The occupiers want their confiscated property organized, of course. Some of the workers manage to come to the pharmacy during their afternoon break, and for fleeting minutes, the Apteka Pod Orłem once again becomes a hub of information given and exchanged, newspapers read and discussed. What food we have, we give them. Some eat it, but most tuck it away to smuggle into Płaszów.

In this way, we learn of conditions in the camp. And what we learn is a nightmare beyond comprehension.

"We will do what we have always done." My voice is firm. "What we can."

. . .

Hania
May 18, 1943

Now when disputes arise over the dividing of the bread, I'm the one to intervene. I miss Fela and the way she could resolve the squabbles that erupted among women frayed by hunger and degradation, how she not only settled disagreements but bonded us together through the poems she recited, a kind word at the right moment, her willingness to share what she had with others.

It's risky to form attachments at Płaszów. The woman you wake up beside in the morning might not return to the barracks at night, her absence marked only by the empty place on the bunk and a few whispered words from someone who heard how she died.

When the ones who don't return are strangers, the pain is less.

"That's enough, Balbina. The pieces are even. We all watched Genia measure them."

Balbina glares at Genia, arms folded across her chest. "I saw her—"

"Enough, I said!" I sigh. "Adela, it's your turn to take your piece first."

One by one, the women take their ration of bread. Balbina takes her time studying the pieces. She grabs one, mutters something under her breath at Genia as she passes.

"What did you say?" Genia grits out, eyes snapping.

"Nothing." Balbina retreats to her bunk, clutching her bread.

Hunger gnaws at not only stomachs but also selves. Before the war these women could never have imagined shouting at each other over whether one slice of bread is a few crumbs larger than another. In the face of the brutality in which we exist, is it any wonder we're becoming people we hardly recognize? What's more remarkable is what we retain, our scraps of dignity a silent defiance of those who purpose to destroy our humanity.

Bending down, I crawl inside our bunk after Adela, resting on the hard boards covered by a single woolen blanket. Some time ago—I've stopped counting weeks—our other blanket was stolen. I could have reported the theft to the block elder but didn't want to make trouble. Doubtless it was not greed but desperation that drove the woman who took it.

As the nights grow warmer, the loss of a blanket is less of a hardship. But even as the days reach toward summer, I fear the coming winter and what it holds for us in Płaszów.

I chew my bread carefully, making each bite last. It will be gone all too soon, but the yawning ache will remain.

Only when Szymon buys a little food from one of the Poles at the nail factory is our hunger briefly eased. He and Romek managed to keep back a few złotys when the SS ordered everyone to hand over all money and valuables a couple of weeks after we arrived. This he exchanges for a couple of potatoes, a hard-boiled egg, a loaf of bread. We gather around our bunk and divide the food into four portions, sharing it with reverence. Szymon risks his life each time he smuggles food into Płaszów. One time they caught a man with a loaf of bread. The guard threw the bread on the ground and shot the man. I begged Szymon to stop, but a few days later, he brought Adela and me an apple.

After weeks of thin turnip soup and claylike bread, the crisp, tart fruit made our taste buds come alive. But as the sweet juice trickled onto my tongue, I thought of the man who lost his life for a loaf of bread and how he could have been my brother.

I slip the remainder of my bread into my pocket to eat with the tepid brown liquid distributed in the morning and stretch out beside Adela. The voices of women—talking, arguing, whispering—blur around me.

"Hania."

I turn.

Genia stands next to the bunk. "There's a man looking for you."

I crawl out of the bunk, adjusting the white kerchief covering my hair, all female prisoners now required to wear one.

"Are you Hania Silberman?"

"Yes." I don't recognize the young man in paint-daubed clothes standing a few paces away. What does he want with me? Has something happened to Szymon or Romek? My heart begins to race, fear a trigger easily squeezed.

"This is for you." He starts to hand me the parcel he carries.

I hesitate. "What is it?"

"A package, courtesy of the JUS."

"Why would they send me a package?"

"Couldn't say. Here." He practically shoves it at me and heads for the door before I can thank him.

The weight of the parcel settles into my hands, my prisoner number and block number scrawled on the wrapping. At the top, my name is penned but in different handwriting.

I stare at the curving script, a memory hovering just out of reach. Drawing me back to another time and place, to two young women a flight of stairs apart. Now a few kilometers separate us. A few kilometers and the chasm of a universe.

Lowering myself to the bunk, I place the package in my lap, brushing my fingers over the crinkled brown paper.

Adela leans forward, touching a corner of the parcel. "What is it?"

"Did someone send you something?" Genia crouches beside our bunk, eyes wondering, eager.

I finger the twine. "The man said it came from the Jewish Mutual Aid."

"Aren't you going to open it?" Adela asks.

Twine tied in a sloppy bow secures the brown paper, as if the parcel was opened and retied in a haphazard fashion, likely searched by the guards.

I undo the knot, the twine catching at my roughened fingertips, and set it aside. Pola and a few others cluster nearby, watching as I unfold the wrapping, whispering together in excitement. Though I long for privacy in which to savor this moment, these women are as starved for comfort as I am. If it helps them to forget the misery around us for a few minutes, surely I can give them this small thing.

"Ohhh," Adela and Genia breathe in unison.

I pick up the first item, a round cake of soap. I hold it to my nose, closing my eyes, breathing in lavender, the soft fragrance banishing the stench of the barracks and my own unwashed body.

"Let me. Oh, please, let me," the women exclaim, eager as children.

I pass the soap to Adela. She holds the small cake with reverence, inhaling deeply. "Mmm. Lavender." She hands it to Genia.

As the women take their turns with the soap, I return to the rest of the parcel. At the sight of the tin of sardines, my mouth waters. The only meat we've had since coming to the camp is a scrap floating in our watery soup from time to time—horsemeat, according to someone who heard it from one of the people in the kitchen. I can almost taste the richness of the oily fish.

Bread, wrapped in a cloth. A real wheat loaf. I breathe in the bread as I did the soap, the aroma of flour and yeast intoxicating.

I run my hand over the blanket, in which everything has been wrapped. It's thick and warm, a beautiful green wool. And it's clean, not infested with lice and bedbugs as our other blanket has become.

Oh, Zosia.

Wrapped in the blanket's folds is an amber bottle. Vitamin drops. I cradle the small bottle as if it holds liquid gold. More than gold: life.

Something white falls to the ground. I reach down and pick up the folded slip of paper, closing my fingers around it.

The women pass around the soap, sardines, bread, and blanket, admiring and exclaiming over them—the unimaginable luxury of these simple items. After each item has been handed around, Genia makes sure it's returned to me. The vitamin drops I tuck into my pocket, out of sight. I can't risk them being stolen, not when Adela needs them so badly.

Shame wells. I'm no more deserving of this bounty than any of these women, yet I'm the one to whom it has been given.

If I'd only myself to consider, I would divide the food with the dozen or so women gathered around my bunk. But I must save it for Szymon and Romek. Everyone receives the same ration, no matter how hard they labor, and constructing barracks and breaking up tombstones to build roads has taken a toll on Romek. He's lost weight, and though he doesn't talk about it, I sense he suffers hunger worse than the rest of us.

Still, there must be something I can share with these women.

"On Sunday, let's all go to the latrine. We can use the soap to wash ourselves." Though there are no showers in the camp, the latrines are now fitted with sinks, out of which comes a trickle of water. Adela and I clean our faces and hands daily, and on Sunday afternoon, the one time we don't work, we wait in line to scrub ourselves and our underthings as best we can.

Genia clasps her hands to her chest. "What it will be to wash with soap."

The women cluster around my bunk, talking about soap. One woman who lived on a farm says her babcia taught her to make her own, another says she bought hers from a shop in the city and it always smelled of roses. For a brief space of time, we forget we're in a labor camp.

For a moment, we remember what it is to be women.

They soon disperse, some to their bunks, others to the latrine, for the bugle signaling lights out won't be long in coming. Carefully, as if it might dissolve under my touch, I unfold the page.

Adela leans over my shoulder, reading the lines penned in Zosia's script.

Dear Hania,

An acquaintance has made it possible for me to send this package in the hope of it reaching you. I will send parcels as often as I can. We are all well. You will be glad to know your robin remains safe in its nest.

My breath catches, and though there's more to the letter, I read the last line again.

"Robin" was Tata's pet name for Rena on account of a red coat she wore when she was small. Zosia couldn't know about that unless Rena told her.

Rena is safe.

At night, lying awake on the hard bunk, the glare of searchlights piercing the barracks windows, surrounded by the sounds of women restless in slumber, a crack opens in the wall behind which I keep the past. I hold their faces in my mind. Rena, Pani Weinberg, Zosia. And I wonder if they are safe and if I will ever see them again. The killing of prisoners is commonplace in Płaszów, but there are others executed here, brought to the camp in lorries— Jews discovered in hiding or with forged papers, Poles caught harboring them or found guilty of some act of resistance. Day and night the shots reach us, but we do not know the names of the dead, their lifeless bodies tossed in a ditch and buried beneath a layer of earth. What if my sister, Pani Weinberg, and Zosia are among them? When this thought rises, I press my eyes tight as if to force it out, begging ADONAI to protect them, wondering if my prayers are too late.

And now, this slip of paper, the sureness of Zosia's script . . .

I must shred the letter tomorrow morning and drop the fragments down one of the stinking holes in the latrine, but for now, I hold it in my hands and read the precious words again and again.

Your robin remains safe.

Something wet trails my cheek, lands on the page, a tiny starburst blotting the ink.

"Hania, you're crying," Adela whispers.

Am I? A droplet slides down my lip, salty and warm. I had forgotten the taste of tears.

I wipe my face with the sleeve of my coat. The contents of Zosia's parcel are spread on the bunk around us. My gaze touches each item, falling last on the letter in my hand.

It is more than soap and vitamin drops, bread and a blanket, words on a page.

It is hope.

CHAPTER TWENTY-FIVE

Hania
October 15, 1943

FATIGUE IS A CURRENT, dragging me down, carrying me away. I blink hard, the two halves of the brush blurring.

Stay awake. Stay alert.

Prisoners labor day and night in Płaszów, and our twelve-hour shifts alternate between weeks. After we finish the night shift and stand for roll call, we're allowed to sleep during the day, but we rarely manage more than a few hours between the bugle blowing at noon, a random inspection of the barracks, the report of shots coming from the hill. They execute prisoners on a different hill now. The other ditch could hold no more bodies.

By the end of a week on night shift, we're exhausted, our minds in a fog, our pangs of hunger sharpened by lack of sleep. It's Thursday. Or is it Friday already? Night has long since fallen, the darkness outside the windows cold and heavy. A stove stands in one corner of the room, but it's seldom lit. The light from the hanging bulbs provides scarcely enough illumination to work by.

Since September, prisoners have not been permitted to work outside the camp, all but eliminating contact with the world beyond the gates of Płaszów. Now working at a sheet metal factory inside the camp, Szymon no longer able to smuggle food to us. I'm relieved he's not taking that risk anymore, but at least working outside the camp meant he spent most of the day in relative safety, away from the countless dangers that accompany us every hour in Płaszów.

In the months since the first arrived, we've received three parcels from Zosia. Without Szymon bringing us extra food and our rations decreased—now one kilo of bread is shared between eight instead of six—each has become even more precious. The last only contained a note, some bread, and a pair of knitted socks, as if someone, most likely a guard, pilfered part of the contents while searching the package. But though the items in the parcels provide sustenance for our bodies, what the arrival of each one does for our spirits is nourishment of another kind. The entire system of life in Płaszów serves as a constant reiteration—we are nothing in the eyes of the Nazis. Zosia's parcels remind us that beyond the fences of this camp someone cares what becomes of us.

Only the forgotten can truly understand what it is to be remembered.

I position the two halves of the brush. I've been promoted—if one can call it that—from threading bristles to joining the halves of the brush with metal fasteners.

My head droops, my eyelids heavy. The drone of the factory lulls me. I'm warm . . . in a soft bed with clean sheets . . . resting my head on a feather pillow . . .

The door bursts open.

I jolt.

Boots thud. Untersturmführer Göth strides into the factory, accompanied by two SS.

"Achtung!" bellows the foreman.

Chairs scrape. I rise, standing at attention behind the worktable along with the others. My gaze flies to Adela, two tables away with the others who thread the bristles. She stands rigid, arms at her sides, eyes straight ahead.

The kommandant's gaze passes over our rows. "Continue."

We sit. I pick up my small hammer and pound the fastener, each strike hitting its metal head.

Faster. Faster.

I grab another fastener, set it in place, and keep pounding. Untersturmführer Göth's unmistakable voice permeates the factory. He's asking the foreman questions about production, which the foreman answers in a deferential tone.

But there's no time to follow their conversation as I snatch another two halves, line them up, take a fastener, pound it in. Fatigue disappears. I work harder than ever, movements frantic, as if the faster I work, the more invisible I will become.

Followed by the two SS and the foreman, the kommandant proceeds slowly among the tables, pausing every so often to watch someone at work.

It's after midnight. Do the SS never sleep? They like making unannounced inspections during the night shift, checking to make sure production continues and the foremen aren't letting the workers rest. Maybe they hope to find us sleeping to give them a reason to punish us. Not that they need a reason.

The measured tread of boots draws closer. My empty stomach cramps as I hammer the fastener.

Perhaps the kommandant will pass by me. Perhaps I truly can become invisible. Perhaps—

"And what are you doing?"

My mouth goes dry. I raise my head. The kommandant stands in front of my table, hands behind his back. I've never been this close to him. He has eyes like a bird of prey. They are blue.

I notice this human detail, the color of his eyes, with a strange detachment. The others around me work without stopping.

"I'm joining the halves of the brush together with fasteners"—I swallow—"Herr Kommandant."

He picks up one off the pile of finished pieces. I don't duck my head, nor do I stare directly at him, keeping my gaze somewhere in the middle. He turns the piece in his hand, studying it.

I taste my heartbeat.

What if the fastener is crooked? He has shot people for less.

The brush clatters as he tosses it onto the pile.

"How many of these have you made tonight?"

Somehow, my voice doesn't shake as I answer. I try to sound confident, a skilled worker assured of my abilities.

"You started at what time, seven o'clock this evening?" His words slur. It's obvious he's been drinking.

"Yes, Herr Kommandant."

He rocks back on his heels, a slight frown creasing his brow, as if he's making some mental calculation or found my answer displeasing.

I hold my breath.

Without another word, he moves on, followed by his cadre of attendants.

I continue working, allowing myself not even a second of relief.

"It's interesting to hear you speak about production." The kommandant stands at the end of a row of tables, speaking to the foreman in a voice loud enough for everyone to hear. "When anyone can see this factory is not producing. I've made the calculations. These workers should have completed twice as much tonight."

"Herr Kommandant, if you wish to see the reports, I think you'll find them most satisfactory."

"There's no point in arguing." He chuckles slightly. "It's simple mathematics. It's obvious you've allowed laziness in these workers, and you will be punished."

I glance up as the kommandant draws his pistol.

"Herr Kommandant, if I might be allowed to explain—"

"Turn around."

The brush in front of me blurs as a shot rings out.

A thud.

My hands shake as I position a fastener and pound it into place.

"Give the rest twenty-five lashes. Perhaps a little discipline will remedy this problem."

"*Jawohl*, Herr Untersturmführer."

The two SS exchange a few words, then one of them pivots and heads out the door.

Like a machine, I keep working, my throat so tight I can barely breathe. Can I stop this? How can I stop this? Twenty-five lashes . . .

The other SS man stands with the kommandant a few paces away from the foreman's sprawled body. They chat and light cigarettes while we work in frozen silence.

The door opens and the first SS enters.

"Everything is ready, Herr Untersturmführer."

"Then take them out. Come on. Let's get going."

"Everyone, outside," shouts one of the SS.

I need to find Adela. I need to tell her she must not lose count.

I push through the crowd, catching sight of her. We reach each other. Terror shines out of her wide eyes. I grab her hand, her sweaty fingers clinging to mine as the SS herd us through the door.

Night air cools my face. The cold beam of searchlights throws light on four tables set up outside the brush factory. Guards stand next to them, holding whips. We form lines four across and the first two lines step up to the tables. We're in the fourth line. We'll be next.

"Look at me, Adela."

Her teeth chatter, her face pale in the white glare of light.

"You must not lose count. Otherwise they'll start over again. No matter how bad it is, you must not lose count."

She nods.

Whips crack. Screams serrate the night.

"Don't watch." We stand, gripping hands, gazes on the ground. The whistle of the whips intermingles with strangled cries and the voices of those being punished counting the strokes.

The first group staggers away from the tables. One woman collapses after a couple of steps.

The kommandant stands to one side, smoking a cigarette.

"Next."

Tears slide down Adela's cheeks. I let go of her hand as we approach the tables. I must spare her. Perhaps I could be punished for both of us. Search-lights sting my eyes. I draw a shuddering breath.

"Bare your legs and bend over the table."

"Please. Might I take her punishment too?"

Adela glances in my direction, eyes wide.

The guard stares at me.

My legs shake.

"Bare your legs and bend over the table."

My hands tremble as I lift my dress and pull down my underthings. The guard grabs my arm, shoving me down hard. I grip the edge of the table, squeezing my eyes shut.

The whip cracks.

A fiery knife rips my skin.

"One," I gasp.

Again, fire slashes my bare legs.

This time, I cannot hold back the cry that tears my throat. "Two."

The lashes land, one after the other, as the teeth of the whip shred my flesh. Dizziness blackens my vision.

Don't lose count.

"Twelve." I wrench out the word.

Blood roars in my ears. The blackness sucks me down. The whip whistles. Agony sears.

I scream.

Adela lies on her stomach as I wash and bandage her ribboned flesh. Whimpers escape her lips, her face pressed into my coat, folded into a pillow under her head.

I soak a cloth in the bowl of water, cleaning the lacerations on her buttocks and legs. I have no iodine or ointment, only water in my soup bowl, carried from the sink in the latrine. There are supplies at the infirmary, but I don't risk taking Adela there. Sometimes the SS charge in and shoot all the patients for no reason. But if I don't get something to put on our wounds, they'll become infected. I'll go to the infirmary alone and ask for ointment.

Adela cries out as I clean a deep gash.

"I'm sorry." My voice is a dry whisper. For what am I sorry? Because I'm hurting her? Because she was whipped?

Because we are alive?

My own lacerations throb, my dress sticking to my raw skin. By the time everyone received their punishment, it was time for the morning count. I don't know how we dragged ourselves to the Appellplatz. Those who collapsed, OD men carried to the infirmary.

Somehow Adela and I stood for roll call. She leaned on me when the guards weren't near, and I supported her as best I could until the woman next to us took pity and whispered for Adela to lean on her.

I bandage Adela's wounds with strips torn from a pillowcase. Then I lie beside her on my stomach. Only night shift workers asleep on their bunks and the block elder remain in the barracks. Pain beats through my body, its own pulse.

I need to go to the infirmary, bring back ointment for Adela and me so our cuts won't become infected. So we won't run fevers. So we won't die.

I rest my head on my folded arms.

Adela turns her head, red-rimmed eyes meeting mine. "I can't go on like this," she whispers. "I don't want to go on."

Someone stronger would find the words to comfort her. Someone better would draw from their own well of resolve so she might gain strength. But my well is empty.

My eyes slide shut, as I will myself to fall into oblivion.

I am not stronger, better.

I am broken.

CHAPTER TWENTY-SIX

Zosia
November 11, 1943

NIGHT OBSCURES THE CITY, gathering up the last remnants of light, as Janek and I walk to my flat.

Every two months, we meet by the statue of Grażyna. I give him a parcel, he brings me news of Leon. Janek assures me the boy is well and my parcels of food and books are passed along. Sometimes we wander the paths stitching the Planty, speaking of the latest reports from the underground newspapers, the situation in the former ghetto. No longer are workers marched each day from Płaszów, putting an end to our contact at the pharmacy with those imprisoned in the camp. The wall and barbed wire that hemmed in the district have all but been removed, the abandoned tenements prepared for new occupants by Polish workmen. Street by street, building by building, the last traces of the ghetto are erased.

Though Janek and I speak of these events, with each meeting, we find ourselves also talking of other things. Of how I grew up in Kraków as an only child while he spent his boyhood on a farm in the country, the second of five children. Of how he left home at seventeen and came to the city to find work to help support his family when the farm fell on difficult times and ended up staying and joining the police after serving his compulsory term of military service. Of how my tata wanted me to marry, but I insisted on attending university to study pharmacy. Of our lives before the war.

Only before.

Tonight Janek arrived nearly an hour late, apologizing but giving no explanation save that he'd had to attend to an urgent matter. After an exchange of my parcel and his news, he said he'd accompany me to my flat. I told him it wasn't necessary—after all, it was barely a quarter of an hour walk, but he answered that he'd been taught to see a lady safely home after dark and would do so if I'd permit him. I could have insisted, but truthfully, I had no wish to.

There's a feeling that comes with being cared for. Safe, like having some-one beside you while crossing an ice-slick street, knowing if you start to slip, you need only reach for their hand. Warm, like nestling beneath an eiderdown on a snowy night.

I've missed that feeling. While caring for others, I've ignored just how deeply.

Walking at Janek's side, I glance at him, his profile shadowed by the brim of his cap. "You seem quiet."

It's not the silence I note but the sense of what lies beneath its surface. Something is troubling him. I've come to know this man who leaves so much unspoken, to understand his silences . . . though sometimes it seems I hardly know him at all and understand him no better than I did when we first met.

"I'm afraid I'm not good company tonight. I apologize."

"No, please. It's all right." I pause. "Would it help to speak of it?"

"I don't know what good it would do. And I do not think you'd care to hear it." For a moment, he does not speak. "Today our commander informed me and a couple of the others that a report had been made about Jews hiding in a certain flat. He ordered us to go and search it. There was a young woman hiding in a cabinet. I'd searched the room before any of the others and I thought—I thought I could protect her. They found her anyway."

My throat squeezes.

"We took them all—there were four of them—out into the courtyard. The other sergeant shot them. That's the order now, anyone found in hiding is to be shot without delay. The way she looked at me, that young woman, as we led them out . . ." In his voice lives deep and bitter anguish.

We reach the corner of Alte Weichselstrasse, deserted in the clutch of darkness. Our steps still.

"In her eyes, I saw the man I have become. If ordered to take an innocent life, I'd sooner give up my own. But even if I am not the one to carry out the act, blood is on my hands, on my conscience. And I don't deserve to live."

In my flat, two women and a child wait for me to return home. Today a young woman and three others died while Janek watched.

He hadn't been the one to pull the trigger.

But does that make him any less complicit in their deaths?

I do not have an answer.

He'd tried to protect her. As he'd protected Hania from the SS man. As he'd aided Pani Weinberg and Rena in leaving the ghetto. As he'd found Leon a place of shelter.

As he has doubtless helped others.

I've seen the police at the gate and in the ghetto. The navy blues who took part in the deportations with as much zeal as the SS. Men who take the power given them and use it to destroy fellow human beings. Those for whom the satisfaction of the act itself is its own reward.

That is not Janek.

"No." I shake my head. "How could you have stopped what happened today? Have you not sought to use your position to protect whomever you could?"

"So many times I've thought about deserting. More than once, I almost did. But then I . . ." He breaks off.

Wind tugs my hair away from my cheeks as we face each other under a darkened streetlamp. "There is not one of us who hasn't learned the truest measure of themselves in this war, and we've all made choices that are nothing to be proud of. But that's not the man you are." The fervency of my voice startles me. "Not to me."

"Thank you for that." He pauses, a softening in his features. "You are a remarkable woman, Zosia Lewandowska."

The note in his tone upends me inside. These words are no pretty compliment, for this is not a man who deals in flattery. The rough edges of his voice hold a tenderness so unexpected it leaves me shaken. I regard him, at a loss. Not because of the words themselves but the way he spoke them. Because of my response to them, how my breath stilled and heat rushed into my chest.

"I've learned we must speak the words that matter because there are few we regret more than those left unsaid. The time may come when words are too late and"—his voice cracks—"we carry the pain of it the rest of our lives."

"What are you saying?" I can barely trust my voice.

"When I lost Celina, the part of me that felt what we'd shared . . . it no longer existed. After a time, I grew used to it, the emptiness. But then I came to know you." The look in his eyes undoes me. "I would never presume to take the place your husband held, but if you were willing to let me love you, I would—"

"Janek, please, I . . ."

He glances away, into the night. "Forgive me. I had not intended this tonight. You deserve better than the ramblings of a desperate man." His eyes find mine, the weathered contours of his face outlined by darkness. "But no matter what your feelings are, know that, in me, you will always have a place to turn."

"Thank you." My voice catches, unexpected tears welling. I reach up and gently touch his face, my fingers against rough stubble, the heat of his skin. He stills beneath the pressure of my hand. My fingers linger against his cheek, my throat tight and burning.

To feel in this way, there's something sharply painful in it. I've grown used to a heart numbed by scars. Learned to live with the familiar void carved by Ryszard's loss. Grieving him became a way of binding myself to him, the one way I had. I gathered up the shards of myself and kept living because I must, but to give anything of myself to another man was something I never asked for. I'm not certain anything remains to give, that the years haven't drained it all away and left behind a husk of the woman I used to be.

My hand falls away, but my fingertips do not forget the touch of his skin. "Good night."

"Good night, Zosia." A trace of sorrow enters his gaze as he regards me.

How easy it would be to let this man love me. To love him in return. Perhaps a part of me already does.

There is much I no longer fear. But this terrifies me.

I turn away and leave him.

• • •

November 17, 1943

The tapping at the door is so faint it takes a moment to register the sound. I glance up from my sewing. Pani Weinberg raises her gaze from the sock she's darning. Rena sits on the rug playing blocks with Sara. We look at each other, silently asking the same question.

Who would be at the door at this hour? It's after dark and nearly curfew.

More tapping.

I rise and leave the sitting room. In the entryway, I crack open the door.

A small shadow of a figure stands outside.

I suck in a breath, open the door, pull the figure inside. I close the door, slide the bolt. Only then do I face Leon.

"I'm sorry, pani." Leon's eyes plead with me.

"What are you doing here?" My voice is a sharp-edged whisper.

Shivers shake his shoulders. He isn't wearing a coat, only a damp shirt and trousers. His lips are pale with cold. "He . . ." Leon's teeth clatter. "He . . ."

"Come with me." I guide him into the sitting room.

Pani Weinberg stands. She and Rena stare at him, this skinny boy eying them like he's ready to bolt.

"It's all right, Leon. You don't have to be afraid." With a hand on his shoulder, I lead him to the sofa.

He sits with his hands between his knees, still shaking.

"Where did he come from?" Pani Weinberg asks, voice low.

"This is Leon."

"Her Leon?" Rena looks between Sara and him. I nod.

Something passes across Leon's face as his gaze fixates on his sister, her little legs sticking out beneath her dress as she happily crams the corner of a wooden block into her mouth.

"Why don't you bring Karolina here?"

Rena scoops Sara up and carries her to the sofa. She lowers herself beside Leon with Sara in her lap.

"Sara-bird." Leon reaches out and touches his sister's hair. "Don't you remember me?"

Sara shies away from him, clinging tighter to Rena.

"It's me, Sara-bird. Leon."

"Her name is Karolina now."

He looks up at me, frowning. "Why is she called that?"

"I'll explain later." I crouch in front of the sofa. "What are you doing here?"

"He didn't come back," Leon says, the words barely audible.

"Who didn't come back?"

"Pan Janek. I waited, but he never came."

"Who's Pan Janek?"

"The policeman."

"Leon, who have you been staying with?" Do I not already, deep down, know the inevitable answer before it comes?

"Pan Janek, the policeman."

The words slam into me.

Of course. I should have known.

"What's happened? Where's Janek?"

"I don't know."

"What do you mean you don't know?" My voice rises.

Leon starts shaking again, hands balled in his lap.

"Leon, listen to me." Somehow I gentle my tone. "It's very important you tell me everything. When was the last time you saw Janek?"

"Yesterday morning. He had on his uniform, like he always does when he leaves for work."

"Did he say when he'd be back?"

"In time for supper. But then the Germans came." He glances up, his young face haggard. "I know because I saw."

"They came to the flat?"

He nods. "I heard them shouting when I was coming down the ladder."

"You weren't in the flat?"

"I wasn't supposed to be up there. Pan Janek said never to go up on the roof without him, but I wanted to watch the clouds. Then it started to snow, so I came down."

"Did they see you?"

He shakes his head. "I hadn't opened the door yet. I—I ran back up to the roof. I saw them down in the street. Aron and Stefcia and Rafał and Estera. The Germans took them outside."

"So many," I whisper.

"The Germans must have found the place behind the armoire. Or maybe they didn't make it inside in time."

I almost force the words from him, driven by the urge to know the truth. Instead I wait, giving him time.

"Then I heard the shooting." He looks down at his hands.

Pani Weinberg stands frozen, face white. Even Sara sits silent in Rena's lap.

"I was scared to come down in case the Germans came back, so I stayed up on the roof all night."

Last night, it had snowed. It's a wonder Leon hadn't frozen to death on the roof without so much as a coat.

"I waited all day, but Pan Janek didn't come back. I didn't know where to go. You told me to come here if I was ever in trouble. I'm sorry if I should not have come, pani."

Months ago, as I sat in the attic, Sara in my arms, the Luminal easing her toward sleep, I'd made Leon memorize the address.

"No. You did well to come here." How is my voice so calm when inside I'm disintegrating? I must not allow myself to absorb the implications of Leon's words. Not now. Not here.

"When you heard the Germans shouting, did they say anything of Janek?"

"I didn't hear much. But one of them wanted to know if Pan Janek was hiding anyone else. He was shouting, so I heard. Rafał knew where I was, but he wouldn't tell the Germans. He didn't. They never came for me." He pauses. "I asked Rafał to come with me, but he doesn't like it when I go up on the roof. He says it's too dangerous. But if he'd been with me . . ."

"I know." I place my hand on his knee. "You don't have to talk anymore."

"How hungry you must be." Pani Weinberg's voice emerges strained. "I'll bring you something." She leaves the room.

Sara has slid down from Rena's lap and plays on the rug with her blocks, clacking them together and babbling to herself. Rena sits, face somber, watching Sara play.

Slowly Leon gets up and crosses the room, crouches on the rug. "What a big girl you are now, aren't you?"

Sara blinks up at him but doesn't cry.

"Can I play too?" Leon places one block on top of another.

I stand, barely noticing the ache in my knees. "I'll get you something warm and dry to put on."

Leon looks up, uncertainty in his eyes. "How long can I stay?"

I swallow. "You will stay for as long as you need."

I leave the sitting room. In the almost darkness of the bedroom, I open the armoire, skim my fingers past the neat row of dresses, skirts, and blouses, reach for the shirt hanging in the back. I undo the buttons and replace the hanger, fold the shirt over my arm. Save for his robe, it's the last piece of Ryszard's clothing that hasn't been sold or made over into a garment for one of us. The shirt will swim on Leon's frame, but it will do until his own clothes are clean and dry. I pull out Ryszard's quilted robe.

I still. My throat constricts. My legs give out. I lower myself to the floor, clutching the robe. Head bent, I press my cheek into the soft, worn fabric from which my husband's scent has long since faded.

A rending overtakes my chest, my breath lost in the swift severing. I muffle my jagged gasp in the folds of cloth.

But why would they do this? How long ago I asked the question.

Because there comes a point when it becomes impossible to do nothing and justify one's existence as a human being.

Janek. The man who wore the uniform of the complicit even as he defied what he was meant to enforce. Risking himself to preserve others. Bearing the weight of all he had witnessed, the guilt of all he had failed to do.

Telling me of regrets, of speaking what matters, of words left unsaid.

If you were willing to let me love you . . .

I didn't let him finish. I wanted him to stop because I was afraid of how his words would unravel me.

"Dear God . . ." I whisper, my voice stifled by the fabric.

I want to summon a prayer, but words fail to form. Every part of me is spent and at the same time screaming. I must not break. To break is a luxury and my life holds no room for luxuries. For the people in this flat, I need to be strong.

A warm hand settles on my head. I turn.

Pani Weinberg strokes my hair with roughened fingers, as if sensing my need for comfort. It's a mother's touch, and I lean into it. She makes no attempt to speak, and I am glad of it, for I am empty of words.

In the stillness and the sifting of her fingers through the strands of my hair, my breathing evens and a semblance of calm returns. "Is Leon all right?"

"When I brought his supper, I found him asleep on the rug." Her face softens. "Poor boy. What a time he's had."

"I'll make up a pallet on the floor. He can stay in here during the day." I don't ask Pani Weinberg whether Leon should stay with us. He will stay.

I rise, the garments in my arms. It's past time for bed and the inevitability of another day will soon be upon us.

Before leaving the room, I pause. Shadows deepen the lines in Pani Weinberg's face, the sunken pouches of skin beneath her eyes, the iron-gray wisps escaping her upswept hair.

"Thank you," I say softly.

"HaShem will give you strength." Her voice is firm, as if she accepts the truth behind her words without question. "We are in His hands, you and I. And this man, Janek, he is too. Yes." She nods. "We are all of us in His hands."

"If I knew what happened to him . . ." I whisper. "I have to know."

Even if I learn the worst, I can bear it better than the unknown.

When Ryszard was in Sachsenhausen, I thought the same, desperate, naïve. I'm still desperate but no longer naïve. There was much I did not know then, about how it's possible to lose a part of oneself and still keep breathing. But I understand now.

There is much that is possible.

CHAPTER TWENTY-SEVEN

Hania
December 7, 1943

STARS BLANKET THE SKY above Płaszów.

They are the same color as the searchlights that sweep across our rows during roll call, only smaller. Brighter. Specks of purest light, as if someone scattered bits of glass across black velvet.

Frost gathers in the air, exhaled with our breath as Romek and I stand outside my barracks, my head tucked under his chin, the warmth of his arms around me.

Love, like everything that gives one a reason to live, is forbidden in Płaszów. Couples caught sharing intimacy, or even holding hands, are punished by execution. But we have lived among death for months. We have watched people lose their lives for the smallest infraction; watched others die for no reason at all. The future consists of surviving from one minute to the next, and we take chances because life itself has become a chance. We ache for a reprieve from hunger and exhaustion, for the comfort of holding and being held. They strengthen us like food, these moments together beneath the stars, so we give into the longing, risking in this when we're careful in so many other ways.

"They can't take the sky from us." My voice is hushed. "The stars shine for us too."

"They shine for you." His lips brush the side of my forehead. "See that one." He points to one of the pinpricks of light. "It's shining just for you. That's why it's the brightest."

"Why?"

"Because you're the brightest. You will always be my brightest star."

His words reach into my heart and settle there. They are beautiful, like the stars, in the midst of so much that is ugly.

His arms fall from my waist as he reaches into his pocket. "Give me your hand."

"What?"

"Come on. Give me your hand." He places something round and cool in the center of my palm.

A silver band glistens in the light. My breath catches.

"Szymon made it for me at the metal factory from an old spoon. I wish it were something better."

"No, it's beautiful."

"Let's see if it fits." He takes my hand, holding it in his as he slips the ring onto my finger. It's too big, but I don't care. To me, it is a treasure.

He stands facing me, my hand in his, his eyes on mine. "Perhaps these are words that should be kept for better times, perhaps it's wrong of me to say them now, but they are the truest words I know." He swallows. "I love you, Hania Silberman. I want to share a life with you, to have a family together, to give you a home. So much I want these things."

I reach up and trail my fingers across his cheek, meeting rough stubble and a jagged scar where a guard hit him in the jaw with the handle of a whip, the sharpness of his bones and the warmth of his skin.

He smiles at me, a fragment of his old smile. So much of who we are now is broken fragments.

But I hold the tenderness in his eyes close, for it is still the same.

"I love you too." My words are a whisper of breath. I've never said it to a man and meant it in this way before. Perhaps I should not do so now. But there's no promise of better times, no certainty we will again see a future that resembles the past we once knew.

If we are to love, it must be as we live. By moments.

He gently tucks a wisp of hair behind my ear, the back of his knuckles lingering against my cheek. Our gazes hold, a wordless question in his.

I nod, my breath shuddering a little, my heart beating fast.

Then his lips brush mine. Our first kiss, my first ever, and it is tender and warm and so very right.

Footsteps crunch, coming around the side of the barracks where we stand.

We start, putting distance between us.

"It's only me." It's a relief to hear Szymon's voice out of the darkness. He makes our few moments alone possible, keeping watch for us, standing near enough he can warn us of a passing guard. "Time to go, Romek. They'll be closing the gate soon." Szymon pauses, looks between the two of us. "Well, did you give it to her?"

Romek nods, the corners of his mouth climbing slightly upward.

I hold my hand in front of me, admiring the ring. "You made this, Szymon?"

"It's just part of an old spoon. It doesn't look very good."

"It's a beautiful gift."

Szymon scuffs his shoe in the snow, a trace of a grin at his lips. "You'd best keep it out of sight."

"I will." My eyes meet Romek's. "Good night."

"Good night, dearest Hania." He squeezes my hand, rubbing his thumb against the ring for an instant before letting go.

I turn to Szymon. "Thank you for keeping watch for us."

He nods. Turns, about to follow Romek, then pauses. "I'm happy for you, Hania." He shifts, one hand in his pocket, ducking his head before his eyes find mine. "Romek and you, what's between you . . . it's a good thing."

The words make me want to smile and cry both at once, perhaps because of how strange it is to feel anything apart from emptiness. Instead I clasp him in a quick, fierce hug, unable to find the words to say how much his mean to me.

The two men walk away, steps quick, down the barracks-lined road toward the men's compound. I stand against the side of the barracks, my ring tucked in my palm, watching their figures fade into the night.

• • •

December 10, 1943

I carry the ring in my hem, a pebble of weight. While standing on the Appell-platz in the hours before dawn, wind stabbing through my coat, I remember it. Bent over endless brushes and fasteners, I think of it. The rest of the time I am in Płaszów, my stomach just as empty, my body just as cold, but in those brief minutes each day, I am somewhere else, thinking of the man I love, wondering if we will see each other later. There's a new sweetness to our moments together. Now we never part without whispered words of love and gentle kisses. At night I slip the ring from my hem and curl my fingers around it, smoothing my fingertip along the small circle, falling asleep with it tucked in my palm.

Adela smiles when she notices. I showed her the ring as we huddled together in our bunk. "Now we'll be sisters," she whispered.

Somehow Adela has not given up. She still relies on me, but there's a new maturity in her, as if she reached a point so low she had to become stronger or else shatter. Our wounds are healing with the aid of the ointment a nurse gave me at the infirmary, but we couldn't sit for over a month because of the bruises and lacerations. Our new foreman drives us without mercy, likely fearing the same fate as his predecessor, but said nothing when we worked standing at our tables for weeks.

Adela and I sit on our bunk, eating our ration of bread and chatting with Genia and Pola. Both girls helped tend our wounds in the days following the beating, and because of their care our cuts didn't become badly infected. To thank them, I gave them some of the jam in Zosia's last parcel. I don't risk saving food for long, for fear it will be stolen, so we shared the small jar between us, savoring each spoonful.

"I have news." Pola's eyes spark as if she has a secret.

"Well?" Genia pops a piece of bread in her mouth as she crouches beside our bunk. "Are you going to tell us?"

Pola takes a bite and chews slowly before answering. "Have any of you heard of the *Deutsche Emailwarenfabrik*?"

"The enamelware factory on Lipowa Street?" I dab a stray crumb from my skirt with my thumb.

"Sure, I've heard of it," Genia says. "There's a subcamp there now, right?"

Pola nods. Then softly, she says, "I'm to go there. My tata got me on the list."

I stare at her. "What list?"

"The list of workers being sent to Emalia. My tata knows the OD man who does the paperwork when people are transferred. Tata had to bribe him, but we're both on the list."

Adela's eyes widen. "You're to leave Płaszów?"

"In a few days." Pola glances down at her hands, almost as if she's ashamed to tell us. "People say it's a good place. They say it's—"

"I know," Genia says, voice a little hard. "They say it's a refuge."

"A chance," Pola whispers.

We look at each other—four girls huddling together—and for a moment, no one speaks.

A chance.

All of us deserve a chance.

"That's good, Pola," I say. "I'm glad for you."

Genia draws a breath. "Yes. We're happy for you. Really."

Romek wends through the crowded barracks, his lean frame standing out in the room of women.

"Your boyfriend's here, Hania," Genia teases.

I put the rest of my bread into my pocket and rise to greet him. "I didn't expect to see you tonight."

Romek meets my eyes, grief raw on his face.

I still. The smile withers on my lips.

I've stood in this place before. Is it any wonder a sure and sudden knowing crashes over me?

"Hania—"

"Where's Szymon?" The question rasps from my throat.

"Hania, I . . . he . . ." He stops, shakes his head.

I press my eyes tight, as if truth can be shut out as easily as light.

On our last holiday before the war, Tata and Mama took us to the seaside. We swam in the surf, waves crashing in our ears, the taste of salt on our lips. Szymon waded to his waist in the spray and stood, face lifted to the sky, arms outstretched, wind licking his hair. He'd turned to me and grinned so wide his eyes crinkled.

It's a grand thing to be alive, isn't it?

His words echo through the corridors of the past.

My little brother.

Szymon.

A cry traps inside my chest. I don't need to release it for its force to shake every part of me.

I open my eyes. Romek stands a pace away, hands fisted at his sides. The others sit on the bunk, silent.

"How?" The effort it takes to force the single word leaves me spent.

Romek shakes his head.

"Tell me." I don't recognize my voice, so hard it is.

"The foreman sent him on an errand to another part of the camp. Szymon was coming back when Göth rode up behind him on his horse. Szymon didn't see him, so he didn't move to the side of the road and take off his cap. Göth drew his pistol." Romek's throat jerks as he swallows. "One of the men in my barracks told me. He saw it happen."

I shake my head. Back and forth, back and forth.

Romek pulls me into his arms.

Tears squeeze past the corners of my eyes, sliding in hot trails down my cheeks, my throat swelling, my sobs noiseless.

Romek crushes me against his chest, whispering against my hair. A moment passes before I realize the Hebrew words are from the Twenty-Third Psalm, often recited at funerals along with Kaddish.

Romek's voice washes over me. There are not ten men to say the Mourner's Kaddish and there will be no grave to place a stone upon. Szymon's body has been disposed of as all bodies are in Płaszów, thrown into a ditch alongside the corpses of those long dead.

Through these words, Romek honors my brother, offering the only service he can perform. ". . . *veh-shahv-tee beh-vayt* ADONAI *leh-oh-rehch yah-mim.*"

He finishes but doesn't step away, as if he senses his touch is all that keeps the numbness from overtaking me completely.

My eyes slide shut. I draw in jagged breaths. Somehow I am still breathing. Somehow I am alive. But how I do not understand.

How can a heart keep beating after it has turned to dust?

CHAPTER TWENTY-EIGHT

Hania
August 6, 1944

BENEATH A SEARING SKY, we stand on the Appellplatz. Fear flicks through our ranks, sharp like the tail of an SS man's whip. The morning count should have ended hours ago. But the command dismissing us doesn't come.

Instead the SS stride slowly along the rows of women. Every so often, they pull someone out of line. Sometimes they select a whole row. Those taken out of line join the column standing in fives facing the road leading to the camp gate. The kommandant and other high-ranking SS oversee the proceedings from tables set up at one end of the broad expanse.

Sun beats down on my head. Adela stands beside me, cheeks flushed and glistening.

What is the selection for this time? A transport?

The camp is full to the point of bursting. Though there are far more barracks than when we first arrived, ours is crowded with more women than ever. Transports come in, others go out, as if the camp is Kraków's Main Station. Only the destination rests in the hands of the SS, not the passengers.

Or is the selection for something else? I swallow, throat parched. Are those chosen intended for the hill?

Three rows ahead of where Adela and I stand, two SS *Aufseherinnen* advance down the line. Since Płaszów's designation changed from a labor camp to an official concentration camp at the beginning of the year, female SS guards have been added to the staff. One might expect women to be less harsh, but there's no softness in these Aufseherinnen. Theirs is a special kind of cruelty, as if the mere fact that we're women too gives them a greater reason to torment us.

Their boot falls pause in front of a woman—an instant's deliberation, then an Aufseherin pulls her out of line. To do this, the guards don't touch the prisoners. Instead they use small canes, catching the back of the woman's neck with the curved end and jerking her forward.

As I do each time there's a selection, I fix my mind on a single purpose. If Adela is selected, I will go with her, no matter what. Even if she's chosen for the hill, I will not let Romek's sister face her last moments alone.

But if I'm chosen, Adela will have no one. Regulations are stricter since Płaszów became a concentration camp, and it's not as easy for men and women to meet. Romek comes to our barracks whenever he can, but we see him less and less these days.

Adela needs me. Without me, who will take care of her? Women with a mama, sister, or daughter take care of each other. Those with no one take care of themselves. Survival requires all one's strength, and though a woman may show kindness to a newcomer or stranger, she cannot bear the burden of their life and hers too.

The Aufseherinnen select the entire row ahead of ours, yanking out each woman. I know many of these women. They're from our barracks. Their faces are familiar, their voices thrum around us in the evenings, their breathing fills my ears as I lie on the bunk. Some I know only by sight, others I've exchanged conversation with, a few were among the women with whom I shared Zosia's soap. Word of Szymon's death had spread through the barracks, and though no one voiced their sympathy, I read sorrowful understanding as their eyes met mine in the days that followed.

How many empty places will there be in our block tonight? Where will the women be who used to fill them?

The Aufseherinnen start down our rank. I pull my shoulders back, stand tall and straight, glancing out of the corner of my eye at Adela. Red blotches her cheeks from the heat, a sunburn peeling on her nose. But she stands erect, shoulders rigid, not staring directly at the Aufseherinnen or lowering her eyes but keeping her gaze straight ahead.

One of the Aufseherin taps her cane against her thigh as she walks. She's young, maybe a few years older than me, elegant in her tailored jacket and skirt, her carefully coiffed hair golden in the sun. She strolls along our row, accompanied by the other Aufseherin, fixing her eyes on each face for a second or two before making her decision.

Sweat slides down my spine.

Please. Don't take Adela from me.

I repeat my clumsy prayer again and again.

The blond SS woman wraps her cane around the neck of the woman standing two places away from Adela. She jerks the cane and the woman steps forward. The other Aufseherin gestures with her thumb in the direction of the growing column and the woman moves toward it.

The pair of Aufseherinnen continue, passing the next woman by.

The blond SS woman stares at Adela with eyes of ice.

She raises her cane, curls it around Adela's neck.

I stop breathing.

The Aufseherin yanks the cane, pulling Adela out of line. Adele's eyes find mine, hers full of panic. The other Aufseherin gestures with her thumb. Adela hesitates, looking back at me.

A crack as the blond SS woman hits Adela across the shoulders with the cane. "Move, you miserable hund."

Adela stumbles toward the column.

The Aufseherinnen stop in front of me.

Instead of making my face blank, I lift my chin and stare directly at her. Somehow I must be selected too. Pleading will have no effect. Perhaps angering her will.

Her gaze flickers as if she cannot believe someone as pathetic as me would dare look her in the face. We stare each other, and for the first time, I let defiance blaze from my eyes.

She raises her cane, dragging me forward with such force I nearly trip. I barely notice the pain in my neck or the other Aufseherin gesturing for me to join the line. I walk toward Adela with quick steps, heart thudding against my breastbone, afraid the blond SS woman will realize I angered her on purpose and call me back.

Opposite us, ranks of men carpet the Appellplatz. I scan their figures as I hurry toward the end of the column. How can I hope to find one face among thousands? Still I search for Romek. One glimpse of him, to catch his gaze for an instant's goodbye.

But the men staring back at me are strangers.

The rank of five where Adela stands is already full, so I take my place in the row behind her. Adela glances over her shoulder. Relief shows on her flushed, sunburned face. I give her a little nod before she faces forward again.

I did what I'd set out to do. Whatever comes, Romek's sister will not face it alone. It's a promise I make to myself as much as to him—to take care of Adela.

My head throbs from the heat. My dress sticks to my clammy skin.

"What will happen to us?" the woman next to me whispers, voice cracking from fear or the heat or both. Her eyes are glazed, her lips blistered and peeling. "What will happen to us?" she repeats.

Is she asking me or talking to herself?

I look away, fixing my eyes ahead, beyond the barbed-wire fences and rows of wooden barracks. Though I do not voice the question, it echoes as I squint against the sun's glare, staring into the vast blue of the sky.

What will happen to us?
I do not have an answer.

We pass through the gates of Płaszów, hundreds of women ahead of us, hundreds—if not thousands—more behind us. I can scarcely believe we're leaving the place that to us has become a cemetery of the living as well as the dead. But to where? And for what?

Flanked by guards, we march to the railroad tracks. My head pounds from thirst. My hollow stomach aches. For hours, we stood in the sweltering heat. It must be past noon, but we didn't receive our portion of soup or food or water of any kind. Of course the SS wouldn't be so wasteful as to allot rations to prisoners being sent away.

A string of rust-brown railcars waits on the tracks, their doors open mouths.

Cattle cars. Built to transport livestock or crates of vegetables or lumber.

I stare at the cars. We have long been reduced to cargo.

"Halt." The SS move along our rows, counting our heads, checking clipboards. We stand waiting while they count and recount us. Sweat trickles down my forehead. I run my tongue across my lips, tasting salt. Like tears. An SS officer takes out a handkerchief and wipes his brow.

Time drags. Finally the loading begins. Guards swarm, herding those ahead of us into the cars at one end.

"Schnell! Schnell!"

Frantic women clamber inside as the guards goad them with whips and rifle butts. An SS officer standing to one side glances at his watch and frowns, as if there's some schedule that must be kept.

Once a car is full, the guards bolt the door and move on to the next. There must be over thirty railcars attached to the train. The voices of the SS lacerate the air. A woman screams. The sun punishes my head. I swallow, trying to work up enough saliva to moisten my throat, but my mouth is completely dry. My mind drifts.

Suddenly everyone around us breaks rank and surges toward one of the cars, driven by the guards. A whip lands on my shoulder, a swift burning, snapping me from my daze.

I grab Adela's hand, so we aren't separated as we're swept up in the fray of women flooding toward the car.

I let go long enough to scramble up the single step. I turn, pull her up after me. Breathless, I pause, standing at the mouth of the car, staring out at the people still below. The winding column seems to stretch without end. How many women are left in the camp?

The women coming up after us force us away from the entrance. Holding hands, Adela and I wend our way through the car. In the semidarkness, I search for a place for us to stand next to a wall, but others already line the perimeter. More and more women crowd in, forcing us to press closer together to make space for them.

Why haven't the guards shut the door? Can't they see this car is full? Still, women keep pushing their way inside. I have to stand on tiptoe to glimpse the entrance of the car above the heads of the women around me.

We'll be crushed if they continue to force women inside. I clutch Adela's hand, dragging in a breath. Already the air is smothering.

The door slides shut with a slam. Darkness closes around us. The bolt on the outside rams into place. Somewhere in the car a woman cries out. I can barely turn around, the bodies of strangers pressing around me. Panic claws my throat. I squeeze my eyes tight.

God is our refuge and strength, a very present help in trouble. Therefore we will not fear, though the earth do change, and though the mountains be moved into the heart of the seas . . .

The words of the familiar psalm run through my mind, becoming a prayer.

Where are You, ADONAI?

Light trickles through cracks in the wooden slats. The pandemonium outside reverberates through the walls. SS shouting. Women screaming.

Heat presses down, a suffocating hand. The scents of sweat and filth and terror, the last sharpest of all, overpower every breath. I pant for air.

How many hours pass inside the car? Two? Three? More?

A whistle pierces the air. The train shudders. Lurches, throwing us to one side, against each other as the wheels grind forward.

Someone coughs. A woman moans. No one speaks, our silence as heavy and airless as the breaths we draw into our lungs. Adela leans against me, her body a brittle leaf against mine. The train gathers speed, flashes of light and shadow passing before me as the rhythm of wheels against tracks becomes one with my pulse.

CHAPTER TWENTY-NINE

Hania
August 6, 1944

THE TRAIN HURTLES INTO the night.

Darkness thickens the air, coats the figures surrounding me. Adela faces me, the whites of her eyes shining out of the shadows. The stench of urine and feces from the bucket in the corner stifles the atmosphere. Time becomes a void of rattling wheels, pressing bodies, overpowering thirst, and the gray emptiness of the unknown.

Twice the train veered to one side, then jolted to a halt, the rushing clatter that trembled through the car minutes later telling us we'd stopped to let another train pass. An indefinite stretch of time passed before our train resumed its journey.

As the hours wear on, some of the women voice questions, seeking answers no one can give. Some are optimistic, saying they wouldn't go to the trouble of transporting us only to finish us off once we arrive at our destination. If they intend to kill us, they could have done it in Płaszów. Perhaps, they reason, the progress of the Allies means Płaszów is being liquidated and its inmates moved to other camps. Others predict we're being taken to be gassed or shot in a pit, spreading fear that infects those around them. Most of the women remain silent.

I've long determined the uselessness of predicting anything the Nazis do. But I cannot stop the question from merging with the rhythm of the train.

Life or death? Life or death?

I reach down and lift my skirt with my other hand. My fingers brush the coin-sized lump in my hem. Romek's ring. I work it through the slit in my hem and curl my sweaty fingers around the metal circle. Remembering Romek's face as he slid it onto my finger, the tenderness in his eyes.

I love you, Hania Silberman.

I must believe liberation will come and we will find our way to one another again. I must keep this belief before me and hold it so tight it gives me strength to survive whatever awaits us.

For Romek. For Adela. For Rena.

A woman coughs, deep and hacking. Liquid pings against tin. Someone must be using the bucket. The odor of urine sharpens, nauseating the airless car.

My body rocks with the motion of the train, my legs wooden from hours of standing. My eyes slide shut, my body lulled toward the haze of sleep.

Blades of light stab my eyelids. I jolt, blinking.

The train slows. Steam hisses. A swath of white light passes over our faces, illuminating the huddled forms of the women around me.

"What's happening? Where are we? What do you see?"

"We're passing under a gate," calls a girl from the direction of the high-set window. "Searchlights. I see searchlights. Barbed wire. It must be a camp."

Brakes screech. The train lurches.

My breath shudders.

Voices. Yelling. Barking dogs.

Fear. The sounds are fear.

Adela shivers, teeth clattering as if she's cold. I'm still clutching the ring in my fist, the metal band embedding itself into my palm. I quickly slip the ring back into my hem.

The bolt on our car clanks. The door crashes open. Light dazzles my eyes.

"Out, out, out!"

Women rush out of the car, stumbling down the step.

I clutch Adela's hand, the seething crowd threatening to tear us apart.

"*Schneller*, schneller, schneller!"

My legs wobble after hours of standing. I trip down the step, the soles of my feet stinging as I land.

"Move. Get in line," someone shouts behind me.

I whirl around.

A man in a striped uniform and cap grips a truncheon, his eyes sunken pits in an emaciated face. "I don't want to hit you," he whispers.

In the next second, Adela clambers out of the car, half falling, half landing. I grab her hand and pull her onward.

Outlines of SS officers stand in the bright paleness of searchlights. Dogs strain at their leashes. Women pour from the cars, herded by men in striped clothing. Someone screams, hysterical.

We reach the end of the column. The ranks move forward.

Searchlights swivel from the watchtower crowning the immense redbrick gatehouse behind us under which the train passed. Barbed-wire fences glisten gray in the blend of light and darkness. Watchtowers rise in silhouette. In the distance, rows of narrow buildings stretch without end.

But it is the sky—the starkness of that terrible sky—that rivets my gaze. Smoke belches from a brick chimney, thick plumes billowing into the night.

The line rushes forward—fast, fast, fast. I need to find out what's happening to the people ahead of us, so I am not taken by surprise, so I can prepare us. We draw closer. I crane my neck, Adela's hand clinging to mine.

SS officers stand at the head of the line, dividing the women, separating them into groups. Some to the left, others to the right.

Selection.

We've scarcely arrived and already they are selecting us. My empty stomach convulses.

The stories the Hungarian women transported to Płaszów told of a camp near the town of Oświęcim return to my mind. *Some they let live, others . . . straight to the gas.*

The dividing taking place at the front of the line soaks me with dread.

Which side is for life? The left or the right?

We're almost there. I meet Adela's eyes, shining with terror in her sunburned face. Does she understand what happens at the front of the line? Do I?

"There are SS at the head of the line. I'm not sure, but it looks like they're selecting people."

"For work?"

I leave her question unanswered. "Pull your shoulders back and stand tall. Listen to me, Adela. You must look strong. Do you understand?"

"What if they separate us?" Adela's voice breaks.

I draw a shaky breath. "Go ahead of me. Whichever way you're sent, I'll follow you. All right? No matter what, I'll follow you."

She nods. Only one row stands between us and the SS.

Shouts and cries and frenzied dogs converge into a single sound. The cadre of SS blur.

One stands in the center—an officer in a gray uniform and black-brimmed cap. In his white-gloved hand, he holds a conductor's baton.

A woman stops in front of him.

A pause—two seconds, no more.

He gestures with the baton.

Left.

Another woman.

Right.

A third woman stands before the officer.

"How old are you?" It's almost polite, his tone. Pleasant. He even smiles a little, his elegant, uniformed figure silhouetted in a glare of white light.

"Fifty-two, sir," the woman answers in a hesitant voice.

The baton motions left.

Our row stands in front of the officer with the baton.

Adela's fingers slide from mine. She steps forward, shoulders straight, chin tipped slightly upward. Pressure builds in my chest, trapped there with my breath.

The officer's eyes fix on Adela. Time stills.

The baton points, sending Adela to the right.

She turns, looks back at me, her slight frame caught in the haze of searchlights.

Is this the moment that separates us?

Adela moves away.

I step up to the officer with the baton. Somehow I stand tall, raise my chin.

Two seconds. No more.

Right.

I walk toward the right, toward Adela. I draw a ragged breath. The air carries a strange sweetness that burns acrid in my throat. Reaching the women standing in ranks to the right, I step into the last place in the row where Adela is, two others between us.

Adela catches sight of me, relief a flicker in her dull eyes.

Was it only this morning I stood on the Appellplatz in Płaszów? The hours seem to expand until they bear the weight of years. Twice in one day we've managed to stay together. It's a small victory, but no pride rises inside me. The SS women with their canes or the officer with the baton could have separated us with a single gesture. How can there be victory when one's fate is sealed by a second's deliberation?

The column grows. One of the men in striped uniforms hurries beside our ranks. Somehow I must find out what this place is. This urgency overpowers my usual resolve to be invisible. How can I reckon with our surroundings if I don't know where we are?

"Please, a moment," I call out softly in Polish as he passes, half expecting him not to understand or to continue without pausing.

He stops but doesn't look at me.

"Can you tell me where we are?"

"Birkenau." His voice is hollow.

"Where?"

"It's part of Auschwitz."

Auschwitz.

"What's happening here?"

"You see the smoke? It's the crematoriums. They never stop burning." His gaze flashes up, his gaunt face hard.

The air tastes charred when I draw it in.

"Want to know why it smells like this? It's because of the ashes. Don't worry, you won't smell it long. One of these days, you'll go into the chimneys too. You breathe ashes until you become ashes. Sooner or later, it will happen to you. Sooner or later, it will happen to all of us."

CHAPTER THIRTY

Zosia
August 30, 1944

THROUGHOUT THE SUMMER OF 1944, a breathless tension hangs in the air, thick and cloying as the heat. Events long awaited burst one after the other, exploding fireworks lighting up the black skies of occupied Europe. Though the *Krakauer Zeitung* and other newspapers sanctioned by the occupiers never fail in their proclamations of ultimate German victory, they cannot keep the truth from reaching us. Even in their propaganda, one can read between the lines. We know the real meaning of phrases like "straightening out the lines" and "strategic withdrawal."

Through the underground press, we follow the progress of the Allies. The momentous day in June, when the news that the Allies had landed in Normandy filtered through the city, Tadeusz opened a bottle of vodka and the four of us clinked glasses in the duty room, toasting the Allies and the liberation of Europe. The Red Army has broken through German defenses and is advancing across Poland. And on the first day of August, the *Armia Krajowa*—the army of the Polish underground—rose up in Warsaw.

The hearts of each of us in the pharmacy were with the valiant men and women who'd joined the fight to free the city from occupation. But within days, heavily reinforced German troops surged in to crush the revolt. Nearly a month later, the battle for Warsaw rages on. We no longer wait for news of victory, only for word the bitter struggle has reached its end.

I step out of the pharmacy into the summer heat. Barbed wire and a wall no longer demarcate the former ghetto, and new occupants inhabit the buildings. The pharmacy functions much as it did before the spring of 1941, serving the residents of Podgórze, though the shortages of occupation are more marked than ever.

Only two fragments of the wall still stand. The rest has been torn down. No one can be seen in the streets wearing an armband with a blue star. They too are gone.

There's no gate with navy-uniformed police standing guard, asking for my pass, searching my bags. Now we come and go freely. I cross the Third Bridge, leaving Podgórze behind.

Propaganda drones from a loudspeaker on a street corner. A German policeman stops a woman and demands her papers. The bleak weariness of war has left its mark on every face, from old men to the smallest children. Everyone walks quickly and avoids the gazes of strangers, grips handbags and parcels close. Thieves roam the streets, especially after dark, despite the curfew.

On an advertising pillar, a notice with the heading ANNOUNCEMENT stands out among sun-bleached advertisements and faded notices in German and Polish. The paper is still crisp, the ink not yet smudged by weather and time. Two columns of black type list the names and crimes of those sentenced to death in the Kraków District, the names of the executed a warning to anyone contemplating similar deeds.

I should continue on. But, as I always do, I pause, running my gaze along the columns.

**Płocki, Stanisław, from Dębica,
participation in a forbidden organization.**

**Leśniak, Michał, from Kraków,
unauthorized possession of a weapon.**

**Majewska, Danuta, from Pilzno,
harboring a Jew.**

I scan the remainder of the list, wearily relieved none of the names are familiar. They are strangers, the people on this list, and so their names mean nothing to me, yet I know for what they died. Perhaps they too had once stopped to read the names of strangers on a list. I wonder if it was worth it to them, what they had done. I wonder if they would have done it still if they had known.

I move away. I should stop reading the lists. Janek's name hasn't appeared on a single one. That means nothing, of course. Many are executed without their names being published. Still, despite what I tell myself, I won't stop searching.

Several minutes later, I reach my flat and climb the stairs. Standing in front of my door, I withdraw the key from my handbag. Tadeusz's news presses against my throat like the tip of a blade.

I know nothing for certain. There's no need to burden them with vague fears. Already, they carry so much.

I twist the key in the lock and open the door. The deeper tones of a man's voice from the sitting room combines with the scent of cigarette smoke and hair tonic. Wariness heightens my senses.

Not today.

I smooth strands of hair behind my ears, away from my sweaty cheeks, and enter the sitting room.

Pan Burzyński occupies the armchair. Rena sits stiffly on the sofa, hands in her lap. Sara plays on the rug with her doll. Leon is nowhere in sight.

"Zosia, you're back." Rena's smile wavers at the edges.

Pan Burzyński rises from the armchair. "Good day, Pani Lewandowska."

I nod. "Pan Burzyński."

"I just dropped by to bring you some tomatoes. I thought you all might enjoy them."

I force a polite smile, sorely tempted to make him aware, in no uncertain terms, how unwelcome we find his presence. With Leon in hiding and Rena alone during the day, it's far too dangerous for Pan Burzyński's visits, the frequency of which has become disconcerting, to continue.

I need to put a stop to it but in such a way that he doesn't become either angry or suspicious. "That's very kind, but I'm afraid we can't continue accepting your gifts. As we have no way of repaying you, it doesn't seem right. You understand, I'm sure."

Pan Burzyński is not a particularly large man—I'm only a few centimeters shorter than he is—but something about his presence makes the room small and oppressive. "Surely there can be no impropriety in accepting a few trifles. These are difficult times. I seek only to share with my friends. Especially as *Panna* Górska has been kind enough to let me bore her with my conversation during your absence."

Rena returns his smile faintly.

A noise—muffled—comes from somewhere in the flat.

Ice slicks my veins.

Leon?

"Ah-ah-ah, two little kittens, ah-ah-ah." Sara rocks her doll, the lullaby high and off-key.

I smile at her, then turn back to Pan Burzyński.

His expression remains the same, open, eager.

"You're right, of course. Please forgive me. You're very kind."

"No need to apologize. You have your pride, I understand. And now I should be going." He turns to Rena. "Goodbye, Panna Górska. Tell your mama I was sorry to have missed her."

She rises. "Thank you for coming. And for the tomatoes."

"Well." He smiles briefly. "I hope you enjoy them."

"I'll show you out," I hasten to say.

"Please don't trouble yourself." He nods. "Good day to you both."

The tread of his footsteps recedes. The door shuts.

I stand unmoving, Sara's singing the only sound. My head throbs in time with my pulse.

"Leon?"

"In the armoire." Rena's voice is drained. It's past time to bleach her hair again. She covers her hair with a kerchief before leaving the house when her dark roots begin to show, but Pan Burzyński's visit was likely unexpected. She wears no lipstick, her face pale without cosmetics. Somehow she looks both older and younger than she really is.

"How long was he here this time?"

"About twenty minutes before you came. I didn't invite him in. I never invite him in, but somehow, he always . . . he told me he'd put the tomatoes in the kitchen for me, and what was I to do?" Her words spill out, a little desperate. "Why does he keep coming here? Do you think he suspects?"

"What reason could he have?" Though, truly, I am not sure. "I think he's fond of your company and that is why he comes."

"The way he speaks to me sometimes . . ."

My stomach coils. "What does he say?"

"Nothing, really. Just that I am very pretty, and he finds me easy to talk to." She glances away. "It's fine. It doesn't bother me, what he says."

But it does and it should, and suddenly, I'm angry. At Pan Burzyński, at myself, but mostly at the life we're forced to lead. Before the war, when we'd nothing to fear from our neighbors and Jews did not have to become invisible to stay alive, I'd confront Pan Burzyński without a second thought. After I finished with him, he'd never come near Rena again.

I still might.

"I won't have him bothering you like this. I'll talk to him. Tell him exactly what I think about men who chase after young girls."

Rena's eyes widen. "No. You mustn't. It will only make him angry. It's best if we go on as we are." She raises her chin. "I should see to Leon." She moves past me and goes into the bedroom.

No matter what Rena says, I won't dismiss it that easily.

Later, while Pani Weinberg puts Sara to bed, I sit at the table, bent over the household accounts. I sigh, rubbing a hand across my blurry eyes. The news from Płaszów invades my mind, making it difficult to concentrate on what I'll need to sell to buy enough coal to keep us from freezing this winter.

"What is it?"

I look up. I didn't hear Pani Weinberg come in. "I'm just tired." I close the notebook. "I should go to bed."

Pani Weinberg pulls out a chair and sits, studying me with a look of concern. "Did something happen today? Have you had some news?"

I hesitate. I should say I'm worried about money, which is true, or Pan Burzyński, which is also true.

"You have, haven't you?" Something changes in Pani Weinberg's face, an opening into the burden she carries but of which she never speaks. It's how we've learned to live, three women bearing our individual burdens and never speaking of their weight. Theirs are greater, far greater, than mine, and never am I more aware of this than now, with Pani Weinberg searching my eyes as if she could read in them the answers she seeks . . . and fears.

If it were my sister and brother, my children, I would want to be told. No matter its cost to me.

Rena comes into the kitchen. She looks between us. "Is something the matter?"

I draw a breath. "I heard something today."

"What?" Rena's voice holds the same apprehension as Pani Weinberg's.

"Magister Pankiewicz told me there have been transports from Płaszów."

"Transports?" Pani Weinberg breathes. "What sort of transports? Where do they go?"

"Other camps . . ." I shake my head. "I don't know. It seems plans are being made to close Płaszów. Even the Germans know it's only a matter of time before the Red Army arrives."

The unknown soaks into the silence. Rena wraps her arms around herself. Pani Weinberg glances away, lips pressed tight.

"There are thousands of people in Płaszów," I say, voice quiet. "This doesn't mean they have been sent away."

Pani Weinberg nods. "That is true. But if they are indeed to close the camp, there will be more such transports." The words are fact and she says them as such.

I can offer them no assurances. No words can lessen the fear for the ones who are as precious to them as their own breath.

Romek and Adela. Szymon and Hania.

What becomes of those inside the gates of Płaszów is as beyond our hands as if the whole of Poland stretched between us and them.

• • •

September 7, 1944

A strange silence pervades the flat. I close the door, its soft click amplified in the stillness, and step into the sitting room. Sara plays on the floor with her doll. She looks up as I come in.

"Hello, sweet one." I drop my handbag on the arm of the sofa and bend to scoop her up. "Where's Jadwiga?" It's not like Rena to leave Sara unattended.

"Iga," Sara repeats.

Carrying her, I step into the curtained darkness of the bedroom. Empty. My skin prickles.

"Leon?" I call softly. "It's Zosia. Are you there?"

From the other side of the armoire comes a quiet tapping.

I cross to the armoire and open its door, push aside the skirts and dresses on their hangers revealing Leon hunched inside, knees drawn up to his chin.

He turns his head to look at me but doesn't move from his cramped position.

"Why are you in here? Where's Jadwiga?"

"In the kitchen," he says in a quiet voice. "Is Pan Burzyński gone?"

"Pan Burzyński was here?"

He nods, face sober.

I put Sara down on the bed. "Stay here. Both of you."

As I near the kitchen, muffled sobbing reaches me, a soft and broken echo. I stop in the doorway.

Rena sits at the table, head resting on her arms, shoulders shaking.

I step inside. "Rena," I say softly, using her name, her real one. I place my hand on her back. "Rena."

Rena raises her head, hair in tangles, face streaked with tears.

"What's happened?" I kneel beside her, voice soothing, heart pounding.

She shakes her head. "It's . . ." Another sob wrenches from her. I pull her into my arms.

"Shhh." I hold her close, rubbing her back, even as panic rises in my throat.

She draws away and swipes the back of her hand across her eyes. "I'm sorry."

I search her face. "Did something happen when Pan Burzyński was here?"

She drags in a shuddering breath. "He said he was going to fix the kitchen faucet. Leon hid, but I was so afraid Pan Burzyński would hear something, so I stayed in the kitchen and scoured the pots, trying to make as much noise as I could. He . . . he came up behind me." She clamps a hand over her mouth.

"Did he"—I swallow, throat dry—"hurt you?"

"He put his hands on me. He tried to kiss me." She gulps back a sob. "I pushed him away, told him to leave me alone. He got so angry. He said I'd led him on, that I'd promised him things." Her eyes meet mine, tears wet on her cheeks. "He knows."

Every part of me goes cold. "What are you saying?"

"He said he should have known better, it was just like a Jew to make promises and not keep them."

"That doesn't mean he knows." My voice is strangely calm. "People talk like that all the time. Saying someone is like a Jew is just an insult."

"It wasn't." She shakes her head. "I saw his eyes. He knows."

I will remain calm. I must remain . . .

"What happened then?"

"He stormed out and slammed the door."

"He didn't say anything else?"

"He just left. He didn't even take his tools."

"When?"

"Twenty minutes ago. I don't know exactly. I didn't know what to do. I was going to take the children and go to the pharmacy to find you."

My breath shakes. If Pan Burzyński is turning us in, it won't be long before the police arrive. At any minute, they'll pound up the stairs, break down the door.

Don't think it.

He may not report us. He may have spoken that way simply because he was angry, a spurned man whose pride had been injured. He may know nothing.

Or he may have already gone to the police.

"We need to leave. We'll go to the pharmacy. You'll be safe there."

"What about Pani Weinberg?"

"We'll go to the hospital and fetch her." She should still be there. I'll tell her to come with us and she can make some excuse to leave early. I don't know what will happen once we reach the pharmacy. I just need to get them away from here. I rise. "Come. Quickly. We'll pack a few things."

Rena stands, moving mechanically. I follow her out of the kitchen. In the bedroom, Sara is asleep atop the eiderdown, the armoire shut. I throw open its door. Leon still crouches inside.

"Get out." I bend down, yank my suitcase from beneath the bed. "We have to leave. Don't ask questions, just help Karolina on with her coat. Hurry."

Eyes wide, Leon climbs out of the armoire and scurries from the room.

I grab dresses and skirts off hangers, toss them into the suitcase. Rena pulls a blanket from the foot of the bed, folds it, adds it to the suitcase. I kneel and jerk open the bottom drawer, pull out nappies, clothes, fling them into the open mouth of the suitcase.

"Bring the little tin from the kitchen. The one in the dresser."

Rena rushes away. Leon returns with Sara's coat.

My fingers bump against something at the back of the drawer. I pull them out.

An album and four framed photographs. I stand, clutching the Silbermans' photographs, throw them into the suitcase, close the lid and latch it. Gripping the suitcase, I run into the sitting room.

Rap, rap.

I freeze.

Rap, rap.

I whirl around, nearly colliding with Leon. "Into the bedroom. Now."

Leon disappears, Sara in his arms.

I return to the sitting room. Rena stands, holding the tin, her face white. The pounding grows louder.

"Go into the kitchen." I thrust the suitcase into her hands. "Don't come out."

She hesitates.

"Go."

I wait until she's gone, then approach the door. The thudding of my heart fills my ears.

I open the door.

Pan Burzyński shoves past me. "A word, Pani Lewandowska."

For a second, I'm so stunned it's him and not the police that I can only stare. I follow him into the sitting room. "Pan Burzyński, what a surprise." My voice doesn't even falter. "You're here for your tools, of course. I'll fetch them—"

"Don't." He grabs my upper arm, his fingers digging into my flesh. "I think we can both agree this game has gone on long enough."

"I don't understand." The scent of him, cigarettes and hair tonic and sweat, overwhelms me.

"But I think you do, Pani Lewandowska. I think you understand very well."

His gaze bores into mine.

I stare into his eyes without flinching.

And there it is. The anger on the face of this small, weak man, but also the truth.

"You're hurting me," I say, voice quiet and shaking only a little.

He releases me so quickly I stumble backward. "I'm a decent man, you know. Someone else would have turned you in already. You and your Jews. Oh, yes. You think I don't know about them?" He gives a faint chuckle. "Because I've not attended university as you have, you think I am without intelligence? But let me tell you what I know. I know that Jadwiga is not Agata Górska's daughter, but both are Jews who escaped the ghetto and came to stay with you only a few days after it was liquidated." He pauses, as if waiting for some reaction from me.

I only stare at him.

"How do I know this? Because Jadwiga is in fact the daughter of that Jew, Dr. Silberman, the same Dr. Silberman who used to live on the second floor of this very building."

My chest tightens. "How dare you make accusations about the guests in my home? You have no proof—"

"I have enough. When I first saw her, I admit I thought nothing more than that she was a pretty young woman. But as time went on, I began to notice something curiously familiar about her. Then one day I was passing the Silbermans' flat, and I remembered the doctor's two daughters. Such polite, pretty girls. Unlike you, who never failed to turn up your nose at me." A hard, angry look passes across his face. "I decided to mention the Silbermans to Panna Jadwiga, told her I wondered what had become of them, and though she was calm, I could tell she was afraid. Not to mention it's obvious she's not a natural blond. Rare for a girl so young to dye her hair, don't you think?"

"That proves nothing."

"It's unfortunate Panna Jadwiga was so cold to me this afternoon. Had she been otherwise, I might have kept your secret, despite the personal risk had it become known I'd concealed knowledge of Jews living under Aryan papers."

I take a step toward him, trembling with anger and fear. "You would have taken favors from a girl who is barely more than a child? And you call yourself a decent man?"

His jaw tightens, his nostrils flare.

"Is that what you want? Is that the price for your silence? Because I . . ." I swallow.

"What? Would you offer yourself to me? You, the proud Pani Lewandowska, who never gave me a second glance, who couldn't be bothered to repay my kindness with so much as civility?" He comes toward me.

I stand completely still, heart pounding.

He stares at me, his breathing ragged. "What have these people brought you to? What would you do for them, I wonder?" He reaches up, his thumb skims my cheek.

I don't move, his breath hot against my face. He leans in. I flinch.

His hand falls away. "You wouldn't be worth it."

I release a shuddering breath.

"But I'm willing to consider another arrangement. Ten thousand złotys in exchange for my silence."

"So you're a common szmalcownik, is that it?" The venom in my voice would have shocked me once but not anymore. That's what he is—a black-mailer who'd prey on anyone so long as it lined his pockets.

"No, Pani Lewandowska. I'm a more decent man than you deserve." The way he says it, it's as if he really believes it. That by making this demand, he really is a decent man.

Perhaps, in some demented way, it is a kind of decency. Our lives for ten thousand złotys.

"And if I won't give you the money?" Why do I say this? Maybe because I'm trying to be strong, and to be strong, I can't let myself admit how cornered I am.

"Then you leave me with no choice. I've no doubt the Gestapo would be interested to hear about you and your Jews." The unsettling calm of his voice frightens me more than his anger. "It's your decision."

I'm trapped. From the pleasure on his face, he knows it and is enjoying it. This is about more than money to him. This is about gaining power and exerting it. About reducing me and taking satisfaction in my weakness.

For that, for everything, I despise him.

But if I told him so, he could take back his offer as easily as he extended it. He will always control us, no matter how much money I give him.

We need to leave, but first I have to deal with him. Once he's satisfied he's cornered me, he'll go and we can get away.

"Very well." My words come out quiet, resigned. "But if you expect me to have that much money at hand, I'm afraid I must disappoint you."

"I'll take what you have now. You can have a month to come up with the rest." He sounds as if he's negotiating a business deal.

"How do you expect me to get that kind of money in a month?"

"That's not my concern, now is it?"

"Wait here." I lower my eyes, defeated, submissive. "I'll get what I have."

I leave the sitting room. Footsteps sound behind me, but I don't give him so much as a backward glance.

I stride into the kitchen. Rena backs against the stove when Pan Burzyński comes in after me.

The tin sits on the table. I pick it up, open the lid, shake the roll of bills into my palm. I turn and face him. "Here's five hundred złotys." I hand him the money. "It's all I have."

"Fine." He shoves it in his trousers pocket without counting it. Then he goes still. I follow his gaze to the suitcase on the floor next to the table.

"What's that for?" His voice sharpens. "Oh, I see. You think you can run? Flee into the night with your Jews, is that it?"

"You must be mad." I laugh. "Where would we go?"

"That's why you agreed so readily to our bargain, isn't it?" His words are low, measured. "You knew you were never going to give me a grosz more than five hundred złotys." He stares at me, strands of slicked-back hair falling over his broad forehead. "I should have known you'd have me for a fool."

"No." I shake my head, frantic. "I admit, yes, we were planning to leave, but that was before. I thought you'd turn us in. What was I supposed to do?"

"You have your money. She's given you every grosz she has. What more do you want?"

I glance at Rena. Strength and fear collide in her eyes.

"You want to know?" He pushes past me. Grasps Rena by the shoulders, pressing her against the stove.

She stares at him, shaking but refusing to cower.

"I don't know what I ever saw in you," he mutters. He grabs her by the arm and hauls her across the kitchen. "The deal's off. I'm calling the Gestapo. She's coming with me. If you care what happens to her, you'd better not think about leaving this flat before they get here."

Feral strength surges through my body. I lunge for him, fighting to tear Rena away—

His fist drives into my stomach.

Air whooshes from my lungs. I land hard on my backside.

"Please let me go." Rena struggles against him, sobbing as he drags her out of the kitchen. "Please don't do this."

"Enough." His hand lashes out, connects with her cheek.

I clamber to my feet, desperation a roar in my brain.

My gaze catches on a gleam of metal. A pipe wrench. On the floor, its end sticking out from under the table.

I reach for it, curl my fingers around the metal handle. Rena's cries tear at my chest as I leave the kitchen.

Pan Burzyński jerks Rena across the sitting room.

Blood roars in my ears. My fingers tighten around the handle.

Pan Burzyński catches sight of me. "What's that you're—?"

I raise the wrench and swing with all my strength.

Steel cracks against bone.

The force of the blow reverberates through my body.

He lurches to one side, eyes glazed, face chalky. For an instant, he stares at me. Blood gushes down his face. He staggers, crumples.

I stand over him, gripping the wrench. My breath heaves fast and hard.

"Is he . . . ?" Rena's voice is far away.

"Get the children."

She doesn't move.

"Now!"

I return to the kitchen, heft the suitcase, and leave the room. In the sitting room, Leon stands with Sara in his arms, only a few steps away from Pan Burzyński's prone body, blood a spreading stain on the rug. Leon looks at me, more shocked than horrified.

"Let's go," I say, voice hollow.

I move to leave the sitting room, then remember I'm still clutching the wrench. It takes effort to loosen my grip and set it on the floor—my mind is so hazy I can think of nowhere else to put it. I pick up my handbag from the sofa, clamp it under my arm, then walk to the door. I open it, ushering Rena and Leon ahead of me.

Gripping the suitcase, I glance over my shoulder to where Pan Burzyński lies on my blood-soaked rug, for what will probably be my last glimpse of my home. Even as I comprehend this, my mind remains blank and numb.

I shut the door and lead the way downstairs, Rena and Leon following. We pass no one, the echo of our footsteps loud as we cross the deserted foyer.

I push open the door and we step onto the street. Leon squints, as if unaccustomed to the brightness. Rena isn't wearing her coat. They follow close beside me as we hurry down the sidewalk.

I left my coat behind too, but I won't go back for it.

There's no returning now.

CHAPTER THIRTY-ONE

Zosia
September 7, 1944

IT'S ONE OF THE greatest ironies of my war—after sheltering others for so long, I now find myself in need of shelter. I've gone from harboring the hunted to becoming one of them.

Stillness drapes the night. I sit in the pharmacy attic, leaning against the wall. Leon and Sara are already asleep, curled up on the floor. Rena lies on their other side, next to Pani Weinberg. Awake or asleep, I can't tell.

Before Tadeusz disappeared down the attic steps, his gaze rested on me, his brow lined, concern on his face. He took us in without question, even after I told him everything. He promised to do whatever he could for us.

We're safe. For the moment, at least. But despite Tadeusz's presence below, and Rena, Pani Weinberg, and the children beside me, I can't rest. I'm not sure I'll ever be able to again.

I killed a man.

Though he might still have been alive when I left, and may survive his injuries, the truth remains. Whether I meant to end his life is of no consequence. I would have done anything to stop him from harming Rena or handing us over to the Gestapo.

During these years, I've made choices, and done and failed to do many things of which I'm not proud. Yet the worst of it is not what I have done but the realization of what I am capable of doing.

How can there be absolution for such an act?

I will protect her with my life, I promise you.

Hania's eyes, so fiercely brave, meeting mine as she asked me to take care of her sister. To do what she could not.

I've fought to protect the lives entrusted to my care. When I wanted to give up, I kept on, and when the struggle for survival threatened to overcome me, I somehow found strength. I've given the whole of myself and would give still more.

Yet I am left in the wreckage of my failures.

I rest my head against the wall, the hush of night broken only by the children's sleeping breaths and a creak from below.

I'm so tired. Of trying and failing. Of witnessing suffering and death and being unable to stop it. Of the life war has handed us and who I have become in that life. Of the ways grief hollows a heart.

Of my own powerlessness.

Again and again, this reality has met me. I stood at the pharmacy window as shots resounded in the square, as children were torn from a world they had scarcely begun to know, as life ran in rivers across the cobblestones. None of it did I prevent. I dispensed sedatives while transports left for Bełżec, and Luminal to desperate parents, but I could not stop the trains or shelter their children. I loved two men but could protect neither of them from the destruction of the Nazis. I could not save Hania from Płaszów.

I cannot preserve even those I've fought most to protect. Pani Weinberg. Leon. Sara.

Rena.

I squeeze my eyes shut and try to pray. What else, after all, is left to me but God?

The words won't come. There simply are none. Somewhere along the way—I'm not sure exactly when—I've ceased to turn to Him.

Perhaps I could no longer bear the silence.

I sit in Mass and listen to the readings and murmur the prayers, but the holy words that once moved my heart have become distant and cold. The echo of His absence, or at least a sense of His presence, has emptied my soul. I believe in Him—that I have not lost—but I want to rage, to accuse, to demand answers, and it both angers and shames me. Once I never doubted His goodness, but how can I trust in it now? The breadth of suffering upon this world is so great, and yet in it, how often He seems distant.

In it, how often I feel abandoned.

Warmth trickles down my skin. I don't brush it away, lingering in the gentleness of it. I close my eyes, the single tear damp against my cheek, waiting for morning, wondering if it will bring the Gestapo and our end. How will I face it, for now not only those in this room will pay a price, but also Tadeusz, for harboring us?

A shadow moves and a floorboard creaks.

I swipe the back of my hand across my face.

Pani Weinberg settles into the space between Sara and me, a blanket around her shoulders. "Can't sleep either?"

I draw a breath. "I'm sorry," I say softly, needing to speak the words, yet ashamed of their insufficiency.

"For what would you be sorry?"

"Rena and I spoke about Pan Burzyński some days ago. I knew he was a danger to us every time he came. I should have gotten us away before or found some way to manage him or . . . something. But I didn't, and now . . ."

"You are not to blame, Zosia. How could you know what he intended? What happened is not your fault, any more than it is Rena's or mine."

The weight of the wrench as I gripped it, the jolt of the blow through my body, the flash of shock in Pan Burzyński's eyes before he crumpled to the ground . . .

"But what I did . . . I should feel guilt, and I do. Still, I would do it again if it meant you and Rena and the children would be safe."

"There is not one of us who does not carry guilt. I think of Romek and Adela, and I tell myself a better mother would have found a way for her children. I should have sent Adela out of the ghetto that day. Instead I thought it would be safer for her if I took the risk first. So many times I've asked myself why I chose to believe there would be a chance for all of us. Why did I leave my daughter behind?" Her voice breaks on the whispered words. "I don't know where my Adela is, my Romek, but if I could, I would take their place. I would give my life for theirs and to do it would be a gift to me." In the quiet anguish of her voice lies a mother's broken heart.

"I would have done anything for them."

"I know. And I want you to know how grateful I am for what you have done for us."

"It wasn't enough," I whisper, more to myself than to her.

"What ever could be? There is no 'enough.' Not in such inhumanity. But 'enough' is not what matters. When the decrees began after the occupation, I watched as those we had lived beside as neighbors turned from us. We'd always known there were those who hated our people, but the Germans made it legal to take from us, to mistreat us, to hate us, and many joined them gladly."

"I remember."

"It was not so bad from people we did not know, but when those we thought were our friends no longer spoke to us on the street"—she glances down at her hands—"it was very hard. When we were forced into the ghetto, it seemed the world had forgotten us. I accepted this because I had no choice." She looks into my face. "But then you came to us and offered to help, not only your friends but me and my children, who were strangers to you. You took us into your home, risked your life for us. You and Magister Pankiewicz and the others have given me hope that there remains something greater than evil. HaShem has not forsaken us. Whether we are left to see the end of this war, I believe this. Just as I believe HaShem led you in what you've done and will lead us in whatever comes."

The depth of her belief stuns and shames me. How can it be possible, after not only witnessing but living the hatred and horror of these years, she holds so fervently to faith? "You still believe? After everything?"

"HaShem is not in the evil of men, the destruction of life, but in it, He is with us. There is no darkness strong enough to snatch us from the hand of the One who created us."

My throat tightens so I can only nod, her words touching the cold, cracked remnants of what once was my faith.

She reaches across the space between us and squeezes my hand, her work-roughened touch gentle. "Perhaps we will both be able to sleep now."

"Thank you," I whisper.

"Good night, my dear." Pani Weinberg squeezes my hand once more, then rises, steps around the sleeping forms to resume her place next to Rena.

I stretch out beside Sara, slipping beneath the blanket she and Leon share, her body warm alongside mine. Her small hand tucked beneath her cheek, lips softly parted, she sleeps, her rest as peaceful as if she were in her crib at home instead of on an attic floor.

I trace a fingertip across her cheek, remembering the nights when she woke crying and I paced the floor with her in my arms until she fell asleep against my chest. Now, though danger surrounds us, she slumbers in spite of it. She was born into the cruelty of war and has no memory of the mother who hid her under the coal and loved her enough to walk away.

Does God look down upon this child, upon all children whose innocent lives have been ravaged by a hate in which they had no hand?

There is no darkness strong enough to snatch us from the hand of the One who created us.

As the night enfolds me, a wakening stirs within my soul.

For the first time in a long while, I turn to Him in the darkness.

• • •

September 8, 1944

Footsteps creak on the attic steps. Tadeusz appears in the opening. In the dimness of the attic, he takes in the sight of us—Rena and Pani Weinberg folding clothes and placing them into the suitcase, Leon crouching against the wall, arms wrapped around his knees.

"It's just after eight o'clock. We'll have you safely away before the pharmacy opens."

"We'll be right down." I lift Sara off my lap and rise. Pani Weinberg closes the suitcase.

Single file, we descend the attic stairs, Rena carrying Sara, Pani Weinberg with the suitcase.

Tadeusz waits for us at the foot. "Come." He leads us through the empty pharmacy and into the laboratory, ushering us in ahead of him, closing the door behind us.

Irka and Helena stand by the table, waiting for us. "Hello, children." Irka approaches, smiling at Leon and Sara.

Tadeusz takes my arm, drawing me aside. "You're to go to Barska 14 in the Dębniki district. Pani Janczyk has a flat on the third floor, first door to the left. When she answers the door, ask if she still teaches music lessons. She's expecting you."

I commit the address and phrase to memory. "How did you manage to arrange it so quickly?"

"Pani Janczyk is a friend of mine. She's sheltered others for brief periods of time. Irka paid her a visit last night. In a few days, you'll be transferred to a more permanent hiding place outside the city or provided with false papers. Pani Janczyk has contacts who will handle the necessary details."

I understand the logic of these plans, even as I struggle to absorb their reality. When we arrived, I told Tadeusz it was urgent we leave the pharmacy as soon as possible. To remain where the police might search for me wasn't safe for him or us.

It won't be enough to move to another city or village under our own identities, not if the police are looking for us. If Pan Burzyński is alive, he'll make certain the authorities learn about me. If he isn't, well, then the police will likely search for me anyway.

We've no choice but to go into hiding. Others will shelter us, risk their lives for us.

There's no time to dwell on this change in my circumstances, so I simply nod. There's no time for further questions either, but I must ask one. "What if the police come here? What if they question you?"

"I'll tell them I don't know. They won't arrest me because one of my staff failed to turn up for work and I don't know what's happened to her."

Tadeusz's words may dismiss the danger, but he's as aware of it as I am.

Though risk has long been part of our lives, for Tadeusz, Irka, and Helena to be endangered by our association shakes me deep down.

Heavenly Father, protect them from harm.

He reaches into his pocket, presses several folded bills into my hand. "You never know when you might need it."

It pains me to take money from him, especially as I remember the złotys in Pan Burzyński's pocket, forgotten in my haste to leave the flat. "Are you sure you can spare it?"

"Yes, yes. Now tuck it away. Quickly now."

I open my handbag and slip the bills inside. When I look up, Tadeusz's gaze rests on me and my throat aches with a rush of remembrance.

When we met at the café, and he shook my hand and I noticed how his smile warmed his eyes. The first time I stepped through the door of the pharmacy and saw him standing behind the counter in his white coat, back-dropped by the cabinet crowned with its outstretched eagle. The party on Sylwester when he poured drinks and mingled with guests as if he were the host of a prewar social event. The years of working side by side as the deportations unfolded beyond our windows. Last night, when he answered my knock and guided us inside, then assured us of his help without hesitation.

"We should go," I say quietly.

His gaze holds mine. "Come back after the war is over."

"I will." Even as I say the words, I wonder if they are yet another promise war will force me to break.

A faint smile creases his face, embedded with new lines and aged by the weary years, but in that smile, he's still the handsome man who could charm a dinner party and dispense prescriptions with the same dash of savoir faire. "Good pharmacists are hard to find. I'd hate to think I was losing you permanently."

I laugh, but it comes out a bit broken. "Yes, I imagine you would."

He reaches out as if to clasp my hand. Instead he pulls me close in an embrace that smells of herbs and medicaments, comfort and home. "Look after yourself, Zosia."

"You too," I whisper. "*Bóg zapłać.*" *God bless you.*

He draws away. "Just come back."

I cross the room, throat aching as I approach Irka and Helena.

"Put this on." Irka hands me the garment folded over her arm. Her woolen coat.

"Irka, no. I'm not going to take this."

"Nonsense," she says, voice brisk. "I won't have you freezing come winter. Don't argue with me. Put it on."

I slip my arms through the sleeves, its warmth settling over my shoulders, then tie the belt at my waist.

She nods. "A little big, but it will do."

I swallow against the tightness in my throat. "Thank you."

"God be with you," she whispers, clasping me tightly.

"And with you." I hug Helena. "Goodbye, my friend." Then I turn, gaze falling on Tadeusz, standing on the other side of the laboratory, watching us.

The years have joined the four of us in a bond deeper than colleagues, closer than friends, as indelible as our shared experiences.

As we have been shaped by it, so too will it remain.

The others wait nearby. "This way." I lead them to the back door and guide Rena and Sara, Leon, and Pani Weinberg into the corridor ahead of me.

One hand on the knob, I turn, looking back at Tadeusz, Irka, and Helena. For an instant, I capture the memory, the image of them standing side by side.

Then I follow the others into the corridor, through the passageway to the back entrance. I push open the door and we cross the empty courtyard and pass through the gateway. I don't hesitate before stepping onto Józefińska Street.

A cart rattles past. Pedestrians hasten along the sidewalk.

Then I notice the scent, the sharp, charred stench carried on the autumn wind. I still, gripping my handbag. My breath catches.

Papery flakes swirl against a colorless sky.

"Snow." Sara's voice is awed. She reaches up as if to touch one of the bits of white floating in the air around us.

Leon stares at the sky, eyes wide.

Rena looks at me.

We walk on as ash rains from the heavens.

CHAPTER THIRTY-TWO

Hania
January 18, 1945

FLAKES OF WHITE SWIRL in the night as we stand in rows of five, waiting to march out of Auschwitz. As they land on my cheeks and lips, they taste of water, not of ash. Smoke no longer billows from the crematoriums, filling our lungs with the bitterness of death. Flames flicker against the sky, but now it's the camp records being destroyed. These files and records, lists and names are the last remnant of the numberless souls who entered the camp.

Though it's paper and ink instead of flesh and bone, lives are still consumed by flames.

The Germans know the war is all but lost. News in Auschwitz-Birkenau spreads the same way as in Płaszów, passed in whispers from person to person. We crave these reports as if they are bread and share them with others in the barracks, the precious crumbs of information nourishing our hopes of liberation. German troops are being pushed back, the Red Army is advancing across Poland . . .

Now we do not need rumors to know the Russians are almost here. The thunder of guns reverberates in the distance. Parts of Poland may already be liberated, perhaps even Kraków, seventy kilometers to the west. Rena and Zosia may be, this moment, free. I let myself imagine it, though the thought is a weightless one. The Allies may not have reached Kraków, and if they have, there's no guarantee Rena and Zosia are still there.

Or still alive.

For days, whispers filtered through the barracks and among our ranks as we stood in line for bread—the SS are making plans to evacuate the Auschwitz camps before the Allies arrive, destroying evidence and blowing up the crematoriums. Those able to walk will be marched to Germany. The ill will remain in Birkenau. It's said after the evacuation, the SS have been issued orders to lock the gates, pour petrol around the perimeter, leave the electric fences on, and set Birkenau ablaze, incinerating everyone left inside.

Join the march or pretend to be ill and stay behind? Will the Russians arrive before the SS can follow through with their plan? We asked these questions of each other and ourselves. To go or to stay?

Adela and I decided when the time came, we would march. If we are to die, let it be outside the gates, not in the flames of Auschwitz-Birkenau.

Earlier today, guards marched us from Birkenau to the main camp, where we stand with thousands of others waiting for the order to move out. It's been hours since we arrived, the sky long since faded to black, snow drifting in heavy flakes. I stamp my feet, wriggle my toes. The artificial glare of searchlights cuts the night.

I glance at Adela. Shivers shake her emaciated frame. She's shrunken and frail, but she's here. With me. Together we survived the months in the camp—the grueling labor, the selections where we stood naked with thousands of other women while the SS chose who would be sent to the gas and who would live another day, the disease that ravaged the bodies of the women around us, the hunger that weakens us until we are shells.

The SS count us, their boots crunching on the frozen ground, breath streaming from their lips in clouds. Smoke from the enormous bonfires rises into the sky to mingle with the falling snow. Dogs bark. Gunfire rumbles in the distance. My teeth chatter.

Finally the order comes. "Forward march!"

We take the first steps. Swirling snow glitters in the searchlights. Countless rows of five ahead of us, countless more behind us, we pass through the gates beneath the iron-welded words.

ARBEIT MACHT FREI

Only the dead are free in Auschwitz.

We leave the gates behind us, tramping down the center of the road as snow falls in sheets. We're marching into a blizzard. Adela and I exchange glances, her cheeks blotchy with cold, both of us wordlessly asking the same questions.

Was our choice right? Is this march to be our end?

Our gazes hold, two women silently offering each other what strength we still possess. Then we set our faces forward into the driving snow.

The feet of those marching ahead of us—perhaps thousands—cut a hard-packed path through the heavy drifts. Some of the SS ride on horseback while others flank our ranks on foot. All are armed.

There's no question about what will happen to anyone who tries to escape, though out in the open, away from watchtowers and high-voltage fences, our chances of succeeding would be greater.

But where would we go? Our ragged dresses, shaven heads, and the numbers tattooed on our left forearms would immediately mark us as escaped prisoners. Would someone show pity and take us in? Not likely, when doing so would mean risking their own lives. Still, I might attempt it while we're yet in Poland if not for Adela. For two to escape would be far more dangerous than for one. All we have is each other. I refuse to be separated from her.

My wooden clogs slip on a patch of ice. I flounder, clutching the bundle containing our blanket and the bread issued to each of us before we left Birkenau. Our blanket, the metal soup bowl attached to a belt of string around my waist, and my clothes form the sum of my possessions. Everything else, including Romek's ring, I lost when the SS made us strip and leave our belongings behind upon arrival in Auschwitz-Birkenau. I tried to conceal the ring under my tongue, but one of the SS saw. I got beaten and the SS got the ring. As if it was worth anything to them, a crudely fashioned circle of metal.

My last link with my brother and the man I love.

Time passes, not in minutes or hours but in frozen darkness and bitter snow. The lanterns and electric torches carried by the SS cast a weak glow. We trudge past houses and farms, their windows dark, smoke purling from chimneys. I imagine their inhabitants sleeping, nestled beneath warm quilts, unaware of the column of humanity tramping down the road only meters from their doorsteps.

Despite those who broke the path ahead of us, the endlessly falling snow reaches almost to my calves, icy wetness seeping through the woolen socks one of the girls who worked sorting the belongings of people transported to Birkenau smuggled to Adela and me. Wind whips my thin dress around my legs, cold stabbing the bare skin above my socks, burning, then numbing my flesh.

I stumble over something in the middle of the path, grabbing Adela's arm to stop myself from falling. I glance down. She does too.

The corpse of a man lies faceup, half-buried in the snow.

Holding hands, Adela and I step over the body.

We plod onward, the women ahead of us dark shapes in the blinding snow. More corpses litter the path, line the sides of the road, lumps soon buried beneath falling snow. The bodies of the male prisoners who came before us. At first, I try my best not to step on them. But I do. We all do. I close my mind off, do not allow myself to think of them as men, only obstacles in my path.

Women and girls struggle to sustain the pace set by the SS. More and more lag behind, losing their places in the rows of five, slipping further back in the column. Somewhere in the darkness, a shot rings out. I keep moving without so much as turning my head, gripping Adela's hand as we plunge into the night.

Don't fall behind.

CHAPTER THIRTY-THREE

Hania
April 3, 1945

BERGEN-BELSEN IS A WASTELAND.

In Birkenau, we slept on shelves, twelve women to a shelf. In Belsen, we sleep on the ground in barracks so crowded we're forced to practically lie on top of one another. In Birkenau, the distribution of rations was daily, orderly. In Belsen, many days there are no rations, and on the days we do get them, the portions are hardly portions at all—a little bitter liquid we call coffee, a ladleful of watery turnip soup, and a couple of times a week, a piece of bread one centimeter thick. I know this because I am good at measuring bread.

There are no hangings as in Płaszów, no gas chambers as in Birkenau, but thousands are dying. From starvation, from tuberculosis, from typhus. Death in Belsen is slow, agonizing. Everywhere there are piles of bodies, fresh corpses intertwined with the long dead. The air does not carry the scent of smoke but of decaying flesh.

In this camp of nothing, we slowly become nothing.

In the months in Belsen, I've wanted to lie down and not get up so many times. I've watched others do it. They simply don't fight anymore, and soon, their bodies are added to the mound. When I wake on the cold barracks floor next to women who died in the night, I wonder how I will find the strength to rise, to stand for roll call, to work, to live. Though the distant thunder of explosions tells us nearby villages are being bombed, it's difficult to believe the Allies will ever reach us. To believe any of us will be alive once they do is harder still. I've heard it said that to live one must have purpose. My purpose is Adela. If not for her, I would have given up long ago. But I refuse to abandon Romek's sister. He loves her as I do Rena. In his place, I care for her, fight for her. And in her way, Adela fights for me.

Maybe I'm simply going crazy, but as I fight for Adela, it's as if I'm fighting for Rena too. As if protecting Adela somehow means my sister too is being protected. Deep down, I know there's no power in such a bargain, if indeed that's what it is, but to exist another day in Belsen means to draw on every last bit of resolve. I pray, asking ADONAI to help me honor my promise to Romek and to help Zosia honor the promise she made to me, to strengthen my body and Adela's, to preserve my sister and protect those I love.

In Birkenau, work didn't make us free, but it gave us a better chance of living. Those too ill to labor went to the infirmary, mostly to die. Work shaped our days, and in a strange way, gave us purpose. I did not realize this until we arrived at Belsen, where only some of the prisoners labor. The rest stay in the barracks, crouching or lying on the filthy ground, one in a heap of starving, sick, weak, shivering, dying women.

After a week of not working, existing on barely existent rations, I knew we had no chance of staying alive if I didn't do something. One morning during roll call, the SS chose some women for the garbage-collecting kommando. I didn't know then what work women were being picked for but decided anything would be better than rotting in the barracks, so I bit my lips to give them color, stood tall, and somehow was chosen.

Our kommando loads garbage from the kitchens onto carts, then, hitched to the carts like draft animals, we pull them to potato pits in fields several kilometers outside the camp. We empty potatoes from the pit, shovel out the garbage from the carts, load potatoes onto the carts, and drag the carts to the officers' kitchen.

If we're caught eating a potato or even a potato peel or any other food found in the garbage, we're beaten by the Aufseherin who guards us. But when you're starving, a beating in exchange for a potato is not a bad trade. I'm careful not to sneak potatoes every day, and I make sure the SS woman isn't watching before slipping one from the pile, but somehow she still catches me, slapping my face so hard my ears ring.

To be caught eating earns a beating, but to be caught smuggling food into the camp is punishable by death—not only for the thief but for everyone in the kommando. We know this, yet still we take chances. When someone you love is starving and when there in front you is a pile of potatoes, how can you not take the risk of smuggling food?

Today when the Aufseherin was smoking a cigarette, I managed to slip a potato into the pocket I fashioned under my dress. Later, I found half an apple in the garbage from the officers' kitchen. The guard at the gate didn't search our kommando thoroughly, so I managed to smuggle my treasures into the camp.

After standing for evening roll call with the others from the garbage kommando, I hurry to the barracks, eager to share the food with Adela. By the time I reach the rows of long wooden huts and find ours, I'm out of breath.

I linger outside for a minute, drawing in sips of air before entering the hut. My eyes adjust to the murky dimness, my senses to the reek of excrement and decay. As I search for Adela, I do my best not to step on the women slumped on the floor or crouching with their knees drawn up to their chests, but there's little space between one body and another, and invariably a moan or curse escapes one of the prone forms as I pick my way through the barracks.

Adela hasn't returned from the Appellplatz yet, so I claim a space on the floor, checking before lowering myself to the ground to make sure I'm not about to sit in a pool of waste, though often I'm too tired to check or care. So many suffer diarrhea. Though latrines are few—mostly outdoor pits—fewer still are those with the strength to reach them every time they're seized with cramps.

I wait, arms wrapped around my knees, watching the door for Adela. Finally she comes in behind another woman, our blanket around her shoulders. I lift my hand, catching her attention, and she makes her way through the barracks.

When she reaches me, she sinks to the ground and curls up on her side, knees tucked to her chest.

"Adela, what is it? Are you all right?" I bend over her, touching her shoulder.

She clutches the blanket to her chin. "I'm so cold."

I adjust the blanket, tucking it around her bony shoulders, smoothing it over her. "Is it because they took so long counting us?"

Her teeth chatter. "I've been cold all day."

I rest my hand on her forehead. Her skin burns my palm.

No. Please, no.

"Turn onto your back for me, all right?" I keep my voice calm.

She does. I unbutton the top of her dress. She lifts her head. "What are you doing?"

I pull her dress away from her skin, exposing her neck and chest.

No rash. But a rash doesn't usually appear until several days after the onset of symptoms. I've seen enough typhus to be familiar with its progression . . . and its outcome.

No. Adela can fight this. She *will* fight this.

I lower the fabric and redo the buttons. "Does your head ache?"

She nods, swallowing. "I ache all over." Her eyes meet mine, glazed with a too-familiar sheen. "You think it's typhus, don't you?"

"I think you need to rest. I brought a surprise for you." I reach inside my dress and pull out the piece of apple. It's mushy and brown and coated in slime from the garbage, but it's fruit. I wipe it on my dress before handing it to her.

Her eyes widen as she takes it. "How did you . . . ?"

"I found it in the garbage. It's your favorite, right?"

"Yes." She cradles it in her hand. "I used to stop by the market on the way home from school. There was an old woman who had a stall. She used to sell the most beautiful apples, so round and golden-red. The taste of those apples, like every bite held all the sweetness in the world." She holds the shriveled apple a moment more before handing it to me. "Thank you, Hania."

"Don't you want to eat it?"

"Maybe later. I'm not very hungry now."

How can it be possible? But typhus has a way of stealing the appetite, even in those previously suffering torturous pangs of hunger.

I glance toward the entrance to the barracks. They haven't brought the vat of soup yet. On the days we receive rations, distribution usually begins once we return to the barracks after roll call.

Another day of nothing.

My stomach cramps. I press a hand to the hollow of my midsection, but it does not ease the emptiness gripping me with its never-ending ache. Only thirst is worse than hunger and the splash of tepid, black-tinted water is the only liquid we're given. The dryness of my throat makes it difficult to swallow and there are sores in my mouth that I think are from dehydration. Our only other source of water is the reservoir a distance away from the barracks. The greenish water it contains has a foul smell, but on the days when coffee isn't distributed, it's all we have.

The grinding of slow starvation and the parched agony of thirst is worse than being beaten by the SS woman, worse than being whipped in Płaszów, worse than any pain I've ever known. Because of it, I have become a shell, one step away from nothing, and I am slipping toward nothing faster than I want to admit. I push away the thoughts crowding in and tuck the apple into my dress. I'll eat a few bites of the potato before sleeping tonight but save the fruit for Adela.

"Are you thirsty?"

"A little." She turns onto her side again, facing me.

"I'll bring you some water." I rise.

"No, don't go. Stay with me." Her voice is pleading. "I've been so alone all day."

"For a little while and then I'll fetch you some water. And you'll eat a little of the apple for me, yes?"

She nods and I settle beside her, the woman slumped at our feet preventing me from fully stretching out.

The woman on my other side coughs, a feeble rattling thick with sputum.

"This morning, on our way to the field with the garbage cart, we passed some men on a work detail," I speak softly, like a mama telling her child a bedtime story. "They must have been from the men's camp."

"Did you see anyone you know?"

"No." I searched their faces for Romek, as I always do when encountering a group of male prisoners. But even if someone from my past had been among them, would I recognize him among the skeletal men in ragged uniforms, their faces dirty and unshaven? I doubt he'd recognize me. "But as we passed, one of the men called out to us. 'Hold on. It won't be long now. Tell your friends to hold on.'" I can still see the fire burning in his hollow eyes, hear his voice carrying across the road to us.

"What did he mean?"

"I think he was trying to tell us it won't be long before the Allies are here."

Hope enters Adela's gaze, a guttering flame. "Can it really be true?"

I leave the story unfinished, how the guard grabbed the man by the collar, threw him to the ground, and beat him. When I glanced over my shoulder as we continued down the road with the garbage cart, the guard was still kicking him.

"It must be. It must be true." I speak the words to give her strength, not because I believe them. I pray this lie will be forgiven me. "Now, rest. I'll get the water."

Adela nods, shivering with fever. She closes her eyes and I tuck the blanket around her, then rise to walk to the reservoir and fill the soup bowl that has hung from a string around my waist since I traded five rations of bread for it in Birkenau.

I step over the prone figures huddled on the barracks floor. The door creaks as I slip outside. Mud sucks at my clogs as I make my way down the barracks-lined road in the gray twilight. I wrap my arms around myself, hunched against the cloying chill. My legs shake. Spots blacken my vision.

Hold on.

The slam of the guard's boot into the man's crumpled body swallows the shouted words of hope.

My foot catches on something. Before I can break my fall, I hit the ground hard, face down in the mud. Breath leaves my lungs in a rush. I raise my head.

A half-naked corpse lies a few centimeters away from my face.

Go to the reservoir. Water for Adela.

I close my eyes, resting my cheek in the mud, tasting dirt.

Hold on.

I'm so tired of holding on.

. . .

April 15, 1945

Water trickles from the rag as I wring it out and wipe Adela's forehead, gently smoothing the damp cloth across her skin. The same motion, over and over. Heat radiates from her body, as if she's burning inside. I dab her chest and neck, where reddish blotches spot her skin, trying to quench the fire, to stop it from consuming her.

Time is blurry. In the first days after Adela fell ill, I continued to report for the garbage kommando, offering a woman in our barracks half a potato each day in exchange for caring for Adela.

While shoveling garbage, I scoured for anything edible—half a lemon peel, a bit of soggy bread, a morsel of some kind of meat—and stole potatoes with stubborn recklessness. But Adela only managed to eat a little of what I brought. Each evening, I found her weaker, her fever high, diarrhea soiling her blanket and clothes. The block elder permits those too sick to report for roll call to remain in the barracks and Adela soon became one of them.

When the woman who'd been caring for Adela fell ill herself, I decided to stop reporting for work. In Belsen, we have no prisoner numbers. It only matters to the SS that each day twenty-four human draft horses report for the kommando, so after I told one of the stronger girls in the barracks about the opportunity the job afforded to sneak extra food, she was more than eager to work in my place.

I remain in the barracks, fetching water from the reservoir, bathing Adela's forehead, emptying her soup bowl of waste, as she no longer has the strength to make it to the latrine, cleaning her as best I can, and lifting her head so she can sip water. I can't remember the last time rations were distributed. Maybe a few days ago, maybe longer, or maybe I am just losing track of time.

Though there's an infirmary in Belsen, I'm afraid for Adela to go there. In Płaszów and Birkenau, those in the infirmary were always the first to be selected, the first to be disposed of.

If they had medicine at the infirmary, taking her there would be worth the risk, but the infirmary in Belsen has nothing—no medicine, few nurses and doctors, and not enough beds. No one goes to the infirmary to get well. They go there to die. And when death comes, they are alone. I won't send Adela there, not when I can care for her, be with her.

I drop the rag into the greenish water in my bowl, squeezing liquid from the cloth with shaking hands. Crouching beside her, I sponge her forehead. Dingy light leaks through the window, casting shadows on the women covering the barracks floor. The heat coming off Adela's body soon permeates the rag and I wring it out again. I need to go to the reservoir for fresh water, but I don't want to leave her, so I keep wiping her skin and wringing out the cloth again and again.

Adela's eyes flutter open. "Mamusia," she breathes, voice as fragile as a wisp of smoke.

"It's me, Adela. Hania." She hasn't woken in so long. The last time, she thrashed with delirium, and I had to hold her down. I brace myself for it again, but she lies still.

"Hania." Adela swallows thickly. "I was dreaming . . . such a nice dream. Mama was sitting next to me with her hand on my forehead. She was singing to me like she did when I was little. I wish I could remember the song. I wish . . ." She fights to draw a labored breath.

"Shhh." I rest my hand on her forehead. "I'm here." I speak the words through chattering teeth. I'm so cold . . . then hot. How long have I been like this?

"Mama told me . . . it will be all right. She said . . ." Her words come in gasps of breath. ". . . we'll be free."

"Yes," I whisper. "Yes."

"You'll find them . . . after it's over. You'll tell them I tried . . . won't you?"

I shake my head. "You'll tell them yourself."

"Tell them . . . remember . . . this is not all there is." Her voice grows weaker, her breaths thinner. "This is not all we are."

"Shhh." I wring out the rag, place it on her forehead, my own body wracked with shivers. "Rest now."

A thready breath shudders from her cracked lips, her glassy eyes unfocused. "Can you help me . . . say the Shema? I . . . have to say it."

I swallow, my throat unbearably dry. "Shema Yisrael."

Hear, O Israel.

"Shema Yisrael," she whispers.

"Adonai Eloheinu." Together, we recite the prayer.

The Lord *our God.*

"Adonai . . . Echad . . ." Her head sags to the side, as if she no longer has the strength to support it, her chest rising with labored breaths.

I've tried so hard and for so long to fight, but I cannot fight this current. It's dragging her down, pulling her under, and I am powerless to stop it.

"Hold on, Adela." My voice cracks. "It won't be long now. Hold on."

The others in the hut, the chills shaking my body, the scent of filth and waste, the passing of time . . . all of these recede. Adela's chest barely rises as her breaths grow farther and farther apart. I keep wringing out the rag and wiping her forehead and chest. There is nothing else I can do, yet I cannot do nothing.

"I'm here," I whisper as she struggles to breathe. "I'm right here."

Is there a space between when her last breath leaves her and when I notice the silence? How long do I wipe her forehead after there is no longer a reason to? I do not know. It does not matter.

Someone moans, another woman is vomiting, but my ears are full of the silence left by the void of Adela's breaths. How gentle it is, the gentlest sound I have heard in Belsen. She's still, her head turned aside, her eyes closed.

Death should bring tears, but my eyes are dry. Perhaps I no longer remember how to weep. I feel emptiness but not grief. My numbness runs too deep to be cut by sorrow.

The rag falls from my hand, useless. My body shakes and my head throbs. Sweat soaks my dress and chills my skin. Typhus. I haven't let myself acknowledge how sick I am until now.

Again and again, I've pushed myself beyond the limits of my endurance for Adela, but now she's gone and I have nothing left with which to fight the fading of my body.

I lie next to Adela, rest my head beside hers, and close my eyes. Somehow I sense I will not get up. I don't care. I only want the pain to end.

In my mind, I see the faces of the ones I love—the smile crinkling Tata's eyes, Mama's gentle gaze, Szymon's crooked grin.

Rena's bright eyes.

Romek, holding my hand, slipping a circle of silver on my finger. Offering me a future as our present was destroyed.

Zosia, facing me as the crowd jostled around us, her gaze flashing with undiluted resilience.

I can't remember what she said to me the last time I saw her, something about a promise. Doesn't she understand by now? Doesn't she know war turns promises to ashes?

Forgive me.

The words are for them all.

I wrap my arms around myself and pull my knees to my chest, shivering. I want only to sleep. The blackness hovering at the edges of my consciousness spreads and widens, until there becomes nothing else.

Voices form a distant blur.

I open my eyes. I don't move my head, just lie there on my side, Adela beside me.

There's something strange about these voices. I'm not sure what it is or where they come from. Maybe they're inside my head. Maybe I'm delirious.

A creak. Light.

"They are here," someone screams in German.

I turn my head.

A woman stands in the doorway of the hut. "They are here!" She clutches a ragged blanket around her shoulders, tufts of gray hair sticking out from her skull.

I wish she would be quiet. All I want is to go back to sleep.

"Who's here?" a raspy voice asks.

"The British. We are liberated!"

Someone releases a strangled cry.

"The Allies? In Belsen?"

"Can it be possible?"

"Come and see." The woman gestures toward the door. "Come."

Women stir, rise from the floor, and make their way to the entrance. I watch them leave with a strange detachment. They're walking into a trap. Probably the guards in the watchtowers will shoot them. The SS likely spread this rumor for that very reason.

I lie on the floor of the hut, one in a heap of humanity. Only a few women left the hut. I wait for the report of gunfire.

It doesn't come. Perhaps they're killing them some other way.

Or else what the woman said is true. But how can it be true?

I'm no longer afraid of anything the SS can do to me. I've accepted death. Does it matter anymore how it comes?

My gaze rests on Adela, motionless beside me, her face turned toward mine. She's already free.

We are liberated.

Deep inside, something sparks.

What is it? What gives me the strength to press my hands flat on the floor and raise myself to my knees? Whatever it is, it stems from that spark.

My vision blurs. My head pounds. My arms shake. Slowly, painfully, I crawl through filth. On my hands and knees, around bodies, through pools of urine and excrement. My chest aches with the effort to breathe.

I raise my head. Meters separate me from the door.

Hold on. It won't be much longer now. Tell your friends to hold on.

I keep crawling, gasping for breath, lifting my head every so often to see how close I am. My teeth chatter. My knees wobble.

By the time I reach the door, my body can barely support itself. Opening the door is like pushing against a brick wall. It creaks open.

I crawl outside. Light stabs my eyes. I raise my head, staring up the stretch of road lined with huts, littered with bodies.

Women wander in groups or alone. Some sit on the ground outside the huts. Two women embrace each other, crying. Another woman leans against the hut opposite mine, eating something out of a tin, using her fingers to shove the food in her mouth.

Where are the guards?

I don't have the strength either to stand or return to the hut. I stay where I am, on my hands and knees. The air is not so bad out here, at least.

Three figures stride down the road. Men in brown uniforms.

Women rush up to them, voices high, excited.

What am I seeing? What's happening?

One of the men breaks away from the group and continues on alone. He carries a rifle. I watch as he walks down the road. He isn't SS.

Strength surges. I crawl toward him. He catches sight of me, stops a few meters away. I keep crawling, shaking with fever. If he wants to shoot me, fine. But he only stands there, watching me. A meter away, I stop.

We stare at each other. He's young. Tall. Clean-shaven.

He says something I don't understand.

He crouches in front of me. Again he speaks, his voice low, strange.

Most of the English words, I do not know. But these I do.

"Corporal William Philips, British."

"You are British?" My voice is less than a breath.

Something wet slides down his cheek. Tears? He is our liberator.

We are liberated.

But he is crying.

CHAPTER THIRTY-FOUR

Zosia
June 11, 1945

WAR HAS LEFT ITS scars on Kraków, but they are not the kind that evidence themselves in mounded rubble and devastated streets. Unlike Warsaw, left in ruins after the uprising, Kraków's majestic architecture and cobbled thoroughfares remain unscathed. The redbrick towers of the Mariacki Church still rise into the sky in the Rynek Główny, and on Wawel Hill, the great castle presides over the city as it has for centuries.

Yet the ravages of war endure. The Red Army entered Kraków on January 18. People thronged the streets to cheer the liberators, but in the days that followed, as soldiers looted storehouses and plundered personal property, the taste of celebration turned bitter. And though spoken of only in whispers, many women were raped by Soviet soldiers in the days after the city's liberation.

For over four months we stayed on a farm outside the town of Wieliczka, hiding in the cellar of an old woman's cottage as the Red Army surged across Poland. Near the end of January, the fighting reached us, the arrival of the Russians soon followed by the retreat of the German army.

At the beginning of February, we returned to Kraków. The moment I stepped through the door of the pharmacy and saw Tadeusz and Irka standing behind the counter was the first time I really believed the war had ended for us. For several days, we stayed with Tadeusz until I found us a room to rent.

Last September, the Gestapo had come to the pharmacy searching for me, but by playing the part of a disgruntled employer and promising to inform them immediately should any information about my whereabouts become known, Tadeusz convinced them he knew no more about my disappearance than they did. Tadeusz later received a similar visit from Pan Burzyński, who'd gladly provided the Gestapo with information about me and the people living in my flat. I'd been dully relieved he hadn't died by my hand, but the thought of him still alive had almost been enough to make me want to return to Wieliczka.

The day after our arrival, Irka paid a visit to my flat. She spoke to neighbors who informed her they'd not seen Pan Burzyński since the beginning of November. One rumor said he'd been deported to Germany as a forced laborer, another that he'd been executed by the underground for blackmail and denouncement of resistance members. No one knew for certain. In any event, my flat had been let to other tenants.

At the end of April, Hitler killed himself in his bunker in war-torn Berlin. In May, we gathered around Tadeusz's radio and listened to Churchill's speech announcing Germany's unconditional surrender. The war in Europe has ended and its survivors are left adrift in its ruins. With the liberation of concentration camps, those who lived to see freedom have begun to seek news of their families and make their way home.

The whole of Europe has become a congregation of the searching and the scattered.

In Kraków, hollow-eyed survivors of the camps crowd the registration office in the old Jewish Community Center. Those who lived in hiding or passed as Polish Christians all find their way there. Desperate for news but more, still, for hope, they fill out forms and stand in front of lists, write letters, and question strangers.

To find someone; that's the thing. Family. Relatives. Friends. A link in a broken chain.

But how many are left? How many survived to be found?

Pani Weinberg, Rena, and I make our way to the registration office—sometimes together, sometimes alone—joining the men and women scanning lists, searching faces, repeating names.

No news. Until one day, the last day of May, we learned Chaim Guterman died at Bełżec.

How do you tell a child their tata isn't coming back? Sara is too young to remember her parents or understand loss, but Leon isn't. He'd come with us to the registration office, squeezed through the crowd, stood on tiptoe in front of the lists, face taut as he scanned the columns of names posted on the wall.

We told them, Pani Weinberg and me. Neither said anything at first. Then Leon asked which camp his tata died in, his voice quiet but matter-of-fact, as if no question could be more natural. Sara looked up at her brother and asked, as she does about everything these days, "Why?"

She's too young to comprehend death and I'm not sure she even understood what it meant that a parent she didn't remember was gone. But Leon told her, explaining it as best as an eleven-year-old could.

That night, I woke to him crying in the darkness. I went to him and knelt beside his mattress. I could not replace the parents he'd lost, but I could hold him through the tears.

Somehow, in the face of it all, life falls into a semblance of ordinary. Our lives before 1939 are not a dropped stitch to be picked up and begun afresh. We do not ask ourselves how to return to them. But, in our own ways, we begin to live again.

In the autumn, Leon will return to school and Rena will start at a secondary school. I spend the evenings tutoring them, so they will not be so far behind. When we stayed at the pharmacy before moving to our rented room, Rena spent hours watching us in the laboratory and wandering the materials room, trailing her fingers across the bottles and tins, curiosity a spark in her eyes. Since then, she's often found her way to Zgody Square in the afternoon, bringing Leon and Sara, never happier than when we let her assist with some small task. Tadeusz lent her some books on chemistry and pharmaceutics, and she pores over them for hours, asking me to explain terms and passages she doesn't understand.

I crowd every moment of the busy days, hoping when night comes and I fall into bed, exhaustion will bring sleep. Sometimes it comes quickly. Other times, thoughts held back by the waking hours refuse to be silenced.

I think of Leon and Sara and wonder what future there is for them, what future there is for all who lost their childhoods to war. I think of their mama, who surely died in the liquidation of the ghetto, and of their tata, one of the countless murdered in the gas chambers at Bełżec.

I think of Romek, Adela, and Szymon.

Of Hania.

They are young and strong. Surely they survived the camps. Surely they are alive, out there, somewhere.

Surely they will come home.

I want to believe this. But I'm not blind to the scenes at the registration office. How again and again the reality of loss severs the journey of reunion.

Still, I pray for their return. And for us, who wait for them.

There is so much I do not understand and will never understand, but perhaps understanding is not what is meant for us. In its absence, I turn to God for the strength to believe. That He who holds the heavens is present in the earth and has not forsaken us. That our tears are not forgotten in His sight. That our grief is joined with His, and His heart breaks at the suffering wrought by evil men.

That no matter how our lives may shatter, in His hand, they remain.

I've learned the process of faith is not accomplished in a single stride but slowly, daily, hourly. Like breath, we are given enough for the moment we are in.

In this, in Him, I find peace.

My prayers include another name, one that returns to me in the sleepless hours. Time has blurred the memory of his face and I have no photograph to remind me. I've lost the cadence of his voice, the way his eyes creased at the corners, the touch of his hand in mine. Only the words that lay between us remain.

If you were willing to let me love you . . . In me, you will always have a place to turn.

I hold them close as the offering he meant them to be. Then I believed my heart held nothing to give him in return, so I turned away. I lost the moment when we had it and war is not generous with second chances.

But if I could stand with him beneath a streetlamp once again, I would not hold back the words that matter.

I've written letters and filled out forms, but the response has been the same: *We have no information on Jan Kamiński.* Still I won't stop searching until I know what happened to him.

In the silent spaces of the night, I remember the man I loved too late.

• • •

June 12, 1945

"Pardon me, please, but have you seen Dawid Ormianer?"

I turn from the lists on the wall of the registration office as the young woman approaches. Her wrinkled summer dress hangs on her rail-thin frame. Her bony fingers clutch the collar as if it's too tight. On her left forearm are numbers in blue ink.

"I saw him last on the ramp at Birkenau. He's sixteen, my brother. Have you seen him?"

"I'm sorry. I wasn't there." How many times have I looked into desperate eyes and repeated those words?

She nods, eyes vacant, and drifts away, clutching her collar.

I wasn't there.

The words taste chalky, bitter. Like guilt.

Two women push in front of me, and I step to one side. The names on the lists are their families, not mine. People crowd around the notice board, craning their necks and jostling for a place. Others stand in front of the typed sheets, motionless and silent, alone in the crowd. Many are painfully thin, their frames little more than flesh stretched over bones, their hair growing back in patches. Some still wear striped prison uniforms.

Every face bears a wordless story of suffering, a rendering of what it cost them to survive. In the void of their gazes, I realize how little I understand of the horror of this war.

I wait for Pani Weinberg and Rena, clasping my handbag in front of me. The hum of voices echoes off the high ceiling. Men and women, a few children, queue in front of desks, waiting to speak with a clerk or fill out a registration card, so their names can be added to records. The Nazis used registration to mark the Jewish people for annihilation. Now, they register again, this time as a confirmation of life.

Throughout the room, people cluster together in little knots. Survivors come not only to register and seek assistance from the committee but in the hopes of encountering a familiar face. Reunions of school friends, of acquaintances from the ghetto, of old neighbors, are small miracles to those for whom life is a column of losses.

But for every cry of recognition and embrace, there are countless scenes of mourning. The man turning away from the notice board, shoulders stooped. The hollow-cheeked woman nodding at a clerk's words, pressing her lips together, hurrying out the door with her head bent. One girl leading another away, silent tears glistening on their cheeks.

The commonplace of grief.

Pani Weinberg wends through the crowd toward me, Rena at her side.

One look at their faces and my heart starts pounding.

Tears shine in Pani Weinberg's eyes. She swallows, gathers herself. "Romek is on the list."

Never will I forget the way she whispers the next words.

"He's alive."

CHAPTER THIRTY-FIVE

Hania
July 17, 1945

I'M ALMOST HOME.

Train wheels clack against tracks as my mind repeats the words, testing them as if they are another language.

I'm almost home.

I'm not sure anymore what those words mean. They are a hazy memory of something distant, as if I stand gazing down a long road, a hand tented over my brow, squinting into the sun, trying to see what lies at the end of it, trying to remember.

There is so much I do not remember and so much I cannot forget.

The memories are strung-together images, sometimes scattered, sometimes so sharp I'm there again in an instant.

White sheets on a hospital bed.

Opening my eyes and looking down and thinking I'd died because there were white sheets.

The weeks after liberation are a blur of memories. This one stands out. I don't know how long we remained in the disease-ridden filth of the huts before being transferred to the hospital. A couple of weeks, at least. Until then, medical personnel treated us where we were. Nothing had prepared them for Belsen. Nothing could prepare anyone for Belsen. But they did the best they could, tireless in the face of an incomprehensible scope of suffering.

I was out of my head with fever most of the time. Maybe if I hadn't been, I wouldn't be here. I was too sick to care about food and so I didn't eat the army rations like those who were stronger. Because their malnourished bodies couldn't digest the food, many of them died.

For so long in the camps, people died because they were starving. After liberation, they died because they were eating.

In the huts, they fed us liquids—watered-down soup and a glucose drink—and did their best to sustain our lives until we could be moved to the hospital. In spite of their efforts, every day they went through the huts removing the dead. So many died in the days after the Allies arrived, having barely grasped liberation.

One time, half-delirious with fever, I felt a tugging on my leg. Some-one—a man in uniform—was dragging me away. I must have made a sound, because he stopped.

He'd thought I was a corpse.

By the time they moved us to the hospital, my fever had broken. At first I had to be fed intravenously, then my shrunken stomach could handle only liquids. My hair fell out in clumps, and I had ulcers in my mouth and infected sores on my body. Slowly, as weeks became months, my strength began to return. The doctors and nurses did more for us than provide medical care. Far more. One does not realize what it does to be treated with dignity, to be cared for with compassion, to be reminded of one's humanity, until one has been devalued as we were in the camps.

As I lay in the hospital bed while fluid dripped into my veins, and I could scarcely lift my head from the pillow, in my mind, I was with Rena. I'd heard Germany had surrendered and imagined my sister in freedom. Safe and well and waiting for me. I couldn't allow myself to consider any other alterna-tive. She would be with Zosia, and I would find them both. Day after day, I repeated this to myself. Would I have fought, had I not this hope? Every day for years had been a fight. Lying in the hospital, I fought another battle, this time against my failing body.

Somehow, impossibly, I won.

Once I could get out of bed for short periods of time, I assisted the nurses in the ward, for the need was tremendous and they were sorely overworked. The rate of death decreased—I overheard one of the nurses say people were dying five hundred a day in the first weeks after liberation—but many were simply too ravaged by malnourishment and disease to recover. Once again, the dead were removed from among the living.

After being released from the hospital, I spent a couple of weeks in the dis-placed persons camp near Belsen. I wandered the camp, searching for anyone I knew. Apart from a few women who'd been in our barracks in Birkenau, I didn't find anyone. Some of those I met from Poland planned to immigrate elsewhere. "Poland is nothing but a graveyard for Jews," one man said. Young people spoke passionately of Palestine, of joining the fight to establish a Jewish state and building a life in this land of promise. Others talked of immigrating to the United States or South America. People set out for other DP camps in search for their families. Many left to begin the journey home.

Once I made up my mind to return to Kraków, it became my sole purpose. In the hospital, I asked one of the nurses to mail a letter to Zosia. I waited but never received a reply. At the beginning of July, I left the DP camp and traveled to Hanover to the Central Committee for Refugees. There I obtained twenty-five German marks and documents stating I was a camp survivor returning to Poland to search for relatives.

I'd heard at the DP camp about the difficulties to expect on the journey, had been told by well-meaning people it wasn't safe for a girl to travel so far alone and I should wait. But there's a strange freedom that comes with knowing nothing can be worse than what one has already faced. I'd survived the ghetto, Płaszów, Birkenau, the march across Poland, Bergen-Belsen, and my weakened body's battle with typhus. Only one thing remained for me to lose, and I would not know if I had lost it unless I returned to Poland.

It took two weeks to reach Kraków, crossing war-battered Germany on trains, military vehicles, and on foot. On the roads, in villages, at the stations, I encountered others like me—crowds of men and women making their way home. Their stories remained mostly unspoken, but it wasn't difficult to distinguish who'd been in the camps. Not just by their emaciated figures and lack of possessions, but by the brand of determination evident even in those whose eyes still held the vacant expression so many had worn in Birkenau and Belsen. Everyone seemed eager to leave Germany, as if a terrible association clung to its soil, even in its defeat.

Steam hisses and brakes squeal, returning me to the present. The train pulls into Kraków's Main Station, the figures standing on the platform blurred by a rise of smoke. I scan their passing faces through the window of the overcrowded passenger carriage, as if searching for someone, as if someone is waiting for me on the platform.

The train jolts to a stop.

In seconds, everyone is rising from their seats, collecting their bags, crowding the aisle. I stand on shaky legs and join the line filing toward the train carriage door, glad all I need to do in this moment is move forward in the queue.

I've spent the past years standing in line. So many lines.

I reach the exit and descend the steps, instantly swept up in the crowd swarming the platform. Passengers pour out of the carriages and hurry past carrying luggage, the smoke-hazed air a din of hurried footsteps and raised voices.

I stand on the platform, a thin girl in a worn gray coat, a kerchief covering the stubble on my scalp, hands empty of luggage.

Two men shoulder past me. I stumble sideways. They stride down the platform without so much as a backward glance. I drag in a breath, adjust my kerchief with a shaking hand.

Then I start walking, one among the crowd, carried down the steps and out of the station by its swell.

Had someone asked where I'm going, I'm not sure I would have been able to tell them. But in my heart, I know.

I turn down Potockiego Street, the cobbled thoroughfare curving around the Planty. The lush green of the Planty, a blue-and-white tram gliding past, the elegance of the buildings with their stucco and brick facades . . . How unchanged it all appears. As if this city had never been touched by occupation, as if I had never left.

I continue on, the far-off clang of a tram ringing out as I pass Kopernika Street. There, I pause.

For years, I've kept my past behind a wall, locking it away deliberately, protecting my precious memories from the otherworld of the camps. Now, like the first crack in a dam, the realization of where I am, the familiarity of all that surrounds me, releases a flood of remembrance and I am powerless against its tide.

Wandering down Kopernika, school satchel in hand, when I should have gone straight home, my feet carrying me past the familiar offices, until I came to a pale stucco building, *Dr. Adam Silberman* in engraved letters on the gold placard.

The scent of antiseptic, the sweetness of the peppermint drops Tata kept in a paper sack in the top drawer of his desk. Me, perched on a chair in the waiting room, flipping through the same magazines I'd read a dozen times while Tata finished a late appointment with a patient.

His voice from the doorway, his white coat exchanged for his suit jacket, a fedora atop his head. "Closing time, Hania. We'd best go home to your mama. She'll be waiting for us." His voice held a smile matching the one softening his eyes. Then he'd turn off the lights and hold the door for me, as if I were a grown-up lady instead of a gangly schoolgirl in plaits.

We'd best go home . . .

My chest aches as I draw a breath, moving onward. I'm suddenly tired, so very tired, as if the kilometers I've walked, the sleepless nights I've spent, the distance I've traveled, has emptied me of strength and left me with none for these last moments.

Still, I keep walking.

Low-hanging clouds fleck the faded sky as I make my way down Starowiślna Street. Starowiślna, the broad thoroughfare bustling with life and color.

Rows of stately buildings in shades of sandstone and brick, iron balconies high above the street, shops with brightly painted signs, manicured trees lining the sidewalk.

And then, before I can prepare myself, I'm there. Standing in front of the place I once called home. It hasn't changed.

Somehow, it would be easier if it had. If the years had left it weathered and scarred, altered in some way.

I stare up at the second-story windows, the last two on the right. The pale film of sheer curtains veil what lies beyond them.

I wonder if they are the same—the draperies and curtains. The draperies were sage green. Mama chose them to match the sofa in the sitting room.

I stand on the sidewalk as long moments pass. I've come so far to reach this place. My heart should take flight, give my feet wings to carry me the final steps.

But I can't make myself move.

I'm afraid to step through the door, to climb the stairs to Zosia's flat, to learn what remains of the ones I love. Of all the kilometers I've walked—on the winter march from Birkenau, on the journey across the ruins of Germany—these steps are the hardest I will ever take.

I beg You for strength, ADONAI.

I can scarcely breathe for how hard my heart pounds as I approach the door, push it open. The foyer is silent, dim, my footsteps soft echoes on the tile.

Suddenly I'm running up the stairs, flying up them, my heart beating so fast it threatens to burst out of my chest. In seconds, I reach the third-floor landing, standing in front of Zosia's door.

I pause to gulp in breaths and smooth a hand down my coat.

Then I lift a shaking hand and ring the bell. My pulse beats fast in the hollow of my throat as I stand, waiting.

What if no one answers? Zosia may still be at work. Rena may be . . . ?

It's been over two years since I've seen my sister. I don't know where she'd be on this summer afternoon.

Then I'll wait. In a few hours, they'll return. When they do, I'll be here.

The door cracks open.

"Yes?" The woman standing inside takes in the sight of me. Her brow pinches.

"I'm looking for Zosia Lewandowska. Is she in?"

No answer, save a slight hardening in the woman's jaw.

"Do you know when she'll be back?"

"She won't. She doesn't live here."

I made a mistake and am at the wrong flat. I should apologize to this woman for disturbing her and—

The numbers on the side of the door stare back at me. There's no mistake.

"Are you certain? It's only I know she used to live here and . . ."

"My children and I are the only ones living here, except for a couple of boarders, and none of them go by that name."

I stare at her as the remains of my heart dissolve.

"Now, if you'll excuse me, I've got work to do."

The door shuts.

I stand on the landing, wondering if I should try again, if it would do any good.

She has no reason to lie to me. She doesn't know me. Nor Zosia, it would seem.

Slowly, I descend the stairs.

There, in the shadows of the second-floor landing, I still, only steps away from the closed door to the left.

I'm home.

Those words meant something. Once.

"I'm home, Mama." My cracked whisper echoes in the empty landing.

But only silence answers me. There are no memories, no remnants of their voices. Their faces are faded, like old photographs bleached by the sun.

Their voices are gone.

I cross the landing. I'm not sure why. Perhaps from a broken hope there will be something left. Something tangible to hold onto. Some small piece of my past. Just . . . something.

I hesitate. Then I press the bell.

No one answers.

Minutes go by, so many I'm about to give up. Likely no one is home. But then I catch a noise from inside. I ring the bell again.

I wait, twisting my hands in the folds of my coat.

The door opens halfway, revealing a woman standing on the other side. "May I help you?" She's not much older than me. Her summer frock falls in graceful folds, accentuating her waist.

"Yes, I . . ." I swallow, my throat suddenly dry. How do I say this?

She watches me expectantly, a trace of impatience on her pretty face.

"My name is Hania Silberman. My family and I used to live here before the war. I was wondering if I might please be allowed to look around, just for a moment." I fix my gaze at a point beyond her shoulder, at the familiar stripes of the beige-and-cream wallpaper behind her.

Seconds pass as she stares at me. "You're a Jew, aren't you?" Her eyes narrow, her red lips twisting as if she's tasted something unpleasant.

I swallow again. "I won't take anything. I want only to look around. My family is gone and I would like to see the place where we used to live one more time." I stand taller, meeting her eyes. This is a reasonable request. I don't need to be afraid.

"I thought the Germans were supposed to have got rid of you people. How many of you are left?"

I blink at her, ears ringing as if I've been slapped.

She takes a step forward, voice low, vicious. "Get out of here, you filthy Jew."

The slam of the door reverberates through the building.

I turn and run, clattering down the stairs. I miss a step, nearly fall, come down hard on my right foot, my ankle wrenching. Sudden, shooting pain. I don't even pause.

I shove open the front door and stumble onto the sidewalk. Pressing a hand to my midsection, I gasp for air, the rhythm of my heart a dull, hard pounding. I'm shaking inside, the way I shook when I heard the crunch of the kommandant's boots on the Appellplatz. I drag in breaths of humid air.

I want to sink down on the stoop, wrap my arms around my knees, and let the tears fall. I should be past the point of breaking by now, but coming face-to-face with the woman who's stolen my dead parents' home and having the door slammed in my face is a pain greater than any beating I received in the camps. I am alone, a stranger in the city of my childhood. What reason is there to be strong?

I stare dry-eyed at the buttery façade of the four-story building so bound together with the innocence of my girlhood.

There is no home for me there anymore.

I turn away. At first, I am simply wandering. I used to dream of strolling along a street in freedom, no more marching in rows of five, able to choose where I will go and what I will do. But after freedom, what then? I've nowhere to go and no one to whom I can turn.

It won't be long before it grows dark. Before boarding the train to Kraków, I exchanged my few remaining marks for złotys, but how long must I make them last? It wouldn't be so bad to sleep on the street—I've slept in places far worse—but I haven't eaten since the hard roll I bought at the station early this morning.

I could ask the caretaker about Zosia's whereabouts. Perhaps he knows where she's gone or at least how long ago she left. But I can't bring myself to go back, not with the vile words spewed from the woman's perfect red lips so fresh. Maybe tomorrow but not today.

Nearly every city has a Jewish committee, a place for the displaced to register, seek news of relatives, and receive aid. I don't know where the one in Kraków has been set up. And—if that woman's reception is any indication of the kind of welcome Jews returning to the city can expect—that's not the kind of question I want to go around asking.

Nearing the intersection of Starowiślna and Miodowa, I pause. I could make my way to one of the synagogues, if any are left in Kraków. Does anything remain of Kazimierz, the once vibrant center of the Jewish community? Or have those who once prayed and worked and lived on the streets and in the buildings the Jews of Kraków called home for centuries simply been replaced by strangers?

I'll walk the streets of Kazimierz, visit the synagogues and the Jewish committee. I'll search every face for one familiar, and I won't stop searching until I learn the fate of the ones I've lost. I may find no one, but I won't give up until I know the truth.

For we who survived, that is what comes after freedom.

And today? There's one place left for me to go. One person who may hold the answers about my friend and my sister and where they've gone.

Clouds bulge in a sky heavy with unspent rain, the air thick, almost breathless as I limp down Starowiślna. A tram clatters past, its blue-and-white body outlined by the gray day. I haven't ridden one since the Nazis banned Jews from public transportation. I used to trudge through the city on aching feet, looking with longing at the trams traveling smoothly along their tracks. One of the first things I'd do when *this* was over, I vowed, was ride a tram. How little I then understood of what *this* would become and how soon being forbidden to ride a tram would seem small and unimportant.

The tram fades into the distance. No matter how worn I am, it's a luxury I can't afford.

At last I reach the Third Bridge, the dark waters of the Wisła rippling like glass. The bridge is passable, but its iron structure has been damaged and repaired. I cross the bridge, steps slow and weary, ankle throbbing.

The sky opens and summer rain pours as the bridge recedes behind me. The droplets fall fast and hard, wet and slightly warm. Still, I shiver as rain slicks my skin and splotches my threadbare coat.

There's no gate at the entrance of the square, no navy-uniformed policemen standing guard, so I simply walk onward. Zgody Square stretches before me, veiled by the falling rain.

The patter of the rain dissolves into a whistle blaring, SS shouting, panicked screaming, a single shot . . . silence. The heat beats down and I glimpse my tata's face for the last time.

The past recedes and I stand alone on the outskirts of the square. Rain glistens on cobblestones marked with memories. Here, illusions died amid discarded luggage. Families torn. Lives ended. Countless single tragedies against the backdrop of a greater destruction. How many witnesses are left to speak of them?

The stones remain and they are silent.

Rain falls as I approach the building at the corner of Zgody Square and Targowa Street. The Apteka Pod Orłem stands unaltered, its facade washed to a dull shade by the downpour, as ordinary as any building in the square. An unremarkable pharmacy. Yet to me and so many others, it stood as a beacon of life at the heart of a raging storm.

I still in front of the pharmacy, rain drenching my skin, fear and hope clashing in my chest. I am used to fear, but I am afraid to hope.

Fear can be endured, but nothing is harder to bear than the loss of hope.

I limp the few steps to the door and open it, rain soaked and shivering.

On the other side of the counter, a woman in a white smock stands on tiptoe in front of the high cabinet. Wisps of blond hair escape the roll at her nape as she reaches for a bottle off the shelf.

My breath catches.

She turns.

"May I help—?" For the space of several breaths, she stands motionless, staring at me as if I'm a stranger. Then the bottle slips from her fingers, crashes to the floor, shatters into fragments.

My throat aches as our eyes lock. There are no words. Only two women separated by a pharmacy counter, the unspoken years standing between us.

• • •

Zosia

For months, I've clutched hope so fiercely my heart ached.

But the lists do not lie. There are so many lost, so few living. Each time I left the registration office, I clung tighter to the belief that Hania would come back, even as it slipped from my grasp.

Now, I round the counter, crunching over shards of glass and spilled tincture, wanting only to reach her, to touch her.

A pace away, I stop, suddenly overwhelmed.

I should have prepared myself for this. For the woman who would return to us.

But all I can think of is the girl standing shyly in the doorway on my wedding day and what the years have done to that girl.

She's thin. So painfully thin. Her coat hangs on her as if she's a child wearing her mother's clothes. A faded kerchief covers her head. The round softness of her features has become sharp angles and hollow cheeks.

"Zosia." Her voice is a broken whisper.

My throat is too tight to form words. I gather her in my arms, pull her close, half-afraid she'll crack beneath my touch. Her arms come around me, and we hold each other in the silent room. She's so fragile, the ridges of her shoulder blades stark beneath her coat. But she clutches me with sudden strength.

We draw away. In her sharply boned face, her eyes are startlingly bright as they look into mine, bright with unshed tears.

"You've come back to us," I say softly.

She tries to smile. It forms as a whisper on her cracked lips. Then her smile fades as her eyes search mine. "Rena?" It's barely more than a breath, the single word, but it holds such desperation. As if wherever she's been, whatever she's done, whatever has been done to her, she's carried the question with her through it all, and now gives it voice.

"Rena is—" I swallow. "She's . . ."

Voices and footsteps echo in the corridor. Tadeusz strides into the dispensing room. He stops, catching sight of us.

Rena hastens in behind him, draws up short.

Hania's face pales.

I see it in their eyes, the instant they find each other again.

All at once, they're moving forward, coming together in the center of the room.

"Renusia." Hania touches her sister's face. "Renusia," she whispers again. Tears fall unheeded down Rena's cheeks and Hania wraps her sister in her arms.

I press my hand to my lips, heat blurring my eyes. *Thank You, God.*

A warm hand settles on my shoulder.

I turn, looking up at Tadeusz.

"It's not all lost, is it?" Our gazes hold and the measure of these years is in his eyes. Of all these days asked of us, of the memories we will never leave behind, of the cost that will be borne beyond our generation.

"No," I say quietly. Hania and Rena stand in the center of the room, sisters joined as one. "Not all lost."

. . .

Hania

We ride the tram to Zosia's flat. I sit by the window as the streets of Kraków pass beyond the rain-blurred glass, Rena beside me. I can't stop looking at my sister. She's grown nearly as tall as me, her childish frame replaced by a young woman's figure, soft curls skimming her shoulders, where long plaits used to fall.

Little has been said of the time we've been apart, but her eyes speak for her. Gone is the innocence of a child's gaze. In its place is a girl thrust into womanhood by war and changed by what survival has taken from her. Rena is here, but my baby sister isn't coming back.

She knows about Szymon. I started to tell her, but she stopped me. Someday I will speak of our time in Płaszów, of how Szymon's courage helped me to be strong, of how proud Tata and Mama would be of the man he became, of the ways he cared for Adela and me. Someday I will tell her how he died. Someday. But not now.

She smiles hesitantly.

I smile back, reaching across and threading her fingers through mine on the wooden bench. Sitting beside her, the warmth of her shoulder against mine, it doesn't seem real. I want to hold her and never let go, but there's a strangeness between us, as if neither of us knows quite how to be around the other.

I sense her watching me, taking me in as much as I'm studying her, the same way Zosia did. In their eyes, I see myself. Shock dawned first, pain followed, and they could hide neither. I did not need to read it in their gazes to know how I must appear to them. I've looked in a mirror. I know what the camps did to me. Even after weeks in the hospital, my body remains ravaged. I've gained a little weight, but I'm still withered. Broken.

I am alive. That is enough. In time, my strength will return and my body will regain its fullness. In time, Rena and I will fall into the pattern of sisters again. There are parts of my past I will always carry but never speak of to her—or perhaps to anyone—and she may never fully share hers with me but, in time, as we talk and as we grieve together, we will grow to understand who the other has become.

In time . . .

After existing for so long in measured minutes, we have time. How impossibly wonderful those words are.

We get off at the tram stop and continue the rest of the way on foot. Zosia walks a pace ahead, a little girl on her hip, a boy of about ten in step beside her. Zosia introduced them to me as Leon and Sara, no other explanation. Leon shook my hand politely, then asked without preamble what camps I'd been in and did I know anyone named Yitzhak and Bronia Guterman? *His uncle and aunt*, Zosia said by way of clarification.

I wasn't shocked by his forthrightness. In the DP camp we were all reciting names to strangers, shaking our heads and murmuring, "No, I'm sorry," in answer to people with eyes as searching as our own. It's what you do—keep asking and asking, each time hoping maybe someone will remember, maybe the next person will know something. I sometimes felt ashamed, staring blankly as someone repeated the names of relatives I didn't know, and I wondered if I *had* known them, if I'd been there as a mother or sister was selected for the gas or carried out of the barracks to be added to the pile of others who'd died during the night.

I told Leon I'd been in Płaszów, Auschwitz-Birkenau, and Bergen-Belsen. The only way I can say the names without the memories is to repeat them in a toneless voice while I let my mind go blank.

At the words *Auschwitz-Birkenau* and *Bergen-Belsen*, Rena and Zosia turned pale.

The rain has slowed to a drizzle by the time we reach the building where Zosia rents a single room within a flat. My ankle throbs with every step as we mount the stairs, but I'm only vaguely aware of the pain. Everything is blurred, the way it is in dreams, as if I'm somehow detached from my surroundings. This has happened before in some of the worst moments. Never the good.

"We'll put a cold compress on that ankle straightaway." Zosia shifts Sara on her hip as she rummages in her handbag. She pulls out a key and fiddles it in the lock. I glance at Rena.

Our conversation in the duty room returns to me.

"Where's Pani Weinberg?" I'd asked after Zosia ushered Rena and me into the duty room as Magister Pankiewicz hastened to wait on a customer who'd come through the door while Rena and I stood hugging and crying in the pharmacy's front room. I hesitated to voice the question but forced out the words, needing to know.

"She's at the orphanage run by the committee. She works there, has ever since we returned to Kraków."

Pani Weinberg was in Kraków. I'd sat in Magister Pankiewicz's leather chair, hands wrapped around a glass of water Zosia had brought me, absorbing this news, when Rena said in a quiet voice, "Romek's here too, Hania."

I couldn't speak, couldn't breathe, just sat, gripping the glass of water. Had I been standing, my legs would surely have given out beneath me.

Romek survived. He survived and he's here.

The memory falls away. I draw a slow breath, but it does nothing to unravel the tightness in my chest as we stand outside the flat. Zosia passes Sara into Leon's arms, then turns to me.

"Do you want to go in alone?" she asks gently.

"Are . . . are you sure he's here?"

"He might not be in yet. He's only been in Kraków a week. Every day he goes to the registration office, searching for information about you and Adela."

The reality pierces my throat. He doesn't know about Adela. None of them do.

"I'll just . . ." More words fail, so I slip past her.

"Our room is the door to the right," her soft voice calls after me.

I step inside the flat and approach the closed door, uncertain whether to knock or simply go in, when I catch the undertone of voices from inside.

Perhaps it's only my imagination, but the familiarity of those voices sends a sudden, powerful surge through me. I nearly fling open the door then and there, but something stops me.

I close my fingers into a fist. Two short raps.

Waiting, the seconds stretching, each heartbeat pulsing with expectation.

As if through a haze, I see myself, the girl in the gray coat standing outside the door. I don't know why she survived. She wasn't stronger or braver or better than the countless untold who did not. She didn't deserve life any more than they. Had the incomprehensible held any logic, Birkenau or Belsen would have ended her as it had so many others.

It's as if I've spent the past six years standing in the center of a whirlwind, and all around me, others were swept away by its vortex while I remained. To understand why would be to place my humanity above the silenced cries of lives consumed by smoke.

I will never understand.

The door opens. A man stands inside. He's shadow-thin, eyes sunken, dark hair stubbly, the taut line of a scar jagged across his cheekbone.

Romek.

He stares at me, gaze raw with disbelief.

I breathe his name.

He searches my face as if memorizing my features. Or maybe remembering. "You're here." His voice is hoarse.

"I'm here." My eyes well up.

He pulls me inside.

The click of the door as it shuts behind us.

Pani Weinberg's stifled cry.

Romek's arms coming around me, mine around him.

The crushing desperation of our embrace.

His stubble against my cheek.

The salt of tears on my lips.

The haze lifts, like sunlight streaming from behind clouds, illuminating everything in sudden, startling clarity.

I rest my forehead against his, our tears mingling. For a long moment, there is nothing else. Only us. The boy and girl who walked together on Krzemionki Hill and fell in love as the world fell to pieces, now older, altered, scarred, but loving each other still.

He brushes his thumb gently against my cheek, wiping away my tears. My breath shudders as he traces the edge of the kerchief covering my head. It slips away, falls to the ground. My eyes sting as they meet his and read the sorrow there.

He touches my hair with a tenderness that leaves me undone, smoothing his fingers softly over the patches and tufts on my scalp. "My beautiful Hania." His lips brush mine and his kiss tastes of tears and loss and love. "My brightest star."

I want to weep for how he has been broken, for how the years have broken us both. But he is here, we are here, and so I smile through my tears.

He smiles back, a trace of his former grin, and it is enough, his smile.

I turn, Pani Weinberg's presence coming fully to my awareness. Once I may have blushed to share such an intimate moment in view of Romek's mama, but now I'm only glad to see her. She's aged, her features worn, wisps of white in her hair. But a soft light fills her gaze as she looks at the two of us.

"Hania, my dear." She comes toward us and embraces me. Her arms are warm and kind and strong, and I lean into her as I once leaned into my mama's embrace. She draws away, then asks, hesitant, "And Adela? Is she with you?"

I hear the falter of hope in her voice, see it on Romek's face. How can I do this? How can I speak the words from which there is no returning?

I must. For Adela. She was strong until the end, and she would want me to be strong for her.

"Adela isn't coming back." My throat burns as the truth comes over their faces, a slow but irrevocable understanding. "She had typhus. She died in Bergen-Belsen a few hours before the liberation."

For a moment, there is only silence. Romek held me as I wept for my mama and my brother, and I want to go to him, to hold him, but he stands, body drawn tight, as if he is not ready to break.

The door creaks. Zosia comes in, followed by Rena and the children. They silently take us in.

"Was she . . . were you with her?" Romek's voice is almost distant. Yet it cracks at the edges with held-in pain.

"To the very end. She . . ." I swallow. The memories I hold of her are theirs, and they are all I have to give. I'll share them, not the worst, not all, but some. Adela would want her family to know. "She was so brave. So many times, she helped me." I meet Pani Weinberg's eyes as they glisten with tears. And I remember Adela's face. "The day she died, she told me she dreamed you were with her. You told her we would be free." My throat aches as I finish. "I saw her face. She was at peace."

Romek turns away, hiding his face. I go to him, put my arms around him, draw his head down to rest against mine. His shoulders shudder.

"She tried so hard," I whisper into his hair. "She tried so hard for you."

I hold him, his bent head against my shoulder, his hands gripping my arms, mine around his shoulders, pulling him tight against me, until he draws away, eyes red.

A thud, then on its heels, a child's cry. We both turn. Sara sits on the floor next to the bed, her legs stuck out in front of her, lip trembling, tears rolling down her cheeks. Leon starts to rush to her, but Zosia places a hand on his shoulder as Pani Weinberg scoops up Sara, cradles her close.

"Did you bump your head?" She smooths Sara's hair, checking for injury. "Shhh. It's all right. I've got you now." The last she says in a voice so quiet I barely catch the words.

Romek crosses to his mama. I watch the four of them together—Pani Weinberg holding Sara, Leon looking up at them both, Romek with a hand on his mama's back. Mother and son lock eyes and there is more than grief between them. There is strength. Tenderness. Love.

Loss remains and we will always live with its ruins beneath our feet. But we will build again. Homes. Families. Women will bring new life into the world and children will grow. The glow of Shabbat candles will light the table, and we will once again recite the familiar prayers.

We will live. And with our lives, we will bear witness to theirs.

Fela. Romek's babcia.

Adela. Szymon.

Tata. Mama.

Each beautiful, undaunted life.

I limp toward them. Rena comes to stand by my side, and I slip my arm around my sister's waist. We share a quiet smile. In her face, I find remnants of the family we lost. The softness of Mama's smile. The strength in Tata's brow. The spark in Szymon's eyes.

I meet Zosia's gaze, the woman who gave what she had to do what she could.

You are a good friend, Zosia Lewandowska.

Romek sweeps Sara into his arms and she giggles, her laughter sweet and pure. I look from one to another, lingering last on my beloved Romek.

We, all of us, are more than we survived.

CHAPTER THIRTY-SIX

Zosia
July 30, 1945

WHAT HAVE THE YEARS made of me?

The woman in the mirror stares back at me; she has no better answer than I. War has formed me into a different shape, into someone I recognize but do not fully understand. Or perhaps it is the woman I used to be—who I was before the choices I made in this war and the questions evil forced me to answer—perhaps it is she I do not truly know. The war is over now, and we are left to live with our regrets. Mine will never leave me.

I did what I could, but it was not enough. I helped a few . . . so few. I would not say I turned my back on the rest, but there's no use seeking a softer term to salve my conscience. In my dreams I see them, and they remain with me when I'm awake. The men and women who made the journey with quiet dignity to the trains that would take them to Bełżec, the march of the children across Zgody Square, the little girl with the blue bow looking up at the pharmacy window, up at me, as she passed by . . .

The silence they left is its own accusation.

I meet the eyes of the woman in the mirror, and I see myself as I am now. How a crease has set itself permanently between my brows. How the stubbornness that once showed itself in my eyes as an occasional flash has hardened into sharp determination. How the sparkle of laughter has left my gaze.

What is my life to be now? I ask as I stand in front of the cracked mirror in the communal lavatory. *What is left for me?*

I've been plagued by these questions since Romek and Hania, Pani Weinberg and Rena told me of their decision to leave Poland. There's nothing left for them here. The Kraków where Jews lived for centuries no longer exists. All that remains of Kazimierz are synagogues desecrated during the occupation and strangers inhabiting the former homes of Jewish families. That isn't all though. One might expect the trickle of returning Jewish survivors to be met with sympathy, or at the least, tolerance. After all, their collective losses are far greater than ours. Instead, a fresh wave of hatred surged. Near the end of June, a Jewish woman in Kraków was accused of attempting to kidnap and murder a Gentile boy, giving rise to rumors of murders of more Gentile children, their blood allegedly used by Jews for transfusions. More than one riot has broken out in Kazimierz as a mob hurled stones at synagogue windows and shouted curses at the people gathered inside.

Romek's jaw was set as he spoke of all this, and I read in his eyes what he left unsaid. He lost his sister, his babcia, and numerous relatives to an inferno of hate. What family he has left, he will protect. He'd found out through the registration office that a cousin from Warsaw had survived the war and is at a DP camp in Austria in the American occupation zone. Conditions there are good, his cousin wrote. Eventually Romek's cousin hopes to arrange for immigration to America or elsewhere.

"It won't be easy, traveling to Austria, but we'll be better off there than if we stay in Poland," Romek said. "It's strange to think of seeking refuge in Austria of all places, but there, at least, we'll be among our own people and can begin something of a life again. In time, perhaps we too can immigrate. Whatever difficulties lie ahead"—he paused—"it can't be worse than what we've already come through."

"We'll be married there." Hania placed her hand over Romek's. "Romek's cousin wrote weddings take place in the DP camp every week."

"And Leon and Sara?" I asked.

"They'll come with us." Pani Weinberg wrapped her hands around her cup of tea. "Now we've had confirmation their aunt and uncle . . . won't be searching for them, and no other relatives have yet been located, there's no reason why they can't go. In the DP camp, we can continue to seek information about their relatives. Some may still be found. Until then, they need to be with a family, even if it isn't their own."

"Leon can go to school. There's one at the DP camp already," Rena said. "I'll take classes too, and they've started vocational training courses, so surely I can learn something useful." She leaned over, voice low, eyes bright with determination. "I won't forget my dream of going to university. Who knows what could be possible in America? I will be a pharmacist someday, Zosia. I won't give up, no matter how hard I must work or how long it takes."

"It will be a chance to start again," Hania said quietly. "For all of us."

They're already preparing for the journey. The sooner they're out of Poland, the better, Romek says.

I return to our room. Tadeusz gave me the day off, and Hania, Rena, and Pani Weinberg are in the kitchen preparing a picnic for us to take to the Planty. Leon and Sara will run and play, and we'll sit on a blanket and let the sun warm our faces, let its rays wash our weariness away.

Romek sits on the edge of the bed, Sara in his lap. From the clumsy way his fingers are twisting her hair and his focused expression, he appears to be attempting a plait. From the state of her tangled curls, he appears to be failing rather impressively.

"Hania just handed me a brush, put Sara on my lap, and said 'do something.' They'd be better off letting me make the sandwiches." He gives me a crooked smile.

"Here." I sit beside him and lift Sara onto my lap. "Let me show you how it's done. Just sit still for another minute, sweet one." I gently comb out the tangles, then demonstrate how to separate the hair into sections and braid the strands.

Romek hands me the ribbon and I tie a bow.

"There." I smooth a hand across the top of Sara's head. "All done." I set her down and she scampers from the room in search of Leon. I stand, smiling at him. "Don't worry. You'll improve with practice."

"Thanks." He rises, starts to move to the door. "I'll go see how else I can demonstrate my lack of domestic talents."

"Wait."

He turns. The years in Płaszów, Gross-Rosen, and Mauthausen sanded away the boyishness of his features and left behind a man who's aged a decade in two years, tall and rail thin, the watchful sharpness in his eyes never fully dissipating, even when he's relaxed.

"I've been hoping to catch you alone the past few days."

"Have you?"

I swallow. I shouldn't need to steel myself. Not after so long. But as I twist the thin gold band off my finger, a prick of loss pierces my chest.

It's fleeting though, like the jab of a needle, an instant's pain and no more. In my mind, Ryszard smiles, a soft, only-for-you smile. Then the image of him fades and recedes.

"I want you to have this." I hand him the ring, still warm from my skin. "For Hania. For your new life."

He stares at it, the gold circle small in his callused fingers. "But it's your wedding band. I can't take this."

"Please take it. It was given to me with love, and I will always hold that love close. But now it should be worn for the future, not the memory of the past. Please, Romek. For your bride."

He nods, slips the ring into the pocket of his trousers. "Thank you." He reaches out and clasps my hand in both of his, gazing steadily into my eyes. "Not only for this."

I want to say I do not deserve thanks—from him or anyone—for what little I did. It wasn't enough, not for his sister or Szymon. If I'd only done more . . .

Why didn't I do more?

Instead I place my other hand over his. "God keep you both in your life together."

The door opens and Leon bursts in, Sara on his heels. "Pani Weinberg said to tell you the picnic's ready. And there's a surprise, but I know what it is." He comes over to me and cups his hand around his mouth. "Raspberries," he whispers. "But you'd better not tell anyone."

I smile. "I won't."

Romek strides toward the door and swings Sara in his arms. "Ready, Sara-bird?"

"Yes!"

Romek chuckles. "Then we'd best not waste any time."

In minutes, we're spilling out into the blue-skied summer day. Romek carries the basket of food, his other hand holding Hania's. Rena has a book tucked under her arm. Pani Weinberg holds Sara's hand, Leon and I walking alongside them.

Leon chatters to Pani Weinberg about how Romek promised to help him practice kicking and passing this afternoon, his prized and battered ball beneath his arm.

I lift my face to the sun, its rays soaking into my skin.

"Pani Lewandowska, look. That man down the street."

My gaze follows Leon's.

A man trudges along the street, the brim of his cap tipped low over his eyes.

My step falters. His stature, the set of his shoulders . . . why won't it stop? Why does my mind persist in seeing what isn't there, catching sight of a wide-shouldered stranger and glimpsing in him the features of another man? Only to be gripped by a wretched sense of my own pathetic inability to stop hoping against all reality each time the stranger comes into focus and he isn't Janek.

Not today. For one day, for just *one day*, I refuse to let the past slip in to taint this simple pleasure.

In the distance, a tram clangs and a woman rides by on a bicycle.

The man raises his head.

My breath stills.

It's not possible.

Janek isn't here. He's not walking along this street, or any street, because he's gone. There is no hope, only finality.

"Isn't that Pan Janek?" Leon's voice is far away.

I stare, squinting against the sun.

Something breaks inside me, and suddenly I'm pushing past Leon, running down the sidewalk, jostling pedestrians, colliding with a woman coming out of a shop, ignoring her startled exclamation, heedless of all else but reaching him.

"Janek!"

The man looks up. Somehow, I didn't expect him to still, for shock and recognition and—yes, it's in his eyes too—hope against all reality, to tangle together.

Somehow, even as I ran headlong down the street, I didn't expect to find him.

I draw up short, breaths ragged, the breeze swirling strands of hair into my eyes.

Slowly, he takes the last steps separating us.

We stand close enough to touch, but I don't reach out. I take in his hollow cheeks, the gray stubble on his unshaven jaw, the thinness of his frame.

"Zosia."

One word, a whisper of breath, and all the nights I pressed my face into my pillow to muffle my sobs, all the days I kept grief shuttered and silent, all the regret I couldn't forget . . . all of it comes flooding over me. "I never thought I'd see you again," I finally whisper. Words too simple to fill years and space and everything that separated us.

"I know," he says quietly.

"Where were you?"

"They sent me to a labor camp near Pustków, then later to Sachsenhausen. I was there until shortly before the end of the war." He pauses, darkness passing over his face.

I'd heard there had been a labor camp in Pustków. He'd been so close, only a short journey by train from Kraków. Then Sachsenhausen, the notorious camp in Germany where Ryszard and untold others died.

"Every day, I thought of you. I carried you with me, held your face in my mind. You were with me, Zosia." He reaches out as if to touch me, then his hand falls to his side. "It doesn't matter how you feel about me, that's not why I'm here. You helped me to live." The steady intensity of his gaze never leaves mine. "I wanted to thank you."

"Janek, I . . ." I take the final step and then I'm in his arms and we're clutching each other as if one embrace could hold every moment of longing from these years. His lips whisper against my temple, the barest brush of a kiss, and my breath catches. My fingers fist his collar as I raise myself on tiptoe and press my lips hard against his.

With this kiss, I give him the whole of myself—the woman shaped by loss and sharpened by war, the woman afraid of love because she knows how easily it breaks and leaves you broken, and the woman offering the only heart she has, in all its calluses and fragments.

He lifts me off the ground as he kisses me with the urgency of a man starved, as if neither of us truly believe we'll be given anything more than this moment.

Finally, he lowers me, draws away, my hands still gripping his collar.

The years left neither of us as we were; even love is not what it once was. Those we first loved are gone, and with them, a part of each of us. We pledged ourselves to them when life was golden in its promise, before we witnessed what a merciless darkness can destroy, before we knew what it meant to be tested to the very substance of ourselves.

Now here we stand. On a busy street as carts rattle past, passersby skirt us on the sidewalk, and a tram clanks in the distance. And none of it matters, because for me, there's only him.

"You once told me we must speak the words that matter because there are few we regret more than those left unsaid. I thought I would always carry that regret." I draw a breath. In all I've done and everything I've feared, the next words are among the bravest I will speak. "I love you." I exhale the words my heart has long kept close beside the memory of him.

Beneath the years-deep weariness, he looks at me with a kind of wonder in his eyes.

No, more than wonder. Light.

"I never stopped," he whispers.

I reach for his hand, my fingertips tracing the hardened surface of his broad palm, the thin ridge of a scar across his knuckles. The years embedded into his skin.

Later we will speak of what we lived. Some memories may always be kept silent, but words are not the fullest measure of understanding. Though the weight of our experiences can never be borne by another, in our bearing of them, we will no longer be alone.

"How did you know where to find me?"

"After I left the station, I went to your old flat. One of your neighbors said—well, she said a lot of things." Janek pauses, his slight hesitation indicating what he'd thought had become of me. "If anyone could tell me what had happened, I figured it would be Magister Pankiewicz. I went to the pharmacy. He gave me your address."

"Come. You look as if you could use a good meal. The room I rent is nearby. It's yours for as long as you need, if you want to stay. It's not much of a home, I'm afraid."

"Then we'll make one." There's a softness in his eyes as they hold mine. "For both of us."

"Yes." I nod. Life floods my veins; suddenly I'm *alive*, and my heart spills over with the joy of it.

We turn.

The others stand gathered nearby.

Romek's lips tilt. "I take it you're acquainted with this man, Pani Zosia."

I laugh—it escapes in an irrepressible burst that's both strange and wonderfully right. "I am. We are"—I smile at Janek—"acquainted. This is Janek Kamiński. He's a . . ." I hesitate, uncertain how to introduce him,

A smile forms on Pani Weinberg's lips. What Janek means to me is likely not a surprise to her.

"Zosia and I used to work together," Janek says.

"It's a pleasure to meet any friend of Pani Zosia's. Romek Weinberg." Romek grips Janek's hand.

Leon steps forward, looks solemnly into Janek's face. "Hello, Pan Janek. I remember you."

Janek stares at the boy with tousled hair carrying a ball beneath his arm. "I remember you too," he says quietly, holding out his hand for Leon to shake. "You've grown so tall. One of these days, you'll be taller than me." He turns to me. "The others?"

I press my lips together, shake my head.

Janek nods, his understanding unspoken.

"Are you coming with us?" Leon asks.

Janek glances at me.

"We were on our way to the Planty for a picnic," I say. "But you must be tired after your journey. There's no need for the two of us to go."

"Why not?" His hand closes around mine, linking our fingers together. "It's a fine day."

"Yes." I smile. "It is."

The sun spills golden light as we make our way down the sidewalk: Sara between Pani Weinberg and Rena, a hand in each of theirs, Hania and

Romek holding hands, Leon at Romek's side. I rest my head briefly against Janek's shoulder, his fingers warm around mine.

There are days of darkness yet ahead. As long as the capacity for inhumanity dwells in the hearts of men, as long as there is hatred, so too will suffering remain. These years have marked the world. Once the horror they held was unthinkable; now it has become possible. Some may seek to sweep the remnants of memory away, but the world has only begun the accounting of its losses. It is for we who are left to remember so the future may never forget.

But there is a greater legacy. It is Sara's sweet laughter and Leon's curious eyes. It is Rena and the bright and determined woman she will become. It is Hania and Romek and the love they share and the children their love may someday bring into the world. It is Tadeusz, Irka, Helena, Janek, and every person who quietly answered with their lives the question *what can I give?*

It is all of us who, in our own ways, choose not to stand in the space between.

I tilt my face to the sky, to cottony billows of clouds tinted by the shining sun.

We are the legacy.

HISTORICAL NOTE

"DESTINY HAD PLACED THE 'Pod Orłem' pharmacy at the very heart of the ghetto, where it bore witness to the inhuman deportations, horrendous crimes and relentless degradation of human dignity perpetrated by the Nazis,"[1] wrote Tadeusz Pankiewicz after the war. When Germany invaded Poland on September 1, 1939, he was thirty years old, the manager of his family's pharmacy in Podgórze, a district of Kraków on the right bank of the Vistula (Wisła in Polish) River.

Irena Droździkowska had been employed at the Apteka Pod Orłem since September 1939. Aurelia Danek-Czortowa joined the staff in May 1941, followed by Helena Krywaniuk in December. All three women were in their twenties when they began working at the pharmacy.

In a rare interview in 1985, Irena spoke about her experiences in the ghetto. "We helped however we could. The truth is that we were doing it selflessly, demanding nothing in return. We saw all the vileness with which people were being treated in the ghetto and knew the same could happen to us anytime. How could we not help?"[2]

Though the experiences of numerous individuals inform the characters of Zosia Lewandowska and Hania Silberman, neither are directly based on specific people. This gave me the liberty to explore their journeys through the lens of a fictional narrative while keeping my rendering of their experiences as historically authentic as possible. I omitted Aurelia Danek-Czortowa to keep the pharmacy staff at the four it was during the period of the ghetto.

Many of the events depicted in the novel actually occurred. SS-Sturmscharführer Wilhelm Kunde really did enter the pharmacy during the June deportations and load his revolver at the front counter—one cartridge for

---

1. Tadeusz Pankiewicz, *The Kraków Ghetto Pharmacy* (Kraków: Wydawnictwo Literackie, 2013), 21.
2. Irena Droździkowska, interview by M. Suda, Kraków 1985, audio recording, in the collection of the Eagle Pharmacy, a branch of the MHK, as transcribed by the author.

each of the pharmacy staff. Propaganda photographs were taken from the balcony of the building where the pharmacy was located, and afterward, the German police brutally forced everyone out of the lorries. The scene where Kunde stamped identity cards for others who happened to be in the pharmacy is inspired by several similar incidents that took place during the deportations. Pankiewicz later wrote that his female colleagues were "wonderful at taking advantage of Kunde's good mood."[3]

In depicting the deportations and the ghetto's final liquidation, I drew from the detailed descriptions in Pankiewicz's memoir, recorded interviews with Tadeusz Pankiewicz, Irena Droździkowska, and Aurelia Danek-Czortowa, and memoirs and testimonies by Jewish survivors of the Kraków ghetto. Irena Droździkowska recalled the massacre that unfolded during the liquidation: "I can still remember this number. One hundred and seventy-six. I counted the shots fired there, but I stopped the count after that number and broke down completely. I was given a tranquilizer while the shooting continued. . . . I don't even know how I can carry on living after all that I saw there."[4] The scenes I chose to include in the novel are only a fraction of the events that occurred, events of horrific inhumanity and immeasurable tragedy. Each account I read and testimony I heard provided insight into both the panoramic view of the historical narrative and the deeply personal experiences of individuals and families.

Hania and Romek's relationship is inspired by the true stories of men and women who fell in love in the ghettos and labor camps of occupied Poland. Love reminded them of their humanity and sustained their hope. To love at such a time was a form of resistance, an act of defiance all its own. These bonds gave people who often found themselves alone after losing their families a reason to endure. Such strength can prove life itself, and many times, it did.

I owe a debt of gratitude to Bartosz Heksel, from the Historical Museum of the City of Kraków, for his insightful answers to my queries about the pharmacy and its personnel, and for sending me invaluable interviews, photographs, and floor plans. Heartfelt thanks also to Terri, for reading the novel with an eye for authenticity regarding Jewish faith and culture.

The role of Poland's non-Jewish population concerning the crimes against the Jewish people has been much discussed by historians. In my research, I encountered examples of cruelty and complicity, but also courage found in unlikely heroes. One such individual is Franciszek Banaś, the inspiration for Janek Kamiński. In 1941 Banaś was posted to the Kraków ghetto as one of

---

3.   Pankiewicz, *Kraków Ghetto Pharmacy*, 119.
4.   Droździkowska, interview by M. Suda.

the "navy blue" police. "The work in the ghetto was against my conscience," Banaś wrote. "At all times I had to look at crime and death."[5] Banaś facilitated the smuggling of food into the ghetto, spread news about upcoming deportations, and aided in the escape of several people. In 1980 Yad Vashem bestowed upon Banaś the title of Righteous Among the Nations.

During the deportations in June and October 1942, approximately thirteen thousand men, women, and children were transported to the Bełżec extermination camp and murdered in gas chambers. In the ten-month period of the camp's operation, approximately 450,000 people were killed at Bełżec.

When the ghetto was liquidated in March 1943, the SS and their auxiliaries massacred two thousand people. Three thousand others were deported to Auschwitz-Birkenau, 2,451 of whom were gassed upon arrival. During the liquidation, approximately eight thousand were marched to the newly constructed labor camp at Płaszów.

Ruling over Płaszów was a thirty-four year old SS-Untersturmführer from Vienna. Amon Göth was appointed kommandant of the camp on February 11, 1943 and soon became notorious for his cruelty. Göth's secretary recalled how in the middle of dictating a letter, Göth would rise from his chair, open the window of his office, and shoot at prisoners passing by. Then he would return to his seat and resume dictation with a bland, "Where were we?"[6]

After the war, Göth stood trial for his crimes. He was sentenced to death and hung in Kraków on September 13, 1946.

In the autumn of 1944, as the Red Army advanced, orders were issued to close the camp and erase evidence of the crimes committed. Prisoners were forced to exhume the dead buried in mass graves and incinerate them on a giant pyre. Few of Kraków's residents knew the source of the flurries of ash that came from the cremation of thousands of corpses only a few kilometers away. This is shown in the scene when ash swirls in the air as Zosia leaves the pharmacy in September 1944.

I sought to handle the scenes depicting the concentration camps with care and for the violence portrayed to show the reality faced by those who lived these experiences. I believe diluting the truth does a grave disservice to the millions who suffered and died as a result of calculated hatred and systematic genocide. Thus I made the decision to include scenes that may be difficult to read and were extremely challenging to write.

5. Franciszek Banaś, *Moje wspomnienia*, ed. Michał Kalisz and Elżbieta Rączy (Rzeszów: IPN, 2009), 131.
6. Mietek Pemper, *The Road to Rescue: The Untold Story of Schindler's List* (New York: Other Press, 2008), 45.

In 1947 Pankiewicz published his memoir *Apteka w getcie krakowskim*, later translated into English and published as *The Kraków Ghetto Pharmacy*. He dedicated it to his colleagues who, "for the entire duration of the Kraków ghetto's existence, risked their lives to bring aid to its inhabitants."[7] In 1983 Yad Vashem honored Tadeusz Pankiewicz as Righteous Among the Nations. Today the Apteka Pod Orłem is a branch of the Historical Museum of the City of Kraków, toured by visitors from all over the world.

Perhaps the impact of the pharmacists of the Kraków ghetto is best captured by a letter Pankiewicz received a few months before his death, written by a man who, fifty years earlier, had been forced to live in the Kraków ghetto as a young boy. "Enclosed please find a modest cheque for $250. Please accept it in the spirit in which it has been sent to you and consider it as a symbolic payment for the three pills of Panflavin, which you gave me in 1943 and for which I could not pay you then. I consider it a great honor to have had the privilege of sharing your warm hand. In fact, I have never forgotten your kindness for all those years . . ."[8]

Three million Polish Jews perished in the Holocaust. That number is a statistic, but behind the statistic are three million human beings, individual lives, lost in the flames of hatred. One might be tempted to wonder what significance the actions of Pankiewicz and his colleagues held when set against the magnitude of such a tragedy. Their efforts did not alter the statistics, at least not noticeably. But every act affirming common humanity, every risk taken to preserve a life, every moment in which decency and compassion were extended to an individual mattered. Not on a vast scale, perhaps, but on a human scale. And as each person chooses to do what they can, the human scale becomes the vast scale.

That is the legacy of the pharmacists of the Apteka Pod Orłem.

7.   Pankiewicz, *Kraków Ghetto Pharmacy*, 5.
8.   Martin Baral, in the collection of the Eagle Pharmacy, a branch of the MHK.